BROKEN

DON WINSLOW is the author of twenty-one acclaimed, award-winning international bestsellers, including the *New York Times* bestseller and sensation *The Force*, and the #1 international bestsellers *The Cartel*, *The Power of the Dog*, *Savages*, and *The Winter of Frankie Machine*. *Savages* was made into a major film by three-time Oscar-winning writer-director Oliver Stone. *The Power of the Dog*, *The Cartel* and *The Border* sold to FX in a major multimillion-dollar deal to air as a weekly TV series beginning in 2020. A former investigator, antiterrorist trainer, and trial consultant, Winslow lives in California and Rhode Island.

🐦 @donwinslow
📘 /DonWinslowAuthor
www.don-winslow.com

Also by Don Winslow

BROKEN

SIX SHORT NOVELS

DON WINSLOW

HarperCollins*Publishers*

HarperCollins*Publishers* Ltd
1 London Bridge Street,
London SE1 9GF

www.harpercollins.co.uk

First published in Great Britain by HarperCollins*Publishers* 2020
1

First published in the United States by William Morrow,
an imprint of HarperCollins*Publishers* 2020

A catalogue record for this book
is available from the British Library

ISBN: 978-0-00-837742-7 (HB)
ISBN: 978-0-00-837743-4 (TPB)

Printed and bound in the UK by CPI Group (UK) Ltd, Croydon CR0 4YY

MIX
Paper from
responsible sources
FSC™ C007454

This book is produced from independently certified FSC™ paper
to ensure responsible forest management.

For more information visit: www.harpercollins.co.uk/green

To the reader.

Simply, thank you.

If you don't have the time to read, you don't have the time (or the tools) to write. Simple as that.

—Stephen King

CONTENTS

———

BROKEN

The world breaks every one and afterward some are stronger
in the broken places.

—Ernest Hemingway, *A Farewell to Arms*

You ain't gotta tell Eva the world is a broken place.

A 911 dispatcher on a New Orleans night shift, Eva McNabb hears humanity's brokenness for eight hours straight, five nights a week, more when she's pulling doubles. She hears the car accidents, the robberies, the shootings, the murders, the maimings, the deaths. She hears the fear, the panic, the anger, the rage, the chaos, and she sends men racing *toward* it.

Well, mostly men—there are more and more women on the force—but Eva thinks of all of them as her "guys," her "boys." She sends them into all that brokenness and then prays they come back in one piece.

Mostly they do, sometimes they don't, and then she's sending more of her guys, her boys, into the broken places.

Literally, sometimes, because her husband was a cop and now her two grown sons are cops.

So she knows that life.

She knows that world.

Eva knows that you can come out of it, but you always come out broken.

Even in moonlight the river looks dirty.

Jimmy McNabb wouldn't have it any other way. He loves his dirty river in his dirty town.

New Orleans.

He grew up and still lives in the Irish Channel just a few blocks away from where he stands now, behind an unmarked car in the parking lot by the First Street Wharf.

Him and Angelo and the rest of the team are gearing up—vests, helmets, shotguns, flashbang grenades. Like a SWAT team, except Jimmy forgot to invite those boys to this party. Like he forgot to invite the Harbor Police or anyone except for his own team in the Narcotics Unit of the Special Investigations Unit.

This is a private party.

Jimmy's party.

"Harbor's gonna be pissed," Angelo says as he climbs into his vest.

Jimmy says, "We'll let them in on the cleanup."

"They don't like being janitors," Angelo says. He fastens the Velcro across his chest. "I feel stupid in all this shit."

"You *look* stupid, too," Jimmy says. Friggin' vest makes his partner look like the Michelin Man. Angelo is slightly built—he went on a crash diet of bananas and milk shakes to make weight for his department entrance physical, and he hasn't gained a pound since. Thin, like the pencil mustache he thinks makes him look like Billy Dee and doesn't. Caramel-skinned, sharp-featured, Angelo Carter grew up in the Ninth Ward, as black as black gets.

Jimmy's vest feels tight.

He's a big man—six-four, with the broad chest and shoulders of his Irish ancestors who came to New Orleans to dig the canal locks with pickaxes and shovels. He rarely had to brawl as a street cop—even in the Quarter—because his sheer size and look were enough to intimidate the most hostile drunk into a sudden change of heart.

But when Jimmy did have to go, it would take a whole squad of brother officers to pull him off. He once wrecked—*wrecked*—an entire crew of bubbas who came down from Baton Rouge and got rude in Sweeny's, Jimmy's neighborhood bar. They went in vertical and loud, went out horizontal and silent.

Jimmy McNabb had been one tough street cop, like his daddy before him.

Big John McNabb was a legend.

Both his sons had no choice to be anything but cops, not that either wanted to be anything else.

Now Jimmy looks around at the rest of his team. He judges that they're tense but not too tense, got just the right edge to them.

You want that edge.

Jimmy's feeling it himself, the adrenaline starting to course through his bloodstream.

He likes it.

His mom, Eva, says that her son always liked the juice—whether it's adrenaline, beer, whiskey or a horse race at Jefferson Downs or a bottom-of-the-ninth at-bat in the police league—"Jimmy likes the juice."

Jimmy knows she's right.

She usually is.

She thinks so, too.

Jimmy and his little brother have an expression for it—"the last time Eva was wrong."

Like, "The last time Eva was wrong," dinosaurs roamed the earth. Or "The last time Eva was wrong," God took the seventh day off. Or, Danny's personal favorite, "The last time Eva was wrong, Jimmy had a steady girl-friend."

Which *was* like, yeah, eighth grade.

"Jimmy's a pitcher," Eva once said, "but he prefers to play the field."

Funny, Eva, Jimmy thinks.

You're a hoot.

He and Danny always refer to their mom as "Eva." In the third person, that is, never to her face. Just like they call their dad "John." It started when Jimmy was maybe seven, he and Danny were being punished by a "lock-down" for some infraction involving a baseball and a broken window, Jimmy said, "Man, Eva was really pissed," and it stuck.

Now Jimmy glances over at Wilmer to check on him. Suazo looks kind of bug-eyed, but the Honduran usually runs a little hot. Jimmy calls him a Honduran, but Wilmer grew up in the Irish Channel, too, in the little sub-neighborhood called Barrio Lempira that's been there since before Jimmy was born.

Short and wide—a refrigerator—Wilmer's a New Orleans guy, as much a Yat as the rest of them, and it's good to have a Hispanic on the team, especially these days, since more Hondurans and Mexicans came in to rebuild after Katrina, and no one was asking to see green cards.

Good to have him tonight, too.

Because the target is Honduran.

Jimmy gives him a wink. *"Tranquilo, 'mano."*

Easy, brother.

Wilmer nods back.

Harold—and do not call him "Harry"—never runs hot.

Jimmy wonders sometimes if Gustafson even has a pulse, he's so laid-back. One time on a drive over to a raid where he could very well have been killed, Harold fell sound asleep in the backseat. To Jimmy he's a "vanilla milk shake"—bland, benign, and very white. Blond-haired, light blue eyes, literally a church deacon.

Even Wilmer curbs his language around Harold, and Wilmer has a mouth like a Third World outhouse. But when Harold is present, Wilmer curses in Spanish, in the correct belief that Gustafson doesn't understand a word.

McNabb is big, Gustafson is bigger.

"We don't need to build a border wall," Jimmy has opined, "just have Harold lie down."

On a bet one time (not between Jimmy and Harold, Harold doesn't gamble), Gustafson bench-pressed Jimmy.

Ten times.

Cost Jimmy fifty Grants, but it was worth seeing.

I have a good team, Jimmy thinks.

Smart, brave (but not fearless, fearless is stupid), their strengths, weaknesses, and talents blend perfectly. Jimmy has managed to hold them together for five years now, and they know one another's moves like they know their own.

They're going to need all of that tonight.

They ain't never done a boat before.

High-rise heroin mills, shotgun-house crack emporiums, biker clubs, gang corners—they done all that, countless times.

But a cargo boat?

That's a first.

But that's what Oscar Diaz is using to bring in his huge shipment of methamphetamine, so that's what they're going to hit.

They've had the Honduran up for months.

Laid way off him, though.

Passed up the small shit, waited for Oscar to make his big play.

And now he has.

"Okay, let's do the thing," Jimmy says. He reaches back into the car and takes out his old, worn Rawlings glove, the same one he's had since high school, a scuffed ball wedged in the webbing.

The others also take out gloves, and they stand a few feet apart, throwing the ball around like it's infield practice. It's almost comical, in their vests and helmets, but it's a ritual, and McNabb respects ritual.

They ain't never lost anyone when they tossed the ball before an op, and he don't intend to lose anyone now.

And it's an unspoken reminder—do not drop the ball.

They do a few circuits, and then Jimmy takes off his glove and says, *"Laissez les bon temps rouler."*

Let the good times roll.

Eva McNabb listens to the child's voice on the telephone.

It's a DV, a domestic-violence call.

The little boy is terrified.

Married to Big John McNabb for coming on forty years, Eva—five-three to his six-four—is no stranger to violence in her own home. John don't hit her no more, but he's a mean, angry drunk, and he's drunk more often than not since he pulled the pin. Now he throws glasses and bottles and punches holes in walls.

So Eva knows something about DV.

This one is different.

They're all bad, but this one is *bad*.

She hears it in the boy's voice, in the shouting in the background, the screaming, the hollow thumps of blows landing that she can hear *over the phone*. This one starts bad, and the only thing she can do is try to see that it doesn't end worse.

"Sugar," she says softly into the phone, "are you listening to me? Can you hear me, darlin'?"

The boy's voice quivers. "Yes."

"Good," Eva says. "What's your name?"

"Jason."

"Jason, I'm Eva," she says. It's a violation of protocol to give her name, but fuck protocol, Eva thinks. "Now, Jason, the police are on the way—they'll be there very soon—but until they get there . . . Do you have a clothes dryer, *cher*?"

"Yes."

"Good," Eva says. "Now, Jason sugar, what I need you to do is climb into that dryer, okay? Can you do that for me, sweetheart?"

"Yes."

"Good. Do it right now. I'll stay on the phone."

She hears the boy moving. Hears more screams, more yelling, more curses. Then she asks, "Are you in the dryer, Jason?"

"Yes."

"Good boy," Eva says. "Now what I need you to do is close the door behind you. Can you do that? Don't be scared, now, sugar, I'm right here."

"I closed the door."

"Good boy," Eva says. "Now, you're just going to stay in there, and we'll have a nice chat until the police get there. Okay?"

"Okay."

"I'll bet you like video games," she says. "What games do you like?"

Eva runs her fingers through her short black hair, her only sign of nerves, and listens to the boy talk about Fortnite, Overwatch and Black Ops 3. Looking at the screen in front of her, she watches the blinking light representing the patrol car moving toward the boy's address in Algiers.

Danny is in a radio car there in District 4, but it's not his.

She's relieved.

Eva is protective of both her boys, but Danny is younger, the sensitive one (Jimmy's as sensitive as brass knuckles), the softer one, and she doesn't want him seeing what the officer going into that house is likely to see.

The car is close now, barely a block away, with two other units—neither of them Danny's—chasing. She sent all three with the warning that there are children involved.

Every cop in the district knows that if Eva McNabb tells them to go fast, they'd better go *fast*. Or they're going to have to answer to her, which ain't nobody want to do.

Eva hears the sirens over the phone.

Then the gunshot.

The round strikes the metal bulkhead *waaay* too close to Jimmy's head and then ricochets around with a randomness that sends Angelo sprawling to the deck.

For a second, Jimmy thinks his partner's hit, but Angelo rolls tight against the bulkhead and gives him a thumbs-up.

It ain't good news, though, the Hondurans wanting to slug it out, lead pinging off steel with a sickening whine, bouncing around like the balls in one of them lottery machines, and Jimmy and his team pinned down in a narrow passageway.

Maybe I *should* have brought the SWAT team, Jimmy thinks.

The bullets are coming from an open hatch thirty feet down the passageway. Someone has to be the first to go through that hatch, Jimmy thinks, or we should just tuck our tails between our legs and slink the hell back off that boat.

That someone is going to be me, Jimmy thinks. He unclips a flash grenade from his belt and tosses it overhand through the hatch. No filth on it, no spin, just a straight-ahead fastball across the center of the plate.

The white light blasts, hopefully blinding the shooters on the other side.

Jimmy bursts in behind it, shooting in front of him.

Some bullets come back, but he hears footsteps on the steel deck running away from him.

"New Orleans Police! Lay down your weapons!" he yells, for the benefit of the shooting review board.

He hears footsteps banging in front and behind him now, doesn't have to turn around to know that Angelo, Wilmer, and Harold are coming up right behind him. In front of him, he sees a guy, and then the guy just disappears, and then Jimmy realizes that he's gone down a ladder.

Jimmy gets to the top of the ladder in time to see the guy banging down the rungs, but Jimmy don't do that. Placing one hand on the railing, he vaults down and lands in front of the guy.

The guy goes to lift his gun, but Jimmy gets off first, a left hook that puts the skell on the deck, unconscious. Jimmy stomps his face for good measure—and by way of teaching a lesson as to what happens when you pull a weapon on a Narcotics Unit cop.

Then it goes black.

Danny McNabb's on the graveyard shift.

He doesn't mind. Most of the action happens on graveyard, and a second-year patrolman needs action if he's going to move up. And he likes his assignment in District 34—Algiers—because Algiers, while technically a part of New Orleans, is a world of its own.

The "Wild, Wild East," as they call it.

It keeps a patrol cop busy, and Danny likes to be busy. But now his long legs are starting to cramp, what with sitting in the car for all these hours.

If his brother Jimmy is a bull, Danny is a Thoroughbred horse.

Long, lean, and lanky.

He still remembers the day he got taller than Jimmy, his mother marking their heads with a pencil on the doorsill of their bedroom closet. Jimmy was pissed, insisted on fighting him. ("You may be taller, but you ain't tougher.") Eva wouldn't let the fight happen, though.

They went out to the ball field for a night game, and on the way Jimmy said, real serious, "You may be bigger now, but you're still my little brother. You always will be. You got dat?"

"I got it," Danny said. "I'm better-looking, though."

"True," Jimmy said. "Too bad you got that mini dick."

"You wanna measure that, too?"

"Just my luck," Jimmy said, "getting a fag for a brother."

When Danny told Roxanne that story, he changed the words to "gay guy." It wasn't as funny, but Roxanne is gay and he knew she wouldn't like "fag." He knew that Jimmy didn't mean anything by it, though. Jimmy doesn't hate gays—he hates *everyone*.

Danny asked him that one time, after Jimmy had gone off on one of his rants. "Do you hate *everyone*?"

"Let me think," Jimmy said. "Gays, lesbians, straights, blacks, Hispanics, white people . . . Asians if there were any here . . . yeah, pretty much I hate everyone. You will, too, a few more years on the job."

Danny's mom and dad told him pretty much the same thing. That the biggest downside of police work is it makes you hate everyone except other cops. He doesn't believe it, though. He just thinks police have a selective experience with people. Cops just see too many bad things and forget that there's good.

Eva didn't want him to be a cop.

"Your husband's a cop," he answered. "Your other son's a cop."

"You're different from them," she said.

"Different how?"

"I meant in a good way," Eva said. "I don't want you to end up like your father."

Angry, bitter, drunk.

Blaming the job for it.

That's him, though, Danny thought. It's not me.

It's never going to *be* me.

He has a sweet life now.

A good job, a nice little apartment in the Channel, a girlfriend he loves. Jolene is a nurse who's on the graveyard at Touro, so even their schedules work out. And she's a sweetheart, with long black hair, blue eyes, and a wicked sense of humor.

Life is good.

The unit is parked on Vernet Street by McDonough Park across the street from Holy Name of Mary Church, because the parish priest complained to the district captain about the "perverts" who are cruising the park in the small hours of the morning.

Like priests should complain about perverts, Danny thinks.

Eva made him go to Mass until he was thirteen, although she never went herself. He and Jimmy went to Catholic school all the way through

Archbishop Rummel High, and Jimmy used to say there were two kinds of Catholic-school boys, "the quick and the fucked."

Jimmy and Danny were two of the quick.

Anyway, he and Roxanne have been parked out here all damn week to keep the priest happy, and they haven't seen one "pervert," and Danny's bored as hell.

Just sitting in the dark.

Someone turned the lights out.

All Jimmy can see now are red lights, tracing through the black like in some sort of stupid laser-tag room, except this is real, the bullets will be real, the dying will be real.

A dot lands on his chest, and he dives to the deck.

"Down! Down! Everyone down!" he yells.

He hears his guys drop.

The red dots search them out.

Jimmy takes out his flashlight, turns it on, and rolls it to his left. It draws fire, and he sights in on a muzzle flash and shoots. Angelo and Wilmer do the same, and Jimmy hears Harold's shotgun boom.

Then he hears a grunt and a moan of pain.

"You ain't want to do this!" Jimmy yells. "Put down your guns! Tell 'em, Wilmer!"

Wilmer yells out the message in Spanish.

The answer is gunfire.

Fuck, Jimmy thinks.

In fact, fuck *shit*.

Then he hears an engine start up.

What the . . . ?

Lights come on.

Headlights.

Looking to his left, Jimmy sees Harold driving a forklift toward them. The prongs have two heavy crates on them, and Harold lifts them like a shield and yells, "Get on!"

The rest of the team hop on like soldiers on a tank, shooting around the crates as Harold drives it right toward the shooters, illuminated by the headlights, backing up toward a bulkhead, with nowhere else to go.

Four of them.

Not counting the two wounded trying to crawl away from the charging forklift.

Fuck 'em, Jimmy thinks.

If they make it, they make it.

They don't . . . oh, well.

Cockroaches anyway.

Jimmy leans out and sees one of the skells backing up, raising an AK like he doesn't know what to do.

Harold makes up his mind for him. Drives the forklift right into him and presses him against the bulkhead. The other three drop their guns and raise their hands.

Jimmy hops down from the forklift and slaps one of them across the face, hard. "You could have done that twenty minutes ago and saved us all a lot of aggravation."

Angelo finds a light switch and turns it on.

"Well, now," Jimmy says.

What he sees is meth.

Stacks and stacks of rectangles, floor to ceiling, wrapped in black plastic.

"Gotta be three tons here," Angelo says.

Easy, Jimmy thinks.

A couple of million dollars' loss for Oscar Diaz. No wonder his boys were willing to slug it out.

Oscar ain't gonna be happy.

Wilmer and Angelo are securing the suspects with plastic ties. Harold still has AK Boy pinned against the wall, although the assault rifle has clattered to the deck.

Jimmy walks up to him. "You got yourself into a real predicament here, ain't you?"

AK Boy squirms.

"What *are* we gonna do with you?" Jimmy asks. "You ever see a tick pop? You know, when a tick gets all swollen up with blood and you squeeze it and it just *pops*? If I tell Harold here to step on the gas . . . pop."

"No, please."

" 'No, please'?" Jimmy says. "You was gonna kill me, man."

"You want me to call this in now?" Angelo asks. "These boys might bleed out."

"Give me a minute," Jimmy says.

He and Harold take AK Boy up onto the deck.

The river is still muddy.

Flowing fast, though.

"What's your name?" Jimmy asks AK Boy.

"Carlos."

"Carlos, can you swim?"

"A little."

"I hope so," Jimmy says. He lifts Carlos over the rail. "Tell Oscar Diaz that Jimmy McNabb says hi."

He drops him over the side.

"Now we can call it in," Jimmy says.

Half an hour later, the boat is awash in alphabet soup.

NOPD, SWAT, DEA, HP, EMTs, even the Louisiana State Police show up, because everyone wants a piece of what might turn out to be the biggest drug bust in New Orleans history.

Biggest meth bust for sure.

On the dock the media's starting to roll up.

Jimmy lights his own cigarette and then Angelo's.

Angelo takes a deep drag and then asks, "What did the boss say?"

"Big headlines, film at eleven, no humans got hurt," Jimmy says. "What's Landreau *gonna* say? 'Congratulations.' "

"But he's pissed."

Landreau's pissed, Jimmy thinks. SWAT is pissed, DEA is pissed, Harbor Police is pissed—Jimmy don't care because he knows . . .

Oscar Diaz is *really* pissed.

He is, and not because the dripping-wet rat is messing up his floor.

The condo is across the river in Algiers Point. Oscar has the penthouse, and the view from his terrace is of the Mississippi and, beyond that, downtown New Orleans, from the Quarter to Marigny to Bywater. Oscar's not focused on that, though. He's focused on his boy Carlos, who just cost him more than he paid for the condo.

Cost him more than that, though.

Cost him more than just money.

This was going to be Oscar's shot—to rise from the middle ranks of drug slingers to the top tier. This was his big chance—to move that kind of weight up the river to St. Louis and Chicago. Prove that NOLA could be a transshipment hub, use the river and the harbor to bring the stuff in, then put it on trucks and send it out on the highways. If he pulled this off, the Sinaloa people would hook him up with a lot more weight, enough meth to make a move into LA and New York.

Now the Sinaloans are going to think he's a piece of shit. That New Orleans is too dangerous. He's going to have to get on the phone and tell them that he lost their drugs, and he knows that's the last call of his they'll ever take.

So his drugs are gone, his money is gone, and his chance is gone. He'll spend at least five more years selling to redneck bayou trash.

He walks back inside to the living room and stands in front of his fish tank, a ninety-one-gallon Red Sea Reefer 350 containing the loves of his life—his beautiful, bright yellow Neptune grouper (cost him $6K), his little red-and-silver bladefin basslet ($10K), the golden with electric-blue stripes carion angelfish (cost him nothing, was a gift from the cartel), and his most recent acquisition and pride, his $30K blue queen angelfish, which cost so much because the gorgeous beauties live in deep underwater caves.

Oscar has a lot of time, money, care, and love tied up in his tank with its expensive, beautiful corals. He lifts open the lid, puts in a few flakes of dried food, and then opens a plastic container holding small chunks of raw clam and tosses them in.

"You're stressing out my fish," he says to Carlos. "My fish are very sensitive to stress, and they're picking it up from you right now."

"I'm sorry."

"Chill out," Oscar says. "Now, *who* said to say hi to me?"

"Said his name was Jimmy McNabb," Carlos says.

"DEA?"

"City cop," Carlos says. "Narcotics Division."

"And he threw you off the boat to give me a message."

"Yeah."

Oscar turns to Rico. "Take Carlos out and kill him."

Carlos turns white.

"I'm *fucking* with you," Oscar says, laughing. He turns back to Rico. "Get my boy a hot shower and some clean clothes. That fucking river is filthy. *Entiendes* Rico?"

Rico understands. Take Carlos out and kill him.

When they leave, Oscar walks back out and looks at the city.

Jimmy McNabb.

Well, Jimmy McNabb, you just made this personal.

You made it personal and took something away from me.

Now I'll take something away from you.

Something *you* care about.

The cop who took the DV comes in to see Eva personally afterward.

She'd heard it all over the radio, but he wants to show respect. "Pretty much the way you'd thought it would go. The perp shot the woman and then himself."

"How about the kid?"

"We found him in the clothes dryer," the officer says. "He's okay."

As okay, Eva thinks, as a little boy who just heard his father shoot his mother to death can be.

"Good thing he did himself," she says. "Save us the trouble of a trial."

"You got dat right."

"And the kid goes into the system," Eva says.

She wants to cry.

But Eva don't cry.

Not in front of a cop anyway.

Rico listens carefully to Oscar and then shakes his head and says, "You can't touch a cop."

Oscar takes this in. Then, "Who says you can't?"

Danny and Roxanne are still sitting in the park, their third night waiting for the no-show pervert.

"Okay," Danny says after a lot of thought, "fuck Rachel, marry Monica, kill Phoebe."

"Poor Rachel," Roxanne says. "Always fucked, never married."

"No, she and Ross got married in Vegas, remember?"

"Yeah, but they were drunk."

"Still counts," Danny says. "You?"

Roxanne says, "Kill Monica, marry Rachel, fuck Phoebe."

"That was quick."

"I've given it a lot of thought," Roxanne says. "I've always wanted to do Phoebe. Since like season one."

"Jesus, you were what, seven?"

"I was a precocious lesbian," Roxanne says. "I played with Barbie dolls."

"Every little girl played with Barbie dolls."

"No, Danny," she says, "I *played* with Barbie dolls."

"Oh."

Roxanne's blood and brains splatter on Danny's face.

It happens so fast.

A hand grabs her short hair and jerks her out.

His car window shatters.

Danny reaches for his gun, but a cloth is already over his mouth and nose. He kicks against the floor, trying to push off, but it's too late.

He's unconscious when they drag him from the car.

The sirens sound like baying hounds.

First one, then another, then four, five, a dozen as the units roll toward McDonough Park. They roll from all over Algiers, then out of the 4th District station house, then across the river from the 8th.

Responding to Code 10-13.

Officer needs assistance.

The sound is horrific.

A chorus of alarm.

Echoing across Algiers.

The party's at Sweeny's of course.

Ain't nowhere else it would be. Jimmy's been going there since he was a kid. Literally—he was eleven, twelve years old when he'd go into the bar to get his old man out.

Or at least get his paycheck before he drank it all.

Now it's Jimmy's home bar and his old man does his drinking at home.

So the night after the big bust, it was only natural that the cops repaired to Sweeny's for the celebration.

The team is there, of course—Angelo, Wilmer, Harold—and all the other guys and gals from the Narcotics Unit, a half dozen cops from SID Intelligence, and a spattering of uniforms and detectives from the 4th, the 8th, and the local 6th District.

Landreau stopped in for a token drink. Even a couple of city and federal prosecutors came by, and two local DEA guys showed up with cowboy hats for the team and gave a toast: "We're like McNabb's dick—no hard feelings."

But most of the guests left early, and now it's just the team, a few cops from Narcotics, and the others that served with them at various times in their careers. The few civilians in the place know enough to mind their own business and just be quietly amused at the raucous storytelling.

"So I'm lying there flat out," Jimmy says, "shitting my pants, thinking, We're fucked, and then Harold . . . Harold comes roaring up on a *forklift*. . . ."

A chant starts: "Har*old*! Har*old*! Har*old*!"

Harold's on the little stage with a mike in his hand, trying to do stand-up comedy. "So I go to my proctologist. He takes one look at my anus and says, 'Jimmy McNabb?' "

"I love you, Harold," Jimmy says, a little overrefreshed. "In a very heterosexual, manly, Christian way . . ."

"Har*old*! Har*old*! Har*old*!"

Harold taps the mike. "Is this thing on?"

". . . like Jesus loved . . ."

"Judas," Wilmer says.

"No, the other one."

"Peter."

"Peter or Paul . . . or Almond Joy," Jimmy says. "Anyway . . . what was I saying?"

"Every cop wants a leader of integrity, courage, and honor," Harold is saying. "But we got Jimmy McNabb, and I say, 'Easy come, easy go.' "

Angelo stands up, his legs wobbly, and pounds the table. "Angelo wants sex! Who wants to sex Angelo?!"

"Jimmy does," Wilmer says.

Lucy Wilmette, a veteran from 8th plainclothes, raises her hand. "I want to sex Angelo."

"Now we're getting somewhere," Angelo says. "So who else?"

" 'Who *else*'?" Lucy asks. "Jesus, Angelo."

Eva watches the blips on the screen.

Like bees swarming back to the hive.

She follows the radio calls.

Officer down . . . Officer lying in the street . . . Ambulance needed . . . Confirm ambulance needed . . . Officer responding . . . Officer responding . . . Officer responding . . . Unit 240 D . . . Where's the other officer? . . . Why isn't he responding? . . . Gunshots were heard. . . . Witness on the scene . . . Christ, it's a kid. . . . Jesus Christ, where's the ambulance? . . . She's bleeding out. . . . I can't get a pulse. . . . Sean, she's gone. . . . Where's her partner? Goddamn it, where's her partner?!

Unit 240 D.

Danny's car.

With her left hand, she punches in Jimmy on speed dial.

Straight to voice mail.

He's at the party.

At Sweeny's.

Jimmy, pick up!

It's your brother.

"This is one of them cops you can't touch?" Oscar asks.

Danny is handcuffed to a steel chair bolted to the concrete floor in a warehouse by the docks on Algiers Point. His ankles are cuffed to the chair legs.

"Wake him up," Oscar says.

Rico slaps Danny until he comes to.

"Jimmy McNabb's little brother," Oscar says.

Danny blinks, sees a moon–faced Hispanic man standing over him. "Who are you?"

"I'm the man who's going to hurt you," Oscar says.

He fires up the acetylene torch.

The flame glows blue.

Jimmy raises a pitcher. "A toast! Here's to taking ass and kicking names!"

He pours the beer straight from the pitcher into his mouth.

"Jim*my*! Jim*my*! Jim*my*!"

Jimmy sets down the empty pitcher, wipes his mouth with the back of his hand, and says, "Seriously—"

"Seriously," Wilmer says.

"—here's to taking dope off the street, guns off the block, and bad guys off the count. Here's to the best damn group of cops in the world. I love you people. All of you. You're my brothers and sisters, and I love you."

He plops down into his chair.

"Was that Jimmy McNabb being nice?" Lucy asks.

"It's the booze talking," Wilmer says.

Gibson, a sergeant from the 4th, walks into Sweeny's and sees a party well in progress. Looking through the crowd, he spots Jimmy McNabb onstage doing a horrible karaoke version of "Thunder Road."

Gibson searches out Angelo Carter and finds him standing at the bar.

"Word with you?" Gibson asks. "Outside?"

"Jesus," Angelo says. *"Danny?"*

The news sobers him up quick. He's known Danny since he was a kid, a pain-in-the-ass little brother hanging around, idolizing Jimmy, wanting to catch on with the department.

And now he's dead?

"It's bad," Gibson said. "We found his body down by the wharves at Algiers Point. He'd been tortured."

Burned.

Every bone in his body broken.

Now Gibson says, "We gotta tell Jimmy."

"He'll go crazy," Angelo says.

Jimmy McNabb loves nothing in the world except his partners and his family. When he finds out that Danny is dead, he's going to go violent.

He'll rip up the place.

He'll hurt other people and himself.

They have to fucking *handle* this.

"Here's what we're going to do," Angelo says.

Angelo goes through the door first.

Followed by Wilmer, Harold, Gibson, three of the biggest uniforms Angelo could find in the 6th, and Sondra D, who has parlayed her remarkable resemblance to Marilyn Monroe into a lucrative career as a thousand-dollar-a-go call girl. She was about to make that much with a visiting fireman at the Roosevelt Hotel when Angelo called.

Everything in the bar stops.

Everything usually does when Sondra walks into a room.

Silver-sequined dress.

Platinum hair.

"Jimmy!" Angelo yells. "Someone here to see you."

Jimmy looks down from the stage and grins.

Sondra looks up at him and says, "I'm Sergeant Sondra from . . . *Internal Affairs. . . .* "

Which gets a laugh from everyone.

Including Jimmy.

"You've been a *baaaad* police officer," Sondra says in her best MM voice. She produces a pair of handcuffs from her décolletage and dangles them from her right hand. "And now you're under arrest."

Harold and Wilmer step onto the stage, take Jimmy by the elbows, and walk him down to Sondra.

"Turn around," Sondra says. "Put your hands behind your back."

"Are you going to cuff me?" Jimmy asks.

"For starters."

"Do what the lady tells you," Angelo says.

Jimmy shrugs. "Far be it from me . . ."

He turns around, puts his hands behind his back, and Sondra cuffs him.

Angelo checks to make they're on tight and locked, then gently bends Jimmy over the bar, leans next to him and says, "Jimmy, there's something I have to tell you."

People in Dispatch later said you could hear Eva's scream from outside the building.

That may or may not be true.

What is known is that after that night she never again spoke above a hoarse whisper.

Jimmy goes berserk.

Swinging his head like a club, he knocks Angelo away from him, then swings the other way and hits Wilmer. He kicks behind like a mule, sending a uniform sprawling.

Then Jimmy starts to bang his head into the bar.

Once, twice.

A third time.

Hard.

Angelo tries to grab his shoulders, but Jimmy, his head streaming blood, pushes up, turns, and bull-rushes him back over a table. Bottles and glasses fly as Angelo crashes to the floor.

Jimmy whirls and kicks one cop in the gut.

Turns and back-kicks another in the knee.

Another cop runs up to grab him, but Jimmy head-butts him across the bridge of the nose and the cop lets go.

Harold bear-hugs Jimmy from behind, traps his arms, and lifts him off his feet. Jimmy wraps his left foot around Harold's ankle and then brings his right heel up into Harold's crotch. Harold doesn't let go, but it does loosen his grip enough for Jimmy to twist his right arm out, stick his palm under Harold's chin, and push. Most guys would give it up before their neck snaps, but Harold isn't most guys. His neck is like a bull's, and he holds on. "I don't want to hurt you, Jimmy."

Jimmy knees him twice in the balls.

No muscles there.

Harold lets go.

Jimmy kicks another table over, two more chairs, runs against a wall, slams his head into it, then knees it, knocking a hole in the plaster.

Angelo taps him in the back of the head with a borrowed baton.

A deft, expert blow.

Jimmy slides down the wall unconscious.

Four guys carry him out and shove him into the back of a cruiser.

They drive him to the 6th and put him in a holding cell.

Captain Landreau doesn't like Jimmy McNabb, but he doesn't like seeing one of his guys sitting on the floor of a cell with his back against the wall either.

"Get him the hell out of there," Landreau says. *"Now."*

They open the door, Jimmy gets up and walks out.

His team's waiting for him, but Jimmy sees two uniforms looking at a cell phone, their faces ashen. They stop and put it down when they spot Jimmy.

"What?" Jimmy asks. "What are they looking at?"

"You don't want to see it," Angelo says.

"What are you looking at?" Jimmy asks one of the uniforms, a scared rookie.

The rookie doesn't answer.

"I said what the fuck you looking at?"

The rookie turns to Angelo, like, What should I do? This is Jimmy freaking McNabb.

"What are you looking at him for?" Jimmy asks. "*I'm* talking to you. Give me that fucking phone."

"You don't want to see it, Jimmy," Angelo says.

"I'll decide what I want to see," Jimmy says. He turns back to the rookie. "Hand it the fuck over."

The rookie hands it over.

Jimmy sees the vid-clip and hits Play.

Sees—

Danny screaming his throat out.

The chair jumping like a windup-toy rabbit.

"Look at him hop!" a voice says.

Another voice: "Fire it up again."

"He might die." A third voice.

"Don't let him," the second man says. "Not yet."

A gap in the clip. A cut, then—

Danny's chin drops.

His body is burned.

And broken.

Every major bone.

"You got all this?" the second man asks.

"It will go viral," a new voice says.

"Get this, too," the second guy says. "T-Ball."

A ball bat swings at Danny's head.

Another cut, then—

Danny's charred body, fetal, his clenched hands reaching toward his face like black claws, lying in tall grass and garbage along the river.

A chyron rolls across the bottom of the screen:

OSCAR SAYS HELLO.

Jimmy McNabb always thought the word "heartbreak" was a metaphor.

Now he knows better.

His heart is broken.

He is broken.

They bury Danny among the tombs in Lafayette Cemetery Number 1 up in the Garden District.

The calling hours were brutal, the coffin closed.

There will be no Irish wake. No one wants to laugh and tell stories. There's no cause for laughter, and Danny's life was too short for many stories. And John McNabb is already drunk—it's business as usual—just angrier, more sodden, more bitter, even more silent.

He is no comfort to his wife or surviving son.

Then again there *is* no comfort.

Police in full dress uniform and white gloves—Jimmy is one of them—carry the coffin to the grave.

The rifles sound, the bagpipe plays "Amazing Grace."

Eva doesn't cry.

A small woman, smaller now, dressed in black, she sits in the folding chair and stares straight ahead.

Accepts the folded flag and lays it on her lap.

Jolene does cry—shoulders shaking, she sobs as her mother and father hold her.

The bagpipe plays "Danny Boy."

The house is a classic New Orleans shotgun close to Annunciation Street off Second Avenue. A small front yard, scrawny grass and dirt, sits behind a chain-link fence that runs along the cracked sidewalk.

Jimmy enters through the front door into the sitting room.

His old man sits in an easy chair.

A glass in his left hand, he stares out the window and doesn't acknowledge Jimmy.

They ain't had a lot to say to each other since Jimmy was about eighteen, finally bigger than Big John, and he shoved his shit-faced old man against the kitchen wall and said, "You ever hit Mom again, I'll kill you."

And Big John, he laughed and said, "You ain't gotta worry about that. I ever hit her again, *she'll* kill me."

Turns out Eva had bought herself a little Glock 19 and told Big John exactly that—"You raise a fist to me again, I'll send you to meet your Maker."

Big John believed her.

Only hit walls and doors after that.

Now Jimmy walks past him, through his parents' bedroom, then through the room that him and Danny shared.

Fuckin' painful, being in that room.

Remembers how he used to clamp his hands over Danny's ears when Big John and Eva was goin' at it. And Danny, he'd ask, "John's hitting Eva again, isn't he?"

"No," Jimmy would say. "They're just playin'."

But Danny knew.

Jimmy was trying to protect him, like he always did, but he couldn't protect him from that.

And you couldn't protect him when he needed you the most, Jimmy thinks as he looks around the room—the old ball gloves, the Jessica Alba poster with the corner peeling down showing the yellow masking tape, the window him and Danny used to go through to sneak out at night and drink beers Jimmy had hidden in the park.

Jimmy walks into the kitchen, where Eva stands at the counter pouring her strong, chicory-laced coffee into a mug.

A pot of chicken gumbo simmers on the stove.

Jimmy always swore that the same pot of gumbo sat on the stove for as long as he could remember and that Eva would just come in from time to time and dump in more water and new ingredients.

She's changed out of the black dress into a dark blue blouse and jeans. Now she holds the coffeepot up to Jimmy, and he shakes his head.

"A drink, then?"

"No."

"You need to check in on Jolene," Eva says. "She's taking it hard."

"I will."

She looks him up and down, a long evaluation. Then she says, "You're an angry man, Jimmy. You were an angry boy."

Jimmy shrugs.

Eva is right.

"You hate for the sake of hating," she says.

Again, Jimmy thinks.

"I tried to love the hate out of you," Eva says, "but you were consumed with it. Maybe it was your father, maybe it was me, maybe it was just your nature, but I couldn't reach you."

Jimmy doesn't say anything.

He knows Eva well enough to know she's not done.

"Danny wasn't that way," she says. "He was a loving little boy, a loving man. He was the best of us."

"I know."

Another long look, another appraisal. Then Eva takes his wrists in her hands. "I want you to embrace everything I tried to love out of you. I want you to embrace your hate. I want you to avenge your brother."

She looks up into his bruised, cut face.

Into his black, swollen eyes.

"You do that for me?" Eva asks. "You *do* that for me. You think of Danny. You think of your baby brother."

Jimmy nods.

"And you kill them all," Eva says. "You kill all the men who killed my Danny."

"I will."

Eva lets go of his wrists.

"And you make it *hurt*," she says.

The crash pad is in the Quarter, on the second floor of an old building on Dauphine Street.

The apartment belongs to a major weed slinger doing eight years in Avoyelles. He's doing his time there instead of in Angola because McNabb put in a word with the sentencing judge, who owed him a favor.

So the team gets to house-sit a place in the French Quarter, near the clubs, the bars, and the streams of tourist women. They took full advantage of all that.

But those were better times.

Now Jimmy stands in the middle of the living room.

"There were four voices on that tape," he says. "One of them was obviously Oscar Diaz. We don't have an ID on the other three."

"The boy you tossed in the river showed up dead," Angelo says. "Bullet in the back of the head. So no help there."

"What about the others we arrested?" Jimmy asks.

Wilmer takes over. He's the Honduran.

"One got shanked in Orleans," he says, referring to the city's central jail. "He bled out before the COs got there. The other two made bail."

"You're fucking kidding me."

"They're in the wind," Wilmer says. "Probably running from Oscar harder than they are from us."

"What about Oscar?"

"I've been all over Barrio Lempira," Wilmer says, citing the biggest Honduran neighborhood. "I've been to St. Teresa's. No one knows where he holes up."

"Or they know and they're not giving him up," Angelo says.

Wilmer shakes his head. "No. I went to friends, cousins, family. The whole community is angry about what happened to Danny. This Oscar asshole is new. No family, nothing. No one really knows him."

"Someone does," Jimmy says. "Someone knows someone. Go back to the neighborhood. Shake it hard."

"It's going to be next to impossible," Harold says, "to find all four of these guys."

"I don't have to find all four," Jimmy says. "I just have to find the first."

Jimmy and Angelo drive out to Metairie, across Highway 61 over in Jefferson Parish.

A green, leafy suburb.

"They didn't used to let brothers buy out here," Angelo says. "You came to Metairie, you came to clean toilets."

"What changed?" Jimmy asks.

"Katrina," Angelo says. "People needed houses, the market couldn't resist."

"Did you want to live out here?" Jimmy asks.

"Hell no."

"So why do you care?"

"I don't," Angelo says. "Just making conversation."

Angelo takes Northline to Nassau Drive, an arc of mansions with big lawns and swimming pools abutted by the country club.

Charlie Corello's red-tile-roofed house is set off the sixth tee. Angelo parks in the curved driveway, and they walk up to the door and ring the bell. A maid answers and leads them out to the swimming pool in a walled courtyard.

Bare-chested, deeply tanned, and slathered in sunblock, Corello sits under an umbrella at a wrought-iron table, sipping an iced tea and looking at his laptop. He gets up and puts a hand on Jimmy's shoulder. "I'm sorry for your loss, Jimmy."

"Thank you."

"Sit down." He gestures to two chairs. "Good to see you, Angelo. You guys want anything?"

"No thanks."

The thick hair on Charlie's head and chest is snow white, and he's put on a few pounds since Jimmy last saw him—what, maybe five years ago. Charlie's grandfather used to run all of New Orleans. Hell, he ran all of Louisiana. Truth be told, he ran a lot of the United States.

Some people say that Charlie's grandfather had the president assassinated.

The Corello family ain't what it used to be, but Charlie still wields a lot of influence in New Orleans. Drugs, prostitution, extortion, protection—the usual mob franchises.

They all pay for Charlie to sit under an umbrella by the country club.

"How's Eva taking this?" Charlie asks.

"Like you'd expect."

"Give her my regards."

"I will."

"What can I do to help?" Charlie asks.

"You do business with any Hondurans?" Jimmy asks.

"We're off the record here?" Charlie says. "I don't have to pat you down for any wires?"

"You know me better."

Charlie does. Him and Jimmy have done business, back in the day when Jimmy was a street cop, later when he was a plainclothes in Vice. Jimmy got an envelope at Christmas, Charlie ensured that his people didn't get violent with the girls or sell dope to kids.

They each kept their word.

Jimmy ain't taken an envelope since he moved to Narcotics, and he's busted a few of Charlie's associates but never worked the case back to Metairie.

"I buy product from some Hondurans," Charlie says, "but not from this cocksucker Diaz."

"So you don't know how to find him."

"I'll put my people on it," Charlie says, "and if they come up with anything, you'll be the first to know."

"I appreciate that," Jimmy says. "Here's something *you* should know. I'm going to put serious pressure on the dope-slinging community, and this time I'm going to follow it wherever it leads me, even if that's to Jeff Parish. *Capisce*, Carlo?"

"Don't threaten me, Jimmy," Charlie says. "We go way back, our fathers before us. Come to me as a friend."

"As a friend," Jimmy says, "there were four men in that room. I'll take any one of them."

Charlie sips his tea and takes a long look out at the golf course, where a foursome of drunk bubbas jack up the sixth green. He turns back to Jimmy and says, "I'll get you a name."

Wilmer and Harold walk into the little club in Barrio Lempira with their badges held out in front of them.

About a dozen people sit at the bar or at tables in the middle of the day. Most are men, all of them Hondurans, none of them happy to see the police.

"Good afternoon!" Wilmer says. "This is a friendly visit from your New Orleans Police Department!"

Groans, curses.

One man bolts for the rear door, but Harold is fast for a big man. He catches him by the back of the shirt, grabs him, and throws him against the wall.

"Empty your pockets!" Wilmer says. "Put everything on the bar or a table! If we find anything in your pockets, that item or items will go down your throat or up your ass, depending on my always mercurial mood! *Hazlo!*"

Hands go into pockets, come out with crumpled bills, change, keys, phones, little bags of weed, pills, a needle, a spoon.

Harold pats down his man, comes out with a flip knife and a bag of marijuana, a roll of bills and some crystal. "Well, well, well, what have we here?"

"It's not mine."

"And that's the first time I've ever heard that." He rips a wallet from his back pocket and finds a driver's license. "If I run you, Mendez, Mauricio, am I going to find an outstanding warrant? Don't lie to me."

"No."

"I said don't lie to me."

The owner behind the bar gives Wilmer an ugly look.

Wilmer sees it. "Are you eye-fucking me, *cabrón*? You got something you want to say?"

The owner mutters something about "your own people."

Wilmer walks over, grabs him by the front of the shirt, and pulls him half over the bar. "Let's get something straight. You're not my people. *My* people have jobs. They're out working instead of drinking in a shithole bar in the middle of the afternoon."

He pulls the owner in closer. "You want to mumble at me some more, boss, or do you want to keep your teeth in your mouth?"

The owner looks down at the bar top.

Wilmer leans in and whispers, "Every day, *cabrón*. I'm coming back every day until these *cucarachas* stop coming in here. The fire inspector, the health inspector, they'll be here every day, too, and a twenty ain't going to stop them from finding violations."

"What do you want, money?"

"You *want* a slap, don't you?" Wilmer says. "I don't want money, *cabrón*, I want names. I want names of anyone who knows Oscar Diaz or anyone who knows anyone who knows anyone who knows him."

He lets the owner go and turns to a young guy sitting on a stool. "I'm going to pat you down, *m'ijo*."

"I'm not your son."

"You don't know that," Wilmer says. "I get around. Hands on the bar."

The guy puts his hands on the bar. Wilmer pats him down and finds a bag of weed in his jeans pocket. "What did I tell you? Huh? What did I tell you?"

Wilmer rips the weed out of the bag and holds it up to the kid's mouth. *"Bon appétit."*

The guy shakes his head and clamps his mouth shut.

"You want it up your *culo* instead?" Wilmer asks. "Because I will do that. Then I'll take you in. Now eat."

The guy shoves the weed into his mouth.

Wilmer addresses the rest of them. "Put your keys and your money back in your pockets! Everything else now belongs to me. You all heard what happened to that young officer. It brings shame on my community. Someone better come to me with names. Or you will have no place to be in the middle of the afternoon. Everywhere you go, there I will be!"

Harold asks, "What do you want to do with this one?"

"Bring him."

They haul the guy out to the car and shove him into the backseat. Harold runs him on the system and comes up with outstanding warrants for parole violation and possession with intent to sell. "What did I tell you about lying to me?"

"Okay, I have warrants," Mauricio says.

"Least of your worries," Wilmer says. "We're taking you to see Jimmy McNabb."

The two cars are parked in an alley over in Algiers.

Jimmy has Mauricio pushed against the front fender.

Angelo sits on the hood, looking at Mauricio's phone. "What's your pass code?"

"I don't have to tell you that," Mauricio says. "I know my rights."

"The man knows his rights, Jimmy," Angelo says.

"Tell me more," Jimmy says to Mauricio.

"Huh?"

"About your rights," Jimmy says. "Tell me about them."

"I have the right to remain silent. . . ."

"And . . . ?"

"I have the right to an attorney," Mauricio says. "If I can't afford one, one will be appointed for me."

"Can you afford one?" Jimmy asks.

"No."

"Then I appoint me," Jimmy says. "And as your attorney, I advise you to give us your pass code before I have Harold there hold your hand in the car door while I kick it shut. Take my advice, Mauricio."

"You wouldn't do that."

"Which hand do you jerk off with, Mauricio?" Angelo asks. "Whichever it is, tell him the other one, because he really would do it."

"One, two, three, four, five, six," Mauricio says.

"Seriously?" Jimmy asks.

"Easy to remember."

"This is what I hate about tweakers," Jimmy says. "You're all so fucking stupid."

"It works," Angelo says. He scans through the phone. "Apparently Mauricio's clever code word for meth is '*taquitos*.' 'I have the *dinero*. I'm coming over for a quarter of *taquitos*.' "

"I'm kind of hungry, I could go for some *taquitos*," Jimmy says. "Mauricio, you don't mind if we text your dealer and set up a meeting, do you? That wouldn't violate your rights?"

Mauricio pouts. "I guess I don't have no choice."

Angelo says, "The guy texted back 'the usual place.' Where's that?"

Mauricio doesn't answer.

"Open the car door," Jimmy says.

Mauricio gives them an address on Slidell Street in Algiers.

"And a name," Jimmy says.

Fidel.

On the drive over to Algiers, Jimmy's phone rings.

"McNabb."

"You don't know me," the man says. "I'm one of Charlie's people. The guy you're looking for is named Jose Quintero. He was there."

"You have a location on him?"

"Sorry, no."

"Tell Charlie I said thanks," Jimmy says. "As a friend."

Wilmer raps on Fidel's door.

"*¿Quién es?*"

"*Es Mauricio.*"

The door opens, but the chain lock stays on.

Harold kicks it open.

Jimmy goes through as Fidel is trying to get up off his back. Jimmy doesn't let him but kicks him square in the chin, putting him down again.

And out.

When Fidel comes to, he sees Jimmy and Wilmer on the sofa, drinking his beer. Angelo stands between him and the next room, Harold blocks the front door.

A pistol—a piece-of-shit old .25—is set on the coffee table.

"Time to wake up," Jimmy says. "You got enough meth in here to guarantee you fifteen to thirty. But you're also within two blocks of an elementary school, Fidel, so that gets you an LWOP. Life without parole."

"You dropped that shit on me!"

"Yeah, I'd go with that," Jimmy says. "See what the jury says. Or we can just walk away, pretend none of this unpleasantness ever happened."

"What do you want?" Fidel asks.

"Jose Quintero."

"I'll do the time."

"See, I thought of that," Jimmy says. "You might be more afraid of what Oscar might do to you, or to your family, whatever. The pistol on the table already has your prints on it. I'll put a bullet in your head and that gun in your cold, dead hand."

"You're bluffing."

"I'm Danny McNabb's brother."

Fidel's eyes get wide.

"Yeah, you recognize the name," Jimmy says. "You still think I won't do it?"

"I swear," Fidel says. "I never touched your brother. All I did was hold the camera."

"That's all you did?" Jimmy asks. "You dumb fuck, I didn't think you were there."

"I swear!"

"Well, if that's all you did," Jimmy says, "just tell me where we can find Quintero."

Fidel tells him.

Jimmy takes the .25 off the table and shoots Fidel in the head.

"Another drug deal gone bad," Jimmy says.

They leave the house.

One down.

Jolene lives on Constance Street in the Channel, within walking distance of the hospital where she works. She comes to the door in a robe, drying her hair with a towel.

She's a classic Cajun—long, lustrous black hair, eyes that Jimmy swears are violet.

As beautiful as Jimmy remembers.

"I just got out of the shower," she says. "Come on in."

Jimmy steps inside.

The front room is a small kitchen.

"Eva asked me to come over," Jimmy says, "see how you're doing."

She laughs. "How do you think I'm doing? I'm a mess. I'm destroyed. You want a drink or something?"

"It's ten in the morning."

"Yeah, I own a clock, Jimmy," she says. She opens a cupboard over the sink and takes down a bottle of Jim Beam. "I just got off two hours ago. Busy night in the E-Room. Couple of stabbings, a shooting, a two-year-old shook into trauma by the boyfriend. You want a drink or not?"

"I'll take a drink."

Jolene pours two fingers into a squat glass and another for herself into an old jelly jar. Hands him his and sits down at the kitchen table.

Jimmy sits across from her.

"You think Danny ever knew about us?" she asks.

"We were over long before you and Danny."

"High-school sweethearts."

"Is that what we were?" Jimmy asks.

"Nah, more like fuckbuddies," Jolene says. "And it didn't end in high school, Jimmy."

"I don't think Danny knew," Jimmy says. "He never would have . . ."

He lets it go.

"Got up in there where his big brother been?" she asks.

"Jesus, Jo."

She drinks and then says, "He wanted to be just like you, you know. I'm glad he wasn't . . . just like you. Would you have come to our wedding, Jimmy?"

"I'd have been the best man."

"Stood there beside your brother and watched my daddy walk me down the aisle," she asks. "Give me to your brother?"

"Yeah." Wouldn't have been the first time. He remembers when she and Danny met, Danny's birthday party at Sweeny's. One of those love-at-first-sight things. Jimmy saw it in his eyes, and in hers. He looked at her like, Olé, darlin', pass on through. You and me were never serious anyway.

"We're just Yats," she says. "New Orleans white trash. Danny was better than that. He was better than us."

"He was."

She polishes off her drink. Gets up from the chair.

"Fuck me, Jimmy."

"What?"

She straddles him and unties her robe. It slips open. "Just fuck me. I want you to anger-fuck me."

"Stop it."

She reaches down and unzips him. "What's the matter? Can't do it? Feel all guilty?"

"Fuck you."

"*There's* my Jimmy."

He shoves into her.

Not gently.

Lifts her up, still inside her, pushes her into the wall and fucks her. The table rattles. The jelly jar falls off and breaks on the floor.

She grips his back, digs her nails into him, and cries when she comes.

He holds her against the wall as she sobs into his neck.

When he finally sets her down, he says, "Be careful. You're barefoot. Don't cut yourself on the broken glass."

Jimmy goes to the house, and Landreau calls him into the office.

"Sit down," Landreau says.

"I'll stand, thanks."

"Suit yourself," Landreau says. "Homicide caught a Honduran meth dealer killed over on Slidell. Looks like a suicide, but it might have been other-assisted."

"Oh."

"You wouldn't know anything about that, would you?" Landreau asks. "Guy named Fidel Mantilla?"

"Garbage taking out garbage," Jimmy says. "Even better when the garbage takes itself out. In any case, NHI."

No Humans Involved.

Landreau looks at his desktop for a few seconds and then asks, "How are you doing, Jimmy?"

"Fine."

"I mean with your brother's death."

"You mean my brother's murder?" Jimmy asks.

"Okay."

"I'm fine." He stares at Landreau, who stares back.

The boss knows that Jimmy killed Mantilla.

He also knows he can't prove it.

"Well, if you hear anything," Landreau says, "share it with Homicide."

"I'll do that," Jimmy says.

That night Jimmy's phone rings.

It's Angelo.

They have Quintero.

Jimmy says he'll be right there.

He meets them at a recycling center in Barrio Lempira off Willow and Erato that belongs to an associate of Charlie Corello's.

Angelo opens the trunk of his car.

Quintero is inside, cuffed by the wrists and ankles, a gag stuffed in his mouth. He's a skinny guy, young, with long black hair.

"Take him out," Jimmy says.

Harold and Wilmer grab Quintero, lift him out of the trunk, and stand him in front of Jimmy.

"I'm Danny McNabb's brother," Jimmy says. "Just so you know I'm not fucking around with you."

Quintero's eyes show the fear they should.

They drag him over to the back of the yard. An industrial trash compactor—a big, ugly green machine—is set along the edge of the fence. Jimmy finds a box of cans, throws them into the compactor. "Watch this, Jose."

Jimmy flips the switch.

The compactor grinds and squeezes the cans flat. A horrible crunching, metallic sound that lasts ten long seconds.

"Put him in," Jimmy says.

Harold and Wilmer lift the struggling, wiggling, moaning Quintero into the compactor.

"I know you were there when they tortured Danny," Jimmy says. "I know there was one other and Diaz. But I know you didn't give the order, so I'll give you one chance—I want a name and a location."

He pulls the gag from Quintero's mouth.

"I don't know where Diaz is," Quintero says. He starts to cry.

"Give me the other name," Jimmy says. "Last chance."

"Rico," Jose says. "Rico Pineda."

"Where do I find him?"

"I don't know."

"Good-bye," Jimmy says.

"He has a black girlfriend!" Quintero says. "Keisha. She dances at the Golden Door. In the Ninth."

"You know it?" Jimmy asks Angelo.

"Yeah."

Jimmy shakes his head. "You know what I think? I think you're lying. I don't think you were there at all. I think you're making this shit up to save your ass. *Adios*, Jose."

"No!" Quintero says. "I was there! I swear!"

"Prove it."

Quintero is breathing hard, hyperventilating. "Your brother, he wore a medal on a chain around his neck, right? A saint."

"Which saint?" Jimmy asks.

"St. Jude!"

"I guess you're telling the truth after all," Jimmy says. "I guess you *were* there."

He flips the switch.

Quintero screams.

Jimmy gets back in his car.

Two down, he thinks.

Angelo sits at the bar and watches Keisha writhe on the stage.

She's pretty.

And young, just nineteen.

Younger than Rico.

They ran his name—he's thirty-eight, with a sheet. Came in after Katrina to do drywalling, found it more lucrative to do stickups and extortion. Got out from a five-spot in Angola just a year ago and then apparently caught on as muscle with Diaz.

Jimmy had wanted to go right at him, but Angelo persuaded him otherwise.

"You're white," Angelo said.

"*I* am?"

"Yes," Angelo said. "A white cop at a titty bar in the Ninth? They'll make you right away. Let me do the approach."

He smiles at Keisha, who wriggles over to him and bends down. He sticks a five in her G-string, and she dances away. But he keeps his eyes on her and none of the other girls, and when the song is done, she comes off the stage to his stool.

"You want to go to the VIP Room, darlin'?" she asks.

"How much that cost me?"

"Fifty and a tip if I'm real nice to you."

"How nice can you be?" Angelo asks.

"*Real* nice, we go into a booth," Keisha says.

"Let's go." He peels three twenties out of his pocket. "Down payment."

She leads him upstairs to the VIP Room, sits him down, and starts grinding on him.

"You *big*," she says.

"Gettin' bigger, darlin'," Angelo says. "You said somethin' about a booth."

"Another hundred."

He gives the money. She gets up, walks to a curtained booth, and crooks her finger at him. Angelo follows her into the little room and sits down on the bench. She kneels in front of him.

He leans down, tilts her chin up, and shows her his badge.

"Shit," she says. "Please, I can't do another bust."

"It ain't that, Keisha."

"How you know my name?"

"I know all about you," Angelo says. "I know you have two priors, I know you live on Egania Street, I know you got a man lying low there with you. Rico Pineda."

She starts to pull away, but Angelo grabs her wrist. Says, "We're going to take him. Without you we take him hard and he dies. With you we take him soft and he lives."

"I can't do that. I love him."

"More than you love your daughter?" Angelo asks. "You have a three-year-old living with a known felon. Drugs in the house. If I come over with CPS, they take DeAnne from you, she goes into the system."

"You motherfucker."

"Best you keep that in mind, too, girl," Angelo says. "You help me, I have bus tickets for you and DeAnne up to Baton Rouge, go live with your mama for a while. But you gotta make up your mind right now, because one way or the other we taking Rico."

He lets go of her wrist.

Jimmy turns around to look at Keisha in the backseat. Three in the morning, they're parked down the block from the shotgun house she rents.

"Tell me again what you're going to do," he says.

"I'm going to go in," Keisha says. "He probably in bed in the back room. If he isn't, I take him in there."

"And . . ."

"I leave the door unlocked behind me."

"Where does DeAnne sleep?" Angelo asks.

"In the front room on the couch."

"We'll try not to scare her," Angelo says.

"We'll give you five minutes," Jimmy says. "Then we're coming in."

"Keisha," Angelo says, "if you warn him and he runs, someone will be out back and shoot him. And you can kiss your daughter good-bye, because you'll never see her again."

"I know."

"Where does he usually keep the gun?" Angelo asks.

"Under his pillow."

"He reaches for it, he's dead," Jimmy says.

"I'll stop him," she says. "But . . ."

"What?" Jimmy asks.

"You won't hurt him, will you?" Keisha asks.

"No," Angelo says. "We just want to talk with him."

She gets out of the car.

"Do you trust her?" Jimmy asks.

"Motherfucker, I don't even trust *you*," Angelo says.

"Remember," Jimmy says, "I need him alive."

They wait the five and go.

The door is unlocked.

Jimmy goes in, sees the little girl sound asleep on the couch, her arm wrapped around a pink stuffed elephant.

Gun drawn, Jimmy moves toward the back room.

Angelo moves along the opposite wall.

Wilmer blocks the front door, Harold is outside in the back.

The bedroom door is cracked open.

Jimmy gently opens it.

Rico is naked on the bed, a big, thick man with tattoos on his arm and chest. He sleeps like a convict, wakes up at the slightest noise, and goes for his gun.

Keisha has a death grip on it.

"Fucking bitch. *Puta*."

"Roll over," Jimmy says. "Put your hands behind your back."

Rico does it, but he's still focused on Keisha. As Jimmy cuffs him, he says, "I'll kill you. I'll kill that fucking brat, too."

"Shut your mouth," Angelo says.

He goes through Rico's pants, grabs his phone, then takes the gun from Keisha.

He and Jimmy haul Rico up by the forearms.

"Can I at least get some clothes on?" Rico asks.

"You won't need 'em," Jimmy says.

They pull him into the front room.

DeAnne is sitting up, gripping the elephant, tears running down her cheeks. She's terrified.

"It's all right, sugar," Angelo says. "Just a bad dream. Go back to sleep."

Jimmy and Wilmer take Rico out to the car. Angelo stays behind and gives Keisha two hundred-dollar bills.

"There's a bus leaving in an hour," he says. "You and the little girl be on it."

Don't let morning find you in New Orleans.

"Where are you taking me?" Rico asks as they shove him into the backseat.

"Where you took my brother," Jimmy says.

The old warehouse is on the river in Arabi, almost over by Chalmette.

Been empty since the storm.

Rico's hands are cuffed behind him, around a steel pillar. He looks at Jimmy and says, "So what are we doing?"

"I recognize your voice from the video," Jimmy says. "You were talking about my brother—'Look at him hop.' You thought it was funny."

"It was," Rico says. "I laughed my ass off. I know you're going to kill me. So kill me. What are you waiting for?"

Jimmy slips a set of brass knuckles onto his right hand and says, "Anyone want out of here, now is the time. No hard feelings."

No one moves.

Harold sits on a pile of crates.

Wilmer leans against another pillar.

Angelo lights up a cigarette.

Jimmy slips another set onto his left hand, lets out a deep breath, and then goes to town on Rico.

Like a workout on a heavy bag, except this is on a human being.

Jimmy digs bone-breaking lefts and rights into Rico's ribs, then steps back and lands a straight right into his liver.

Rico bellows.

Jimmy rolls his left shoulder over and throws a hook into Rico's cheek. Then a right uppercut into his chin, then pulls it back and smashes it into the bridge of Rico's nose.

Blood spurts on Jimmy's face.

He doesn't notice.

Sweat pouring off him now, breathing heavy, he moves in again and smashes his fists into Rico's ribs, turns him and pounds his kidneys, turns him once more and launches a vicious uppercut into his balls.

Rico's chin drops to his chest.

Blood runs over his tats.

"That's enough," Angelo says.

"It ain't enough," Jimmy says, his chest heaving. "It ain't near enough."

"We need him to talk," Angelo says. He steps between Jimmy and Rico. "Where do we find Oscar?"

"You don't," Rico says.

Wilmer slides down the crates. "Let me have a crack at him."

He gets up in Rico's ear and says quietly in Spanish, "That man beating you, he's El Cajedo."

It's part of an old Honduran folklore about a black dog, created by Satan, and a white dog, created by God.

"The black dog and the white dog are always fighting inside him," Wilmer says. "Right now, the black dog is winning, which is very bad for you. You want the white dog to win, tell us what we need to know."

"They fight inside me, too."

"I know," Wilmer says. "You did a very bad thing, and you're going to die for it. You're going to die, and then you're going to hell. But maybe if you let the white dog win, God will forgive you."

"There is no God."

"There better be, *'mano*," Wilmer says. "The only other choice is the black dog."

Rico's head drops again. He whimpers in pain. Then he looks back up and says, "Go fuck yourselves."

"Y'all leave now," Jimmy says.

The team walks out.

Jimmy walks around and finds a three-foot-long iron pipe on the floor. He picks it up, hefts it in his hand, and walks back to Rico.

"You broke all my brother's bones before you burned him to death," Jimmy says. "Bad news, Rico. The black dog won."

He goes at it until he can't swing the pipe no more.

Three down.

One to go.

"He give it up?" Angelo asks.

"No."

Driving away, Angelo says, "You ever think maybe we're doing the wrong thing here?"

"No." A few minutes later, he adds, "They got what's coming to them."

"It ain't them I'm concerned about," Angelo says. "It's you."

"That's sweet."

"What you're becoming," Angelo says. He waits for a long time before asking, "I mean, is this what Danny would really want?"

"Dunno," Jimmy says. "I can't ask him, can I?"

They drive a few more blocks before Jimmy says, "I know something's broken in me. I know that. You want off this train, Angelo, jump off. We're still friends."

"You're not my friend, you're my partner," Angelo says. "I ride to the last stop."

This might *be* the last stop, Jimmy thinks. Rico didn't give it up, and now we have no way of finding Oscar Diaz.

I fucked up, I lost my temper, and now I can't avenge my brother.

It's over.

Two murder cops—Garofalo and Perez, look at the body cuffed to the pillar. The man—or what used to be a man—was beaten to death.

To say the least.

His arm and leg bones poke through the flesh. His face has been pounded into something resembling a smear of putty.

"This isn't your usual drug execution," Garofalo says. "This was personal."

They're both thinking the same thing.

Jimmy McNabb.

Jimmy drinks hard.

The kind of drinking meant to drown a pain that just won't stay under. Memories of Danny that float to the surface like all them broken pieces that ran down the streets after the storm.

Him and Danny walking down Third Street, his brother singing along with the choir music coming out from the Grace & Glory church.

Him and Danny lying in their beds at night, listening to the old man knock against the furniture when he came in off shift, and Danny looking at him all scared and Jimmy saying, "It's okay. I'm here."

I'll protect you.

Or him and Danny arguing about po'boys, which was better, roast beef or oysters, and Danny saying, "Oysters look like snot, probably taste like it, too."

"You *would* know what snot tastes like, you booger-eating little prick."

"At least I eat my *own*."

And them laughing and laughing until the Big Shot creme sodas came out their noses.

Sitting in his chair now in his apartment in the Channel, Jimmy looks at his hands. They're cut and swollen, his knuckles purple.

The pain feels good.

He wishes it were worse.

He wants to hurt.

The word in the precinct house locker room is that McNabb is ticking off the boxes.

"Bullshit," one cop says.

"Yeah?" another says. "Look at it. There were four guys on that tape. One of them was Diaz. Maybe the other two were Mantilla and Pineda."

"Dispatch had a call the other night," another one says. "Someone heard screams coming from the recycling plant over on Willow."

"Honduran neighborhood."

They keep on about it until Angelo walks in.

"You boys have something you want to talk to me about?" he asks.

It gets quiet.

"No one has anything they want to say?"

No one does.

"Good," Angelo says. "Keep it that way."

It stays that way until he grabs his gear and walks out.

The knock on the door wakes Jimmy up.

He's still in the chair.

Reaching for his gun, he holds it behind his back, goes to the door and opens it.

"Señor McNabb."

The guy looks to be in his forties, Hispanic, solidly built. Well dressed in a khaki linen suit, blue shirt open at the neck.

"What do you want?" Jimmy asks.

"Something that would be best discussed in private," the man says. "May I come in?"

Jimmy ushers him in, makes sure he sees the gun.

"I assure you that won't be necessary," the man says.

"Who are you?" Jimmy asks.

"You don't need to know my name."

"How do you know what I need?" Jimmy asks.

"I know you need the location of Oscar Diaz," the man says. "I've come all the way from Culiacán, Sinaloa, to give you what you need."

"Why would the cartel do that?"

"Diaz crossed the line," the man says, "murdering an American police officer in the United States. And in such a sadistic manner. We'd like to do business here, and we'd like to do it under the normal adversarial relationship with the police, not one unnecessarily exacerbated and emotionally laden."

"If you wanted Diaz taken out so bad," Jimmy says, "you'd do it yourselves."

"We will if you prefer," the man says. "But we thought you'd rather do it personally. We understand *sangre,* family. And we're confident in your abilities—Diaz is the last on a list, isn't he? Mantilla, Quintero, Pineda . . ."

"What do you want in return?"

"As I said, a normal relationship," the man says.

"Business as usual."

"Business as usual."

"Where is he?"

The man hands Jimmy a slip of paper with the address of a high-rise in Algiers Point.

"Diaz is in the penthouse with an army," the man says. "He's frightened and desperate."

"If I catch you with dope," Jimmy says, "I'll still bust you."

"I would expect nothing less," the man says. "But I'm in management, I never touch the product. Good hunting, Señor McNabb. I hope you succeed. Diaz is a piece of shit."

He shuts the door behind him.

Landreau looks across his desk at Hendricks, the chief of Homicide.

"We have a problem," Hendricks said.

"Don't we always."

"One of your men is a person of interest in three homicides," Hendricks says.

"McNabb."

"No one wants to see the murderers of Roxanne Pulaski and Daniel Mc-Nabb brought to justice more than I do," Hendricks says, "but a narcotics cop can't just go around executing people."

"Do you have proof?"

"If I did," Hendricks says, "McNabb would be in lockup. Along with the rest of his team."

"If you can prove it, arrest them," Landreau says. "Until then . . ."

Hendricks stands up. "We're old friends, Adam. We've always worked well together. I just wanted to give you a heads-up. Chief's retiring next year. Word is you're on the short list, and I'd hate to see something like this—"

"I appreciate you looking out, Chris."

Hendricks leaves.

Landreau gets on the horn to another one of his teams and tells them to get on McNabb and stay on him.

The condo building is ten stories high and overlooks the river from Algiers Point.

Angelo pulled the plans from the City Planning Commission, and now the team sits in the crash pad and goes over them.

A ground-floor lobby, no doorman but security cameras.

"He'll have monitors in his unit," Jimmy says, "so he'll see us come in."

There are two elevators, but only the one on the right goes up to the penthouse, and it requires a key card.

"Can you deal with that?" Jimmy asks Harold.

"Power drill."

The elevator opens inside the penthouse unit.

"Nice when you got groceries," Angelo says.

The other elevator only goes to the ninth floor.

"There'll be interior staircases," Jimmy says, "by code."

"Here they are," Wilmer says, pointing.

The plans show two sets of staircases that run from the roof into the basement, one on the west side of the building, the other on the east. Exterior fire escapes parallel the staircases, so the choice is whether they go up inside or outside.

"Outside would be easier," Angelo says. "We go up to the penthouse—there's a terrace."

The plans show a terrace that wraps around three sides of the penthouse, giving the occupant panoramic views of Algiers, the river, and the city beyond.

"Did you have a terrace in the Ninth?" Jimmy asks Angelo.

"We called it a 'porch,' " Angelo says. "After Katrina it had a view of the river, too. From underneath."

"Diaz will have a lookout on the roof," Wilmer says. "He'll make us if we go up the fire escape."

Everyone in the fucking world will see us, Jimmy thinks. Department choppers with cameras will be there before we can get to the sixth floor, or you got some citizen with a cell phone. He doesn't want to see those vid-clips in court—if they survive the raid, they're most likely to be indicted for murder.

"We go up inside," he says.

That has its own set of problems. The building has a 90-percent occupancy rate, so there'll be civilians in the lobby, the elevator, and the hallways. Not only will they be witnesses, but they could be put in danger, and Jimmy doesn't want any collateral casualties.

The right thing to do would be to go in with overwhelming force of SWAT, DEA, U.S. Marshals, and uniformed cops, cordon off the building, clear it of civilians, have helicopters drop men on the roof and then hover for protection.

That's what we should do, Jimmy thinks.

Landreau would greenlight it, and the other agencies would trip over their own dicks to get involved. It would be terrific footage for the ten-o'clock news, which would make the chief and the mayor happy.

The problem with that is that Landreau would insist on going to a judge and getting a warrant, which would bring up some awkward questions about how they know where Diaz is and how they have probable cause that he ordered the cop murders.

Well, Your Honor, I went to some mob connections, and then I put this guy in a trash compactor. . . .

And even if they got the raid papered, the goal would be to *arrest* Diaz, walk him out in front of the cameras with his hands up—another victory for the forces of law and order. But Jimmy doesn't want Diaz coming out of that building anything but dead, and he wants to be the one to do it. Landreau would probably give him the chance to go in first, but Jimmy doesn't want to risk some SWAT sniper taking Diaz out clean and quick with a head shot.

It ain't gonna be clean, it ain't gonna be quick, and it ain't gonna be no one but Jimmy McNabb.

Question is how to make that happen.

"There has to be a service elevator," Angelo says. "Rich people need service, and they don't want the lower orders dirtying up the passenger elevators. Say Diaz needs . . . I don't know, a fifty-thousand-dollar designer sofa delivered. . . ."

They find it in the plans, running up the north side to the roof, with an entrance outside the penthouse.

"It'll have the same key-card problem," Wilmer says.

"Ain't no problem," Harold says. "It puts us outside the penthouse, though. Door goes into the kitchen. It's sure to be locked."

"Plastic charge?" Jimmy asks.

"Shotgun breach," Harold says.

"We'll go in as HVAC guys," Jimmy says. They have the uniforms from surveillance work, and no one in New Orleans is ever going to turn an air-conditioning guy away. "The overalls will cover up the weapons, and we wear the vests underneath."

They decide that Jimmy and Harold will go to the service elevator, Harold will blow the door, Jimmy will go through first. Wilmer will go up the interior stairs in case Diaz tries to bust out that way, and Angelo will cover the fire escape.

"You'll be seen," Jimmy says.

"One guy on a big building?" Angelo says. "Maybe not."

"Diaz will have men stored in units all over the building," Wilmer says. "It's going to be whack-a-mole. Shooting breaks out under him, he's going to be ready."

"Any of y'all ain't wanna go, I'm fine with it," Jimmy says. "We go in, ain't no guarantee we're coming out. Even if we do, our careers are fucked."

They know all this.

Know there's never a guarantee.

Know they'll lose their jobs, their badges, maybe go to jail.

That this could end in Angola or in a box.

"Angelo?"

"You know where I stand, Jimmy."

"Wilmer?"

Wilmer says, "It's an honor thing."

"Harold?"

Of them, Harold is the straightest, the most likely to want out. He stands up, pushes out a ceiling panel, reaches up, and hands down an arsenal— an HK MP5K, a Steyr machine pistol, a Glock 9mm, a Benelli M-4 Super 90 semiautomatic shotgun, a GS-777 shoulder-fired grenade launcher and an M16 antipersonnel mine.

All are weapons they've taken from *narcos* over the years and not turned in. Instead they warehoused them in the crash pad against the day they'd need to slug it out with untraceable weapons. For the day they'd need fire-power the police department doesn't offer.

Diaz has an army? Jimmy thinks as he watches.

Fine.

We *are* an army.

They get dressed in the technicians' uniforms, put the weapons into duffel bags, and go out to the cars.

Landreau takes the call.

"They're leaving the Quarter."

"Keep me in the loop."

One of them nights, man.

One of them steamy, hot, pressure-cooker New Orleans nights when the lid is on the pot, but *just*.

Could blow off any second.

Might come out in a trumpet riff.

A bad look or the wrong word.

A blade comes out, a gun gets pulled.

Kind of night when you're better off keeping your eyes to the ground, your ears open, and your mouth shut.

The night might come down on you anyway.

Jimmy's crew takes St. Philip's to Decatur.

Decatur to Canal.

Canal to Tchoupitoulas.

Then onto the bridge and across the river.

"They're headed for Algiers."

They park on Patterson a block away from the high-rise and wait for Harold to come back.

Takes him twenty minutes, then he gets back in the car and tells them that he had no trouble getting down to the basement and shutting off the air-conditioning.

"Anyone see you?" Jimmy asks.

"The cameras."

"Gustafson went into a building and came out again."

"Just in and out?" Landreau asks.

"He was in there maybe fifteen minutes."

What the hell, Landreau thinks. "Stay on them."

They toss the baseball around.

Call it tradition, call it superstition, it's what they do.

Toss it around like an all-star infield.

"They're playing ball."

"What?" Landreau asks.

"They're playing catch."

Landreau knows that means they're going in.

Jimmy drops the fuckin' ball.

Everything stops. They stand stock-still.

Jimmy picks up the ball, jams it into his glove, and then shoves his glove under his arm. "Fuck it. *Laissez les bon temps rouler.*"

They head for the high-rise.

Oscar Diaz is sweating like a motherfucker.

"What happened to the *pinche* AC?!" he yells.

"I called down," Jorge says.

Jorge is Rico's replacement. Not as tough, but a lot more tech-savvy, which Oscar considers an asset.

"Call down again!" Oscar yells. It's not just being uncomfortable—the air in the room could stress out his fish. They're very sensitive to any change in their environment.

"No, they're here," Jorge says, looking at the monitors. "Three Joe Lunch-buckets in overalls."

"McNabb, Suazo, and Gustafson went in. Carter's on the outside. They're dressed like HVAC repairmen."

Landreau takes this in.

"Boss, you want us to grab them?"

Landreau doesn't answer right away. Jimmy McNabb is about to commit real or career suicide, he thinks, and take me with him. I let this guy do what I think he's about to do, I'll be lucky to be a mall cop in Dogshit, Alabama. "Hold off."

He gets on the horn to the division commander in the 4th over in Algiers.

"I want a cordon thrown around that building," Landreau says. "Nothing goes in, nothing comes out. And no sirens."

"What—"

"McNabb's going after his brother's killer."

Eva watches the blips move toward Algiers Point.

Looks like every radio car in the 4th.

She locks in on the calls. *Cordon around that building. Nothing goes in or out. . . . The guy who did Danny . . . Roxanne . . .*

Her chest tightens, she feels like she can't breathe.

Jimmy McNabb . . .

Hendricks bursts into Landreau's office. "What the hell do you think you're doing?!"

"Stay out of this."

"You're making yourself an accessory to homicide!"

"Arrest me."

"I'm sending my people in," Hendricks says.

"The guys in the Fourth won't let them through," says Landreau.

"You've lost your goddamn mind," Hendricks says. "I'm taking this up to the chief."

He doesn't have to.

The chief appears in the doorway. "Someone want to tell me what's going on here?"

Hendricks tells him.

The chief listens, nods, then says, "The man in that building killed one of my female officers and tortured another one of our officers to death. So here's what we're going to do—the cordon stays around that building. Our radios are going to go on the fritz. And you're going to go home, have a beer, and watch a ball game."

"You're just going to wash your hands of this?!"

"Don't make me wash yours," the chief says. "Because if I do, I'm going to use some very harsh soap. I hope we have an understanding here."

The chief walks out.

The lookout on the roof can't believe what he's seeing.

But it looks like every cop car in the city is headed toward the building. Then the stream of cars parts like water hitting a rock and swirls around it.

We're surrounded, he thinks.

He gets on the phone and calls down.

"The fuck you mean we can't get out!" Oscar yells.

Jorge has fucking had it. He screams, "Which word didn't you understand?! We're fucking surrounded! Every cop in the city is going to be in here in about *five fucking minutes*!!!"

The bladefin basslet, acutely sensitive to noise, starts to dash around the tank. The blue queen angelfish scoots into her little cave.

"I ain't going to no prison," Oscar says. He'd been to prison already, in Honduras. It was not a good experience. "Alert all the guys. We're going to slug it out. You seen *Scarface*?"

Yeah, I seen that shitty movie, Jorge thinks. "It's a fucking *movie*, Oscar!"

"Make the call! DefCon 4!"

Jorge makes the call. Or calls, plural—they have guys on the fourth floor, the sixth, and a fucking squad on nine.

Oscar rips the cushions off the gray Henredon sofa and pulls out an AK-47. He ain't going out easy.

Then the lookout calls down.

"What?!" Jorge yells.

"They ain't coming in."

"The fuck you mean?!"

"They ain't coming in," the lookout says. "They're just standing around their cars, facing the other way."

Oscar runs out to the terrace.

Sees the necklace of cop cars around the building.

What the fuck are they doing? he wonders.

Why aren't they coming?

Jimmy steps into the service elevator.

Harold removes a battery-powered drill out of his toolbox and opens the panel. Takes a quick look, cuts one wire, and then touches another like he's boosting a car.

Jimmy hits the P button, and the elevator starts up.

Jorge remembers the Joe Lunchbuckets coming up here to fix the AC. He goes to the monitor, clicks to the service elevator, and sees two repairmen and the ripped-out panel.

"Oscar, come look at this."

Oscar comes and looks.

Sees a guy who very much resembles the cop they made hop.

Jimmy McNabb.

Oscar gets it now.

Jorge is already on the phone.

The elevator doors slide open on the fourth floor.

Harold's shotgun is at his hip.

It blasts the would-be shooter into the wall.

The doors close.

"Going up," Jimmy says.

Wilmer starts up the stairs.

The Steyr held in front of him.

The first three flights are quiet, but Wilmer hears a door open above him on the fourth floor.

Footsteps on the landing.

He takes another couple of steps then says, *"¿Está bien Oscar?"* Is Oscar okay?

A guy steps onto the landing, a 9mm Glock in his hand.

Wilmer shoots first.

And last.

Angelo is on the fire escape.

Hears the Steyr burst from inside and knows the show has started.

The scene outside is pretty amazing. When he saw the cordon of radio units, he thought the show had been preempted, but then the officers just sat or stood outside the cars. Some civilians in the building have figured out that something is wrong and are emerging, the cops walking them through the cordon.

But no one's coming in.

They're going to let Jimmy do his thing.

Angelo keeps heading up.

He's on the sixth floor when he gets shot.

The elevator doors slide open again on six.

Oscar's guy doesn't see anyone in it, so he sticks his head in.

Jimmy blows it off.

The doors bang against his body.

Jimmy kicks it out, and the doors slide shut.

The noise is unreal.

Gunshots boom in the staircase from the sixth floor down. Wilmer on his stomach, wriggling up like a Slinky.

Has nowhere to go but up.

Fires, crawls, fires. Shoots at the walls so the rounds ricochet around the corner.

Seems to be a good idea, because the shooting stops.

Angelo lies fetal, crumpled up against the fire-escape railing.

The *narco* comes out the window to give him the head shot.

Angelo fires from underneath his arm and gives him one instead.

Then he gets up and keeps climbing, thanking God and Jimmy that they both made him wear that vest.

Elevator door doesn't open on seven.

Jimmy and Harold get out on eight.

Decide that the elevator car is a moving, vertical coffin for two.

So when the doors start opening on nine and Oscar's guys blast it with AK and MAC fire, they don't see any bodies.

What they do see is an M16 "bounding" mine that goes off and releases a few thousand shards of shrapnel into them.

Wilmer is pinned down between eight and nine.

He's been hit twice in the vest and once in the left hand, and it's only a matter of time, and not much, before he takes one in the head. The fuckers are yelling at him, too, taunting him.

¡Vamos, sube, cabrón! ¿Porqué no subes?! Come on up, asshole! Why don't you come up?!

Then he hears a different voice. Jimmy's. "Wilmer, you down there!? Move down a floor! Now!"

Wilmer rolls down the stairs, leaving a smear of blood behind him. He hears Jimmy yell, "Cover up!"

Wilmer throws his arms over his head.

Harold stands in the ninth-floor doorway and shoulders the rocket launcher. He aims the barrel down the stairs and pulls the trigger.

The explosion is horrific.

But the shouting stops.

A few moans, no shouting.

"Wilmer, you good?!" Jimmy yells.

Wilmer can't hear a thing.

Just loud ringing in his ears.

He gets up climbs over a stack of bodies on his way to the ninth floor. The stairs are slick with blood and other stuff.

Jimmy and Harold pull him in through the doorway.

"You're hit," Jimmy says.

"Stairs or elevator?" Wilmer asks.

"I don't think the elevator's going to work anymore," Jimmy says. "And you stay in the stairs, get anyone coming down."

"I want to—"

"I know you do," Jimmy says. "Stay in the stairwell."

He and Harold start up to the penthouse.

The police radios are silent, but Eva's board is lighting up like a Christmas tree on crack. Concerned citizens calling: gunshots . . . explosions . . . screams. what's going on? . . . another explosion . . .

And she wishes, profoundly, she hadn't sent him on this mission, this crusade.

You lost one son, she tells herself, so you go ahead send the other to his death? Her mother was a gambler, taught her since she was a little girl that you don't chase bad money with good. You never catch it, you never get it back.

Now she doesn't take the calls but prays instead.

Please God, please Mother Mary, please St. Jude, the patron of lost causes, please send me my son back.

The explosions have rattled Oscar.

Literally.

The walls shook, a miniature tidal wave roiled the fish tank, and the grouper is going batshit crazy.

Jorge's not far behind.

He sees the images on the monitor—his boys splattered over walls, pieces of them like a box of spare human parts falling out of the ceiling—and says, "I'm turning myself in."

"The fuck you are," Oscar says.

"The fuck I'm not." He heads for the door.

Oscar puts half a clip in his back. Then he looks at the other eight guys who have assembled in the penthouse for a last stand. "Anyone else want to turn himself in?"

No one does.

"There's nine of us and four of them," Oscar says. "Only three ways in here. We take care of these *pendejos* up here, we go down to the basement, then make a break for it. We still have a chance. Split up, cover the lobby door, the back door, and the terrace."

He moves to the center of the living room.

If Jimmy McNabb wants me, he has to go through the others.

Not two of them.

The two *narcos* covering the terrace decide to go down the fire escape, wait until they're out of Oscar's sight, throw their hands up, and take their chances with the police.

They meet Angelo coming up on eight.

Everyone fires at once.

Harold stands to the side of the back door, points the shotgun at a forty-five-degree angle toward the lock.

Jimmy presses himself against the wall on the lock side of the door, ready to go in.

Always the first one through the door, right?

Harold blasts the lock and jumps back.

The door swings open.

A wall of bullets blasts out.

Jimmy doesn't go in first this time.

He sends grenades instead.

Sidearm pitches through the doorway.

First a flashbang to blind.

Followed by a fragmentation to kill.

Then he goes in.

Eva used to say, when the boys made a mess in the kitchen, that it looked like a hurricane hit it.

This kitchen looks like a hurricane punched it in the face.

Backsplashes splashed with blood.

Stainless-steel refrigerator stained.

Oven door hanging open, crooked on one hinge, like a broken jaw.

Three dead, or getting that way. Two on the floor, one leaning over the counter. A survivor crouches behind a butcher block in the middle of the floor. Rises up to shoot Jimmy, misses, hits Harold instead.

Straight in the forehead.

The big man's knees buckle, and then he topples onto the butcher block, then slides off, dying on the way down.

Vengeance always has a cost.

Jimmy swings the HK butt, crushes the shooter's skull, and moves through the kitchen. Harold is dead, and there ain't nothing Jimmy can do for him except grieve, and that will come later.

No time for sorrow now, or regret.

Later, later.

He shoulders the HK and fires in front of him until the clip is empty.

Angelo wipes the blood from his eyes.

Head wounds bleed like crazy.

A "grazing" bullet plows a deep furrow, and he's going to have an ugly scar, but he's alive, unlike the guy who shot him and his buddy, both draped over the fire-escape railing like ghetto laundry.

Dizzy, sick from a concussion, Angelo climbs.

Stay in the stairwell?

Wilmer ain't staying in no fucking staircase.

Qué carajo.

Jimmy or no Jimmy.

White dog, black dog, it's a dog.

Clutching his nine in his one good (left) hand, he goes up the stairs into the penthouse lobby.

Sees the open door.

Hears the firing and steps in.

Jimmy whirls.

Ain't no one supposed to be behind him.

Fires.

Misses Wilmer's head by an inch.

Wilmer smiles with relief.

Then a bullet hits him in the throat, another one in the mouth, a third between the eyes, and just like that, Wilmer is gone from this world.

Jimmy turns and fires.

The shooter rattles and falls.

No time for regret, or sorrow.

Later later later later.

Jimmy steps into the living room.

Firing from the hip, sweeping from right to left, just laces it with fire, shoots up chairs, sofas, tables, windows, fish tank. Ninety gallons of water spill out, fish flop on the carpet.

The clip empty, Jimmy drops the HK, pulls his 9mm Glock, and scans the room.

Where is Oscar?

Lying flat behind the sofa, Oscar sees his precious blue queen angel gasp for air, its mouth sucking, its beautiful azure scales shimmering.

He's outraged.

What he wants to do is stand up and blast the man who killed his fish and destroyed his life. That's what he wants to do, but Oscar Diaz is a coward, so what he does is crawl on his belly toward the terrace.

Jimmy sees him, just as he's slithering through the shattered slider.

He walks over and steps on the small of his back.

"Where you goin', Oscar?" Jimmy McNabb is a big man, his foot is heavy. He raises it and brings it down on Oscar's spine again and again, like to break it. "No, you and me got a date, man. We got us an appointment."

He stomps his back, his legs, his ankles, his feet. "This is for Danny. This is for my brother. My mother. My old man."

Eva's voice:

I want you to embrace everything I tried to love out of you. I want you to embrace your hate. I want you to avenge your brother.

Oscar grunts in pain. His hands still grip the AK, but Jimmy stomps on his fingers, breaking some, twisting some, bruising others. Keeping one foot on Oscar's hand, he kicks him in the face with the other.

You do that for me? You do *that for me. You think of Danny. You think of your baby brother.*

Jimmy kicks him in the mouth, shattering his teeth.

And you kill them all. You kill all the men who killed my Danny.

Stomps on the back of his head.

I will.

Kicks him in the temple.

And you make it hurt.

Jimmy stops kicking him. "I ain't done with you, Oscar. You gonna stay conscious, you gonna stay awake. I'm going to set you on fire and throw you over the side like the garbage you are. You're gonna burn like you made—"

The blow hits him in the back of the neck and drives him forward, off Oscar. Then a forearm wraps around his throat, another locks it from behind, and he's in a choke hold.

The guy that was bent over the kitchen counter.

Jimmy can't breathe.

About to black out.

He drops his gun, stabs backward with his fingers and hits the man's eyes. It loosens the grip just enough for Jimmy to get a breath, get one hand inside the choke, and get it off his carotid artery, and as he does, he staggers onto the terrace, toward the edge.

The guy leans back with all his strength, trying to snap Jimmy's neck, but Jimmy's left hand grabs a finger and snaps it. The man screams, Jimmy turns in his grasp, facing him, and then lifts him. Hefts him over the side, and the man is in the air, legs kicking, arms swimming, screaming for ten long stories down.

Jimmy struggles for air.

Through watery eyes sees Oscar on his feet, staggering toward the fire escape, the only thing in his way—

Angelo, just come over the top, his face a bloody mask, his legs wobbly.

Oscar gets off a shot.

It hits Angelo below the vest, in the thigh, and the femoral artery spurts like a hose. Oscar stumbles over him and gets on the ladder, and now Jimmy has a choice.

Kill Oscar or save Angelo.

Angelo yells, "Get him!"

Jimmy crouches beside Angelo.

"Get him," Angelo says, voice weakening.

"No," Jimmy says. "I got *you*."

He presses hard on the wound, stopping the bleeding. With his other hand, he reaches inside his clothes for his cell phone and calls dispatch.

Eva hears, "Officer down, 2203 Morgan Avenue, Algiers, penthouse. Get EMTs up."

She sends them and then thanks God.

"I got you," Jimmy says. "You're gonna make it, hang in."

"He's getting away."

"Fuck dat."

Because sometimes you're broken, broken so bad you don't know yourself, and then suddenly you do. You're stronger than you ever were, strong enough to take all that anger and hate and rage and stop the bleeding.

You're stronger in the broken places.

Oscar makes it down the fire escape.

On bruised and broken feet, he hops toward the river.

Fifty-eight cops open fire, lighting up the New Orleans night.

Jimmy McNabb stands on the terrace as the first responders load Angelo onto a gurney.

They say he's probably going to make it.

But not Harold, not Wilmer.

They're gone—like Danny—and Jimmy doesn't know if it was worth it.

He turns and looks out at his city.

Even in moonlight the river looks dirty.

You ain't gotta tell Eva the world is a broken place.

She knows life, knows the world.

Knows that no matter how you come into it, you come out broken.

FOR MR. STEVE MCQUEEN

CRIME 101

C rime 101: Keep it simple.

...

Highway 101.

The Pacific Coast Highway.

Aka the PCH.

It clings to the California coast like a string of jewels on an elegant neck.

Davis loves this road like a man loves a woman.

He could drive it all day and all night.

...

Davis sits at the wheel of a black Shelby GT500 Mustang hardtop with a rear spoiler, Gurney flap, 550 HP and 510 ft./lb. of torque.

Crime 101: When you need to get away, you need to do it fast.

He drives north past a stretch of coast where the sun is setting like a busted blood orange in the clouds over the ocean.

To his left the waves crash onto Torrey Pines Beach. To his right the railroad tracks cross Los Penasquitos Creek, and Carmel Valley Road runs along the ridge that flanks the northern edge of the lagoon, where the old car-repair shop has one of the best views on the coast and the pizza joint has been there as long as Davis can remember.

Like a woman of changing moods, Highway 101 changes its name frequently. Now it's North Torrey Pines Road, and in a few yards it will shift to South Camino del Mar.

It's always the 101 to Davis.

Davis follows a white Mercedes 500SL up the hill into the town of Del Mar.

He'd watched Ben Haddad come out of the store in La Jolla with a sample case in his hand.

Davis has watched Haddad come out of Sam Kassem's store dozens of times, but he still looked down at the iPad in his lap and checked the photos of Haddad at the annual jewelry show in Las Vegas. Davis has photographs of Haddad at the Vegas show, the Tucson show, and the Gem Faire in Del Mar.

In the last one, Haddad sits in a banquette at Red Tracton's with Kassem and their wives. They're holding up martinis, smiling at the camera.

The photo was posted on Gem Faire's website.

Davis knows that Haddad is sixty-four years old, married, with three daughters, the youngest of whom is a freshman at UC Santa Barbara. He knows that Haddad likes baseball, plays golf mostly to be social, and hasn't quit smoking despite assurances to his doctor and his wife. He knows that Haddad is fully bonded and insured and never carries a firearm.

Now Davis lets a couple of cars get between them in case there's a follow car. Haddad has never used one before, but you never know. Anyway, Davis doesn't have to stay close to Haddad because he knows where the courier is headed.

Davis saw the email between Kassem and John Houghton, a jewelry-store owner in Del Mar:

Ben is on his way now.

The Mercedes pulls off to the right—at Houghton's Fine Jewelry.

Then Haddad does what he always does, what he believes is the prudent thing for a courier to do. Instead of parking out front along the street, he pulls in to the small parking lot in back.

Davis knows the drill, because it's an article of faith among jewelry couriers and salesmen that theft rings put store*fronts* under observation.

So Haddad pulls in to the back and calls Houghton to tell him he's coming in.

Houghton will buzz him in through the front door.

This is the anomaly—the conflicting agenda of couriers and store owners: The courier wants to protect his merchandise, the owner his store. The store owner's most valuable stock is in the back room, separately locked from the front of the store. The safe is also in the back room.

If a theft ring has followed the courier (or a salesman making his rounds), the store owner doesn't want to let him in through the back door, where the thieves could rush in behind and get the really valuable merchandise or force him to open the safe.

So the courier parks in the back but then walks to the front.

This is the seam.

The crack.

The *edge* that Davis always looks for.

And he won't do it if it's not there.

That's Crime 101.

That and the cigarette.

Davis hears what Haddad tells Houghton on the phone. *I'm just going to have a quick smoke, and then I'll be in.*

Because it's the family car, and Ben doesn't want Diana smelling the smoke and chewing his ass. And unless Diana is out at one of her club meetings or something, this is his last ciggy of the day, because this is his last stop.

So what Haddad does—what he always does— is get on the horn and tell Houghton he's just going to have a quick smoke.

But it's a few drags, not the whole cigarette, so Davis will have, at most, a minute before Houghton wonders what's keeping the courier and comes out to look. Houghton is also fully bonded and insured, but he does carry a weapon—a 10-millimeter EAA Witness.

But a minute is more than enough time.

Crime 101: If you can't do it quick, don't do it at all.

Haddad steps out of the car, lights up, takes a few precious beautiful drags, and stomps out the cigarette under his shoe.

Davis hits the gas.

He takes the SIG Sauer P239 pistol from the center console and holds it in his right hand as he steers with his left.

Davis has the clock in his head as he rolls into the parking lot and gets out. He's dressed all in black—black lightweight pullover sweater, black jeans, black shoes, black gloves, black baseball cap, unmarked with any logo.

Holding the SIG below his waist, Davis comes up behind Haddad just as he's grinding the cigarette butt into the pavement. Sticks the pistol barrel behind his ear and says, "Keep your eyes forward."

Without turning around, Haddad hands him the sample case. "Just take it and go."

Bonded and insured.

It isn't worth it.

Take the sample case and go with God.

Except Davis says, "Not the cheap stuff in the case, Ben. The 'live goods' in your ankle pouches. The papers."

Haddad hesitates. This is where it can all go sick and wrong. This is where it can shift from eight-to-thirty to life-without-possibility-of.

Davis isn't going to let it go there.

"I want to send you home to Diana," he says. "I want you to walk Leah down the aisle in . . . what is it, three weeks?"

Haddad wants to take that walk, too. He bends downs, rips the Velcroed pouches from his ankles, and hands them back over his shoulder.

"Your phone," Davis says.

It will only buy an extra few seconds, but those seconds could be crucial.

Haddad hands him the cell phone. Davis rips the battery out, tosses it into the bushes behind the lot, and hands the phone back. There's no sense being a dick about it and costing the guy all his contact information and his family photos.

"If you turn around," Davis says, "it's to see a bullet come into your brain. Personally, I wouldn't die for an insurance company."

Haddad doesn't turn around.

Davis gets back into his car and drives out.

Elapsed time: forty-seven seconds.

He drives just three blocks north and then pulls in to the underground parking structure of the vacation-rental condo complex. His slot is #182, he's rented it for the month, and he has two spaces.

In his other slot sits a silver Camaro ZL1.

6.2 SC V-8 engine.

Four-lobed Eaton supercharger.

Magnetic ride technology.

The parking structure is about half full.

As usual, Davis sees cars but no people.

He gets out, quickly removes the stolen plates from the Mustang, and re-places them with the genuine ones. He takes the gem papers from the ankle pouches, puts them in his jacket pocket, and throws the pouches into the dumpster. Then he takes the SIG out of the Mustang, gets into the Camaro, and pulls out onto the 101.

If anyone is looking for a getaway car, they're looking for a black Mustang, and now it's literally underground.

With nothing in it that connects to him.

Even if they find the car, it gives them nothing.

He paid for it in cash, registered it under a false name. All they get is a PO box in San Luis Obispo that he'll never go back to.

Sure, he'd lose the car, but it's a good trade.

Couldn't drive it in prison anyway.

He pulls out and heads north on the 101.

Through Del Mar, past the racetrack.

Past the pink neon sign by Fletcher Cove that proclaims SOLANA BEACH,

past the Tidewater Bar, Pizza Port, Mitch's Surf Shop, and Moreland Choppers. Down the hill to the long stretch of beach at Cardiff, then up past
Swami's and Encinitas, past Moonlight Beach, the old La Paloma Theater,
underneath the sign that arcs over the 101 and reads ENCINITAS.

Then along the railroad tracks and eucalyptus trees of funky Leucadia,
up to old-fashioned Carlsbad, past the old power station, its smokestack
evocative of both Springsteen and Blake.

Davis follows the 101 as far as he can go but then has to turn east on
Oceanside Boulevard and get on the 5 North to go through Camp Pendleton,
the Marine Corps base that is a blockage in the artery. He gets off the 5 as
soon as he can, at Los Cristianitos in San Clemente, wends his way through
the old surf town and down along Capistrano Beach, up through Dana Point,
Laguna Niguel, South Laguna, and finally into Laguna Beach.

Davis never tires of this drive, never tires of the constant but ever-changing
ocean, the landmarks, his small gods of place.

He pulls in to the parking structure of another condo complex on the east
side of the 101 overlooking Main Beach and the Laguna Art Museum.

Davis hits the button attached to the windshield visor, the metal gate
slides open, and he pulls in to the concrete underground parking structure
into one of his two assigned slots, marked on the wall as Unit 4.

Beside him sits a black 2011 Dodge Challenger SRT-8.

Hemi V-8.

Chin spoiler.

Variable camshaft timing.

Davis likes his cars American, fast and powerful.

He gets out of the Camaro, walks over to the little elevator, takes it to the
third floor, and lets himself into Unit 4.

The condo is typical—an open floor plan with a small kitchen and breakfast bar at one end, a living room that runs to a set of glass sliders opening
onto a narrow balcony with a table, chairs, and a gas grill. On the south side
of the condo, a corridor leads to a guest bedroom, two baths, and a master
bedroom that looks out on the ocean.

You buy this unit, it's going to run the north side of a million.

Davis doesn't buy, he doesn't own.

Any of his places.

He rents.

Furnished, turnkey vacation rentals. They come with everything—TVs,
stereos, pots and pans, dishes, glasses, cups, coffeemakers, toasters, silver-
ware, towels, washcloths, even soap.

Davis rents them in different names and always pays in cash.

In advance.

Crime 101: People who get their money rarely ask questions.

Here's the deal.

There are condo complexes all up and down the 101.

People buy them, but most don't live in them year-round. A lot of them serve as places for families to gather in the summer or for people from the frigid states to come to in the winter. The rest of the time they sit empty, so a lot of the owners rent them out to pay the mortgage.

Because it's a genuine pain in the ass to do this for yourself, most of the owners use a management service that takes a percentage.

They rent by the month, the week, even the day if they're right on the beach, and all you have to do is establish your credit with one of these management companies and you can change condos as often as you like.

The populations of these condo complexes are mostly transient and faceless. Some of them are refugees from the cold winters of Minnesota or Wisconsin, others are waiting for escrow to clear on the house they've just bought or sold. Some are the recently divorced "in transition." Some just like living by the beach. They come and go. You could live there for years without meeting a neighbor, except maybe to say hi in the parking garage or at the pool.

This works for Davis. He deals with five different management companies under five different names. He never stays in any one place more than a couple of months and rarely goes back to the same condo twice.

What he's learned is this:

If you live everywhere, you live nowhere.

Your address is the 101.

Davis goes to the refrigerator and grabs a bottle of Pellegrino. Then he sits down on the sofa, takes the papers from his pocket, and opens them.

Five small packets of neatly folded, thin white paper. Inside the white paper is a layer of thin blue paper.

Inside each blue paper:

An emerald-cut diamond.

Total value:

One point five million dollars.

Davis gets up, goes out onto the balcony, and looks out at the ocean and the 101.

• • •

Lieutenant Ronald—"Lou"—Lubesnick stands in the parking lot in back of Houghton's Fine Jewelry and looks at Ben Haddad.

"I guess this is what I'm trying to say," Lou repeats. "You make dozens of runs a month between Sammy's La Jolla store and here. Most of the time it's with a few thousand bucks' worth of merchandise. But on the *one night* you're carrying one and a half million in stones, *that's* when you get hit?"

Lou shrugs.

His partner, McGuire, smiles. Lou's shrugs are famous. The word around the Robbery Unit is that Lou says more with his shoulders than with his mouth. Which is a lot of action, because Lou talks a lot.

Like now, Lou saying, "I mean, is there anything about this that *doesn't* say 'inside job'? What, the guy just got lucky?"

"He didn't get any information from me," Haddad says stubbornly.

They go over it again.

Houghton had a customer who wanted to look at some stones that Houghton didn't have but Sammy Kassem did. Sammy chose a sample of five stones from his La Jolla store for the customer to look at. Haddad drove them over and got popped in the parking lot. The robber apparently knew that the sample case was a dummy and that the stones were in the ankle pouches.

Haddad can't give them a face, a license plate, a car—even the color or make of a car.

"He just came out of nowhere," Haddad says. "And he told me not to turn around."

"You did the right thing," Lou says. He'd much rather work grand theft than a murder. Lou did five years on SD Homicide before transferring over. The worst part was informing the families.

"Did you get a sense, was he about your height?" Lou asks.

"Maybe taller."

"His accent," Lou says.

"He didn't have one."

"Everyone has one," Lou says. "Are you saying it wasn't black or Spanish?"

"That's right."

McGuire knows where Lou is headed. Almost all the jewelry-courier robberies in the country are committed by Colombian gangs connected with the drug cartels. A year or so ago, they were banging the East Coast like ten-year-old boys playing whack-a-mole at Chuck E. Cheese. If they've moved out west now, it's very bad news.

Lou Lubesnick and Bill McGuire make an odd-looking team. Lou is five-ten with some salt creeping into the pepper of his ink-black hair and a gut that's making some advances over his belt. McGuire is a six-four, rawboned redhead with freckles and a frame like a wire coat hanger.

Together they look more like a comedy team than a pair of detectives, but there are a lot of guys in the joint who don't find anything funny about the team of Lubesnick and McGuire, especially now that Lou is head of the Robbery Division with five other veteran detectives under him.

Even at this moment, some of the team are canvassing the neighborhood to find out if anyone saw anything, while the rest work the parking lot for tire tracks or shoe prints.

Lou turns his attention to Houghton. "Have you noticed anybody hanging around, watching the store?"

"I think I would have mentioned that," Houghton says.

Lou is immune to sarcasm, totally tone-deaf. "Any customer come in, look around, didn't buy anything?"

"Every day," Houghton says. "This economy, people are lookers."

He says "lookers" with disdain.

"But no one in particular," Lou says.

Houghton shakes his head. This is no mean feat—he has a big head with fatty jowls. His skin is as white as milk—again, no mean feat when your business is a few hundred yards from the beach.

"I want to see your security tapes," Lou says.

They go inside and look at the tapes, which aren't tapes at all anymore but, like everything else these days, a digital record on a computer. Houghton has cameras covering the front door, the inside of the store, and the back entrance, but nothing on the rear parking lot.

"Why not?" Lou asks.

"Because nothing ever happens there," Houghton says.

Lou shrugs.

Something happened there.

Lou looks down and sees the cigarette butt. He looks up at Haddad. "Yours?"

"Does this have to go in your report?" Haddad asks.

Lou shakes his head.

He's married, too.

McGuire slides into the passenger seat of Lou's car. "Twenty bucks says Sammy lays those stones off in Brazil within six weeks."

"Would we be thinking that if he weren't Middle Eastern?" Lou might not be the only cop in SDPD who contributes to the ACLU, but he is the only one who'll admit it. "You can't tell me we don't look at them harder."

"Who knew about the delivery?" McGuire says. "Sammy, Haddad, Houghton. Could have been Houghton for all we know. He said it himself, business is bad. Maybe he tipped off the robbers, got a cut."

"Robbers? Plural?" The theft rings don't work this way, Lou thinks. They're smash-and-grab. They literally smash in the courier's car window, reach in, and take the merchandise. Half the time they beat him up, stab him, or shoot him.

They're violent.

This guy gave back the cell phone.

"Don't," McGuire says.

"Don't what?" Lou asks, even though he knows.

"Don't do your Lone Ranger thing."

Lou is by himself in thinking that there's one guy pulling off a series of high-level jewelry heists.

Eleven jobs over the past four years.

Consistent—always on couriers or salesmen who are carrying value.

Efficient—in and out so fast even if there are witnesses who don't know *what* the fuck they saw.

Patient—the merchandise doesn't show up on the illicit market for months, if at all. So our boy is in no hurry to get paid.

Discreet—none of the usual fences know anything about him.

And clean—there's been more blood spilled at a kids' soccer game than in all these robberies combined.

At first no one thought the robberies were related. No one put them together because they were scattered over jurisdictions—San Diego, LA, Orange County, Mendocino—and no one shared the information.

The received wisdom was that it was a "ring." (Prosecutors *love* rings. Rings make headlines, with a nice series of pictures on the front page.)

It was Lou checking insurance stats that put them together, Lou who introduced the theory that they were looking at one individual.

"A lone wolf," his boss said when Lou first brought it up.

"If you have to," Lou said.

"Bullshit," his boss said.

If it was a ring, Lou argued, someone would have slipped up by now—bragged in a club, pissed off his old lady, or gotten busted on another charge and tried to trade up.

But one guy, keeping his own counsel, staying clean . . .

That guy's not going to give you anything to help you catch him.

It's Crime 101.

Lou is generally mocked for his "pet theory" about the Lone Gunman.

From his bosses, from the insurance companies, even the guys in his own unit bust his chops for having a "man crush," a "bromance" with Robie "The Cat" after the old movie about the jewelry thief.

What was it called? Lou wonders now.

To Catch a Thief, that's it.

Yeah, Lou thinks. *To Catch a Thief.*

Not thieves.

Thief.

Singular.

"Even if there was a real theft here," McGuire says now, "and I'm not saying that there was, it's probably Colombians. And I say this because it almost always is."

"How do we know?" Lou asks.

McGuire hates it when Lou goes into his rabbinical mode. "How do we know what?"

"How do we know they're almost always Colombians?" Lou clarifies. Then, as McGuire knew he would, he answers his own question. "Because they get caught."

"So?"

So, Lou thinks, this guy doesn't.

• • •

Davis walks into the Cliffs wearing a white dress shirt (tailored but not monogrammed), cuff links, and a black three-button wool gabardine Hugo Boss suit.

Black Church oxfords.

Davis owns few clothes, but they're all good.

Classic.

Versatile.

A little retro.

Like Davis.

His brown hair is cut short, like pre-Beatles sixties, like he came out of a Kennedy campaign meeting or the Peace Corps.

Or a Steve McQueen movie.

Davis has seen every Steve McQueen movie ever made, most of them multiple times. Davis would *be* Steve McQueen except Steve McQueen already was Steve McQueen and there's never going to be another one.

But to Davis, McQueen was the living definition of California cool.

If the 101 were an actor, it would be Steve McQueen.

The woman with the shoulder-length brown hair is the hottest woman in the restaurant.

Which is saying something.

All of the dozen or so women sipping white wines or dirty martinis at the bar of the trendy place are gorgeous and yoga, cross-trained, and spin-class fit because that's how they get through the door.

Davis edges his way beside her and says, "It must be a lot of pressure, always being the most beautiful woman in a crowded room."

She turns to him and answers, "Where have you been?"

"I made reservations here," Davis says. "Is this okay, or would you like to go somewhere else?"

"How do you know I'm not waiting for someone?" Traci asks.

"I don't," Davis says. "I'm just hoping you're not."

"And if I am," she says without a trace of rancor, "you'll ask one of these other skinny bitches."

"It's just that I hate eating alone."

A few seconds later, Derry, the manager, comes over and says, "Mr. Delaney, your table is ready. Good evening, Traci."

Davis gives him a fifty-dollar handshake, and they go to their table.

Traci consumes an entire dinner made up of small appetizers—veggies, fish, chicken—nothing that would add an ounce of fat to that body.

"So where *have* you been?" she asks him with a stick of chicken satay perched on her lips. "It's been . . . what, two months or something like that?"

"Something like that," Davis answered. "I've just been out of town on a consulting job."

"How'd it go?"

"Fine."

Traci gets that Michael doesn't like to talk about work. He likes to talk about music, films, sports, news, cars, art, surfing, yoga, triathlons, food, bicycles, but not work. So she switches it up to talk about the sprint Ironman she's training for.

When the bill comes, Davis lays some twenties in the folder.

"Why do you always pay in cash?" Traci asks.

"I hate paying bills."

"As much as you hate eating alone?"

"Almost."

"Do you hate sleeping alone, too?" Traci asks, with a look in her eye that some guys would pay a thousand bucks to see just once in their lives.

Lou is glad to see that the Daily Grin is open.

Guy keeps irregular hours.

The hot dog truck, parked on a vacant lot on the corner of Lomas Santa

Fe and the 101, is actually called the Daily Grind, but some joker removed the *d,* and the new name stuck.

Lou pulls his Honda Civic into the little lot.

His ride is the subject of constant ballbusting.

"Why don't you buy a new car?" McGuire has asked on more than one occasion.

"Why?" Lou answered in return.

"Because it's twelve years old," McGuire said.

"So is your daughter," Lou said. "Are you going to trade her in?"

"Lindsey doesn't have two hundred thousand miles on her," Lou said.

"Two hundred and thirty-seven," Lou said. "And I think I can get three. I mean, you put oil in these things, they run forever."

But it's unseemly, McGuire has maintained, a San Diego police lieutenant driving a car that looks like it should have a Domino's placard stuck on top. And the interior is no better—the seats are worn and sun-faded, crumbs from Lou's many peripatetic meals (In-N-Out Burger, Rubio's, Jack in the Box) are ground into the seams, and the dashboard is Neanderthal— no hands-free phone, no Sirius radio, no navigation.

"I've lived in San Diego my whole life," Lou said. "I know how to get where I need to go."

"What if you leave San Diego?" McGuire asked. "Go on a road trip?"

"In *this* car?"

Angie flat-out refuses to get into the Civic. They usually take her Prius on the odd occasions they go out together.

Now Lou walks up to the hot-dog truck and looks at the trivia question handwritten on the board.

"Alaska," Lou says.

"Huh?"

"The answer to your trivia question," Lou says. "State with the most surface water. What do I win?"

"Free mustard on your dog."

"My lucky day," Lou says. "One chili dog, angioplasty on the side."

"Yeah, I never heard that one."

"And a Coke," Lou says. "No, a Diet Coke. No, a Coke."

Because what the hell, right? He's trying to keep the stomach down and was going to make it home for dinner when Angie called and told him she was going out with friends.

Lou gets his dog and steps over to the end of the truck where the condiments are. He smothers the dog with onions because, again, what the hell. He's thinking this happy thought when the phone rings and it's McGuire.

"You wanna grab a beer?" McGuire asks.

"Not tonight."

"Lou?"

"Yeah?"

"Don't," McGuire says.

"Don't what?" Lou asks.

"You know."

Yeah, Lou knows.

Just like he knows he's going to.

Don't do it, Lou tells himself as he drives down into Del Mar.

McGuire is right for once—don't do it.

But he does. Turns off the 101 on Tenth Street and parks a little way down the street where he can keep an eye on the front door. Goddamn lawyers can afford houses in Del Mar. Cops with twenty-plus years on the job live in Mission Hills.

Del Mar, Lou reflects, is one of those California beach towns that tried to class up its true nature by putting up Tudor-style buildings, replete with hammerbeam roofs (sometimes with fake thatch), half-timbers, and cross gables.

Lou has always half expected to see plaques claiming that Shakespeare had once slept here. Anyway, it's always amused him, although the time he went into one of the restaurants and tried to order spotted dick amused neither the waiter or Angie.

"How about bangers and mash?" Lou asked.

"How about acting your age?" Angie asked.

Which was hypocritical, because one of her standard complaints against him was that he acted too old—i.e., precisely his age.

Lou has a nice house in a nice neighborhood, but apparently not nice enough for Angie. Because her car, the fucking Prius she had to have, is out in front of the lawyer's. She's not even bothering to be discreet anymore.

He allows himself the fantasy of going up and rapping on the door, sticking his shield in the lawyer's face, and asking him, *What the fuck are you doing with my wife?*—pun intended—but the last thing he needs in the world right now is a suspension and a letter in his jacket.

So he sits.

Lou has been on a hundred stakeouts.

Never thought he'd be on this one.

Angie comes out of the lawyer's house at 10:10.

Lou makes a mental note of this, as if it mattered, as if he were going to have to testify in court in cop-speak—*Subject exited the premises at 10:10.*

He leaves some distance but follows her all the way east on 56 to the 163 and then Friar's Road and finally home, pulling off a couple of blocks and waiting for her to get into the house for a few minutes.

Then he pulls up and goes in.

Angie's sitting in the living room sipping a red wine and looking at a magazine when he comes through the door. He can't blame the guy for wanting to bang her—she's still a looker in her early forties—trim legs, nice rack, auburn hair.

She works out.

"How was your evening?" he asks, sitting in the chair across from her.

"Nice," she says.

"*Who* were you out with?"

"I told you—Claire."

"Yeah," he says, willing himself to stay in the chair. "When did Claire move to 805 Tenth Street in Del Mar?"

She shakes her head. "Cops."

That gets him out of the chair. He feels himself coming up as if a wave pushed him, and then he's right in her face yelling, "What the *fuck*, Angie?!"

She doesn't back down.

One of the things that attracted him to her a thousand years ago back at San Diego State.

She just sits there, looks him right back in the eye, doesn't say a thing. What Angie should have been, he thinks now, is a hit man, because she'd be ice in the interview room. Seeing a video of herself whacking some guy, she'd look across the table and say, *"So?"*

"I watched you come out of his house," Lou says.

"I'm sure you did."

Like it's *his* fault, right? Like he's some schmuck making himself ridiculous sitting in his car while his wife cuckolds him. Which is exactly what he feels like.

"Do you love him?" Lou asks.

He can't say the guy's name. It would make it too real.

"I don't love *you*," she answers.

"I want a divorce."

"No, Lou," she says. "*I* want a divorce."

Because she has to win, right? She can't even give him *that* moment.

Traci gets up early and leaves.

A personal trainer, she has several clients who come in before they go to their offices, so her working day starts at 5:00 A.M. Davis kisses her goodbye and then goes back to sleep.

He gets up around eight, pulls on jeans and a hooded Killer Dana sweatshirt, grinds some coffee for the French press, then goes out to the little balcony to look at the ocean.

Opens up the iPad and sends all the surveillance pix of Haddad into the ether. Likewise the emails between Sam Kassem and John Houghton.

Davis hacked Sam's email account months ago and tracked it the way a stockbroker follows the market, getting to know Sam's business as if he were thinking of buying it. He learned that Sam routinely shifted merchandise from store to store, using his brother-in-law, Ben Haddad, as a courier.

Usually the deliveries amounted to more than a few thousand dollars in merchandise—thirty or forty grand at most—well below Davis's risk/ reward equation.

Davis has rejected scores of potential hits—the location was on a busy street, too close to a police station, too far from an available underground garage to stow the work car. The couriers carried weapons or used follow cars—the potential take wasn't worth the risk.

Davis has criteria.

Standards.

Rules.

He never compromises them.

Crime 101: Laws are made to be broken, with rules that are made to be followed.

Crime 101: Get there before the other guy.

Davis drives north past Point Reef, El Moro Canyon, Corona Del Mar, Newport Beach, all the way up to Huntington Beach.

He finds a parking spot near the pier, sits and waits.

Davis always gets to meetings early. Never *at* the meeting point but *near* the meeting point. Near enough to observe the guy he wants to meet or a whole committee. He always parks where there are at least two routes out.

It's a pretty view, the long stretch of beach and the pier that reaches out into the ocean. Quiet today—the surf isn't going off, and there are just a few fishermen and tourists on the pier.

He watches Money walk onto the pier, go about halfway, and lean against the north railing. Davis scans the terrain behind and in front of him, sees no one follow him, no one look up, none of the tourists or old strollers who are more than they seem to be. Nobody speaks into his hand, into his collar, into a book or a magazine.

So Davis gets out of the car, walks down to the pier, and stands along the railing beside Money.

Money is tall, with sandy hair, an unlikely goatee, but neatly trimmed. Gray sport jacket over jeans. Blue shirt, no tie. They call him Money because that's what he does—he takes the raw merchandise and converts it to money.

"Another day in paradise," Money says.

"Why we live here," Davis says. He slips the gem papers into Money's jacket pocket. "One and a half mil."

This isn't just a matter of trust, although Davis has worked with him for years. It's business—Money would never rip Davis off, because Davis makes him . . . money.

Money has only a handful of clients, each of them among the best thieves in the world. He's impeccable about where he fences the merchandise, immaculate about the accounts.

Minus Money's commission this score nets Davis one million flat.

Money is full-service: He fences the rocks, washes the proceeds, sets up overseas accounts under a variety of aliases. He doesn't know Davis's real name, where he lives, what he drives.

"I'll be back to you in a few weeks," Davis says.

"You have an idea how much?" Money asks.

"More than this."

"That puts you close," Money says, smiling.

Close to retirement.

Their deal.

Davis has a number in mind. The amount he needs to live well but not lavishly.

Then he's done.

Retiring young.

Crime 101: Getting out one job too early puts you on the beach. Getting out one job too late puts you in a cell.

Then Money says, "This next job, it's not down south, is it?"

"Why do you ask?"

"No, just some shit I heard."

Davis waits him out.

"There's this San Diego cop," Money says, "apparently has developed a hard-on for you. Pushing a theory about the 'Highway 101 Bandit.' "

Davis feels an electric jolt. "Does he have an ID?"

"No, nothing like that," Money says. "Just a theory."

Yeah, but the theory is right, Davis thinks.

"This cop have a name?"

"Lubesnick," Money says. "Lieutenant Ronald Lubesnick. He's very good."

"How do you know all this?"

"It's my business to know," Money says. "Anyway, you might want to stay away from Dago for a while."

Money enjoys the view for a few more seconds and then walks away. He always leaves the meeting first, and Davis always waits and walks around a little bit before going back to his car.

• • •

Crime 101: "Trust" is a word generally used by convicts and usually in the past tense—i.e., "I trusted him."

• • •

Money gets into his Jag, drives to the Hyatt Regency, and sits in the parking lot.

Fifteen minutes later Ormon opens the passenger door and slides into the seat beside him.

Ormon has yellow hair.

Not blond—yellow.

Short—five-six or -seven—and thin.

Early thirties.

Black leather motorcycle jacket, black jeans, black Doc Martens.

"That was him, huh?" Ormon asks. "Beside you on the pier."

"That was him."

"Did he say anything about another job?" Ormon asks.

"He's doing one in a few weeks," Money says.

"Did he say what it is?"

Money just stares at him.

"But you'll let me know," Ormon presses.

Money nods.

Because Ormon isn't Davis, not by a long shot, but Ormon isn't one score from retiring either.

Money watches a lot of football. He knows the game. He knows you have to trade a star veteran when you can still get something for him.

• • •

Sam Kassem's base store is in El Cajon, or "*Al* Cajon" as the locals call the east San Diego neighborhood since the Iraqi immigration came in.

Lou will never forget the time he went into a convenience store on El Cajon Boulevard to get a Coke and found a goat hanging upside down in the cooler.

"You have a goat in the cooler," Lou said to the Chaldean owner as he checked out. Increasingly, the convenience stores, liquor stores, and other small businesses in the San Diego satellite neighborhoods are owned by Chaldeans, Iraqi Christians who came during the war.

"My daughter's wedding," the owner said, giving Lou his change. "Have a wonderful day."

Now Lou pulls in to Sam's parking lot.

Sam has high-end stores in all the trendy zip codes—La Jolla, Fashion Valley, Newport Beach, Beverly Hills—but he's kept his base here in the old, run-down neighborhood that first took him in when he came over from Iraq.

Lou respects that.

"Why do you let me get robbed?" Sam asks when Lou comes in.

Lou sits down across the desk from him in the office in back of the shop. Sam looks over his shoulder through the one-way mirror so he can keep an eye on things.

"Why do *you* let you get robbed?" Lou counters, taking a page from Angie's book. "Why don't you use a real courier service?"

"He's my brother-in-law."

Lou lets the unspoken question sit.

Sam says, "The insurance people already asked."

"I'll bet they did."

Lou is not without affection for Sam. A handsome man, always immaculately dressed, full head of distinguished silver hair, Sam came here from Baghdad and opened a jewelry store. Twenty-some years later, he has seven stores in Southern California.

It's the kind of American immigrant story that Lou is still a sucker for.

His great-grandparents came from some Polish shithole and worked the tuna boats in San Diego. His grandfather opened a sandwich shop, his father was a professor of literature at UCSD.

"Trust me," Sam says. "Ben was terrified. Diana had to give him a what-do-you–call–it, an Ambien, last night."

"That shit will mess you up," Lou says.

It's Sam's turn to shrug.

"So how?" Lou asks.

"Did the robber know what Ben was carrying?" Sam asks, finishing Lou's question. "You're the detective, you tell me."

"Who knew about the shipment?"

"Me, Ben and Houghton."

"You trust Houghton?"

"I've done business with him twenty years," Sam answers.

I've been married almost that long, Lou thinks. "Walk me through it again."

Sam sighs but takes him through it. "Houghton got hold of him—"

"How?" Lou asks.

"He telephoned," Sam answers. "Said he had a regular customer who was looking for a certain kind of stone—an empress cut—six carats or bigger. Asked me if I had such an item."

"And you did."

"Sure," Sam says. "Five of them that would fit the bill."

"So . . ."

"So I told him so. He asked for pictures, so I sent them."

"How?"

"Email," Sam answers, "and he asked me to have Ben take them over."

"You do that? Just on trust?"

"Twenty years."

Yeah, Lou thinks. "Then . . ."

"Then Ben comes by on his route," Sam explains, "I already have the stones wrapped up in their papers, Ben takes them, and I let Houghton know he's on the way."

"You phone or email?"

"Email," Sam says. "Then I get a call from Ben, his voice is shaking. I was afraid he was going to have a heart attack."

So the robber hacked Sam's emails, Lou thinks. He gets up from his chair. "Hire a service. One of them with an armored car."

"Do you know what that costs?"

"I'm guessing less than one and a half mil," Lou says.

The insurance guy wants to talk with Lou.

Of course he does, a seven-figure hit.

They meet at a taco stand in old downtown El Cajon. Lou makes sure Mercer pays. They sit at a picnic table outside, and Mercer says, "It had to be an inside job."

A scam as old as time, Lou thinks. Shop owner colludes in his own robbery, gets paid for his loss by the insurance company, buys the merchandise back from the thief at a discount, and sells it again on the black market.

Everyone wins except the insurance company, and everyone hates them anyway.

"Before we pitch our tent on the grassy knoll," Lou says, "let's consider the possibility that this *wasn't* an inside job. Let's consider the possibility that we're looking at a real pro who knows his business and does his homework."

Mercer unwraps his second taco from its paper, looks at Lou and says, "You gonna bring up your Superman theory again?"

"Same MO."

"Say you're right," Mercer argues. "That still doesn't preclude your lone guy using inside sources. I think you need to lean on Sam and his extended family a little bit."

"You wanna know what *I* think?" Lou asks. "I think you want to deny this claim while pushing me through the door ahead of you, and I think you can go fuck yourself—I'm not putting my unit between you and your insured."

"I'm just making a suggestion."

"Don't," Lou says. "You have information I can use, give me the information and I'll use it. You want to be *really* useful, get the insurance council to offer a reward, put some heat on this guy. But don't tell me how to do my job, Bill."

Mercer crumples up the paper and tosses it into the trash can.

"Is that a no on the reward?" Lou asks.

"I'm going to polygraph Sam and Haddad," Mercer says.

Lou isn't surprised. The insurance company has the right to demand something called an Examination Under Oath and question its insured under penalty of perjury.

It's the right move.

If Sam and Haddad flunk the poly, it will give the insurance company grounds to deny the claim. Mercer can't demand a polygraph from Houghton because he didn't suffer a loss and isn't making a claim.

But Lou is betting that Sam and Haddad pass the test. Sam is a sharp businessman but honest and hardworking, and Lou really does believe that the insurance companies are prejudiced against Middle Easterners because the Iranian carpet merchants really hosed them back in the nineties. And when the needle doesn't move on the Chaldeans, it's going to point at Houghton.

If, Lou thinks, this was an inside job.

Which it kind of is, if the guy is reading their mail.

• • •

Davis stops by the fish market in Dana Point Harbor, asks what's fresh, and buys two yellowtail fillets. Then he goes to Trader Joe's and picks up a bottle of imported lemon-infused olive oil.

The asparagus he gets from Von's, ditto the dark chocolate (85 percent cacao) and some cream and fresh raspberries for the mousse.

He's cooking dinner for Traci tonight.

• • •

Lou gathers his team in the staff room and stands by the whiteboard, where he's listed every courier robbery in California over the past four years and where he's just finished writing down the latest.

"I *want* this guy," Lou announces in the staff room.

This gets a collective, albeit suppressed, moan from the detectives, not one of whom believes there's a "guy." They also know where Lou is headed, and it's going to be a bitch, because of the eleven robberies on the board only three of them are in the unit's jurisdiction.

Lou jabs his finger at the board. "And to get this guy, we can't just look at this robbery. We have to look at all these robberies for patterns."

Another groan.

Lou and his patterns.

• • •

Crime 101: Every series of acts creates a pattern.

• • •

Lou knows that there are two ways to solve a crime:
1. A snitch.
Someone talks.

You can do all the CSI razzmatazz you want—that voodoo is for juries—but most crimes are solved because someone yaps.

2. Patterns.

With a serial criminal, unless you get a snitch, this is the ball game. A smart criminal can leave only minimal clues, but he can't help leaving patterns, any more than you can help leaving footprints on the beach.

And the patterns always mean something.

That's the good news.

The bad news is that investigators also have patterns—ways of working, ways of thinking, ways of doing, and their patterns sometimes make it harder for them to *see* patterns, to look at a set of facts in a fresh way, to discern new patterns from the expected ones.

It's like looking at a painting that's been in your living room for twenty years—you see what you've always seen; you don't see what you haven't seen.

Like a marriage, Lou thinks.

Now he pushes his team to look at the facts again.

"I don't want anyone to do anything today but *think*," Lou says. "Sanchez, look at every unsolved courier robbery in California over the past five years, eliminate any that wouldn't fit the lone-perp theory. Rhodes, get that smirk off your puss and see what the vics have in common. Ng—MO—look at verbs—he does this, he doesn't do that. Geary, go over the geography—I want a map. McGuire—you review the time factor—there's a pattern in the space between robberies."

"What are you going to look at, boss?" McGuire asks.

"I'm going to look at all of it," Lou says.

I'm going to stand back from the painting.

Lou is a bookish guy.

How Angie describes him anyway, and maybe this is one of their problems. In his rare free time, he'd rather get into a chair with a book, she'd rather go out. He usually yields and goes out, but she senses his resentment and resents it in turn.

"You're becoming your father," she told him one night after leaving a party early because he was sulking.

Don't we all? he thought.

Maybe lawyers in Del Mar don't.

But this is what he intends to do when he retires, sit back and read books.

Mostly history.

Lou just likes history, but he also *believes* in history, believes that most of the present's answers can be found in the past. So that's what he does now—he gathers stacks of old files and starts reading.

April 22, 2008:

A jewelry-store owner in Newport Beach goes to FedEx a custom watch—worth $435,000—to a customer. He gets hit in his own parking lot as he climbs into his car to drive to the FedEx facility.

September 15, 2008:

A salesman from New York flies into San Francisco with a suitcase full of mixed goods—colored gems, diamonds—to visit a number of regular clients in the Bay Area. He gets robbed at gunpoint in the parking lot of his hotel—$762,000.

January 11, 2009:

A diamond dealer from Belgium sells an inventory worth $960,000 to a store in Malibu and gets paid in cash. On the way back to LAX, he stops at a hotel on the PCH to meet a call girl and gets popped on the way out.

(At least, Lou thinks, the guy let him get laid.)

March 20, 2009:

A jeweler in Mendocino drives to FedEx to pick up a package of colored stones shipped from a store in Tucson. He gets hit just as he pulls back in to his shop—$525,000.

October 17, 2010:

Lou's personal favorite. A local dealer goes to Lindbergh Airport in San Diego with a carry-on shoulder bag filled with custom watches, rings, colored gemstones and diamonds. He has to put the bag on the X-ray conveyor belt, then gets stopped and patted down as he goes through the line. When he gets to the conveyor belt, his shoulder bag is gone—$828K.

But Lou doesn't know if he should add this to his list, because it doesn't fit the pattern.

January 14, 2015:

San Luis Obispo. A South African diamond dealer comes into a shop and insists on only getting paid in Krugerrands—pure gold coins. He gets paid and then gets hit in the parking lot of the hotel at 4:00 A.M. when he leaves to catch an early connecting flight—$943,000.

May 2016:

A female store owner takes a range of sample diamonds to the home of a regular customer in Rancho Santa Fe. Gets a flat tire on the road up to the ranch, gets robbed as she goes to change the tire—$645,000.

Then there was this.

September 27, 2016:

A diamond dealer from Brazil comes into Los Angeles with merchandise he claims to U.S. Customs to be worth $375,000. He rents a car at Alamo and drives the Pacific Coast Highway up toward a jeweler in Marina del Rey, his first stop on a sales tour. He meets the jeweler on his fifty-foot fishing boat in the harbor, because why not? Well, because the robber walks onto the boat, takes the suitcase and walks off. Now the Brazilian is fucked because he can't file an insurance claim on the merchandise he didn't declare, rumored to be worth over $2 million.

February 3, 2017:

A Newport Beach jeweler gets a call from a regular customer in Pelican Bay to come to the house with a selection of diamond necklaces for a twenty-fifth anniversary. He pulls in to the driveway and gets hit as he's ringing the doorbell. Turns out the customer and his wife are celebrating their anniversary in Paris and the call was a fake. Call it $500K, give or take.

May 18, 2017:

San Rafael. A San Francisco jewelry store owner shifts some unsold merchandise to his store in Marin County. The courier gets hit as he arrives at the store—$347,000.

And now October 17, 2018:

Del Mar. One and a half mil in Sam Kassem's diamonds.

If it is one guy, Lou thinks, he's taken down something around $8,600,000 in the past four years. Even after expenses and a commission to a fence, well . . .

The cases could be unrelated, Lou thinks.

Which is the received wisdom.

Lou doesn't believe the received wisdom, because there's too much of a pattern.

The robber has done his homework, is getting inside information from somewhere because he just doesn't miss. Every hit is at least mid–six figures, and now he's busting into seven. He knows who is carrying what where and for how much.

The guy has found a niche, Lou thinks, a very specific place in the criminal ecosystem. He hits the jewelers at their most vulnerable point—when they're moving merchandise.

He's selective—two or three jobs a year, always for big money and that's it.

He knows his terrain—the most they have is a video-cam shot from the back, a man in a black hood. Useless. He hits and then just seems to disappear.

He's mixing it up, never hitting the same jeweler or even the same insurer more than once. And moving around geographically, between police jurisdictions, up and down the California coast.

And always near a highway—never in the middle of a city.

What we have here, Lou thinks, is a highway robber.

And a specific highway robber.

Highway 101.

Lou's torn between an iced tea and an Arnold Palmer.

On the one hand, the Arnold Palmer would taste better, but on the other hand the lemonade in it has sugar, which converts to fat, and the fucking lawyer in Del Mar looks like he has negative body-fat percentage from riding his seven-thousand-dollar Italian bicycle up and down the 101.

Lou goes with the plain iced tea.

And a turkey burger.

"Fries or a salad?" the waitress asks.

"Why do you think I'm having a turkey burger," Lou asks, "instead of a real burger?"

"A salad," the waitress says. "What kind of—"

Lou is staring at her.

"No dressing, right?"

Lou nods, and the waitress walks away to put in the order.

A hockey game drones on a TV above the bar, and Lou wonders who watches hockey in October.

The guy is going to hit up north, he decides.

His next job.

That's his pattern.

Then Angie comes in, sits down across from him and says, "I'm guessing you ordered already."

Lou shrugs. "You're late."

"At least you didn't order for me," she says, scanning the menu.

He didn't, but he could have, because he knows what she's going to have—a Caesar salad with shrimp, no dressing. Lou's tempted to tell her this, but he doesn't want to piss her off so he keeps his mouth shut.

But she sees the look on his face when she orders a Caesar salad with shrimp and no dressing. "We've been married too long."

"Apparently that is your opinion."

"So who's going to move out?" Angie asks. "You or me?"

"Me."

"It should be me," Angie says. "I'm the adulteress."

"Hester Prynne."

"What?"

"Nothing," Lou says. "No, I'll go. I could use a change. I think I'm in kind of a rut."

"Sure, *now*," she says. "Is that what it took, Lou, me having an affair? I wish I'd known that sooner."

"Is this your first?" Lou asks.

"Would you believe me if I said it was?"

"Sure," Lou says. "I mean, what do you have to lose?"

"Such a cop."

Lou shrugs again. To annoy her this time, because she has taken to saying lately that his shrugs are both very "cop" and very "Jewish." He wonders if the lawyer shrugs.

"I mean, am I in the room now?" Angie asks. "All your cop buddies tell me you're very good 'in the room.' I guess they didn't mean the bedroom."

"I'll move out," Lou says.

"Where will you go?"

"As if you care?"

"I care, Lou."

"I'm thinking the beach."

She actually laughs. Off his look she says, "I can't picture you at the beach, Lou. You're maybe the least beach person that I know."

Which is maybe why I should go, he thinks.

• • •

Davis rubs freshly cracked black pepper on the fish, then walks out onto the deck and checks the heat on the grill.

Satisfied that the temp is perfect, he lays the fillets on the grill and goes back outside. He pours a thin layer of lemon-infused olive oil into a pan, snaps the asparagus stems in half, washes the top halves, then sets them into the hot oil.

Traci watches all this.

"You're going to make someone a wonderful wife one day," she says.

Davis scorches the asparagus stems, takes them off the heat, dumps them into a colander, and puts a few ice cubes on top of them to stop them from cooking in their own heat. Then he walks back out onto the deck and turns the fillets.

Looks across the 101 and sees the guy standing in the park by the Main Beach basketball courts.

Short guy with the weird yellow hair.

Davis doesn't like it because he saw the guy earlier in the afternoon in Huntington Beach. When he sees someone he doesn't know more than once in the same day—especially in two different locations—he wants to know why.

Crime 101: There's a word for a man who believes in coincidence: the defendant.

Then he sees the guy glance up at his balcony.

Is it Money? Has he flipped on me?

Or did I make a mistake somewhere?

Could he be a cop? Davis asks himself. He mentally retraces his steps since the Del Mar robbery, checking to see if he possibly could have been followed.

He doesn't think so, but who is this guy?

You can't take a chance, he tells himself.

You have to move.

Going back into the condo, Davis says, "Dinner's almost ready."

"I'm starving."

He pulls a bottle of Drouhin Chablis out of the ice bucket, opens it, and pours them each a glass.

Davis takes the chocolate mousse out of the refrigerator, puts a small spoonful of whipped cream on each one, and then places raspberries on the cream.

"You *made* this?" Traci asks when he sets them on the table. "From scratch?"

"It's not hard," Davis says.

Her spoon poised over the bowl, she says, "I shouldn't."

"Dark chocolate," Davis says. "Very good for you—full of antioxidants."

"Well, in that case." She takes a bite. "OMG, Michael. An orgasm on a spoon."

Later, in bed, he says, "I have to leave again soon."

Feels her stiffen in his arms. "How soon is soon?"

"Tomorrow."

"You just got here," Traci says. "I thought you'd stay longer."

"So did I," Davis says.

Until I spotted surveillance on me.

Then Traci asks, "Where are we going with this?"

"Not every trip needs a destination," Davis answers.

You drive the road to drive the road.

"But it's nice to have a direction," Traci suggests. She's not asking for a ring and a date, just an idea if this is headed somewhere. They've been seeing each other on and off for coming on two years, and she just wants to know which it's going to be.

Davis is a player, but he plays straight. One of his rules is never to lie to a woman. So he says, "You're looking for gold on a beach, Traci."

"Are you calling me a gold digger?" she asks, eyes flaring.

"That was a poor analogy," Davis admits, feeling bad that he hurt her feelings. "What I was trying to say is that you're looking for something where it doesn't exist."

"What does that mean, exactly?"

"That I have a lot of 'like' in me," Davis says. "I don't have a lot of 'love.' "

"Got it," she says. "Nice twist on the 'It's not you, it's me.' "

"I like you very much," Davis says.

"Quit while you're behind," she says. And later, "I'm thinking the next time you come back, maybe you don't look me up, okay?"

Okay.

It's too bad, but it's okay.

It's the 101.

Not the 102.

• • •

The complex is called Seaside Chateau, but as the metal gate of the underground parking structure slides open, Lou thinks it looks more like the Solana Beach Federal Corrections Facility.

It's grim in there.

Gray walls, dark.

Then again it's an underground parking lot, Lou thinks as he pulls in. What's it supposed to look like, Shangri-la?

He finds his slot, #18. Actually, the rental comes with two parking slots, but he's only going to need one because he doubts that Angie is going to come for overnights.

What do they call them in the joint?

Conjugal visits?

Lou pulls in next to a black 2011 Dodge Challenger SRT8 that looks like it's in cherry condition. He's careful not to open his door too wide and scratch it. Taking his suitcase and shoulder bag out of the car, he walks to the entrance of the complex, guarded by another metal screen door.

It's depressing, and he wonders what he got himself into. He'd rented the place sight unseen, just off some pictures on the management company's website. The condo itself looked pretty nice from the pictures, but they always do, don't they?

McGuire flat-out laughed when told Lou was renting a place on the beach. "Middle-aged divorced guys, they always think they're going to move to the beach, score some young surfer chick."

"I'm not divorced, and I don't think that."

"*Part* of you thinks that."

"My brain knows better."

Lou has seen those guys. They start going to the gym, they get their teeth whitened, they buy new clothes, maybe a sports car, and the young women look at them like just what they are.

Pathetic.

He has no such illusions. He just thought it would be a nice change—kind of a treat, if you will—to live on the beach for a while, until he sees how all this works out.

Or doesn't.

Lou has lived in San Diego all his life and has never had a place by the beach, so if this is the extent of his midlife crisis, so be it.

Yeah, and okay, if he meets some woman—not some hot twenty-something but an attractive forty-something who happens to take a shine to him—well, okay.

"You can't swing a dead cat in Solana Beach without hitting a yoga studio," Lou says, "so maybe the odds aren't all that bad."

"Yeah, they are," McGuire said. "Why do you think the hot forty- and fifty-somethings torture themselves in the first place? Those yoga pants are only sliding down those tight butts for twenty-three-year-old guys with six-packs."

"Leave a man his illusions," Lou said.

They can't all be trophy wives cheating on their husbands with young studs. There have to be one or two maybe divorced and lonely, looking for a nice guy, maybe a nice dinner out, maybe a roll in the hay.

"Roll in the hay?" Lou thinks as he pushes the door open with his hip. Christ, I'm going to get a hot *eighty*-year-old.

A set of steps lead up to a common area—the standard pool-and-hot-tub combo behind yet another gate, a community grill, a few tables under a roof for the odd occasions when it rains.

He walks past the pool and finds Unit 18—actually, "Chateau 18"—up a flight of stairs on the second floor. A pedant like Lou would have thought "Seaside Chateau" linguistically impossible, especially in Southern California. He's never seen a less French-looking place in his entire life.

He fumbles for the key and opens the door.

And instantly gets it.

Why people do this. Why they spend a fortune—Lou is really splurging on the rent—to get a "whitewater view"—because the floor-to-ceiling windows at the front of the condo look out at the ocean and the beach. It's like a wall of blue—the sky, the water, and then the aforementioned white foam breaking onto the sand.

Just the view is worth it all.

The kitchen is small but looks recently remodeled, there's a small sitting room with a flat-screen TV and a sofa. Lou walks into the bedroom—again small, but with an optimistic king-size bed and an en suite bathroom with a shower and . . . a Jacuzzi tub? Really?

He plops his bags down and feels . . .

Utterly depressed.

Two suitcases on the floor and a cardboard box of books on the backseat of the car.

That's my life now, Lou thinks.

I'm the pathetic middle-aged about-to-be-divorced guy moving into a rented condo on the beach.

• • •

Ormon meets Money on Newport Beach Pier.

"I can understand how you lost him," Money says, gazing out at the blue water. "What I can't understand is why you think it's my problem."

Ormon has an answer to this. "Because you want to make money, and that guy isn't going to make you any more money. Not in the long run. For that you need me. And I need him."

"I don't know where he is," Money says truthfully.

"You've worked with the man for fifteen years," Ormon says. "You must know something."

Money digs deep.

He doesn't like Ormon, who's a violent, impulsive, greedy little creep. Money prefers the steadier, older guys who don't enjoy hurting people. But they're not making them like that anymore. And the violent, impulsive, greedy little creep is right—Davis has come to his sell-by date.

Money gives him a name.

• • •

Sharon Coombs is totally SoCal.

Blond hair, cut short, with highlights.

Trim late-thirties body, honed with yoga, barre classes and Peloton. High, surgically enhanced rack, toned butt, literally sculpted nose. Thin lips she's thinking about making fuller the next time she has some spare cash.

She has a towel wrapped around her neck as she comes down the stairs from yoga, walks into the Solana Beach Coffee Company, orders a latte with soy milk and goes outside to sit down.

Seeing Lou sitting alone at a table, she instantly sums him up as neither a potential customer or a lover and moves on. Sharon is efficient—in her work, her exercise, her sex life. She's not going to waste a second on anything or anyone that doesn't have potential.

And she has business here.

So she walks up to a chair at a table where another man is sitting and asks, "Is this chair available? Do you mind?"

"Not at all," Davis says.

Like, what guy would?

She sits down, looks out at the PCH and says, "I just wrote a new policy. Five and a half million."

Sharon is an insurance broker to companies that write high-limit "excess liability" policies.

If you have a five-bedroom house on a bluff over La Jolla Cove, a garage full of Lambos and Maseratis, some diamonds worth more than a cul-de-sac of suburban homes, you don't call a gecko, you don't call Flo, you don't call a guy who's seen it all because he's covered it all—none of those guys will underwrite that level of risk.

You call Sharon Coombs, who will speed-dial the high-risk, high-roller insurance companies with elite clientele that *will* write insurance against megabuck losses and charge you a huge premium to do it. But if you can afford the seaside palace, the Lamborghini, the rocks, you can afford to insure them.

Sometimes these companies, like mob bookies, will lay off part of the risk to other high-roller companies, and this is what Sharon helps to arrange. Sometimes she'll put together three or four insurers to cover a risk.

To do that she has to verify the value of the property being insured. She has to know its actual worth, its venue, its provenance. She has to make sure you're not getting her to write three mil of insurance on a two-million stone, because then, shit, you'd steal it yourself, throw it in the ocean and make a cool mil.

She has to know that you're taking reasonable precautions to protect the property. If you don't have a security system on the mansion (or you're in the habit of grilling burgers in the living room), you park the Maserati on the street (or you think it's fun to enter it into demolition derbies), or you keep the diamonds in a candy dish on the kitchen counter (or you wear them while getting falling-down drunk slumming in an after-hours club), even Sharon is going to have a tough time getting you insurance.

And she checks on these things—her business depends on it. So Sharon knows what you have, what it's worth and where it is.

And how you protect it.

Sharon makes good money on commissions.

But on the 101, good money isn't always good enough.

It takes money to live here, and it takes more money to live well here, and Sharon likes to live well. And she knows that for Southern California, she's coming up on *her* sell-by date.

She's a thirty-eight-year-old ten, but that's not the same as being a twenty-eight-year-old ten, or even a twenty-eight-year-old nine. And there are some twenty-four-year-olds out there who don't mind hunting in the forty to fifty-five reserve either.

And the men on that reserve? If they have enough money and haven't let their looks go completely to hell, they can hunt anywhere they want. The men are hitting the gym, too, going to yoga, watching their nutrition, even hitting the Botox. Fifty-seven-year-old stockbrokers are now comparing exfoliants.

Sharon needs a big score.

They met at an art-gallery opening five years ago over plastic cups of middling wine and hors d'oeuvres. He was charming, she accepted his invitation to dinner, and he opened the door to his Shelby Mustang for her and took her to the Top of the Cove, and after dessert she took him to her place and was going to fuck him except he said no.

"It's not that I don't want to," Davis said. "It's just that I have a rule about mixing business and pleasure."

Crime 101: Don't stick your dick where it doesn't belong.

"I'm sorry?" Sharon asked.

"You're an excess-liability broker, right?" Davis said. "I think we could do some business together. You can get sex from anyone, but I can make you money."

He explained how.

She's given him three tips in the five years. Any more, someone would put the pattern together and plant her in the middle of it.

The first one bought her new boobs. The second was bigger, a down payment on her condo. The third was her Lexus.

Now she wants to do one more.

The biggest.

And the last.

She makes this clear to Davis. "I give you this and I'm out."

He doesn't tell her he's doing the same thing. Crime 101: Never tell anyone anything they don't need to know.

"What is it?" he asks.

"Arman Shahbazi, an Iranian billionaire, is coming in from Tehran," she says, "for his niece's wedding. He's buying presents for the bride, the groom, the whole family. Watches, diamond necklaces, a diamond ring for the bride."

"Insured value?"

"Five and a half mil."

That would put me over, Davis thinks. Even with her cut, Money's, the discount to the buyer . . . I still clear two million.

Walkaway money.

"The courier is flying in from New York," Sharon says, "and they're going to make the transfer at L'Auberge, where the wedding is."

The luxury hotel in Del Mar, Davis thinks.

Not good.

It would mean consecutive jobs in San Diego, in the same jurisdiction, and that would violate one of his cardinal rules.

Crime 101: The second trip through the buffet line ends in the prison cafeteria.

Especially when you consider this San Diego cop—what's his name?—Lubesnick—who has his sights on you.

But five million . . .

"The carrier has insisted on an armed guard to escort the courier to the transfer," Sharon says. "They'll use a local who'll pick him up at the airport, drive him to L'Auberge and stay until the sale is concluded."

"After that?"

"It goes into a safe in Shahbazi's suite," Sharon says. "There'll be armed security at the wedding and the reception. Israelis."

So there are two moments to do it, Davis thinks. When the courier is on his way from the airport to the hotel or inside Shahbazi's room at L'Auberge, when they're making the transfer.

But the armed guard is problematic—Davis doesn't like the possibility of violence. He's gone his entire career without getting hurt or hurting anyone else. It's a point of personal pride as well as a professional mandate.

Crime 101: If you can't do it without pulling a trigger, you shouldn't be doing it.

So Davis is going to take a pass on this one.

Then Sharon says, "There's something else—Shahbazi's paying in cash."

A little smirk comes across her lips. She knows what Davis knows—the seller doesn't want the IRS finding out about the transaction.

"So he'll have his own security," Davis says.

Sharon shrugs. "We don't insure the cash."

So five and a half mil just became eleven mil, Davis thinks.

Half of it in cash—no need for a fence, no commissions, just three or four points to Money to launder it.

That's a very nice house on the beach.

By the 101.

• • •

As it turns out, life by the beach is pretty good.

This is what Lou is thinking as he enjoys his breakfast burrito. It surprises him—first, as a devoted bagel-and-cream-cheese guy ("Is there a stereotype you won't traffic in?" Angie had asked him one morning), he would never have heretofore combined the words "breakfast" and "burrito," and he certainly wouldn't have thought he'd enjoy the result.

But this is his new life, right? So a couple of weeks ago he wandered into the Solana Beach Coffee Company, just a block inland from his condo in a little strip mall flanking the 101, looked at the menu, thought What the hell, it's my new life, right? went way out on a limb and ordered the breakfast burrito.

Now he's hooked.

Crisp bacon, scrambled eggs, lettuce, tomato and salsa, the goddamn things are delicious.

Who knew?

And the setting can't be beat.

He's now accustomed to getting his coffee and food and stepping outside into the little courtyard, which is bordered on three sides by two-story buildings that house, among other things, a climbing gym, a barre studio, a yoga place and a dermatologist who seems to treat only women who by all superficial (as it were) evidence need no treatment whatsoever.

Lou sits at one of the wrought-iron tables and lets the sun hit his face as he takes in the 360-degree view—there's not a bad seat in the house—as the women come and go from their classes and appointments, many of them stopping into SBCC for a quick coffee or smoothie. The customers who aren't beautiful women are mostly beautiful men—surfers, climbers or just workout junkies, although there's one table of middle-aged men with bicycles who seem to use this as a morning meeting place, retired guys who have coffee and heart-healthy oatmeal here before they go off on their ride.

No, life on the coast is getting good to Lou.

At first the constant sound of the surf bugged him, but now it's become a lullaby that soothes him to sleep. He's come to like getting up in the morning and making that first cup of coffee, then stepping out onto his small balcony to look at the ocean.

Then he gets dressed and goes to the SBCC before he heads to work. There's a newspaper rack in the strip mall, and Lou puts quarters in to buy an actual, physical newspaper, his beloved *Union-Tribune*, which he reads as he has breakfast and checks out the locals.

Sometimes he makes it home from work in time to catch the sunset from the balcony, and it's—as the kids would say—*amazing*. If you can't believe in God the Father, Lou thinks—and as a nonobservant Jew he doesn't really know what he believes in—watching the sun sink over the ocean, you have to believe in God the Artist.

The weekends he dreaded as solitary, divorced, angst-ridden loneliness marathons haven't been so bad. He usually starts them with a later, more extended session at the coffee place, then takes a walk up the PCH or over to the Cedros District, which has some interesting shops, more coffee places and a decent bookstore.

Or he walks on the beach.

Which is as surprising a development to him as the breakfast burrito.

Lou has never been much of a beach person. He doesn't really swim, doesn't surf, and the thought of "laying out" and tanning sounds like brain death.

"Jews are more of a desert people," he's explained to McGuire, who also spurns the beach because his Irish skin burns like . . . well, crispy bacon in a breakfast burrito.

"But they both have sand," McGuire said. "Beaches and deserts."

Lou wasn't convinced.

But now the sand is just down a set of stairs outside his condo, so one day he walks down and finds he enjoys walking in the sand, smelling the salt air, feeling the ocean breeze on his face. And if he thought the people at the coffee company were beautiful, it's mostly the same people on the beach except with a lot less clothing.

It's not just the hard bodies.

Lou starts to like the whole scene—the blue water, the open sky, the families out there just having fun, the surfers, the Frisbees—the whole beach scene.

"You'll be buying a surfboard next," McGuire said.

No, Lou thinks now, but I might get a boogie board.

It looks like fun.

So the weekends aren't bad. Actually, he starts to enjoy them. This stretch of the 101, from Via del Valle in the south to Cardiff Beach, starts to become his turf. He likes driving home on it at nights, on weekends he goes to Pizza Port, or Chief's sports bar over by the train station to catch a game on television, and there's always the hot-dog truck.

He misses Angie, but, to be honest, not as much as he thought he would. Yeah, okay, he's a little lonely and Seaside Chateau is kind of a lonely place. Lou finds it fascinating that, since moving there, he's seen a lot of cars in the subterranean garage but very few people in the actual complex.

They must be there, he thinks, because the cars are there, and they come and go, but he doesn't see the people who should go with them. As far as he can discern, the residents fall into several groups: retirees who live there full-time, owners who apparently only come in the summers, and transients—some of them tourists, others transients who are between full-time homes and/or marriages, who have done just what he has—rented from a management agency.

Whoever they are, at least not the few of them he sees in this off-season—ever start conversations. They'll nod hello if you pass them by the pool or in the garage, but that's about it.

Lou finds it curious, but he doesn't really mind. He's kind of enjoying the anonymity in which to explore his new life. If you ever wanted to just get lost, he thinks, you've come to the right place at Seaside Chateau.

The one source of real unhappiness in Lou's life is the Haddad robbery.

For which he does not have a single lead.

The case is as cold as an ex-wife's heart.

Both Ben Haddad and Sam Kassem passed their polygraphs, so the idea of an inside job was out the window. Lou was just as glad—he didn't want them to be implicated. John Houghton, the store owner in Del Mar, had volunteered to take a poly—because he was sick of the insurance company's shit—and also came out clean.

Which left the insurance company on the hook for the money but also left Lou with exactly jackshit.

Lou is more convinced than ever that it's one guy, the "101 Bandit," and that the guy is very good and very careful. He pulled off the Haddad job in less than a minute and then simply disappeared. Like the earth swallowed him, as if there's some kind of subterranean . . .

Parking structure?

He flashes back on the Solana Beach Federal Correctional Institute.

If you ever wanted to just get lost . . .

Is that what his guy is doing? Making his hits, driving into a subterranean garage and switching vehicles?

Lou makes a mental note to check out the structures nearest Houghton's jewelry store. Maybe someone saw something.

Maybe there's something still there.

This is what Lou is thinking as he watches the woman get up from the table. He knows that she's out of his league—she made that abundantly clear by blowing him off with barely a glance, but he also knows that he knows her from somewhere.

Old-school, Lou has a Rolodex in his head, and now he mentally flips through it. She's not a friend of Angie's (or she would have come over out of curiosity or to gloat), she's not anyone he's ever arrested or . . .

Questioned.

Yes you did, Lou thinks.

You interviewed her about a diamond job seven years ago. The woman who was taking diamonds to the house in Rancho Santa Fe, got a flat tire and was robbed of stones worth $645,000. Coombs wasn't the store owner, she wasn't the vic, she was . . .

With the insurance company, and you interviewed her to establish the value of the merchandise and the security precautions . . . but she wasn't with the actual insurance company, she was . . .

A broker.

Sharon . . .

Carter.

No—Cole.

No—*Coombs.*

Sharon Coombs.

So who's the guy? Lou wonders.

They seem to have just met, they had a five-minute conversation, and she picks up her healthy, fancy-ass latte and walks away. No exchange of phone numbers that Lou could see. Just another failed flirtation on the PCH, he thinks. They summed each other up, it didn't pan out, and they moved on.

But there's something in his gut—and it isn't the breakfast burrito—that tells him he was looking at something else.

Because Lou doesn't believe in coincidences.

Crime 101: There's a word for a man who believes in coincidence: the defendant.

From the inside of his car, Ormon watches Coombs walk away and get into her Lexus.

Davis drives.

What Davis does.

When he needs to think.

Crime 101: If a job feels wrong, it is wrong.

He knows this, he *knows* it, but—

There are no buts, Davis tells himself, there are only the basics—Crime 101, *but* . . .

This job is his out. If you were going to make an exception to the rules, this job is . . . well, exceptional. It's risky, Davis thinks, but is it riskier than turning it down and doing three or four jobs to make the same money?

Then he knows he's going to do it.

As he drives past the big smokestack in Carlsbad, he knows that he's going to break his rules and do this one, last job.

Now the question is how.

There are two moments I can do it, Davis thinks. One is in the hotel suite itself, when the courier is turning over the merchandise. There'll be three people in the suite—Shahbazi, the courier and the security guard.

So you have to get into the suite (not a real problem) and cover three men. Then you have to take the jewels and the cash, and you literally don't have enough hands to do that and hold a gun.

Think it through.

The courier will go in, make the exchange and come back out with the cash. You take him in the hallway, disable him, then go into the suite and take the stones. Either in the hallway or in the room, you'll be one on two, depending on whether the security guy stays with the cash or the merchandise.

Better, but still not best.

Think.

What's the critical flaw, what are you not thinking of? He's all the way up in Oceanside before it hits him.

Don't *take* the security guard, *be* the security guard.

The 101 always has the answer.

When Sharon steps out of her shower that night wrapped in a towel, a man is sitting on her bed. The little SIG Sauer 380 she keeps in her nightstand is in his left hand, resting on his lap.

"Don't scream," he says.

Her chest tightens. She feels like she can't breathe. Her fingers touch her throat, and she manages to say, "I have herpes."

"Don't flatter yourself," he says. "I don't want what's between your legs, I want what's between your ears."

She's terrified, quivering, and she can see in his eyes that he likes that.

He taps the side of his head with the gun barrel and rubs it into his weird yellow hair. "You have something in there. Something of value. Something you shared with Davis."

"I don't know what you're talking about."

"I'll tell the police all about you," he says. "You'll do ten years minimum, and those dykes in the joint? They're mostly Mexicans, and they'll make a meal of a *guera* like you, oh, boy."

I can't, Sharon thinks.

I can't go to jail.

I won't.

Ormon smiles. "I know what you're thinking, Sharon. You're thinking you'll bat those eyelashes at the judge and he'll give an Orange County white woman like you probation."

Pretty much what she was thinking.

"And if that does happen, Sharon?" he says. "If that happens, I'll come back, and then I will really hurt you. I'll make it so no man will ever give you a second look again. They'll turn their heads."

"Please . . ."

"You don't have to beg," he says, "you just have to make the smarter choice. I'll pay you the same money Davis does. You won't be out a penny, and you'll keep that pretty face. So what's it going to be?"

Lou decides to try yoga.

Which amused McGuire no end. "Yoga? Really? You're about as flexible as a cinder block."

"Which is why I'm going to try yoga."

"And you have that gut hanging over your belt," McGuire said.

"Which is why I'm going to try yoga."

"What kind of yoga?" McGuire asked.

"There are kinds?"

"Sure," McGuire said. "There's like this hot yoga where they crank the thermostat way up and you sweat like a whore in church, there's a yoga where they do the poses real fast—"

"There are poses?"

"—where you do them real slow," McGuire said. "There's meditation yoga, there's street yoga, there's even goat yoga."

"What's that?"

"I don't know," McGuire said, "and I don't want to know. And you don't want to do yoga, you just want to get laid."

"There's getting laid?"

"Any straight guy who goes to yoga," McGuire said, "is going there to meet women and get laid. Any gay guy who goes to yoga is going there to meet men and get laid. In fact, the word 'yoga' is Hindi for 'getting laid.' "

"No it isn't."

"Might as well be," McGuire said.

"What about women?" Lou asked. "Do they go to yoga to get laid?"

"You better hope so."

Actually, Lou's hopes are a little less ambitious.

If he drops a few pounds in the process, good.

If he meets Sharon Coombs, better.

So now he shoves his ass up in the air doing something the instructor calls "Downward-Facing Dog," and if yoga isn't about sex, Lou thinks, you couldn't prove it by Downward-Facing Dog, or Upward-Facing Dog, or any of the dogs.

To make it all the more so, the ass facing up and down directly in front of him belongs to Sharon.

Upward, Downward, Warrior I, Warrior II, Sun Salutation, —Lou about dislocates his eyeballs trying to keep them off Coombs's ass.

And decides that Lululemon should require a license.

By the time class is over, Lou is sweaty, tired and horny. And Coombs hasn't even glanced at him. But when he's coming out of the locker room, fixing his badge on his belt, she gives him a first look.

Then a second.

And actually speaks to him. "Your first class?"

"That obvious, huh?"

"No, you did great."

"That's a very kind lie," Lou says.

Now she takes a real look at his eyes and then asks, "You want to get a smoothie?"

"I *want* to get a pastrami on rye," Lou says. "But I'll have a coffee with you while you get a smoothie."

"You don't like smoothies?" Coombs asks.

"I don't even like *saying* 'smoothie.' "

Coombs laughs.

As they walk down the stairs together, Lou already knows that what she was looking at wasn't him.

She was looking at the badge.

A few minutes later, they're sitting outside Solana Beach Coffee Company, she's sipping on some green concoction that looks to Lou like vomit run through a lawn-mower bag, and she asks, "So what do you do, Lou?"

"I'm a cop," he says. "And I guess you don't remember me."

She looks at him blankly.

"It was a few years ago," Lou says. "I interviewed you about a diamond theft."

"I'm sorry," she says. "But did I do it?"

"You know?" Lou says. "I never found out who took those stones."

"No?" she says. "That surprises me."

"Why's that?"

"You just strike me as the kind of guy who's very good at what he does."

McGuire was right.

Yoga *is* all about sex.

"You *are* good," she says later, on her back on his bed looking out the window at the ocean.

"You said that about yoga."

"I was lying then," Sharon says. "I'm telling the truth now. How did your wife ever let you get away?"

"She liked a lawyer better."

"Yuck."

"Exactly my opinion." They're quiet for a few minutes looking at the great view and then Lou asks, "Hey, Sharon? Would you have dinner with me sometime?"

"I don't know, Lou," she says. "I mean, I'll *fuck* you, but dinner . . . that's pretty intimate."

Lou can't tell if she's joking or not.

Fucking is a meeting of the genitals, dinner a meeting of the minds, and Lou gets the impression that the former is more common on the 101.

She slides down and starts to administer oral resuscitation.

"That's a little optimistic," Lou says.

"I'm an optimist."

"Hey, Sharon?" Lou says, "why don't you tell me what you really want?"

She looks up at him.

"Why are you telling me this?" Lou asks.

Sharon had just confessed to one felony and conspiracy in another. She could go away for twelve to twenty.

"I'm scared." She looks scared now. Maybe being naked makes her look more scared, certainly vulnerable. "Will you protect me?"

"I'll protect you." You didn't have to sleep with me to get protection, he thinks.

But you sure as hell thought you did. Or you thought you did to make a deal, because now he hears Sharon say, "I gave you this information. Will that keep me out of jail?"

"I think we can work something out," Lou says. "What did you tell this guy? The one who threatened you?"

"Everything I told you."

So "Davis," as Sharon calls him, is going to take down Shahbazi in the hotel room, and then the yellow-haired guy is going to take down Davis as he leaves.

Except, Lou thinks, Davis isn't walking out of that hotel room.

The security guy's name is Nelson.

Robert David Nelson.

Bob.

Davis got his name from Sharon and runs the guy down so he knows everything about him—retired Milwaukee cop come to San Diego for the sun and the good life, married, two grown kids.

Clean record.

A straight shooter.

He's watched Nelson for three days—watched him go out on a courier job with Ben Haddad (so Sammy has smartened up), watched him grocery-shopping with his wife, Linda, at Albertson's, watched him go to the gym and sweat on the exercise bike.

Watched him go to a bar afterward and have one beer.

Then the guy went home.

No drinking problem.

No girl on the side.

He's in bed by nine-thirty.

This is not a guy who's playing an angle or who's going to do something rash or stupid.

Which is good, Davis knows.

Crime 101: Always better to go up against smart than stupid.

Davis has disappeared.

Doesn't matter to Ormon.

He might not know where the man is, but he knows where he's going to be.

And when.

Which is, like, better.

McGuire gets the call. "Lou—"

"What?"

"Sam Kassem is on the line," McGuire tells him. "Says he's got a guy hanging outside who's wrong."

They're on the roll in a minute.

Just Lou's unit, in unmarked cars.

If this is his guy, he doesn't want radio cars spooking him away.

But it shouldn't be my guy, Lou thinks, his stomach churning as it seems to take forever to get to El Cajon. My guy doesn't hit the same vendor twice. And my guy has a much bigger job in the works—he's not going to jack it up with a low-level smash-and-grab.

This is just Sam getting hinky from being hit.

Lou gets on the horn to his people. "Give it a wide berth, but surround the block. McGuire and I will go in."

McGuire pulls up at the end of the block and sees a late-model Camaro parked outside Sam's store.

"He went in," McGuire says. "If it's going to go down, it's going now."

Goddamn it, Lou thinks. Has my guy lost his shit?

Lou gets out of the car, draws his Glock 9 and holds it behind his back. He hasn't drawn his weapon in action . . . well, ever.

Just then a guy bursts out of the store.

A bunch of Sam's watches in one hand, a pistol in the other.

Lou goes into the standard shooting position, aims center mass, and yells, "Police! Stop! Drop the gun!"

Hears McGuire shouting, "Get down on the ground! Down on the ground!"

The guy freezes.

Hesitates.

Making his choice.

"Don't do it!" Lou yells. "Don't do it!"

Please, don't do it.

But the guy does it.

Swings the pistol toward them.

Lou pulls the trigger and keeps pulling it.

So does McGuire.

The guy melts to the sidewalk.

"It's your guy," McGuire says, standing over the body.

"It's not my guy," Lou says, suddenly exhausted, the adrenaline surge crashing back down.

"How do you know?"

"I just know."

A few watches against ten mil?

It's not even Crime 101.

It's Math 101.

Looking out the big window at the Pacific pounding the rocks below, Lou feels sick and disgusted.

He's never killed anyone before.

It feels awful.

Not just that there'll be a shooting board—he knows it will clear him—and that he'll be off duty until it does, but because he took another human's life. That's not why he became a cop. He became a cop to help people, and now there's a person dead over some lousy watches.

It makes him want to pull the pin.

Lou knows what he should do.

Well, he knows what he *should* do.

He's lived by the rules his whole life.

He thinks about it, though.

About going the other way with it.

Because his robber left a seam in his plan, and Lou has found it.

Ten mil in cash and merch?

Those are serious numbers.

Life-changing numbers.

Quit-the-job-and-live-on-the-beach-the-rest-of-your-life numbers.

He gets it now, why people choose to live in places like this. Beautiful views, beautiful people.

Beautiful sunsets.

Insane splashes of reds, oranges and purples as the sea turns from blue to gray to black. I mean, Lou thinks, if you're going to ride off into the sunset, this would be the sunset to ride off into.

He's thinking this when the doorbell rings.

It's Angie.

"Hi," she says.

She looks great.

New hairstyle. A little shorter, a few highlights. Looks like she's dropped a couple of pounds.

"To answer the question behind your cop eyes," she says, "someone was coming through the gate, and I walked in behind them."

"I wasn't going to ask."

"Can I come in?"

He steps aside and lets her through.

She gazes out the big window. "Wow . . . look at you, Lou. A beach dweller. Is this what they call a 'whitewater view'?"

"I think so, yeah."

"Can you afford this? I mean, the rent must be. . . ."

Like it's any of your business, Lou thinks. "For a while."

"Then what?"

He shrugs. "Then we'll see."

"Oh, you *are* becoming a beach bum," Angie says. "Tell me you haven't started surfing."

"I haven't started surfing," Lou says. "But I'm thinking about it. You want a smoothie?"

"No, I don't want a smoothie."

"What *do* you want, Angie?" Lou asks. "Why did you come here?"

She looks at him for a long moment, her eyes filling. Then she says, "I came to see if you want to get back together."

Oh.

That's unexpected, he thinks. What he's really wanted, but not at all what he expected. Of *course* I want to get back together, he thinks, but then he hears himself say, "You know what, Angie? I really don't."

Going, you know, the other way with it.

Crime 101: Never be predictable.

• • •

Davis never feels nervous the day of a job, just an adrenaline jolt, which is necessary. This morning he does feels nervous, though, edgy. Is it because this is his last job, he wonders, or because it's a job his gut knows that he shouldn't do?

It's not too late, he tells himself, looking out the picture window at the ocean.

You can still just drive away.

Go north up the 101 and get lost.

Don't do this thing.

Lou, standing on his balcony sipping his first cup of coffee, is thinking pretty much the same thing.

Don't do it.

He's telling himself this even as he climbs into a suit and straps his weapon—a Glock 9—on.

He walks down into the garage and gets into his car.

A new car is parked beside his.

A dark green Mustang that looks retro.

Like that movie, Lou thinks. What was it?

Oh, yeah, *Bullitt*.

Steve McQueen.

Davis drives the Mustang to the airport.

In a 2019 *Bullitt* Mustang.

Dark green. (Of course.)

5.0L Ti-VCT V8.

3.73 Torsen limited-slip rear axle.

6-speed manual transmission with rev matching.

Dual exhaust with quad tips.

Lou sees the courier come down the escalator.

He walks up to him. "Mr. Perez?"

Perez nods.

His right hand clutches a Halliburton briefcase.

"The car is just outside," Lou says, and walks Perez out to the sidewalk.

The courier balks when he sees the old Civic. It isn't right, it doesn't fit. He turns and looks at Lou, who shows him his badge.

"Trust me," Lou says. "It's in your best interest to get in the car."

Perez gets into the passenger side, Lou slides into the driver's seat. "We can play this one of two ways, Mr. Perez. I can arrest you now for interstate transportation of undeclared valuables—"

"I'm just a courier," Perez says. "I don't know the provenance of these—"

"And I'm sure an ambitious young prosecutor is going to believe that," Lou says. "Or we can play this my way."

Perez takes Door Number Two.

The seam.

Davis waits in the cell phone lot of the airport.

He watches Nelson pull in.

The security guard is early, like they always are, well before the courier's flight is due to land. What he doesn't want is someone standing on the sidewalk outside the terminal with two suitcases worth five mil in his hands.

Davis has the flight info, too.

From Sharon.

The flight info, the courier's name (Perez), even a photo of him.

Davis is dressed for the job. Black suit, white shirt, red tie, black leather shoes. The security guys always look tight, to give the client a sense of professionalism.

A guy is going to protect your life and your money, you don't want him looking like a bobo or a clown. And you want your security guy to look like your standard car-service driver.

Davis gets it—loose clothes, loose work.

McQueen always looked tight, sharp.

He knew what Davis knows.

Crime 101: Dress for your business.

The courier won't have any luggage. He'll walk straight off the plane to the street.

About six minutes at a decent pace.

Davis checks the flight-tracker app on his phone. The flight has landed. He gets out of the car, walks over to Nelson's Lincoln Town Car, smiles and raps on the driver's-side window.

Nelson rolls it down.

Davis angles his body so only Nelson can see the SIG pointed at his face. "Put your hands on the steering wheel, Bob."

Nelson does.

Davis holds his cell phone up with his left hand, shows Nelson a live feed of his house—Linda trimming the hedge along the driveway.

"Here's how it's going to work," Davis says. "You're going to slowly hand me your phone. Then you're going to sit here for two hours and keep your mouth shut. After that you drive home to Linda, because if you do sit here for two hours, she'll still be there to go home to. You'll lose your job, but you'll still have your wife and your Milwaukee pension. Are we good?"

"Yes."

Davis thinks so, too. A guy might risk his own life, but he won't risk his wife's. "Okay, your phone."

Nelson slowly reaches to the console and hands Davis his cell phone. "Don't hurt my wife."

"That's up to you."

As Davis walks back and gets into his car, a text comes on Nelson's phone. I'M DOWN AND HEADED OUT.

Davis types, WILL BE RIGHT THERE, SIR.

Ormon's not at the airport.

He's skipping the prelims.

Ormon's outside L'Auberge, waiting for the main event. Got him a MAC-10 under his red faux-leather jacket, itching to do its thing.

And Ormon, he don't care how many people he scratches off.

For eleven mil, are you kidding me right now?

He looks at his phone.

The plane has landed.

Davis should be going into his act.

His . . . what-do-you-call-it? Finale.

Davis is waiting when the courier emerges from the terminal.

He gets out of the car, signals him, and holds the passenger door open. The courier looks a little askance at the Mustang.

"If I need speed, sir," Davis says, "I want to have it."

The courier gets in.

Davis closes the door, walks around, slips back behind the wheel, checks the rearview mirror, and pulls out.

"There's congestion on the 5," Davis says, "so I thought I'd take the 101, if that's all right."

"I'm from New York," the courier says. "I wouldn't know the 5 from the 101 from a hole in the ground. You all talk in numbers out here. Let's just take the fastest route."

"I believe this will be."

Bullshit, Lou thinks. The guy is a freak. For one of the best, smartest criminals Lou has ever known, this guy just loves the PCH. Or maybe this is a valedictory ride, a sentimental last journey up the 101.

Maybe mine, too, Lou thinks, if this doesn't go down the way I've planned.

"This is the *Bullitt* car, right?" Lou asks.

I know this guy, Davis thinks.

I've seen him before.

When Davis sees someone he doesn't know more than once—especially in two different locations—he wants to know why.

Crime 101: There's a word for a man who believes in coincidence: the defendant.

But he can't place the guy.

Doesn't matter, Davis thinks. What Crime 101 demands is that he pull over, get out of the car and walk away.

But he doesn't.

Lou says, "*Bullitt* or *The Getaway?*"

"I'm sorry, sir?"

"You're obviously a McQueen fan," Lou says. "Which was the best movie, *Bullitt, The Great Escape* or *The Getaway?*"

Keep the guy talking, Lou thinks. Because he's getting hinky. Lou can feel it. The guy has glanced in the rearview mirror twice now, stealing a look, and Lou's a little worried that he's recognized him from the coffee place. If he puts me together in the same spot as Sharon Coombs, he'll pull out of this now.

Crime 101.

"I have to go with *Bullitt*," Davis says. "Although they're all pretty great."

He takes the opportunity to really look in the mirror and try to figure out where he knows this guy from.

"That car chase, right?" the courier says.

"Right?" Davis asks.

"I have to go with *The Getaway*," the courier says. "McQueen's character."

"Doc McCoy."

"Doc McCoy."

Davis pulls off onto Grand Avenue and drives west through Pacific Beach and then turns north onto Mission Boulevard, which is what the PCH is called in this neighborhood. From Mission he takes the left dogleg onto La Jolla Boulevard, up through Bird Rock and into the oh-so-ritzy "Village" itself.

Then it hits him.

The coffee place.

The guy was sitting at a table across from him and Sharon.

He's made me, Lou thinks. Can see it in his eyes in the mirror, see his hands grip the wheel a little tighter.

Lou decides to push it, because it's better to know now than later. "You know my favorite McQueen movie?"

"What's that?"

"*The Thomas Crown Affair*," Lou says.

Smiling at him.

"McQueen was an art thief, right?" Davis says.

"That's right," Lou says. "Faye Dunaway was an insurance broker."

Get out, Davis thinks.

Pull this car over and get out.

Or turn around and shoot this guy in the face.

Lou sees Davis's hand slide over to the center console.

So that's where the gun is, he thinks.

He slides his own hand under his jacket to the Glock.

This could go down right now.

Maybe it's the eleven mil, the walkaway score, maybe it's that he just doesn't like getting played, but Davis keeps driving and says, "I don't think she was a broker, I think she was an investigator."

"You're right," the courier says.

They head up La Jolla Boulevard, past La Jolla Cove, turn onto Prospect, then onto Torrey Pines, all through UCSD, past Torrey Pines Golf Course, then down the long hill that bursts open onto Torrey Pines State Beach, then up the steep hill into the town of Del Mar.

They each know now that they're going to see this thing out.

Playing chicken on the 101.

Now Davis says, "We're almost there, sir."

Yes we are, Lou thinks.

We are almost where we're going.

Lou rings the doorbell to Suite 243.

Davis stands behind him, facing backward, looking back down the hallway.

Shahbazi comes to the door. He wears a gray linen suit with a white shirt open at the collar. "Mr. Perez?"

"Yes."

"Please come in."

Davis goes first, checks the room and then waves Lou in.

Lou shuts the door behind him.

Davis's gun, a SIG Sauer, is already out. "No one has to get hurt here. The gun, under your jacket. Set it down on the bed."

Shahbazi looks at Lou. "Do something."

Lou does. He takes out his Glock and gently sets it on the bed.

"Open the case, let me see," Davis says.

Lou puts the case on the bed, twirls the combination lock and opens the lid. He takes out his pistol and points it at Davis.

Crime 101: Always have a backup.

"Drop the gun," Lou says. "I'm a police officer. I've been looking for you for a long time."

"I'm not going to prison," Davis says. "I'll shoot before that."

"You've never killed anyone," Lou says.

"First time for everything." Davis gives him a long look. "But you have."

"And I hated it."

Davis knows he's fucked up. Violated the rules of Crime 101, and now his only chance is to get back to them.

Crime 101: Everyone has a price.

"I'll tell you what," Davis says. "I take the jewels and leave the cash. You do what you want with it."

Lou juts his chin at Shahbazi. "What about him?"

Everyone has his price, Davis thinks. Crime 101. "What's he going to do? File a complaint on a case full of illegal stones? Five million, you can disappear wherever you want."

The gun is getting heavy in Lou's hands. He feels them start to quiver. "You remember how *The Getaway* ends?"

Davis is puzzled. "Yeah. Doc gets away."

"That's in the movie," Lou says. "In the book there's an epilogue. Doc disappears, but it doesn't end well."

"So that's a no?" Davis asks.

His finger tightens on the trigger.

The door crashes in.

Ormon has the MAC-10 up, sees Lou first and swings it on him.

I'm dead, Lou thinks.

Except Ormon's head explodes.

Lou turns to see that Davis has fired.

Davis turns the gun back on him.

But he doesn't pull the trigger.

"So," Lou says, "what are we going to do?"

"Arrest him!" Shahbazi yells.

"Shut up," Lou says. "Sharon said this was going to be your walkaway job. You have enough stored away to live?"

"Not lavishly."

"But enough to live," Lou says. "Then get in your car and drive. Don't ever come to San Diego again."

"*What?!*" Shahbazi says.

"Did I not tell you to shut up?" Lou asks. He says to Davis, "Let me put it this way—what would Steve McQueen do?"

Davis smiles. "He'd drive."

"So drive," Lou says. "It's Crime 101."

Crime 101, Davis thinks.

Always do what Steve McQueen would do.

Lou keeps the gun on Davis as he walks out the door.

"You're letting that thief get away?!" Shahbazi yells.

"The thief is lying on the floor," Lou says. "The infamous 101 Bandit."

He looks down at the small young man with the bright yellow hair. The young man isn't going to get any older.

"I'll have your badge," Shahbazi says.

"You'll have jackshit," Lou says. He already hears the sirens coming, so he has to make this fast. "What you're going to do when the cops come is listen to what I tell them, nod, and say, 'What he said.' Then you're going to go to your niece's wedding, give out the gifts and be the big man. Do we have an agreement here?"

They have an agreement.

Davis drives.

North, up the 101.

Through Del Mar, past the racetrack.

Past the pink neon sign by Fletcher Cove that proclaims SOLANA BEACH, past the Tidewater Bar, Pizza Port, Mitch's Surf Shop and Moreland Choppers. Down the hill to the long stretch of beach at Cardiff, then up past Swami's and Encinitas, past Moonlight Beach, the old La Paloma Theater, underneath the sign that arcs over the 101 and reads ENCINITAS.

Then along the railroad tracks and eucalyptus trees of funky Leucadia, up to old-fashioned Carlsbad, past the abandoned power station, its smokestack evocative of both Springsteen and Blake.

A sight he knows that he will never see again.

He drives through the day and through the night, stopping only for gas. Through San Clemente, Laguna Beach, Newport Beach, Huntington Beach, Seal Beach, Long Beach, Redondo and Manhattan. Around Marina del Rey, through Santa Monica, Malibu, Oxnard and Ventura.

Then the westward jog past Santa Barbara, north to Pismo and Morro Bay. Daylight finds him in Big Sur, then Monterey, then Santa Cruz.

San Francisco, across the bridge.

Stinson Beach, Nick's Cove, Bodega Bay.

Jenner, Stewarts Point, Gualala.

Point Arena, Elk, Albion.

Little River, Mendocino.

He stops in Fort Bragg.

A small Craftsman house just east of the highway north of town. He bought it years ago and, to keep it clean and safe, has never gone back.

Until now.

Now it will be home.

Crime 101: If you can get away, get away.

Lou finishes the last bite of his hot dog and wipes the mustard off his lip with the back of his hand.

Behind him the Solana Beach sign glows pink like sunset.

They bought his story. Why wouldn't they? "Legendary cop foils jewel heist, kills 'The 101 Bandit.' " The suits in the department weren't happy at all about his "lone wolf, cowboy" tactics and his grandstanding, but what were they going to say? He had cleared a dozen major jewel thefts and now taken two dangerous criminals off the count.

Bob Nelson had been more than willing to play ball, to go along with the story that Detective Lubesnick had deliberately replaced him that day in order to set up the sting. The ex-cop's bosses at the security agency weren't thrilled about it either, but they couldn't very well fire an employee who had helped to stop a multimillion-dollar robbery.

The last Lou heard of Sharon Coombs, she'd gotten a job adjusting auto claims with an insurance company in Pittsburgh.

And Angie?

They went through with the divorce, and he heard she was dating some financial adviser.

Lou stayed in Solana Beach, not in the apartment with the whitewater view—he couldn't afford that for too long—but one in Seascape Chateau that has no view but is still close to the beach. He likes the lifestyle, likes going to the Solana Beach Coffee Company for the breakfast burritos. He even takes in a yoga class about once a week.

Now he pulls his Honda Civic onto the PCH and drives north, past the Tidewater Bar, Pizza Port, Mitch's Surf Shop and Moreland Choppers.

Lou has come to love this road like a man loves a woman.

He could drive it all day and all night.

His new license plate is one of those black retro California jobs.

It reads:

CRIME 101.

FOR MR. ELMORE LEONARD

THE SAN DIEGO ZOO

———

No one knows how the chimp got the revolver.

Only that it's a problem.

Chris Shea didn't think it was *his* problem, though, when the call first came over the radio that a chimpanzee had escaped from the world-famous San Diego Zoo.

"Call Animal Control," he responded, not considering runaway monkeys to be a police matter.

Then the dispatcher added, *"Uhh, the chimp appears to be armed."*

"Armed?" Chris asked. "With what, like a stick?"

He'd seen something on Animal Planet about chimps using sticks as tools or weapons, which apparently was significant for some reason Chris missed because he got up to make a sandwich.

Or maybe it was baboons.

Or maybe it was the National Geographic Channel.

"Witnesses are reporting that the chimp is carrying a pistol," the dispatcher said.

Well, Chris hadn't seen *that* on Animal Planet. "What kind of a pistol?"

"A revolver."

Well, that's a break anyway, Chris thought. It could be worse—a Glock or a SIG Sauer. "Where's the chimp now?"

The dispatcher cannot get off the track of copspeak. *"Suspect was last seen heading east on The Prado."*

Which is *not* a break. The central walkway of Balboa Park is squarely within Chris's zone in Central Division, and he has to respond. It's also bad news because on a hot July night a lot of people will be strolling in the park, including a lot of tourists, and the last thing the chief or the mayor wants are CNN headlines about a visitor to "America's Finest City" getting gunned down by a chimpanzee.

"Responding," Chris said, and rolled into the park.

Now he's standing beside five other cops watching the chimp climb up the wall of the Museum of Man. That's what I need tonight, Chris thinks, a chimp with a firearm and a sense of irony.

What makes it even worse is that Grosskopf is standing there shouting into a megaphone. "Drop the weapon and come down!"

Chris likes Grosskopf, who is always more than sincere about trying to do a good job, but the cop isn't the sharpest spoon in the drawer. "Fred?"

"What?" Grosskopf lowers the megaphone and looks annoyed.

Chris says, "I don't think it understands English."

"You think . . . what," Grosskopf says, "some African language? Don't we have that Somali guy in Anti-Crime?"

"I don't think it understands any language except, like, chimp," Chris says. And he's pretty sure they don't have a single chimpanzee in the entire department. A few gorillas, maybe, but no chimps.

There follows a brief discussion about calling Fish and Game, but a chimp is neither.

Harrison suggests the fire department. "They do cats in trees, right?"

He calls the fire guys, explains the situation, listens for a second and then hangs up.

"What did they say?" Chris asks.

"To go fuck myself."

"They *said* that?" Chris asks.

"Not in so many words," Harrison says. "What they said was that, yes, extracting an animal from a tree or a building is generally their business, but the fact that said animal possesses a firearm makes it our business. I don't know, it was hard to hear through the laughing."

A crowd has gathered.

Chris looks at Harrison. "You'd better move them back. Set up some barricades."

"Why?" Harrison asks.

"What if the chimp pulls the trigger?" Chris asks.

"Why would it do that?"

"Because it's a chimp, I dunno," Chris says. "Crowd control. Now."

The crowd has started a chant. *"Don't shoot the chimp, don't shoot the chimp."*

"We're not going to shoot the chimp!" Chris yells. Although he's not so sure. If it starts pulling the trigger . . . they're going to shoot the chimp.

A woman in a safari jacket pushes her way through the crowd and comes up to Chris.

"Carolyn Voight," she says. "I'm with the zoo's Primate Department."

"How did the chimp get a gun?" Chris asks.

"I blame the NRA," Voight says. She's pretty. Tall, blue eyes, her blond hair pulled into a ponytail under her official zoo ball cap.

Chris says, "Seriously, though . . ."

"I have no idea," Carolyn says. "I also have no idea how Champion got out."

" 'Champ the Chimp'?" Chris asks.

She shrugs, like it wasn't her idea.

Grosskopf has overheard the conversation and tries to establish rapport. With the chimp. "Champion, drop the weapon and come down! No one has to get hurt here."

Again, Chris is not so sure. Champion is hanging from a security camera by one hand (or paw?) and is waving the pistol around with the other, and the weapon could easily go off.

"Did you bring a dart gun?" Chris asks Carolyn.

"No."

"I mean, isn't that what you guys do?" Chris asks. "Like, shoot them with a dart and knock them unconscious?"

"Even if we could," Carolyn says, "it would get hurt in the fall."

"Should we bring the hostage guys in?" Grosskopf asks.

"To negotiate?" Chris asks.

"Yeah."

"With a chimp." Although, to be honest, Chris thinks, they've negotiated with a lot of guys who had lower IQs than Champion here, who is at least smart enough to figure out how to break out of a cage. "What would we offer him?"

"Bananas?" Grosskopf asks.

"Actually, that's a myth," Carolyn says. "Chimpanzees and bananas. Kind of a stereotype."

Chris can see the editorial now. SDPD PROFILES PRIMATES. CHIEF PROMISES FULL INVESTIGATION.

With utter seriousness Grosskopf asks Voight, "Do you have any idea as to what motivated Champion to escape?"

"It could be sexual," Voight says.

"Sexual," Grosskopf repeats.

"Alicia recently rejected his mating overtures," Voight says, "and he took it very badly. We had to separate them."

Better and better, Chris thinks. Now we have a heartbroken, horny chimp with a gun and anger issues. He asks Carolyn, "Did Alicia file a restraining order?"

"What?" she asks. Then, realizing he's joking, adds, "I don't think that domestic violence is a laughing matter."

"Nor do I," Chris says, desperately hoping that Sergeant Villa will stir himself from the station house and come over to take charge.

"Maybe," Grosskopf says, "we could bring Alicia here, and that might tempt him to come down."

"So this is your plan," Chris says. "You want to bring *another* chimp onto the scene, hope that the original, *armed* chimp will climb down from that tower and fuck the unwilling female chimp in front of a crowd of dozens of citizens and tourists."

"I can't allow that," Carolyn says. "Anyway, Alicia is not in estrus at the moment."

"What does that mean?" Grosskopf asks.

"She's not in the mood," Chris says. I dunno, maybe dinner and a movie. Or maybe there's such a thing as "chimpanzee porn," although he's afraid to ask, because if there is, it's not knowledge he wants taking up residence inside his head.

Grosskopf is on another bent. "Does Champion have access to television?"

"I don't think so," Carolyn asks. "Why?"

"I'm wondering if he could have seen anything that would teach him how to handle a firearm," Grosskopf says.

Chris is about to say something sarcastic when Carolyn says, "Actually, the custodian's booth in the night house has a television. Champ might have seen that."

"Does it have premium cable?" Grosskopf asks. "Because HBO and Cinemax can be very violent. If Champion was watching, say, *Game of Thrones*—"

"He has a revolver, not a Valyrian blade," Chris says.

"I'm just saying, the gratuitous bloodshed—"

Sergeant Villa has rolled up. He gets out of his car, takes in the situation and says to Chris, "Shoot the monkey."

Harrison says, "Actually, Sarge, it's not technically a monkey, it's a chimpanzee, which is a—"

Villa's glare stops him.

"Sergeant Villa," Chris says, "this is Carolyn Voight from the San Diego Zoo."

"Please don't shoot him," Carolyn says.

"Ma'am, he's armed with a deadly weapon," Villa says. "I can't allow him to put civilians in jeopardy."

"How about you go get a dart gun and we put a net up?" Chris asks. "Champion goes to sleep, falls into the net, we all go home."

"A dart won't reach him from down here," Carolyn says.

Chris looks at the building. "I can climb partway up."

Villa grabs him by the elbow and walks him a few steps away. "Are you kidding me, Shea? You want to take all this trouble for a goddamn monkey?"

"Well, yeah."

Villa looks over toward Carolyn. "Why do I think it's not the monkey you're interested in?"

"That's deeply cynical, Sarge."

Villa walks back to Carolyn. "You have ten minutes to get the dart gun and the net set up. But if Cheetah up there as much as touches the trigger . . ."

"Cheetah?" she asks.

"Tarzan? No?"

Carolyn shakes her head.

"Ten minutes," Villa says.

Carolyn takes off.

A news truck rolls up.

"Why doesn't life just bend me over and fuck me in the ass?" Villa asks. He says to Chris, "Go talk to them."

"Why me?"

"Because I hate them."

A reporter gets out of the truck and walks over, followed by a cameraman shouldering the camera like it's a rocket launcher or something. Chris recognizes the reporter—he's seen him on the late news.

"Bob Chambers," the reporter says. "We heard something about a chimp?"

Chris points up at the Museum of Man, where Champ is hanging by one paw, gesticulating with the other, and screaming noises that Chris interprets as simian for "Fuck you!"

"Shit," Chambers says. "Is that a gun?"

"I'm afraid it is."

"What's your name?" Chambers asks.

"Shea. Officer Christopher Shea."

The cameraman says, "Rolling."

"I'm standing with Officer Christopher Shea outside the Museum of Man in Balboa Park, where a chimpanzee armed with a pistol has scaled the building. Officer Shea, what are we looking at here?"

"What you just said," Chris says.

The camera pans the crowd as Chambers says, "Protesters have gathered, chanting, 'Don't shoot the chimp—'"

"Well, they're not protesters exactly," Chris says.

"No? What are they?"

They're people with nothing better to do at night than prowl Balboa Park, Chris thinks, but he says, "They're bystanders. I mean, they're not actually protesting anything."

"They're demanding that you don't shoot the chimpanzee."

"We're not planning to shoot it. Unless—"

"Unless what?"

"It shoots first," Chris says.

"Is that official SDPD policy?" Chambers asks.

"I don't think we have any official policy on armed primates," Chris says. "I mean, it's not really the sort of thing you'd—"

"So you have *no* policy?"

Chris is fucked, and he knows it.

Then he hears a voice say, "Well, the King Kong regulation—which mandates air support—only covers *giant* apes. And as you can see, this is a pretty *standard*-size ape, so . . ."

The cameraman swings around to the person who's talking and Chris sees that it's Lou Lubesnick. *Lieutenant* Lubesnick, the legendary detective of the Robbery Unit and a major hero of Chris's, is apparently one of those people who have nothing better to do at night than prowl Balboa Park, and he's wearing a loud Hawaiian shirt over baggy khakis, and are those . . . ? Yes, they are.

Lieutenant Lubesnick is wearing Crocs.

Orange Crocs.

With white socks.

He says, "Come on, give this kid a break, Bob."

"Can I get a statement from you, Lou?"

"Sure." Lubesnick looks into the camera and says, "Bob, department policy is to always handle every situation with the least amount of force necessary, consistent with the safety of the San Diego public and the visitors who flock to America's Finest City."

"Do you have any idea how the chimpanzee got the gun?"

"That is the subject of an ongoing investigation," Lubesnick says, "so I'm not really free to comment. Suffice it to say that everything that can be done is being done, and I have every confidence that we will have those answers in a reasonable time."

"Thank you, Lieutenant."

"You got it."

Chambers and his cameraman step away to get a better angle on Champion, who is still screaming imprecations from the side of the building.

Lubesnick steps over to Shea. "The key to talking to the media is bullshit, then some more bullshit, then conclude by sprinkling some bullshit on the bullshit. What's your name?"

"Shea, sir."

"Shea, in the future? Let your sergeant handle media relations."

The crowd shouts as Champion launches himself from the building and lands in a palm tree.

Without dropping the gun.

Chris is impressed.

"If you'll excuse me . . ." He walks to the base of the tree and looks up, assessing it for routes. He spends every Saturday morning on the faux-rock wall in a climbing gym, so he likes his chances.

More than on the building anyway, so things are looking better.

Then things look worse.

SWAT arrives.

They pile out of an armored car, and the officer in charge—clad in black with a Kevlar vest and a combat helmet—starts deploying his men to nearby buildings to take up sniper positions.

What has been a farce now has all the potential for tragicomedy.

The SWAT commander is in earnest conversation with Villa, who doesn't look earnest.

He just looks disgusted.

More uniforms have come in, and they start moving the crowd farther back, behind barricades. Which is great, Chris thinks, because a shocked and horrified populace will be a little farther from the sight of Champion getting blown to bits with automatic-weapons fire and high-powered sniper rounds.

With film at eleven.

"We want to warn our viewers that the following footage is considered graphic. If you're shitty parents with young children still up at this hour, you might want to move them away from the television set while the SWAT team blows up Curious George."

Chris walks over to Villa. "I can climb that tree."

"It's a little late for that," the SWAT commander says.

Chris talks to Villa. "Sarge, do you really want these guys to shoot that animal in front of all these people and the media?"

"Don't fall," Villa says.

Carolyn picks the perfect moment to get back with the dart gun—actually a "VetGun Delivery System" that looks a lot like a MAC-10 machine pistol. Chris is relieved to see that he can fire it with one hand.

Some of her staff start setting up the net at the bottom of the tree.

"He might interfere with a shooting angle," the SWAT commander says.

Pretty much the idea, Chris thinks, although he's too smart and career-minded to say it. He wants to get out of uniform patrol and catch on with the Robbery Unit, where maybe he can make detective.

Chris loves being a cop, even in a radio unit, because he really likes helping people. It's physical, it's active, and it's something different every night.

Usually not *this* different, but still.

"If he gets in the way of a shot and the animal kills him," the SWAT commander says, "it's not on me."

"*I* should go," Carolyn says. "It's my responsibility."

"I got this." Chris slings the VetGun Delivery System across his back, walks back over to the base of the tree and starts to shimmy up.

The crowd applauds.

Wrapping his legs around the trunk, Chris pulls himself up with his hands. The trunk is virtually vertical, and Chris's grip is at best tenuous. But it's too late to back down now. The crowd is chanting, "Go, cop!" and the television cameras are rolling, and Chris knows he's faced with a binary choice of hero or zero.

He looks up to see Champion staring down intently at him with an expression Chris chooses to interpret as concern.

It might be contempt, but Chris prefers concern.

Climbing to what he judges as VetGun Delivery System range, Chris pulls the gun off his shoulder, takes a deep breath and aims at Champion's left shoulder, at which point it becomes apparent that the chimp has had access to television, because he does what a thousand perps have done on a thousand cop shows.

He drops the gun.

Ten feet down.

Right on Chris's face.

Chris loses his grip and falls.

Into the net.

The crowd boos.

Then cheers again as Champion jumps down after him, onto the net, with—as witnesses other than Chris, who is barely conscious, would aver—his hands up.

Villa stares down at Chris.

Scowling.

"Which word in the two-word phrase did you not understand?" Villa asks. " 'Don't' or 'fall'?"

The E-Room nurse is simultaneously skeptical and amused. "A chimpanzee dropped a pistol on your face."

"Yes."

"While you were climbing a tree."

"That's right."

"That's real YouTube stuff."

I hope not, Chris thinks.

He hopes in vain—two dozen versions have already gone viral, some of them set to music like "Welcome to the Jungle."

"Is my nose broken?" Chris asks.

"Oh, yeah."

"Do I have a concussion?"

"I don't know," she says.

"Is my nose broken?"

"And you have a concussion," she says. "Do you have anyone who can drive you home?"

"How did I get here?"

"In an ambulance."

"Can't they take me home?"

"Sure," the nurse says. "We'll get you one of those Uber ambulances. Who's the chick in the safari suit standing over there looking concerned?"

"I don't remember her name."

"You don't remember *your* name," the nurse says. She looks over at Carolyn. "Can you drive him home?"

"It's the least I can do."

"Yeah, well don't even think about doing the *most* you can do," the nurse says. "He needs to stay sort of quiet."

"Shouldn't you check him for, like, brain damage?" Carolyn asks.

"He's a cop," the nurse says. "He already has, like, brain damage. If he passes out, starts projectile vomiting or thinks he's Jay-Z or something, call 911. Otherwise give him some Tylenol and an ice pack and let him get some rest. Then, if you're smarter then you look, you'll make your escape."

"That's kind of mean," Carolyn says.

"Yeah?" the nurse asks. "I take it you're some kind of zookeeper?"

"I work at the primate house."

"Good experience for dating a cop," the nurse says. "Most of them are about a one-half evolutionary step up. I've dated several of them, including my ex-husband. It's a bad idea."

"Is my nose broken?" Chris asks.

Chris has a one-bedroom apartment in a group of bungalows off Kansas Street above University Avenue in North Park. He feels lucky to have it, what with rents in San Diego going up like they're on Viagra and the neighborhood, once a funky semi-ghetto, becoming trendy and gentrified.

A lot of SDPD can't afford to live in San Diego at all but have a ninety-minute-each-way commute from Escondido, Temecula or even Riverside.

As a general rule, cops don't like living near where they patrol, but Chris enjoys living in North Park. It has coffee places, fun restaurants where he goes for brunch with his group of friends, cool bars when he wants a beer, and it still feels like a neighborhood instead of a tourist destination, although more and more people are renting out their places with Airbnb.

Most people in his immediate neighborhood, and certainly in his building, know that Chris is a cop, and most of them like it, even if they won't admit it. Chris thinks that they like the security of having a policeman in the vicinity and indeed have called him at home when there's been a domestic disturbance or a break-in.

They basically know Chris as a good guy.

Which he is.

Which Carolyn starts to learn as she gets Chris through his front door and onto the sofa in his tiny living room.

She already liked him, of course, because he saved Champ from execution, but as she settles him on the couch and goes into the kitchen, more of a narrow galley, to make an ice pack, she likes him even more.

First, there are the framed pictures on his walls.

Chris with his mom and dad.

Chris with what has to be a sister and two little girls who must be Chris's nieces and who are looking up at him adoringly.

Chris, a big smile on his face, bending over an elderly lady in a wheelchair who Carolyn guesses is his grandmother.

So Chris is a family guy.

Then there's the certificate of appreciation for Chris officiating at the Special Olympics, a photo of *Chris* in a wheelchair at an Over The Line tournament, Chris arm in arm with a bunch of friends (who all look like happy, normal, disgustingly healthy people who just came out of a CrossFit session) at an outdoor table somewhere, and the woman next to Chris is incredibly attractive, Carolyn observes with what she is embarrassed to admit is a twinge of jealousy.

Pump the brakes, she tells herself.

Chris Shea is too good to be true.

There has to be something seriously wrong with him.

Either he's a major player (he's good-looking enough to qualify), or he's divorced with a couple of kids, he's a closeted gay guy, or he's hopelessly in love with a coke-addicted stripper.

The kitchen is neat.

No dirty dishes in the sink or the drainer, no dirty pots or pans left on the stovetop.

Although she doesn't need to open the refrigerator to get ice, she does anyway, but the fridge holds no clues. A carton of milk, a six-pack of Modelo, a plastic container full of what looks like leftover (she opens it), yup, spaghetti bolognese.

So he cooks, too?

The freezer is likewise barren of any revelations about Chris Shea's actual dark, brooding, secretive soul. (What did you expect, Carolyn asks herself, body parts?) A couple of Stouffer's dinners, a pint of Ben & Jerry's Cherry Garcia, some more plastic containers of—oh, my God, they're labeled with masking tape—"Tuna Cass" "Marinara Sauce" and "Chili."

So either Chris's mother makes him meals and brings them over—a definite red flag—or he makes dinners and freezes them. And *labels* them—the writing on the tape looks like a man's handwriting.

Carolyn thinks a little shamefully about her own freezer, which has in it . . .

Ice.

Speaking of which, she finds a dish towel, holds it under the ice maker and wraps it into a pack that should fit over his nose. She goes back into the living room, sits down next to him and gently lays the ice pack on his face.

"Does it hurt?" she asks.

"Yes."

"Do you have any Tylenol?" she asks.

"I don't think so," Chris says. "I don't get a lot of headaches."

Of course not, Voight thinks, starting to get a little annoyed with this perfect specimen. "Do you mind if I look in your bathroom?"

"Go for it."

She goes for it.

The bathroom has no incriminating evidence.

For one thing, it's clean (the bathrooms of Carolyn's previous relationships have been . . . well, *not*), the one piece of art is not a poster of some Victoria's Secret babe but of a classic Mustang, and there's one of those toilet-brush containers by the stool.

Now she's pretty sure he is gay.

The medicine cabinet, behind the mirror over the sink, is innocuous. No Vicodin or Oxy, no antibiotic prescription that might betray a recent STD (or sinus infection, girl; Jesus, settle down), no stack of condoms.

No Tylenol, though, either.

Not as much as an aspirin.

A tube of toothpaste (Optic White), some deodorant, and some bottles of vitamins, which she opens to see if there are really vitamins in them.

There are.

Carolyn goes back out into the living room.

"No luck on the Tylenol," she says. "Oh, wait, I might have some in my bag."

She digs around and finds one buried in a crease at the bottom under some tissue and what had at one time been a cracker of some kind. She wipes it on her sleeve and hands it to him. "Take this. I don't think you'll get addicted."

"Are you a doctor?"

"Actually, I am," Carolyn says. "I mean, I'm not a medical doctor, I have a Ph.D. in zoology."

He swallows the pill and closes his eyes.

"You want to watch TV or something?" Carolyn asks.

"I don't watch a lot of TV," Chris says.

Of course you don't, Carolyn thinks as she finds the remote.

She watches a lot of TV.

A lot of bad reality TV.

Carolyn watches, among other things, *The Bachelor, The Bachelorette, Bachelors in Paradise* (anything Bachelor), *Married at First Sight, 90 Day Fiancé* and a geographical smattering of *Real Housewives*. She watches these shows because, as she is very aware, she has no life outside her work and because voyeuring other people's love lives is less painful than brooding about her own.

Or lack thereof.

She hasn't dated since the breakup with Jon.

Who cheated on her.

Who wasn't there, as they say, for the right reasons.

The pretentious, bicycle-pedaling, soy-milk-latte-drinking, small-plate-consuming, spelling-his-name-without-the-*h* slimy butthole. A tenure-track professor of comparative literature at UCSD and the perfect guy for her, right? Educated, intellectual, knew his way around a wine list, saw a future for them together but saw a present comparing more than literature with a grad student, which he defended by pompously declaring that at least she wasn't an undergraduate.

That would have been, you know, unethical.

Anyway, he broke Carolyn's heart, a fact that she's embarrassed about because he wasn't (isn't) worth the heartbreak.

So maybe an academic, pretentious wannabe hipster doofus isn't the perfect guy for me, she thinks as she scrolls through the DirecTV guide. Maybe—the ER nurse notwithstanding—it's a whole-milk-drinking, rock-wall-climbing, neat-freak cop who loves his grandmother.

And what a "meet-cute" story to tell our grandchildren.

Whoa, girl, she thinks, slow your roll.

You hardly know this boy.

She finds an episode of *Cops*.

Chris wakes up in his bed.

His face hurts when he gets up. He shuffles into the bathroom and looks into the mirror. Both eyes are black and swollen, and his nose bone looks a little flattened.

He steps into the shower and lets the hot water pound him. He dries off, puts on a sweatshirt and jeans and goes into the kitchen. A note is propped against his French-press coffeepot:

I put you to bed. Hope you feel better. Thanks for saving Champion.

Best,
Carolyn Voight

PS—Can I take you to lunch to thank you? 619-555-1212.

Huh.

He makes coffee and gets on his laptop.

Sort of a mistake.

He's made the headlines of the *San Diego Union-Tribune*: POLICE OFFICER INJURED APPREHENDING GUN-WIELDING CHIMP.

With a photo of him falling out of the tree.

Great, Chris thinks.

He goes on Twitter and finds out that he basically *is* Twitter, that he and Champion are blowing up the internet.

Taking his coffee into the living room, Chris turns on the local news to see a pretty reporter standing in front of the Museum of Man describing what happened last night. Then it cuts to a clip of Champion brandishing the pistol at the crowd below, then SWAT arriving, then Chris shimmying up the tree. . . .

Then falling.

He shuts the TV off as he hears her say, "YouTube sensation."

Calling into the station house, he gets the news that he's on mandatory seventy-two-hour health leave. So it would give him time to take Voight up on her offer.

Does she really just want to thank me (which is unnecessary, he thinks, because I didn't really do anything except fall out of the tree while Champ pretty much turned himself in), or is she sort of asking me out?

And do I want to do it either way?

She's really nice and really pretty. And obviously really smart (did she tell me that she has a Ph.D.?), but maybe too smart to be interested in a cop with a B.A. in criminal justice.

I mean, what would a zookeeper and a cop have in common?

A lot, actually, he decides when he thinks about it.

He decides he'll call her when he looks a little less like a raccoon that just got a nose job.

In the meantime he's more or less obsessed with the overriding question:

Where did the chimp get the revolver?

There are only so many possibilities, all of them exhaustively covered and debated on the Net.

Some commentators go with a conspiracy theory, that animal-rights activists tossed the pistol into the ape enclosure. Like what? Chris thinks, dismissing the argument. The Primate Liberation Front?

Others have it that it was just a wacko, a sick headcase or just a practical joker who wanted to see what would happen if you gave a handgun to a chimp. Of course it gets political. These days everything does. The right-wing nuts connect the incident to Hillary Clinton, claiming that she was trying to make some kind of point about gun control and at the same time deflect attention away from her thirty-three thousand missing emails, the left-wing nuts blame the NRA, claiming that it was trying to make some kind of point about gun control and deflect attention from Trump's . . .

Well, everything.

Chris isn't buying any of it.

He thinks the real explanation is more mundane. It's just a matter of finding out what it is.

But really, what kind of total dumb-ass would toss a revolver away in a zoo?

Hollis Bamburger is thrilled.

Looking at Twitter on his phone, he sees that he's finally gone viral. Twitter, YouTube, Facebook, you name it—the chimp with the revolver is on it.

Not *the* revolver, Hollis thinks.

My revolver.

For his entire twenty-three years, Hollis Bamburger has wanted to be special for something. He wasn't special at home, where he was just one of six kids by three different fathers, none of them conspicuously present, and a meth-head mother. Wasn't special in elementary school, middle school or high school, which he dropped out of after his third unsuccessful try at tenth grade. He wasn't special at the East Mesa Juvenile Detention Facility, aka "Birdland"—named for its location, not its inhabitants—just there for truancy and a B&E. Wasn't special at Chino, where he went at eighteen for sticking up a liquor store.

If you asked anybody at those institutions about Hollis Bamburger, you'd probably get a blank stare, and then a check of their records would reveal a skinny, undersize white kid whose only evolution would seem to be a growing catalog of bad tattoos that started on his arms and now run up his neck.

Hell, even if you asked his family about Hollis, you'd probably get the same blank stare.

His younger sister, Lavonne, even once vocalized this to a probation officer.

"There's nothing special about Holly," she said. Then she thought for a second and added, "Except that he's really stupid."

Sad but true.

The only thing that ever made Hollis exceptional was his uncannily stupid screwups. So much so that at Clark Middle School any phenomenal act of idiocy became known as a "Bamburger."

You shoved enough toilet paper down the john to cause a flood?

A Bamburger.

You downloaded a term paper and turned it in with the Wikipedia heading still on it?

A Bamburger.

You broke into a teacher's car and fell asleep in it?

Bamburger.

But even that distinction faded by high school, leaving Hollis with . . .

Nothing.

But now . . .

Now Hollis is special for something. He's responsible for the "Champ the Gunslinging Chimp" vid-clips.

Which are being seen all over the world.

Like, people in Africa, China, Europe and France are seeing his handiwork, laughing at the chimp, getting off on the cop falling into the net. That was the best part, the monkey making the cop a bitch.

Hollis hates cops.

The only thing he hates more than cops are COs. Correctional officers are just assholes even too brutal and dumb to be police. But Hollis is too happy right now to be eaten up by hatred. The bright white heat of his newfound internet celebrity has washed away all darkness.

He holds the phone up to Lee. "Dude, check this out!"

Lee Caswell, who has twenty years, six inches, thirty pounds and two felony beefs on Hollis, looks at the vid-clip and then hands the phone back.

"I'm famous," Hollis says.

"*You're* not famous," Lee says. "The monkey is."

"Yeah, but I set the monkey up," Hollis says.

"But you can't tell anyone about it," Lee says.

This is a real kick in the gonads.

Hollis hadn't thought about that.

Now it drops him into a deep pit of despair. Finally, after *twenty-three years*, he has done something special and he can't reveal it. The whole world is watching his achievement, and none of them can ever know that it was Hollis Bamburger.

He's devastated, his short-lived joy now ashes in his mouth.

"*And* you lost the gun," Lee says.

"You *told* me to get rid of it," Hollis says. More like whines.

"Not like that!" Lee yells. He yells at Hollis a lot, in fact, ever since the first moment when Hollis became his cellmate at Chino. Now he starts yelling again. "You think this is funny?! First thing, we're out a gun! Second thing, you embarrassed a cop! You think cops forget that kind of thing!?"

It's been Lee's experience that you can lie to a cop and he'll think it's just business as usual, you fight a cop and he'll forget about it, but you show one up and he'll hate you for life.

"They've got the gun," Lee says. "They'll be tracking it down."

"They can't track it to us."

"You mean they can't track it to *you*," Lee says.

This is true, Hollis thinks. He's the one who bought the gun from a Mexican in a vacant lot on Thirty-second Street, not far from the shitty motel they're staying in now.

Montalbo assured him it was clean.

"What if the cops track the gun to the Mexican?" Lee asks. "And the Mexican gives you up?"

"I used a fake name," Hollis says.

"Yeah?" Lee asks. "Did you use a fake appearance?"

Hollis hadn't thought of that.

"The tattoo on your neck?" Lee asks.

The one that reads HOLLIS. He was going to have it read BAMBURGER, but his neck isn't that long.

"How many Hollises do you think there are in the system?" Lee asks.

"Probably not very many," Hollis says.

Sadly.

"So when you go out to get another gun," Lee says, "cover your damn neck."

"Why do *I* have to do it?" Hollis asks. Again, more like whines, but then he turtles his head when he sees Lee's face get all red and threatening.

"Because you're the one who threw our gun away," Lee says. "And we can't very well do a stickup with just our dicks, can we? At least not with yours."

A comment Hollis feels is unnecessary.

He's miserable now.

This was supposed to have been a triumphant moment, something really special. And now it's turned into a . . .

Bamburger.

The reaction to Chris's return to duty is pretty much what he expected.

Brutal.

He's greeted with, "Welcome back, Monkey-Man!" "Hey, Donkey-Kong!" and guys scratching their armpits while making ape sounds. He loses track of the times he's told not to "monkey around" on his shift.

Herrera holds up his phone to show Chris a vid-clip of him falling from the tree with the chyron NO ACTUAL CHIMPS WERE INJURED IN THE MAKING OF THIS FILM.

His locker is festooned with bunches of bananas.

Chris opens it to find a paperback volume of Jane Goodall's *My Friends the Wild Chimpanzees*, DVDs of *Planet of the Apes*, a *King Kong* poster, a photo of Michael Jackson with Bubbles, several monkey masks, a full gorilla suit on a hanger and a can of grape soda with the *GR* crossed out.

On a piece of tape stuck on the locker, his name reads CHRIS "COCONUT" SHEA.

"Why Coconut?" Chris asks.

"Because," Harrison says, "coconuts drop out of palm trees."

Lieutenant Brown wants to see him. "You're famous now. A celebrity cop."

"I just want to do my job, sir," Chris says.

"We've had a request from the *Tonight* show," Brown says. "They want you and Champion to appear together. Public Affairs wants you to do it."

"I don't want to, sir."

"I nixed it," Brown says. "You're a joke already. A cop who falls out of a tree going after a monkey. It's all over social media."

Chris feels sick to his stomach.

"And you've made enemies in the department," Brown says.

"What enemies?" Chris asks, feeling sicker. "Who? How?"

"The SWAT guys think you made them look bad."

They can do that without *my* help, Chris thinks, but he's smart enough not to say it. He just wants to get out of the lieutenant's office without hearing anything more about how his career is toast.

"You feel good enough to do your shift?" Brown asks.

"Absolutely."

"Okay, go," Brown says. "But do me a favor? If Shamu escapes from Sea-World, you stay out of the water, okay?"

Okay, Chris thinks.

He leaves the office feeling as low as he has in his life. He'll never get the bump to Robbery now.

Lou Lubesnick is never going to take on a joke.

Chris gears up.

It's a lot of gear.

First there's the soft body armor, aka bulletproof vest (Chris knows there's no such thing as bullet*proof*—bullet-*resistant* would be more accurate) with front and side panels. Chris has opted out of the rear panels in favor of less weight and greater flexibility. Then there's a flashlight, a can of OC spray (basically tear gas), a PR-24 side handle baton, handcuffs, and his radio.

A waist holster with his Glock 9mm and spare ammunition.

Then there's the badge over his left breast pocket and an ID tag, gold with black lettering, over the right pocket.

Central Division patrols the neighborhoods of Balboa Park, Barrio Logan, Core-Columbia, Cortez, East Village, the Gaslamp, Golden Hill, Grant

Hill, Harborview, Horton Plaza, Little Italy, Logan Heights, Marina, Park West, Petco, Sherman Heights, South Park and Stockton.

This basically means that if anything violent, twisted, gang-related, random or just plain strange happens in San Diego, it's very likely to happen in Central.

Which is why Chris loves working it.

That night, cruising Fifth Avenue west of the park, he sees:

A WM, who can't go five-three, dressed only in a gold lamé jockstrap and a dog collar, crying, being led down the sidewalk on a leash by a six-five BM, muscled like an NFL linebacker, wearing a Superman costume complete with cape.

Which would all be okay with Chris except Superman is flogging the WM with a silver cat-o'-nine-tails. Chris pulls over, gets out of the car and puts his hand up for them to stop walking.

"What is this, gay Comic-Con?" Chris asks the floggee.

"He came . . . to my apartment," the guy blubbers, "made me wear . . . just this . . . put on this collar . . . and he's been walking me down the street, whipping me."

"Why didn't you call for help?" Chris asks.

"Because . . ." He stops for a couple sobs and a deep sniff. "I'm . . . *enjoying* . . . it."

The black guy says, "He's my slave."

"And you're Superman?" Chris asks.

"What, a black man can't be Superman?" the black guy asks. "Who says Superman has to be white?"

Chris regrets it the second it comes out of his mouth. "But he was. In the comic books, Superman was a white guy."

"In the movies, too," the black guy says. He starts counting off on his fingers. "Christopher Reeve, Dean Cain, Henry Cavill, Tyler motherfucking Hoechlin of *7th Heaven* fame. Eleven Supermans, all white. It's a conspiracy."

"Okay."

"Why not Jim Brown?" the black guy says. "What's wrong with Idris Elba, how about Denzel?"

Chris says, "I could see that."

"Batman, too," the black guy says. Same thing—Adam West, George Clooney, Ben Affleck, *Michael Keaton*. Why not Jim Brown, Idris Elba—"

"Or Denzel," Chris says.

"That's right." Superman turns to his slave and says, "Next time I'll be Batman, you be Robin."

"Why can't *I* be Batman, *you* be Robin?"

"Because that would be ridiculous."

These guys are both higher than kites, Chris thinks. He doesn't know what they're on, but it must be pretty good.

"Yeah," Chris says, "you guys can't be out here doing this."

"Why not?" Superman asks.

"Come on," Chris says.

"We have a right to our sexual self-expression," the slave says.

"Not on a public sidewalk you don't," Chris says. "Look, Spartacus, I'm trying to cut you a break here. Go home. Put some clothes on. If I see you out on the street again like this tonight, I'm taking both of you in."

"For what?" Superman asks.

"Disturbing the peace," Chris says. "Public indecency . . ."

"Are you calling us indecent?" the slave asks.

"You only doing this because I'm black and gay," Superman says. "You're a hater."

Chris sees this blowing up. People across the street are starting to stop and look, and it will be a matter of minutes at most before another car rolls up. It could be Harrison or, worse, Grosskopf or, worst, Villa—who really does hate gays and blacks, more so gay blacks, and probably superheroes, too, because Villa hates . . . well, everybody—and then Superman and Spartacus are both going to jail, and Chris will have a pile of paperwork to do.

But if I have to put this guy in cuffs, I'm going to need backup, because Superman here—big as he is, high as he is—if he wants to, will kick my ass.

He pulls a desperation play. "Look, don't make me break out the Kryptonite."

Superman looks concerned. "You got Kryptonite?"

Chris nods. "In the car."

Superman gets skeptical. "Red or green?"

"Both," Chris says. "Of course."

"Red makes me crazy," Superman says.

Yeah, Chris thinks, *that's* what makes you crazy. "But green could kill you, right?"

"Let me see it," Superman says, calling Chris's bluff.

Chris shakes his head. "If I let you see it, I have to let you *have* it. Department rules."

"*Y'all* cops got Kryptonite?"

"Only the good ones," Chris says. Which is sort of true. "So what's it going to be? You going to go home, or do I have to go all Braniac on you?"

Spartacus, apparently unaware of Jim Croce, tugs on Superman's cape. "We'll go home."

Chris watches him lead Superman back up the street.

It's sort of sad.

One of those nights, one of those shifts.

They're always worse in summer, when air-conditioners strain to work, or there's no AC at all, and people are on the street or in the parks instead of at home in bed.

Tempers are short and fuses shorter.

Arguments all too quickly become fistfights, fists yield to knives, knives to guns, and it happens *like that.* In an ill-considered second, lives are changed forever. People are scarred for life, or maimed, or killed, or they spend what would have been their best years in the purgatory that is the prison system.

Add alcohol and drugs to the summer heat and you have a combustible brew, always just a spark from flaming up.

So after the benign Superman/Spartacus situation, Chris rapidly and in short order pulls a domestic in Golden Hill in which a drunk middle-aged husband was beating the shit out of his drunk middle-aged wife, who in response smashed a beer bottle (Heineken) on the kitchen counter and jammed the jagged glass into hubby's face. Chris rolls up in support to find that Grosskopf and Harrison already have both parties cuffed, the husband (understandably) howling in pain and the wife, despite both her eyes being swollen to slits, screaming at Grosskopf, "Leave him alone! He didn't do nothin'!"

"Don't say that again," Chris says to her. "You'll blow your self-defense case."

She doesn't care. "Don't hurt him! I *love* him!"

It's unreciprocated. "That dumb bitch poked out my eye!"

"Your eye is still there," Chris says.

For how long is another issue.

"We're taking you both in," Harrison says.

"For *what*?!" the woman screams.

"Seriously?" Harrison asks.

The EMTs arrive. Grosskopf takes the husband and cuffs him to the gurney and then supervises as they put him in the ambulance. Grosskopf is pissed, because now he'll have to go to the ER.

Harrison and Chris walk the wife out to Harrison's car and put her in the back.

"This is the third time we've been to your place for this kind of thing," Chris says to her.

"And it don't do no good!" she says.

"I guess that's my point," Chris says. "When you talk to the detectives, tell them you were in fear of your life."

"I love him."

"Okay." Chris shuts the door.

"Why are you trying to help her out?" Harrison asks him.

"Did you see her face?"

"She's safer in jail," Harrison says.

Probably true, Chris thinks.

The evening's next event is a liquor-store robbery on Twenty-eighth and B in Golden Hill.

Chris responds and rolls up just after Grosskopf.

The clerk knows the drill, because robberies at this location are a semi-regular occurrence.

"About five-ten, wearing a denim shirt, cargo pants and work boots. Sounded white."

"What do you mean, 'sounded'?" Grosskopf asks.

"I didn't see his face," the clerk says. "He was wearing a mask. One of them ski masks."

The robber stuck a pistol in his face and told him to open the till. The clerk did the right thing and let him have the money. The robber got about a hundred twenty in cash and also scooped up some of those little airline bottles of vodka and a 5-hour ENERGY.

The clerk saw him turn left—north—when he "exited the premises."

Chris doesn't wait for the interview to end but goes back to his car and rolls north on Twenty-eighth, betting that the robber is headed for the park. He calls it in, knows that other units will be coming, but hopes he finds the guy first.

After the Champ incident, he could use an armed-robbery arrest.

Sure enough, he spots a white male, about five-ten, wearing exactly what the clerk described, walking fast on the pavement that edges the east side of the park. Chris slows and follows at a distance, then sees the guy go into the "goose walk," that stiff-legged gait that perps get when they sense a cop behind them.

Chris hits the microphone. "Stop right there."

The guy takes off running.

Chris pulls over and goes after him.

He knows he should stay in the car and call for backup, but if he does that, the guy will disappear into the park and they'll spend the rest of the shift looking for him and probably not find him.

Besides, let's face it, this is fun.

He sees the guy's hand go into his pocket and dump something in the bushes. That's going to be the gun and the mask, Chris knows, but he doesn't stop for them. He gains on the guy, who's moving none too fast in work boots, reaches out and gives him a hard shove.

The guy falls face-first on the ground, and Chris is on top of him.

"Give me your hands!" Chris yells.

This isn't the perp's first prom. He gives up his hands, Chris cuffs him, and pulls him to his feet. "Why didn't you stop when I told you to? Why did you run?"

"I was scared."

"Of getting arrested for robbery?" Chris asks. He sees flashers back where he left the car and knows it will be Grosskopf. "You just robbed a liquor store."

"No I didn't!"

"Yeah, right," Chris says. "What did you drop back there?"

"Nothing!"

"You took something out of your pocket and threw it into the bushes. You really going to make me dig around for that?" Chris pushes him up against a tree. "Anything sharp in your pockets? Anything that's going to hurt me?"

"No."

Grosskopf walks up. "That looks like our guy."

Chris digs into the cargo-pants pocket and comes out with a bunch of bills. "You didn't rob the store, huh? Where did you get this?"

"It's mine."

Chris finds the little bottles. "These yours, too? You have ID?"

"I left my wallet at home."

Chris shines his flashlight in the guy's face. He's maybe forty, looks like he's lived a hard life. Probably no stranger to the system, and Chris guesses that if they look at his arms, they'll find cheap jailhouse tats.

"You going to tell me your name?" Chris asks.

"Richard."

"You have a last name, Richard?"

"Holder."

"You're just messing with me now," Chris says.

"No, I'm not."

"Did your parents just, like, hate you or something?" Chris pulls up

Holder's sheet. To his intense lack of surprise, Richard James Holder has a record longer than a Queen song. Burglary, robbery, drugs, he's done stretches at Victorville and Donovan.

Chris hasn't been on the job all that long, just three years, but long enough to know the secret that Richard keeps so deep inside that even *he* doesn't know it.

That what Richard wants most in the world is to go back to the joint.

It's his world, the only place he feels at home.

All Chris has to provide Richard with is an excuse, and he'll take it.

Grosskopf comes up to the car. "You going to take him in or you want me to?"

"I have a better idea," Chris says.

If they take the guy straight in and book him, it's just going to come down to an evidentiary fight. They'll probably get him on the possession of the stolen goods but could lose him on the armed robbery and the gun.

"Okay, Richard, we're going back to the liquor store," Chris says.

"I was never there," Richard says.

Chris drives back to the liquor store and walks Richard in. Shows him to the clerk and asks, "Is this the guy who robbed you?"

"Yes, it is."

Richard is indignant. "He can't ID me! I was wearing a mask!"

You have to love these guys, Chris thinks, you just have to love them. And it explains why so many chairs at prison Mensa meetings go unclaimed. He says, "Bullshit, you were wearing a mask."

"I was!" Richard yells.

Chris looks at the clerk. "Was he wearing a mask?"

"No, Officer."

Richard is filled with righteous indignation. "He's lying! I *was too* wearing a mask."

"Prove it," Chris says.

"I will."

They get back in the car, drive to the park, and get out where Richard threw stuff away. He walks to a line of bushes and juts his chin. "There."

Chris bends down and picks up the ski mask. "This isn't yours."

"Yes it is!"

"It won't even fit you."

"Put it on me and you'll see."

Chris slides the ski mask over Richard's head. They get into the car and go back to the liquor store. Chris walks Richard in and asks, "Okay, is this the guy who robbed you?"

"Yes, it is," the clerk says.

Fred's chin drops to his chest. "Okay, you got me."

Chris drives back to the park again, gets out and walks along the route where he chased Richard. Shining his flashlight into the bushes near where they found the mask, he sees something shiny. He gloves up, reaches down and comes up with a .22 Long AMT Backup, a little semiautomatic job, and drops it into an evidence bag.

Back in the car, Chris shows Richard the gun. "Is this what you used to rob the store?"

Richard thinks about this and then asks, "Can I have one of those vodkas?"

"Yeah, okay." Chris opens one of the little bottles, Richard opens his mouth, and Chris pours it in like he's feeding a baby bird.

Then Richard says, "Yeah, that's the gun."

Chris takes him back to the house and books him. He's just finishing up this process when he gets the word that Lieutenant Brown wants to see him. Chris goes into his office expecting a "great job" pat on the back. Good job getting a recidivist robber off the street, good job getting a gun off the street . . .

No.

Instead—

Brown asks, "Do you just want to piss *everyone* off?"

"What did I do?"

"It's what you didn't do," Brown says. "You didn't bring the suspect directly back and turn him over to Robbery. It was their investigation."

"But I got a confession, I got the gun—"

"And I got phone calls from Robbery asking me why one of my uniforms is showing them up," Brown says. "Robbery will take it from here."

"Yeah, sure—"

"Oh, that's okay with you?" Brown asks. "I'm so glad. Do your job and not other people's. And, Shea, if I have to hear your name again tonight, it's not going to be a good thing. Now, get out of here."

He's not out of there thirty minutes when he gets another call, this time a bar brawl in the Gaslamp that has spread out onto the sidewalk.

The Gaslamp, aka just "the Lamp," downtown bordering the harbor, is San Diego's original sin district, since the founding of the city an area of bars, strip clubs and brothels. The story goes that the town fathers tried to clean it up in 1915 and threw all the prostitutes out but then had to invite them all back in when the navy said it wouldn't send ships anymore, which would have destroyed the city's economy.

It's pretty cleaned up now, a tourist destination, but it's still an area where people go to get shitfaced.

By the time Chris rolls up, the street is already a festival of lights with cop flashers and onlookers holding up cell phones to get video souvenirs of their wild night in the Lamp.

Dinner, drinks, a floor show . . .

Which, strictly speaking, is on the sidewalk.

SDPD already has most of the action under control, with combatants pressed up against the wall and cuffs being applied. Villa has other troops gradually pushing the lookie-loos back, but the main event is still ongoing, two guys rolling around on the concrete.

Sort of graceless jujitsu, Chris thinks as he nudges through the crowd.

One of the fighters is obviously the bouncer, with the semiofficial security-guy uniform of a black T-shirt tight around his chest and arm muscles. The other is pure chucklehead, with a shaved head and a Tapout T-shirt indicating that he's an MMA fan who thinks that because he watches mixed martial arts and hits the gym a couple times a week that he can *do* mixed martial arts and hit something that hits back. Which the bouncer is doing right now, slamming elbows into his opponent's face in your basic ground-and-pound.

"Crowd control," Villa says to Chris, who therefore turns his back on the fight to face the street.

A good thing, because right then a humongous drunk comes rolling down the sidewalk throwing air punches and getting ready to jump into the fight.

Chris puts his palm out. "That's enough, right there."

"Fuck that!" the guy yells. "That's my friend!"

The drunk has to be six-four, two and a half bills, and most of it is muscle. He looks like he could actually be a cage fighter, and Chris has no desire whatsoever to find out.

"Stay out of this," Chris says.

"He's my buddy!" the drunk yells. "I'd take a bullet for him!"

"That's a real possibility," Chris says. "Back off, sir."

"Fuck you."

The drunk charges, blasting Chris's left shoulder.

Chris pivots with the force, sticks out his leg and throws all his weight into the drunk's back.

They fall to the sidewalk together, Chris landing on top as he tries to grab the drunk's right hand to twist it behind him.

Un-unh, the guy is too strong.

It's a rodeo now—all Chris can do is try to hold on until help comes in, and then Perez is down there beside him, pulling the drunk's left arm back like it's an oar on a rowing machine, but this guy is strong and anesthetized, gets up on his knees and then to his feet with Chris still hanging on.

Chris "has his back," as they might say in MMA. Wrapping his legs around the drunk's waist, he tries to apply a choke hold, which seems to arouse the outrage of the crowd but does nothing to the drunk, who starts to spin as Perez pulls his Taser and waits for a shot that will hit the drunk and not Chris.

"Hey, that's the monkey guy!" Chris hears someone say. "That's that monkey guy!"

Perez gets his shot.

Chris feels the drunk shake.

Actually more like rattle.

But he doesn't go down.

Villa shoots his Taser.

So does Herrera.

The drunk is pincushioned, wires sticking out of him like a bad ham-radio set as his eyes go all wide and he shrieks.

Then he falls.

Forward.

Like a felled tree.

With Chris still on top of him.

It's a hard landing.

Chris feels the impact jar his chest, his spine. And his head, which explodes in pain from the broken nose and the concussion.

He goes blind for a second but stays conscious.

Climbing off the still-quivering drunk, he sees that the main event is over, the bouncer on his feet, his opponent in cuffs, as Herrera and Perez rush in, handcuff the drunk behind his back and pull him to his feet.

No one's in any hurry to get the Taser darts out of him.

"You all right?" Perez asks him.

"Yeah, I'm good," Chris says.

Herrera's reading the drunk his rights. If there weren't a crowd around, he and Perez might very well get out their batons and beat the living shit out of him, because they don't play, and Villa would simply have walked around the block.

But now Villa is glaring at him and says, "You don't fight any better than you climb."

Chris doesn't know what to say, so he doesn't say anything.

The drunk's face is scraped and bloody.

"Perez will do the paper," Villa says. "You take your guy to the E-Room. What happens on the way, I don't need to know."

Chris, Herrera and Perez walk the guy to Chris's car and shove him in the back. Herrera is a little surprised when Chris buckles the drunk's seat belt, because the other option is to leave it off, hit the gas and then hit the brakes, slamming the drunk's face into the partition.

And it's tempting, Chris thinks.

God, is it tempting.

He gets behind the wheel, drives to the hospital, and walks the drunk into the E-Room.

The admitting nurse is the same woman who took care of Chris four nights ago. "Is this just a lame excuse to see me again? Because I don't date cops."

"Neither do I," Chris says.

She looks at the drunk's face, sees that it's not serious, and then asks Chris, "How about you? You okay?"

"I'm good."

"How's the zoo lady?" she asks. "You going to get with her?"

"No, I don't think so."

"You're even dumber than you look," the nurse says.

I don't know, Chris thinks, I look pretty dumb. First I get clowned by an ape, then I get on the wrong side of Robbery, *then* I get into a roll-around with a drunk. My sergeant thinks I'm a chronic screwup, and he might not be wrong.

"Anyway," the nurse says, "she's probably better off."

Probably, Chris thinks.

Then he gets a call to go back to the station.

Lieutenant Brown holds up his phone and shows Chris the vid-clip of him being spun around on the drunk's back.

"What did I tell you about hearing your name again tonight?"

"That you didn't want to."

"You are becoming a YouTube sensation," Brown says. "Is this your intent, to build your followers?"

"No, sir."

"I do not like to see my officers in the media," Brown says, "social or otherwise."

"I understand, sir."

"Do you?" Brown asks. "I wonder if you do. Do you think you can come in tomorrow and do your shift without making a public spectacle of yourself or stepping on anyone else's shoes?"

"Yes, sir."

"We'll see."

He starts to drive home to get some sleep. He could use some unconsciousness, because consciousness is painful right now.

I've pissed off my lieutenant he thinks, I've pissed off Robbery—the exact people I least want to piss off—and my fuck-ups have gone viral. I'm going to stay in a radio car for the rest of my career, unless they force me to quit first.

The E-Room nurse was right.

I'm a moron.

He gets on the phone.

"I know you said lunch," Chris says, "but how do you feel about breakfast?"

Okay, it turns out.

They meet at the aptly named Breakfast Republic on University.

It's a bright, cheerful place with big windows facing the street, yellow wooden chairs and funky sculptures of broken eggs.

Chris is already there when Carolyn arrives, politely waiting outside the front door. Of course he is, she thinks.

"This is a nice surprise," she says.

Yeah, a nice surprise that left her very little time to decide what to wear. She sure as hell didn't want to show up as "zoo lady" in her safari suit, but she didn't want to overdress either and tip her hand that she possibly thought of this as more than a gesture of gratitude and something like maybe a date.

Carolyn isn't going to lay *that* card down first.

So she decided on a nice black silk blouse over a pair of tighter-than-truly-necessary jeans and a pair of sandals. And she wore her hair not in her on-the-job ponytail but loose and long, falling over her shoulders.

The zoo mandates that all its female employees look "wholesome."

She doesn't want to look wholesome this morning. But she doesn't want to look slutty either, like this is a post-booty-call breakfast, so she took it easy on the mascara.

"I'm glad you could make it," Chris says, holding the door open.

This is different, Carolyn thinks. Professor Asshole would never hold a door open, considering it a condescending, paternalistic passive-aggressive gesture perpetuating the male power structure. He was *complimenting* her by not opening a door.

Chris goes to the hostess and gets a table for two by the window.

He pulls out her chair.

Professor Asshole would never pull out a chair, considering it a condescending, paternalistic . . .

"You're so polite," Carolyn says.

He looks at her curiously.

The boy literally doesn't understand, she thinks, why I would find this remarkable.

Chris sits down across from her. There's an awkward moment of silence before he says, "You look nice. Pretty."

So maybe this is a date, Carolyn thinks.

Or maybe he's just being . . . polite.

"You look less like a raccoon," she says. Then feels really stupid. *You look less like a raccoon?*

"That's good, I guess," Chris says.

"So how *are* you feeling?" Carolyn asks.

"Yeah, good."

Carolyn already knows him well enough to sense that this means, *I don't want to talk about it.* She's surprised she finds this refreshing. Professor Asshole wanted to talk about everything—his career, his ideas, his choice of clothes, his fears, his anxieties, his sinus infections, his *feelings.*

Christ, I was dating a woman.

This boy fell out of a tree, just finished an all-night shift—and from the looks of him it was a hell of a shift—and all he has to say is, "Yeah, good." Stoic, which could be a good or a bad thing. It might be hard to have a real conversation with him when he comes home—

When he comes *home?*

Slow your roll, girl.

Fortunately, the server arrives with the menus.

Chris orders a chicken-mango-sausage scramble with cheddar and onion, Carolyn gets pineapple upside-down pancakes topped with pineapple butter.

"So how's work?" she asks. And why am I starting every sentence with "So"? And please don't say, *Yeah, good.*

To her relief he doesn't. What he says is, "Well, I had something funny happen to me last night."

He tells what is actually, yes, a funny story about Superman and Spartacus.

"You really said you had Kryptonite?" Carolyn asks.

Chris shrugs. "I didn't know what else to do."

The food arrives.

Carolyn notices that Chris waits, his fork poised, for her to take a first bite before he starts eating.

I want to meet this guy's mother, she thinks.

Slow . . . slow . . . the roll.

"How's yours?" Chris asks.

"It's great," she says. "But the sugar crash is going to be brutal."

"Right?" Chris says. He takes a bite of the sausage, then a sip of coffee, and then says. "Tell me about you."

She goes with the auto-cliché response. "What about me?"

"Where you're from," Chris says. "Where you went to school, how you got into your work, what you like to do when you're not working . . ."

She finds herself telling him, going into a monologue about being from Madison, Wisconsin, going to undergraduate school there and then deciding she'd had enough cold weather and snow to last her, like, forever, so she got her master's at Stanford and then her doctorate at UCSD and fell into her dream job at the primate house at the zoo. How her parents are both professors at Wisconsin, her father in chemistry, her mother in French literature, and how she has an older sister, by two years—married, kids—and a younger brother, and when she's not working, she likes to run, go to movies, go to the beach, the usual stuff, and then she realizes that she's been talking nonstop for at least ten minutes and that he's just sitting there listening and probably knows more about her from those ten minutes than Asshole learned in three years.

Carolyn feels herself blush, and then she says, "I'm sorry. I've just been talking and talking."

"I asked," Chris says.

Yes, she thinks. You did. "So . . . your turn."

"Not much to tell." He shrugs again. "I was born and raised here, in Tierra Santa. My dad is a software engineer, my mom teaches third grade. Good people. I have two older sisters—I'm the baby of the family. Went to SDSU. I'm a cop, I've always wanted to be a cop. That's about it."

"What do you like about being a cop?" Carolyn asks.

"Everything," Chris says. "It gets me out and around, every shift is something different, and I guess I like helping people."

Yeah, I guess you do, she thinks.

"What do you like about *your* job?" Chris asks.

"I love the animals," she says. "They can't speak for themselves, so they kind of need me. And they're always real. Never phony. You know, sometimes I think I like apes more than I like people."

Carolyn worries about why this is. Is it because apes don't reject you, don't cheat on you, that they give "unconditional love"? Is it because she needs to be needed? Is she going to become one of those lonely middle-aged women who can only relate to animals? Then she says, "Even though they do throw their poop at me sometimes."

"I've had *people* do that," Chris says.

"No shit?"

They both laugh.

They've finished their food, and if this was him politely accepting a thank-you gesture, then they each get up and go their own ways.

She signals for the check, but when it comes, Chris reaches out and takes it.

"This was supposed to be a thank-you," Carolyn says.

"It was also supposed to be lunch," Chris says. "I *asked* you."

Another passive-aggressive assertion of the male power structure, she starts to think, and then remembers that Professor Asshole isn't here to say that and that she really doesn't mind Chris picking up the check.

"Can I at least leave the tip?" she asks.

"Okay."

"Five?"

"Maybe more like ten?" he says.

She lays down a ten and gets up. "Well, this has been—"

"Yeah, this has been nice."

Nice, she thinks. Kiss of death. Nice is taking your grandmother to Olive Garden, or—

"You want to go to the beach?" he says.

"I'm sorry?"

"You said you liked going to the beach," Chris says. "I was asking if you want to go to the beach."

"You mean now?"

"It's a nice day," he says.

Yes, it is, Carolyn thinks.

Yes, it is a nice day.

Hollis Bamburger really is stupid. *So* stupid that he goes back to the same park, to the same guy, to buy a new gun.

Well, a *used* gun.

Hopefully just one that wasn't used in a previous crime. Hollis is scared enough about the crimes *he's* committed, never mind the ones other people did. So he's counting on Montalbo to sell him a clean gun.

He meets him in the same vacant lot.

"I need a piece," Hollis says.

"Why are you wearing a turtleneck?" Montalbo asks. "It's a hundred and three out."

"I haven't had a chance to do laundry," Hollis says, thinking fast.

"You hiding a mike under there?" Montalbo asks.

"No," Hollis says, thinking fast. "I need a piece."

"I sold you one," the Mexican says.

"I need another one."

"How come?"

It's a good question, because if this *guero* used the gun in a crime and if it gets tracked back to who sold it to him, Montalbo could be on the hook for whatever stupid shit this guy did.

Which is probably very stupid.

"I got rid of it," Hollis says.

"Why?"

"Why do you think?" Hollis asks.

Now Montalbo is more nervous, because it's also possible that the *guero* has been busted for something and he's traded up for a Mexican gun dealer. It's been his experience that there are few things San Diego cops like to get more than Mexican gun dealers. Montalbo ranks it:

Krispy Kremes
Mexican drug dealers
Mexican gun dealers

"I can't help you," Montalbo says. "Tell the cops no sale."

"Come on, man."

"Get out of here before I beat the shit out of you."

Hollis glances around and sees the Mexican's buddies starting to circle like wolves, behavior he's familiar with from the yard at Chino. He's scared, but not as scared as he is of going back to Lee without a gun.

Lee does not handle frustration well.

Thinking fast, Hollis comes up with a genius idea. "I'll cut you in on the take."

Montalbo asks, "How big a cut?"

Because Montalbo has conflicting needs—he needs not to get busted, but he also needs cash—and now these needs are in direct conflict with each other. Montalbo has a bad gambling problem, or more accurately he has a problem with bad gambling, and owes money to Victor Lopez, a loan shark who's running out of patience. Montalbo owes him a couple of grand, but if he could give him just a few hundred, it would buy some more patience.

"Ten points," Hollis says.

"I can lay my hands on an S&W 39 automatic," Montalbo says.

"That's older than dirt."

"You want it or not?"

"How much?" Hollis asks.

"Five hundred," Montalbo says.

It's worth at most two-fifty.

"I'll give you three," Hollis says. If he pays five, they did the last job at a loss, and that will not make Lee happy, and Lee is already going to be unhappy about giving Montalbo a cut of the job.

Lee has a low tolerance for unhappiness.

But Hollis has a solution to this problem—he'll pay Montalbo out of his own share.

"Four," Montalbo says. "Plus the ten points. Final offer."

"Is it clean?" Hollis asks.

"As a nun's chocha," Montalbo says. He has no idea if it's clean or not. For all he knows, it could have been used in the Lincoln assassination.

"Give me your number," Montalbo says. "I'll text you when I have it."

"What about bullets?"

"You bought a gun," Montalbo says. "No one said nothing about ammunition."

"What good is a gun without bullets?" Hollis asks.

"Not much, I wouldn't think."

Hollis sighs. "How much?"

"Ten bucks apiece," Montalbo says.

"That's a rip."

"So do a robbery without bullets," Montalbo says. "See how it goes."

Hollis thinks about it. Actually, he has done a robbery without bullets because usually the gun alone is enough to scare people into opening the till.

Lee does not share this philosophy.

"The only time an empty gun works," he's said, "is in *Dirty Harry*."

Hollis gives Montalbo his number.

Chris takes a deep breath and then makes himself walk into police headquarters on Broadway.

He's still not sure this is a good idea.

Carolyn thought it was.

It was actually her idea.

To his surprise they'd spent the whole afternoon walking Pacific Beach, and more to his surprise he found himself telling her all about his problems on the job.

"Why would the Robbery people be unhappy at you for solving a robbery?" she asked.

"Because it's their job," he said. "And I guess I made them look bad. It's like maybe if you went over to . . . I don't know, the reptile department or something and solved a problem with a boa constrictor."

"Yeah, they wouldn't like that."

"Right?" Chris said. "The really bad thing is that this is the unit I really want to catch on with, and now they're pissed off at me."

"Go talk to them," Carolyn said.

"It doesn't work that way," Chris says. "We talk when we're talked *to*."

"And how is *that* working?"

Not great, Chris had to admit. He also had to admit that he was starting to really like Carolyn Voight. Smart, pretty and . . . nice. And maybe just being nice to me because I tried to rescue her chimp, because the woman has a Ph.D. and is probably way too intelligent to want to date a cop. She probably came to the beach because she felt bad about my broken nose.

By the end of the afternoon, he really wanted to ask her out again, but the last thing he wanted was a pity date.

So he didn't.

But he did decide to take her advice about going to talk to Lubesnick, because she was right—what did he have to lose?

Now he shows his badge, walks into the Robbery Unit, and asks the receptionist, "Is Lieutenant Lubesnick in?"

The receptionist smiles at him. "And who may I say is calling?"

"Officer Shea," Chris says. "Christopher Shea."

"Okay, Officer Christopher Shea," she says, "let me see if he's available for you."

But just then the door opens and Lubesnick comes out. He sees Chris and says, "I know you."

"Yes, sir."

"But where from?"

"Uhh, we met in Balboa Park."

Lubesnick stares at him for a second, then breaks into a big, crooked grin and says—loudly, "Monkey Man! Hey, everyone, we have a celebrity in our midst!"

A bunch of detectives look up from their work and either smile sardonically or frown at Chris. He feels himself turn red—these are the same people he hopes to work with someday.

He hears himself say, "Actually, that's not what I wanted to talk to you about, sir."

"Okay, come on in," Lubesnick says. He looks at the receptionist and says, *sotto voce*, "Give it two minutes, then buzz me and pretend there's a call I have to take."

"You bet, Lou."

Lubesnick leads Chris into his office, gestures for him to sit down and says, "So?"

"It's about the robbery arrest I made the other day," Chris says. "I want to apologize. I was out of line."

"Do you watch football, Officer Shea?"

"Until the Chargers left, sir."

"So do you know what happens when one defensive back leaves his zone to go into another back's zone?" Lubesnick asks. "The other side scores a touchdown. See, if you do our job, what are we supposed to do? We'd be out of work."

"I understand, sir."

Lubesnick looks at him for a long moment. "Actually, you worked the perp pretty well. You have some game. Brown tells me you want to come to Robbery for your next assignment."

"That's what I'm hoping for, sir."

"And you think showing us up is the way to do it?" Lubesnick says.

"I wasn't trying to show anyone up."

"Like you weren't trying to fall out of a tree?' Lubesnick asks. "Like you weren't trying to go WWE down in the Lamp? Yeah, I've had my eye on you, Shea."

Which could be a good thing or a bad thing, Chris thinks. Good thing if he's talent-spotting me to maybe bring me into his unit, bad thing if he's looking at me with an eye to make sure he never, ever brings me into his unit.

The buzzer sounds.

"Lou, you have—"

Lubesnick winks at Chris. "Ellen, tell the pretend caller I'll pretend to call him right back."

"You got it, boss," Ellen says. "I'll take his pretend number."

Lubesnick clicks off and says to Chris, "Anyway, I'll relay your heartfelt apology to the unit and make sure they know you meant no harm. I respect your coming in—that showed me something. Now go away."

Chris stands up. "Thank you, sir."

"You know the question that has yet to be answered?" Lubesnick asks. "Where did that gun come from?"

Chris walks out of the unit, feeling the amused stares on his back.

But what he's really thinking about is Lubesnick. What was the lieutenant telling him? To chase the gun down? Or *not* to chase the gun down? It's ambiguous, because he clearly heard Lubesnick tell him to stay in his lane.

Yeah, Chris thinks, except the lane I'm in doesn't lead to where I want to go. And maybe Lou Lubesnick is telling me to pull in to the lane that does.

Carolyn is pissed.

And pissed at herself for being pissed.

That Christopher Shea dropped her off at her place, thanked her for the nice afternoon, and then didn't ask for another date.

She spent that whole night—and it was a Saturday night, another Saturday night with solo Netflix and solo chill—being pissed off, had a shower and went to bed (by eleven, for God's sake) and woke up the next morning pissed.

Spent her long Sunday run being pissed.

Watched *90 Day Fiancé* (maybe she should find a nice Nigerian prince to go out with) pissed.

Woke up Monday morning and went to work having made the slight but important transition from being pissed at Christopher Shea to being pissed at herself.

Why should I care? she asked herself.

If he's not interested in me, I'm sure as hell not interested in him.

Who does he think he is?

He's not a good tree climber, that's for sure. Probably a lousy kisser, too. She realizes that she's gone back to being angry at Shea and forces herself to return her negative attention where it belongs.

What did I do? she asks herself. What didn't I do?

I talked about myself, I let him talk about himself (the man spilled his professional guts to me), I looked really cute walking on the beach, I thought I made it clear that I was there for the right reasons.

What don't I have that he wants?

"What's wrong with me?" she asks.

Champ doesn't have an answer.

But he reaches his hand out.

The gun, Chris learns, was registered to a solid citizen and stolen in a home burglary that the solid citizen dutifully reported to the police.

So that's a dead end.

Chris visits the Laboratory Unit and gets a little pushback as to what a uniformed patrol officer was doing asking these questions. Luckily for him, the woman on duty realized that he was the Monkey Man, took some pity on him and showed him the test results.

"Actually," she said, "you're the first one to ask."

The gun in question is a .38 Colt Cobra Special with double action and a Hogue Overmold grip.

The grip has Champ's prints all over it, but that's all.

So Chris has to take a different tack—i.e., what was happening in the vicinity of the zoo that night?

He goes to Data Systems and asks for a printout of calls that came into Central Division prior to the Champ call.

"Did a detective send you?" the DS officer, Schneider, asks.

"No."

"Then no can do," Schneider says. "Unless you're the investigating officer on an active case, and you're a patrol officer, right?"

"What if Lubesnick sent me?" Chris asks.

"Did he?"

"You want to call him and ask?" This is Thanksgiving-turkey stuff, this is him stretching his neck way out on the block. If Schneider calls Robbery and Lubesnick answers WTF, Chris's career is a carcass.

He's betting Schneider won't make the call, because if Lubesnick did send him, he's going to chew Schneider a new one.

"Central?" Schneider asks.

"Right."

A few minutes later, Chris is looking at all the radio calls to Central Division before Champ went into his Scarface routine. A couple of domestic disturbances, a creep exposing himself in Balboa Park, the mandatory fistfight in the Lamp, but nothing about an armed robbery or a gun.

Maybe it *was* an animal-rights activist, Chris thinks.

But then he thinks it through. Balboa Park is the easternmost border of Central Division.

It borders Mid City Division.

So if something happened in, say, North Park, the suspect could have run into Balboa.

"What about Mid City?" he asks Schneider.

Hendricks sighs the sigh of the put-upon and gets him the data from Mid City.

And there it is.

Well, there it *could* be, Chris thinks. A liquor store on Thirtieth and Utah was robbed at gunpoint an hour and a half before Chris got the Champ call. Just eight blocks from the eastern edge of the park.

The record shows that two officers responded—Herrera and Forsythe—but by the time they rolled up, the suspect was gone.

So the case is open.

Robbery would have taken it over, but so far there's been no arrest.

The radio record won't show what has been done on it since—that information would only be in Robbery, and Chris doesn't have the balls to go back there yet and ask. But it's curious that no one seems to be working on the gun.

No one went in to look at prints.

Chris thinks he gets it—the whole Champ thing was an enormous embarrassment to the department, which would probably just hope to let the story fade out.

But Lubesnick is nudging me into it, Chris thinks.

Why not his own guys?

He's off-duty the next day, so he waits for the night shift and goes over to Mid City.

Chris finds Forsythe by his locker, getting suited up to go on shift.

"Officer Forsythe, Chris Shea. Central Division."

"I know who you are," Forsythe says. "You're that monkey guy. What can I do for you?"

"You answered a robbery call on Thirtieth the other night."

"What about it?" Forsythe says.

"Can I ask what happened?"

"Nothing much," Forsythe says. "I responded. Herrera rolled up a second later. The perp threatened the clerk with a knife, the clerk handed over the cash. We did an area search, didn't come up with the guy. Turned it over to Robbery."

"It was a knife?" Chris asks. "The radio call said it was a gun."

"No, that's right," Forsythe says. "The clerk thought we'd get there faster if he said gun. You know how it is."

Chris does. People overbid their calls all the time, thinking the cops will come quicker.

"Why are you asking?" Forsythe says. "You have a lead on the guy, a related case?"

"No."

"I mean, you're on radio patrol, right?" Forsythe asks. "You have some sort of personal interest?"

Forsythe is pushing pretty hard on an open door, Chris thinks. "No, I live in the neighborhood. I was just curious."

It's bullshit, and Forsythe knows it's bullshit. "Do everyone including yourself a favor. Don't be curious."

"No?"

"No," Forsythe says. "Go back to Central, chase apes, whatever you guys do over there, but don't be coming around Mid City poking your nose in where it doesn't belong. No offense, huh, Shea?"

"None taken."

No offense taken, but Chris drives over to the liquor store to talk to the clerk.

"Hell yes, it was a gun," the clerk says. He's a sandy-haired guy in his fifties. "You think I wouldn't know a knife from a gun?"

"No, I—"

"I'll tell you what else," the clerk says. "It was a .38 Colt Cobra Special."

Exactly the gun that Champ was waving around.

"An automatic, right?" Chris asks.

The clerk looks at him with contempt. "What the hell kind of cop are you? A .38 Colt Cobra Special is a revolver. Double-action. Two-inch barrel, Hogue Overmold grip. I own guns."

"I figured."

"I have one right under the shelf here," the clerk says. "A Glock 9. So do you think I'd let some guy rob me with a knife? The only reason I didn't pull it was he had the drop on me."

"Can you describe the suspect?"

"Suspect?" the clerk asks. "It was no 'suspect.' He did it."

"Can you describe him?"

"I already did to the detectives," the clerk says. "Don't you guys talk to each other?"

Apparently not, Chris thinks.

"White guy," the clerk says. "Around five-six. Brown hair cut real short. One of those Hawaiian-print shirts, jeans and Keds. Do you want to know about distinguishing marks?"

"Sure."

"A tattoo on his neck. H-O-L."

" 'Hol'?" Chris asks.

"That's all I saw over his collar."

"And you told this to the detectives," Chris says.

"Of course I did."

"And about the gun?"

He already knows the answer. This guy couldn't wait to share his knowledge about guns.

"Sure did."

"So the two officers who responded," Chris says, "they took a report—"

"When they came back," the clerk says.

"Came back?"

"From chasing the guy," the clerk says. "I mean, he had just made it out the door when they came. Took off running. They took off running after him. Tell you the truth, I thought they'd catch him."

Yeah, so did they, Chris thinks.

So the gun that wound up in Champ's hand (paw?) clearly came from the liquor-store holdup.

The question is how it ended up with Champ.

The other question is why Forsythe is lying that it was a knife.

Next shift Chris is walking out to his radio car when Sergeant Villa comes up to him.

And asks, "What the fuck were you doing over in Mid City?"

"Forsythe reached out to you?"

"Herrera did," Villa says. "We were in Eastern together. He's good people. So is Forsythe."

"Sarge—"

"Whatever you're about to tell me," Villa says, "don't. Whatever you were about to say, don't say to anybody."

Chris's sergeant just told him to keep his mouth shut, so he keeps it shut.

"You're a decent guy," Villa says. "A good cop. Don't be a dick."

Great, Chris thinks as he gets into his car. My sergeant is telling me to do one thing, a lieutenant telling me to do another. Villa has the ability to make my life miserable at my present job. Lubesnick has the ability to see that I never get a new one.

But the fact is that he hasn't really connected the dots about what happened with the gun, and he's not likely to. The Robbery detectives aren't offering any information and don't seem to care. Herrera and Forsythe aren't going to come forward, the suspect is in the wind, and Champ isn't saying anything.

And the department would seem to prefer to let it lie.

So let it lie, Chris thinks.

Except he can't seem to do that.

Lubesnick answers his eighth phone message. "Why are you bothering me, Monkey Man?"

"I need to see Robbery's file on a liquor store hold-up."

"Why?"

"You were wondering about a gun?" He tells Lubesnick the address.

A silence, and then Lubesnick says, "I'll call you back."

To Chris's mild surprise, he does, about five minutes later. "That's Detective Geary's case. He's a fine investigator."

"I'm sure he is, sir, but . . ."

"Every word you say after 'but' means every word you said before it is bullshit," Lubesnick says. "But . . . if you want to come in and have a look—"

"I think it would be better if I could see the file without Detective Geary and the others knowing about it," Chris says.

"So you want me to screw my own team," Lubesnick says.

"I want to answer your questions about the gun."

Another silence, then, "You remember my receptionist, Ellen? Meet her at the Starbucks on Broadway and Kettner in an hour. Don't keep her waiting."

"Thank you, sir."

"Don't thank me," Lubesnick says. "Because if you fuck me on this, I'll sink your career so deep that James Cameron couldn't find it."

Chris hustles to the Starbucks. Is there and waiting when Ellen comes in, sees him, and hands him a manila file folder.

"Sit there and read it," she says.

"Then what?"

"Then give it back to me," Ellen says. "You have ten minutes."

She goes up to the counter and orders a latte. She doesn't ask Chris if he wants anything.

It doesn't take him ten minutes. The file is thin, and it says pretty much what Chris thought it would say. It quoted Forsythe's report about arriving on the scene and the clerk saying he'd been held up at knifepoint. It said that the suspect had already fled, that Forsythe and Herrera had done an area search but didn't see the suspect.

Detective Geary had no further leads.

So, Chris thinks as he hands the file back to Ellen, Geary conspired with the two Mid City cops to cover up what really happened. And Lubesnick wants me to answer questions he can't ask his own people.

"You do know that this didn't happen," Ellen says.

"I do," Chris says. Then, "Can I ask you a question?"

"You can *ask*."

"Where was Geary before he came to Robbery?"

"Eastern, I think," she says.

So the Eastern Division old boys' network has circled the wagons to protect whatever Herrera did or didn't do that night, Chris thinks. And the only shot that Chris has to find out what that was is to find a guy with H-O-L tattooed on his neck.

But how the hell, he wonders, am I going to do that?

Richard Holder, unconsciously happy to be back behind bars, is consciously happy that he has a visitor.

Until he finds out it's a cop.

"What do you want?" he asks Chris.

"I want to help you."

"That's what cops always say," Richard replies. "Help me how?"

"Who sold you the gun?" Chris asks. "The little .22 AMT."

"Good gun," Richard says.

"I guess if you're robbing a pigeon," Chris says. "Where did you get it?"

Richard shakes his head. " 'Snitches get stitches.' "

Chris has heard that one a hundred times and has a ready answer. Normally he would answer, *Snitches get time off their sentences,* but with a recidivist like Richard he goes with, "Snitches maybe get to choose where they do their stints."

This does get Richard's interest.

"You could do that?" he asks. "Could you get me Donovan?"

So Richard has buddies and maybe a boyfriend in Donovan, in which case going there would be like going home.

"Here's what I could do," Chris says. "I could write a cooperation memo to the sentencing judge with a recommendation that you do your time in Donovan. Or . . . I could write a different letter requesting that a repeat offender like you should be in the Q."

San Quentin.

Chris sees the flash of anxiety go across Richard's face.

"You get me Donovan," Richard says, "I'll give you the gun dealer."

"No, I need it now."

"How do I know I can trust you?"

"I gave you that vodka, didn't I?" Chris asks. He senses he's near closing, so he pushes a little. "Look, we both know you're going to plead out, because you already confessed, we have the gun with your prints on it. You're going, so you might as well go where you want."

"I don't know the guy's name."

"Give me a location and a description," Chris says.

Vacant lot off Thirty-second, Richard tells him. Tall, thick Mexican guy in his thirties with a goatee, gang tats on his arms, wears a Raiders ball cap.

"The Raiders," Richard says with a snort.

"Hey, the Chargers left."

"Broke my heart."

"Mine, too," Chris says. "One other thing. In your travels through the system, did you ever run across a white guy, about five-six, with H-O-L tattooed on his neck?"

"You mean Hollis."

Chris shrugs. "Maybe."

"No, that's him," Richard says. "Hollis Bamburger. Sure, I knew him at Chino."

"Is that b-*e*-r-g-e-r or b-*u*-r-g-e-r?" Chris asks.

"*U*, I think," Richard says.

"Would Bamburger know your guy on Thirty-second?" Chris asks.

"*Everyone* knows the guy on Thirty-second," Richard says.

Okaaaay, Chris thinks. Then he asks, "What else can you tell me about Hollis Bamburger?"

Richard laughs. "He's an idiot."

Low praise indeed, Chris thinks, from Richard "I Was Wearing a Mask" Holder.

You have to love these guys.

Chris takes his own car to the vacant lot off Thirty-second and sees a bunch of Latino gangbangers hanging there.

They see him, too.

Never mind he's in plain clothes in his own car, they make him for cop right away.

Practice, practice, practice.

They all eye-fuck him, especially a tall, thick guy with a goatee, Raiders cap and tats on his arms.

Chris gets out of the car, holds his hands up by his shoulders like, *I don't mean any harm*, and walks up to the guy. "I just want to talk."

"Talk about what?" the guy asks. "The weather? It sucks. The Padres? They suck. Your sister? She sucks my dick."

"How about a guy with H-O-L tatted on his neck?"

It lands.

The guy has a smart mouth but dumb eyes. They give him right away.

And he knows it. "What about him?"

"Did you sell him a gun?" Chris asks. "A Colt Special?"

"Like I'm going to tell you that."

"Look, I already have a line on him," Chris says. "If I find him without your help, I make him give you up and I jam the baseball bat all the way up your ass, thick end first. But if I catch him *with* your help, maybe you slip my mind."

"I'm no *dedo*," the guy says.

No snitch.

Chris can see that the guy means it. The threat isn't going to work.

"What's your name?" Chris asks. When the guy balks, Chris says, "Come on, can't we do this the easy way? Or do I find some sleazy excuse to bust you and then I get it anyway?"

"Fucking cops."

"Right?"

"Montalbo. Ric."

"I'm Chris Shea. Officer Christopher Shea."

"You ain't no detective?" Montalbo asks.

"Not yet," Chris says. "So, Ric, can we do some business?"

Montalbo stares at him for a few seconds, then says, "Every morning I get up, I ask myself the same question. You know what it is?"

"I can't wait to find out."

" 'What can other people do for me?' " Montalbo says. "What can you do for me, Christopher?"

"I'm open to ideas."

Actually, Montalbo has one.

It hits him like a bright, shining light.

A solution to all his problems.

"There's this guy Lopez?" he says. "If you pop him in his car, he'll have felony weight *hierba* in the trunk."

"Do you owe him money," Chris says, "or did he fuck your girlfriend?"

"Money," Montalbo says. "My girlfriend is the happiest woman in America."

"You have a location on Hollis Bamburger?"

"Oh, I got better than that."

Chris takes down the info on Lopez.

Then Montalbo is looking at him funny. "Hey, I know you."

"I don't think so."

Montalbo grins. "You're the cop with the chimp."

"No I'm not."

"Yes, you are," Montalbo says. "You're the monkey guy."

Chris might be the monkey guy, but he's not stupid. He isn't going to commit the same error twice by making a bust out of his lane.

He calls a high-school friend—a senior when Chris was a freshman—he played baseball with who's now in the Narcotics Division. "Could you use a bust?"

"Could I ever," his friend says. "My boss is up my ass."

Chris gives him the details on Victor Lopez, make of his car, plates, whereabouts—the whole nine. This would be Lopez's fifth arrest, so he isn't going to make an affordable bail, which is doubtless what Montalbo is counting on.

"Thanks, Chris," the friend says. "Anything I can do for you?"

"Just call me when you've booked him."

"You got it."

Not yet, Chris thinks.

But I might be on my way.

Hollis gets a text.

I HAVE YOUR MERCH. MEET ME AT TEN TONIGHT.

He answers. GRATE. SAME PLACE?

It comes back. NO. ZOO PARKING LOT.

OK.

Montalbo turns to Chris. "Happy?"

"Not yet," Chris says.

Chris is ambivalent.

He knows that what he should do is walk his ass into Robbery and turn this potential bust over to them.

A sting like this, involving a gun sale with armed career criminals normally demands real manpower—undercovers, backups, maybe even SWAT. It's against every procedure to go ahead with this solo, without command's permission and a tactical plan.

But there are problems with that approach.

For one, he'd have to admit that he's been doing exactly what he was told not to do—work a Robbery case. He's looked at files he wasn't supposed to see, interviewed witnesses he wasn't supposed to talk to, made an offer to a convict he wasn't authorized to make (or, for that matter, even talk to the skell in the first place), then made a deal with a criminal to arrange the arrest of another criminal in exchange for setting up the original criminal for a sting that he shouldn't be doing.

So there's that.

The other thing is that he'd have to take it all to Detective Geary, who's in on a cover-up that Chris is trying to uncover.

So that wouldn't go well.

His other option would be to take it to Lieutenant Lubesnick, who could override Geary and bring in any manpower he wanted to do the sting on Hollis, but Chris isn't sure the man wants any part of this unless or until it's brought to him all tied up with a bow.

Another possibility is to keep it inside Central.

But then he'd have to go to Villa.

Who wouldn't be happy.

Or go over Villa's head to Lieutenant Brown, who has already told him to stay off the radar and wouldn't in any case be happy to see the whole Champ the Chimp fiasco brought back into the public eye.

The other choice, Chris thinks, is to stop it right here and let the whole thing die.

But Lubesnick doesn't want me to do that.

And you don't want you to do that either, he thinks.

You started this—you want to see it through.

Not to mention get an armed robber off the streets. Which is, after all, the job they pay you to do.

So at nine forty-five that night, he rolls into a corner of the zoo parking lot.

Lee drives toward the zoo.

"Tell me," he says.

"I already told you," Hollis says.

"Then tell me again."

Lee sighs. "I give the Mexican the money. He gives me the gun. I point the gun at him and tell him to give the money back."

It's beautiful, Lee thinks, using the gun the gun dealer sold you to rob him of the money you paid him for the gun. Lee doesn't know the meaning of the word "symmetry" (or, for that matter, "irony") but unconsciously appreciates the concept.

Hollis isn't as enthused. "You know this means we can't go back to him for another gun."

"It was a mistake to go back to him the *second* time," Lee says.

And fuck him anyway, Lee thinks. Charging us three hundred dollars plus points on a piece of shit like an S&W 39. He's robbing us, he deserves to get robbed back. It's justice, is what it is.

Lee believes in justice.

And the Golden Rule.

They are simply doing unto the Mexican what he's doing unto them.

But he can tell that Hollis is scared. For one thing, his foot is tapping like a rabbit on crank. For a second thing, Hollis is *always* scared.

"Don't worry," Lee says. "I've got your back."

"I know."

He doesn't sound that sure.

"When haven't I had your back?" Lee asks, again without the slightest awareness or sense of irony.

This is true, Hollis thinks.

On the yard if anyone except Lee tried to beat the shit out of me, Lee beat him up.

If anyone except Lee tried to make me his baby, Lee beat him up.

Lee has always had my back.

Now Lee is getting positively sanctimonious about it. Emotional to the point of tearing up. "You're my brother. I love you. No matter what happens, I will always be there for you. If this motherfucker tries something with you, I'll take care of it."

How? Hollis wonders. Lee doesn't have a gun.

He points that out to Lee.

Lee thinks about it for a second, frowns, then brightens and says, "I have a car, don't I? This guy tries anything, you just step aside and I'll run him over. Stop worrying. It'll be fine."

Hollis doesn't stop worrying.

I mean, he's not an idiot.

Chris slumps behind the driver's wheel and watches Montalbo pull in to the parking lot in a white Toyota pickup.

Montalbo gets out and leans against the driver's door.

A minute later a green Nissan Sentra with a loose front left fender pulls in to the parking lot about five yards away from Montalbo.

Chris watches Hollis Bamburger get out of the passenger seat and come around the car. Something Chris hadn't figured on, a second guy driving, and he feels stupid because now he'll have to bust two guys instead of one, and he has no backup.

It seems, he thinks, that Hollis and I are in a dumb-off.

Not too late to do nothing, he thinks.

Not too late to simply drive away and turn all this over to Robbery or just forget it.

Except he knows that Hollis and his associate are buying a gun for a reason, and that reason is probably another holdup, and this time someone might get hurt.

And you can't drive away from that, Chris thinks.

You got yourself into this, now you have to see it through.

The only preaching his father gave him: Finish what you start.

So he eases his sidearm into his right hand and lays his left hand on the door handle, ready to go as he sees Hollis walk up to Montalbo.

Hollis hands Montalbo money.

Montalbo reaches back into his truck, comes out with a pistol and hands it to Hollis.

Hollis points the pistol in Montalbo's face and says something.

Montalbo hits him in the jaw with a left hook.

Hollis goes down like he's been poleaxed.

Chris gets out of the car, carries his gun at his side, holds his shield up and yells, "Police! Stop!"

Montalbo is apparently too resentful at Hollis's attempted betrayal to listen. He grabs Hollis by the front of his shirt and bitch-slaps him back and forth.

Hollis screams, "Lee! Lee! Help!"

Lee hits the gas.

And races out of the parking lot.

Chris moves forward. "Police! Freeze!"

Montalbo drops Hollis, gets back into his truck and drives away.

Hollis is on all fours.

He looks up, sees Chris coming, staggers to his feet . . .

And does a Bamburger.

He raises the pistol.

Chris stops, points his own gun, and yells, "It's not loaded, Hollis!"

Hollis looks puzzled as to how this guy knows his name. But if the guy knows his name, he must have other inside knowledge, like that the Mexican son of a bitch sold him an unloaded gun.

He drops it.

And, adrenaline being a wonderful thing . . .

Runs.

Sort of.

More like loops, a pigeon-toed lurch, because Montalbo caught him pretty good. So Hollis doesn't get far before Chris jumps on top of him and drives him into the asphalt.

"Give me your hands," Chris says.

Hollis gives up his hands along with the classic lifelong loser response. "I didn't do nothin'!"

"You're a felon who just bought an illegal firearm," Chris says. "You're under arrest. You have the right to remain silent, you have the right—"

"I know my rights," Hollis says as Chris finishes cuffing him and hauls him to his feet. "I was entrapped."

"You're also under arrest for armed robbery," Chris says.

"I didn't do that either."

Chris walks him back toward the car. "And Penal Code 2876."

"What's that?"

"Leaving a gun where a chimpanzee could get it."

Hollis goes wide-eyed. "You're that cop! The Monkey Man!"

"Fuckin' A," Chris says. He gets Hollis into the back of his car and asks, "Why did you do that, Hollis?"

Hollis clams up.

"Come on," Chris says. "We've got you. The liquor-store clerk will ID you and the gun. And I've got you buying this piece of shit here. Either way you're looking at a long stint. So why don't you just tell me what happened that night?"

"Why should I?" Hollis asks.

Chris thinks about this a little, because there really is no reason for Hollis to tell him anything. Then he says, "Hollis, you've been around. You know the system. So let me ask you something. Is this a police car? Have I radioed this in? I could take you for a drive in the canyon, I could give you some backseat therapy. . . ."

Then he plays a hunch. "I could even drop you over to Mid City, bring Officers Forsythe and Herrera out to the car, see if they'd like to talk to you. Because right now nobody knows we have you."

Hollis looks scared. "You'd do that?"

No, he wouldn't.

Chris would never do any of those things. He just hopes that Hollis doesn't know that. He says, "Or you can tell me what happened that night, and I'll take you to my house in Central, where no one is mad at you."

Hollis tells him the story.

"Okay, I robbed that place," he says. "The cops came so fast I didn't have time to get to the car. I just ran. One of the cops, the Spanish guy, got out of his car and chased me. I jumped the fence into the zoo, figuring he wouldn't follow me, but he did. I was out of breath, so I pointed the gun at him."

"And?"

"He stopped." Hollis smirked. "He backed off. So I waited a few seconds and ran some more. I didn't want the gun on me, so I threw it into that, what do you call it, enclosure."

So that explains it, Chris thinks.

Herrera got scared, and his old Eastern buddies covered for him.

"Are you telling me the truth, Hollis?" Chris asks, although he already knows he is.

"I swear."

"I need to know one more thing," Chris says. "The driver. Who is he, and where do I get him?"

"I'm not telling you that."

"What, out of loyalty?" Chris asks. "Like he just showed you, running away and leaving you in the lurch?"

"Lee," Hollis says. "Lee Caswell."

He gives Chris the name of the motel.

Lee is probably too smart to go back there, but Chris has the license plate. And now he has the story he can bring to Lubesnick. It might take some time to get it punched, but he has his ticket into Robbery.

He says, "That story you just told me? Don't you tell that to anyone, ever again. You robbed that store with a knife, do you understand?"

"Sure," Hollis says, happy to oblige. A knife gets him considerably less time than a gun.

Chris drives to Central Division and walks Hollis in.

"What you got, Shea?" the desk sergeant asks. "I didn't think you were on duty tonight."

"I'm not," Chris says. "Can you keep an eye on this guy? I need to talk to Villa for a minute."

He goes in to find his sergeant.

When she sees the caller ID, Carolyn thinks about letting the call go to voice mail.

Chris Shea has let more than the statutory three days go by without calling her, and she's convinced herself that if he's not interested, she's not either.

But if he's not interested, why is he calling?

She picks up and says professionally, "Dr. Voight."

"Officer Shea."

"Oh, hi, Chris." In that tone like, *Whatever would you be calling about? But I don't really care. I'm a little surprised after five days.* A lot to get done in three syllables, but she manages.

All good cops are connoisseurs of verbal nuance, and Chris is impressed. She hears that in his tone as he asks, "Do you like baseball?"

"I guess." Perfect. Noncommittal, unenthusiastic, yet leaving the door open.

"My lieutenant had a couple of really good seats to the Padres tomorrow afternoon," Chris says. "The Diamondbacks. I was wondering if you'd like to go."

She can't resist. "With your lieutenant?"

"No, with *me*," he says quickly. "He gave them to me."

"You mean, like a date?" she asks.

She's going to make him do this right. The door might be unlocked, but he still has to ring the bell.

"Like a date," Chris says. "I'm asking you out. Would you like to go to a baseball game with me?"

"I *am* off tomorrow afternoon."

"Great," Chris says. "So would you like to?"

She'd like to. In fact, she's a little surprised how much she'd like to. "Should I meet you there?"

"No," Chris says. "It's a date. I'll pick you up. If that's all right."

It is.

He picks her up the next afternoon, and he's cute—dressed a little formal for a ball game. Khakis, a nice shirt, tucked in, and a Padres ball cap. She's a little overdressed, too—an off-the-shoulder peasant blouse atop a pair of True Religion jeans she knows do nice things for her butt.

He's prepaid for parking at the Omni Hotel, just a short walk from PetCo Park, but goes over to a CVS first.

"You're going to need sunblock for your shoulders," he says.

"Did I dress wrong?" she asks.

"No, you look beautiful," he says. "I just don't want you to get sunburned."

He buys a tube of SPF50, and they walk to the ballpark.

"Have you been here before?" Chris asks.

"No," she says. Professor Asshole was always going on about baseball as a metaphor and owned a faux-vintage Brooklyn Dodgers jersey, and he used to talk about visiting every ballpark in the country, but they had never gone to an actual game.

The ballpark is beautiful.

The green of the field, so lovingly tended, is like an emerald. An old red-brick factory building, Western Metal Supply, makes up part of what even she knows is the left-field wall. Behind the stadium are high-rise office and condo buildings and, beyond them, San Diego Harbor.

"Wow," she says.

He sees the enjoyment in her eyes and is charmed by it. "We need to get you a cap."

"You think so?"

"Absolutely."

He walks her to a vendor stand and picks out a blue cap with SD on it. She ties her hair into a ponytail, puts it on and even though there's no mirror to look into, she knows she looks damn cute.

She can see it in his eyes.

He looks happy and proud.

"Our seats are along the first-base line," he says with what she finds to be boyish enthusiasm. "Just a few rows up."

"Great."

They go to their seats: Section 109, Row 12.

"Wow," she says, "these *are* great seats."

"I'm usually up in the bleachers," he says.

"Do you come here a lot?"

"Well, I work nights," he says, "when most of the games are. But I come when I can."

He pauses for a second and then says, "It might be my favorite place in the world."

Carolyn feels that he's told her something important, something intimate.

"Would you like a hot dog and a beer?" Chris asks.

"I would love a hot dog and a beer," she says. Then she laughs at herself. "Not very ladylike, I'm afraid."

"No, it's great," he says. "I'll be right back. Mustard? Ketchup? Relish? Onions?"

"Hold the ketchup."

She sits and takes in the field, the stadium filling with people, the general sense of . . . what is it? . . . *gladness* that pervades the place. Then Chris comes back clutching two plastic cups of foamy beer and two hot dogs.

"Thank you."

"My pleasure."

She studied up last night and learned that the Padres are firmly in last place with little chance of escaping "the cellar," but it doesn't diminish Chris's pleasure in being there.

"We should get that sunblock on you," he says when they finish eating. Then he gets all shy and says, "I mean, you should, you know. . . ."

"No," she says, turning so her back is toward him. "Would you mind?"

He's so gentle, so . . . *respectful* . . . and at the same time so . . . thorough. She loves the feel of the lotion warming onto her skin, the feel of his hands. . . .

"Turn around," he says. "Let me get your nose."

She turns to him and tilts her chin up. He squeezes a drop of the lotion onto his index finger and carefully runs it down the bridge of her nose.

Then he gently smears it in. "There."

There indeed, she thinks.

It might be the sexiest she's ever felt.

Then he says, "Uh-oh."

"What?"

He subtly points to three men with beers in their hands, edging their way to their seats just two rows below them.

"Who are they?" Carolyn asks.

"The first one is Lieutenant Lubesnick," Chris says. "I hope he doesn't see me."

"Why?"

"I just really disappointed him on something," Chris says.

"Oh."

"You know the guy next to him."

"I do?" She looks at the big, florid, middle-aged guy with curly brown hair.

"Sure, his face is on TV all the time," Chris says. "It'll probably be up on the screen at some time today. That's Duke Kasmajian, the bail-bonds king. 'Call the Duke'?"

"Oh, yeah."

"I don't know the other guy."

The other guy turns around, and Carolyn says, "I do. That's Professor Carey. I had a class from him. Eighteenth-century English lit."

"How did you do?"

"Aced it, of course."

Carey spots her, recognizes her, and waves.

Kasmajian and Lubesnick look up to see who he's waving at.

The lieutenant sees Chris, frowns and turns his back.

Carolyn sees the look on Chris's face.

He's devastated.

Which makes it all the more awkward when Chris hits the men's room to offload the beer and Lieutenant Lubesnick is standing there doing the same thing.

Chris doesn't know what to do.

Say something?

Don't say something?

Nod?

Don't nod.

Chris thinks that he should acknowledge the man somehow.

Or does he?

Lubesnick breaks the ice, so to speak. "So, Monkey Man, I talked to your lieutenant about you."

Shit, Chris thinks. He'd like nothing better than to get out of there, but he's in midstream (so to speak). So he says, "Oh."

"He's agreed, starting next month, to loan you to me for sixty days." Lubesnick shakes, zips up and walks over to wash his hands. "Call it a try-out. You do okay, and I think you will, we'll make it permanent. You good with that?"

Chris is shocked. "Yes. I mean, yes, sir."

"Pay attention to what you're doing there." Lubesnick cranks down a paper towel and wipes his hands. "You did the right thing, kid. You could have stepped on a brother officer to get a leg up, and you didn't. That showed me something. You start next week. Buy a sport coat and a tie."

He tosses the towel into the trash and walks out.

It was a test, Chris thinks.

Lubesnick was testing me to see what I'd do.

And I passed.

Top of the seventh, Padres up 4–2. Craig Stammen taking the mound.

Chris says, "Something beautiful might happen here."

"What's that?" Carolyn asks.

Chris says, "Stammen is going to throw the batter a sinker, try to get him to hit a ground ball. If he does, you're going to see something beautiful."

Sure enough, second pitch, Stammen throws the sinker and Descalso hits a sharp bouncer to the shortstop, Fernando Tatís Jr., who runs, scoops up the ball and makes the throw to first for the out.

"He's the most beautiful ballplayer I've ever seen," Chris says.

Chris was right, she thinks.

It was graceful, maybe even elegant.

Certainly beautiful.

Carolyn hears herself say, "Something else beautiful might be about to happen."

She leans over and kisses him.

So life is good for Chris Shea.

He goes into his last week in Central on a high. Lieutenant Brown is off his ass, the monkey razzing is starting to fade, and he comes off shift to a beautiful girlfriend.

Even the Padres put together a little winning streak.

He's half an hour before end of his last shift—*that close*—when another radio call comes in.

A 10/35.

Dangerous, armed person alert.

In this case a man with a knife on Cabrillo Bridge, which connects the halves of Balboa Park over Route 163.

Chris gets there first this time to see a man slashing at the air with not a knife but a machete. He radios a 10-97—arrived at scene—and gets out of the car. No one else is on the bridge. If there had been anyone there this time of the night, Machete Man must have chased them away.

The guy looks to be in his forties—his hair is shaggy, his shirt wrinkled, and he wears baggy khaki trousers held up by a piece of rope in place of a belt. He swings the blade in a wide figure-eight pattern as he yells at an invisible (at least to Chris) adversary.

It's obvious to Chris that the man sees his enemy very clearly.

Chris sends an 11-99—officer needs help—on his radio, then pulls his gun but holds it low at his hip. Right hand on the pistol, left held out palm forward, he walks slowly toward Machete Man. "Put down the blade!"

The man turns his head and looks wild-eyed at him. Chris has seen eyes like that a hundred times. A lot of the people he has encounters with are psychotic, and they have a certain look in their eyes when they've gone off the meds.

And now, Chris thinks, his enemy is me.

Machete Man walks slowly toward him, swinging the blade, yelling, "I know you, devil!"

Chris raises his gun and aims at center mass.

Three years on the job, this is the first time he's pointed his gun at anyone. He hates the feeling, the awful, very real possibility that he might actually have to pull the trigger to protect himself.

Civilians are always asking about these situations, why the cop doesn't shoot the guy in the hand or in the leg. But the public doesn't know anything about situations like this, the nauseating rush of adrenaline coming up, your heart racing. They don't understand how hard it is for even highly trained police to hit someone in the hand, or even in the leg, in a combat situation. You aim for center mass—for the chest—because if you miss, you might be dead.

Chris stops, but Machete Man keeps advancing.

"Don't!" Chris yells. "No! Stop right there!"

His finger tightens on the trigger.

Machete Man stops.

Thank God, Chris thinks, but he keeps the Glock trained on the man's chest. "Drop the machete!"

But Machete Man doesn't. Instead he yells, "Leave me alone!" turns away from Chris and runs to the north railing of the bridge, starts swinging the blade again, yelling at the devil.

I'd love to leave you alone, Chris thinks, but that's not the job. He walks steadily but slowly toward the man, who turns to see him again and then backs to the bridge's railing and swings one leg over. "I told you to leave me alone!"

"I know what you told me, but I can't do that," Chris says. "Let me get you some help."

The man looks at him sadly. "It's too late."

"No, it's never too late," Chris says. "Come on, let me help you."

Machete Man swings the other leg over, and now he's precariously perched to jump.

Or fall, Chris thinks.

Either way he's going to plunge a hundred feet down onto a freeway with traffic coming both ways.

Chris is maybe ten feet from him now, close enough to make a lunge if he has to. But he'll need both hands, so he holsters his gun. The man can't swing the machete from that position anyway.

He looks at Chris again and holds his hand out, as in don't come any closer, and then he says, "The devil's inside me. I have to kill him."

"No," Chris says, edging forward. "I know a priest . . . uhh . . . exorcist. We'll go see him. He'll help you."

Machete Man thinks about it. He looks down at the highway beneath him and then back at Chris. "Are you telling the truth?"

"The truth," Chris says.

Machete Man nods.

Then the lights hit as Grosskopf's squad car speeds in from the opposite direction in response to Chris's radio call. The flashers cover Machete Man in a red demonic glow.

He turns back to Chris with a look of betrayal.

Then pushes off from the railing.

Chris lunges.

His right hand manages to grab the rope belt and hang on, but Machete

Man is already in midair, and his weight and momentum pull Chris over the top of the railing.

Chris reaches back and grabs the railing with his left hand.

Holds on, as it were, for dear life.

Because this time he won't fall fifteen feet into a net but a hundred feet down onto a concrete highway and oncoming traffic.

What he should do is let go of Machete Man, but he doesn't do what he should do and feels his grip on the railing start to slide off, his arms burning, his fingers going numb, and he knows he's going to fall, him and Machete Man, and then—

A hand grabs his left wrist.

Chris looks up and sees—

Batman.

He's five-three and skinny, but definitely Batman. Then Robin, all six-five of him and muscled, takes firm hold of Chris's forearm, and the Dynamic Duo pull him and Machete Man up and over the railing back onto the bridge.

"Holy cocksucker, Batman!" Robin says.

"We should have them over for dinner," Carolyn says.

"At the least," Chris says.

He's strolling through the zoo on a Saturday afternoon after his first week in Robbery with his beautiful, smart, warm and charming girlfriend instead of being a stain on the 163, so yeah, they should have the two guys who saved his life over for at least a major taco night.

"I'll make beef stroganoff," she says.

"Better than what I was thinking."

They stop by the primate environment.

Champ looks out at them, recognizes Carolyn and lets out a scream of greeting. He doesn't seem to recognize Chris.

Oh, well, Chris thinks, it's a thankless job.

Nobody ever finds out how the chimp got the revolver.

FOR MR. RAYMOND CHANDLER

SUNSET

———

C hewing on an unlit cigar, Duke Kasmajian sits on his deck and looks out at the beach where he never goes.

"Too much sand," he answers when asked why not.

Sand is hard to walk on, especially if your five-ten frame has to carry 287, your knees are shot, your new heart valve has no warranty, and sixty-five is getting smaller in your rearview mirror. Add all that to the fact that Duke likes expensive shoes and doesn't like them full of sand, and you got the reason he looks at the ocean mostly from the deck of his home in Bird Rock.

Even though his cardiologist tells him to walk.

Duke has a treadmill and a stair-stepper and doesn't use either of them. They're the world's most expensive clothes hangers.

He *has* stopped smoking.

Also doctor's orders.

Hence the unlit cigar.

A squat glass of scotch sits on a stool by his left hand. Duke's not giving that up for anything—not for the doctor, not for his kids, all adults now, not even for the dozen employees he has in the largest bail-bonds outfit in San Diego, if not all of California.

The Duke is a San Diego legend.

His face is on highway billboards and local TV and radio ads.

"Need to juke? Call the Duke."

He sponsors Little League teams ("Caught stealing? Call the Duke"), OTL tournaments for the wheelchaired ("Over the line? Call the Duke"), and a safe house for battered women that his tougher bounty hunters guard on his dime (no advertising on this; its existence and location are on a strict need-to-know basis).

Duke also doesn't advertise the college tuitions he's laid out for, the twenties he drops at kids' lemonade stands, the Christmas boxes to the families of slain cops and firefighters, or the employees' medical bills he's hijacked at the hospital billing desk.

Nobody knows about those.

Nobody needs to.

All anyone needs to know is that if you have to make bail, phone Duke Kasmajian's office and he'll get you out. The Duke is an equal-opportunity bondsman who doesn't discriminate on the basis of race, gender, sexual orientation, relative degrees of guilt or innocence or criminal history. Duke, in fact, prefers recidivists, because they're a steady income base, and he even offers discounts to "frequent fliers."

"But don't fly on the Duke," he warns.

Don't be fooled by the round, friendly face, or the soft, curly salt-and-pepper hair, or the curmudgeon's smile twisted around the cigar. You run on Duke Kasmajian, he'll hunt you down. Because you're running with his money in your pocket. You take off on one of Duke's bonds, he'll track you until he finds you or one of you dies.

He'll never give up.

Just like he's not giving up his beloved scotch.

Or his vinyl.

Which, the younger people tell him, is coming back again.

Bullshit, Duke thinks as he listens to the Jack Montrose Sextet play "That Old Feeling" (Pacific Jazz Records, 1955)—vinyl records never went anywhere. Duke's collection of the genre generally known as "West Coast jazz" takes up most of the second floor of his house, and his nephew-in-law—his sister's daughter's well-meaning but idiotic husband—is afraid that the weight of all those albums is going to collapse the floor.

Also bullshit, Duke thinks.

His house was built in 1926, when they built things to last.

When most guys his age look out at the ocean, the soundtrack in their minds is the Beach Boys, Jan and Dean, Dick Dale or maybe the Eagles.

Not Duke.

He hears Cool School.

Pacific Jazz Records.

Art Pepper, Stan Getz, Gerry Mulligan, Hampton Hawes, Shelly Manne, Chet Baker, Shorty Rogers, Howard Rumsey's Lighthouse All Stars, Lennie Niehaus, Lee Konitz, Bud Shank, Clifford Brown, Cal Tjader, Dexter Gordon, Wardell Gray, Harold Land, Dave Brubeck, Paul Desmond, Jimmy Giuffre, Red Mitchell, Stan Kenton, Benny Carter . . .

Charlie Parker blew here.

They all did.

Bird played the old San Diego Boxing Arena back in 1953, too long ago for even Duke to have been there, but it means something to him. Just like it means something to him that Harold Land was from San Diego.

This album?

Jack Montrose on tenor sax, Conte Candoli on trumpet, Bob Gordon on bari, Paul Moer on piano, Ralph Pena on bass, Shelly Manne, of course, on drums. Duke knows this without looking at the album cover, he knows most of these details by memory because it's important, goddamn it, to know the sidemen on recordings. Just like in his work, details are important, details are everything, you don't get the so-called small things right, you'll screw up the big things. So Duke remembers who plays on almost every album, but if he doesn't, he can look at the goddamn liner notes, which you can't do on the iPad or mePod or shitPot or whatever they call the thing that his nephew-in-law is always trying to sell him on.

"But, Duke," the kid says, "you can take all your music everywhere."

But I don't want to take my music everywhere, Duke thinks now. I want to listen to it in my home, sipping my scotch, on vinyl the way it was meant to be heard.

I'm old-school that way.

A dinosaur.

In more ways than that, he thinks as he chews the cigar and looks out at the Pacific, because the state of California has just passed a law banning cash bails, which is going to put Duke out of business and all his employees out of their jobs.

Duke's not worried about himself—he knows his money is going to last longer than that heart valve.

But the business he built, the life he built, is about to be gone.

And gone is gone—you can't track it down.

Life isn't vinyl.

It doesn't spin round and round until it comes back again.

Duke knows this all too well.

How many times did he and Marie sit on this deck and watch the sun set? It was a near-nightly ritual. She would come out with his scotch and her glass of red wine, he'd put on some jazz, and they'd stand and watch the blazing reds and oranges, bask in the sheer peacefulness of the oceanic dusk.

It seemed as if the world stopped for those ten or fifteen minutes of awe.

Other couples would come outside, stand silently, and watch. Even the surfers would stop trying to catch waves, turn their boards toward the setting sun, and sit in quiet admiration, maybe even worship.

Later, when Marie was so sick and they both knew that their sunsets together were numbered, he would bundle her up in a coat and a blanket, a knit cap for her bare head, make her a cup of hot tea because she was always cold, and they would sit and watch the sunset, knowing it was their own as well.

Now he sits and watches alone, although he still pours a glass of red wine for her, which he tosses over the deck into the bushes when he's ready to go inside.

It's always beautiful and sad, the sun going down.

Duke goes inside and, reluctantly, picks up the Maddux file.

Terry Maddux is a dirtbag.

Short in stature, baby-faced, killer handsome, with shaggy blond hair, startling blue eyes and a grin that could charm a rock, Terry is also, Duke thinks, looking at his file, a junkie skell. A thief, an addict and therefore a liar, and Duke loves him.

Everyone does.

So much that Boone Daniels, one of Duke's bounty hunters, pinned the name ELT on him, as in "Everyone Loves Terry." Because Terry is charismatic, funny, incredibly kind when he's not jonesing, and he used to be the best surfer that anyone had ever seen.

A legend.

Duke has never been on a surfboard in his life, but he knows beauty when he sees (or hears) it, and watching Terry on a wave was pure beauty. He had a grace about him, a style. He rode a wave like a great trumpet player doing an extended solo, riffing, taking an old tune and making it new, making it his, creating art.

Breaking barriers.

According to Boone—a surfer himself and an ardent surf historian— every big wave on the West Coast had Terry's footprints, as it were, on it. Terry was just a kid, literally a kid, when he paddled out at Trestles. Not much older when he was the first to ride the big wave at Todos Santos. One of the early guys at Mavericks.

He was older when the boys took a boat sixty miles out to the mystical break at Cortez Reef, and it was Terry Maddux who was the first to jump into that sixty-footer, in cold, sharky water, and ride it.

All with that grin on his grill.

"Joyful" was how Boone put.

"He was joyful on a wave."

And off it.

Terry never met a party he didn't like.

Whether it was beers on the beach or shots in a bar, Terry was in it—laughing, joking, slinging back booze and chatting up girls, many of whom went home with him, home being a van he lived out of, taking it up and down the 101, riding waves, causing parties to break out, never causing them to break up.

Terry was on a high—the whole world loved him. The surf mags, the photogs, the clothing companies, they all loved Terry. He was on magazine covers, in surf videos, he had sponsorships and endorsements. When he needed cash to finance his surf jones, all he had to do was put on a wet suit with a logo, a hat, a pair of shoes, and they gave him money for it.

Money to surf.

Money to party.

And that was the problem.

Terry loved to party too much.

It was like he was looking for a bigger and bigger wave. Booze wasn't a big enough high, and then weed wasn't. And then coke didn't give him the rush it used to, and then speed failed to get him high.

Heroin did.

Heroin is the big wave of the drug world.

The undefeated macker.

You don't ride that big wave, it rides you.

Rode Terry Maddux down, blew him off his board and held him under, tumbling him around until it spit him out on the beach.

Washed up.

He'd get high and blow off tournaments, personal appearances, photo shoots. At first the surfing world would make excuses for him—"That's just Terry being Terry"—so as long as he could ride and look good, it was cool.

But then he couldn't.

The thing about surfing—it was Boone who explained this to Duke—is that you have to be in shape to do it well. And to ride big waves, you have to be in fantastic shape—you have to be able to paddle, to swim, to hold your breath for as long as three minutes if one of those giants keeps you under.

You have to be strong, and heroin makes you weak.

Makes you skinny.

You need total, *insane* focus to ride those waves, and heroin makes you *un*focused and *in*sane.

Plus, it makes you look like shit.

Not like a cover boy.

Or a vid-clip hero.

Behavior that made Terry cool when he could surf well made him uncool when he surfed badly. His charm became manipulation, his stories bullshit, his jokes pandering, his pickup attempts creepy, his explanations excuses.

That's the thing about aging, Duke thinks now as he goes over the file again. Behavior that was cute when you were in your twenties becomes aggravating in your thirties, pathetic in your forties and tragic in your fifties.

Nobody loves a fifty-four-year-old child.

Especially not when he's a dirtbag.

A three-time loser:

One conviction for possession.

Another for burglary.

A third for felony possession with intent to sell.

And now Terry has skipped.

Didn't show for trial.

Duke has to find him before the cops do or take a hit for three hundred large. Which would be financially irresponsible, which Duke never is. Especially now that he's looking at the end of his business and has to make sure that he takes care of the files that he has out there before the new law goes into effect.

Duke calls Boone.

About the last thing Boone Daniels wants to do is put Terry Maddux in prison for the rest of his life.

Terry was one of his heroes.

Boone grew up hearing Terry Maddux stories. As a grem he once pedaled his bike furiously up to Bird Rock when he heard that Terry Maddux had gone out there, stood on the bluff for hours just to get a glimpse of the legend. Remembers to this day when Maddux came in, his board under his arm, nodded at Boone as he passed by.

The next day Boone went out and tried to imitate what he saw Maddux do in the waves.

Couldn't, of course, but that wasn't the point.

Boone was a rookie patrolman the next time he saw Terry Maddux.

They say "Never meet your heroes," and maybe they're right. Maddux was so drunk he could barely stand up, never mind ride a wave. The owner of the bar wanted him *out of there*, and Boone and another cop walked Terry to the car, where he threw up all over Boone's shoes and then apologized with such humble sincerity that Boone couldn't stay mad at him. They didn't take him to the house—because he was Terry freakin' Maddux—but to his girlfriend's place, because he couldn't remember where he'd parked his van.

It was maybe three years later, a cloudy winter's morning, when Boone went out to surf at his home break north of Crystal Pier and saw Terry standing there sipping from a cardboard cup of coffee and looking kind of sick.

"You going out?" Terry asked.

"Yeah," Boone said, a little stunned. "You?"

Terry grinned his famous grin. "I seem to have misplaced my stick."

"You can borrow one of mine," Boone said.

"Yeah?" Terry said. "That's very decent of you."

Boone walked him over to his van, opened the rear door and showed Terry his quiver. Terry picked out a six-foot tri-fin. "You sure you don't mind?"

"I'd be honored."

Terry stuck out his hand. "Terry Maddux."

Clearly he didn't remember Boone, much less puking on his shoes.

"Yeah, I know," Boone said, feeling like some stupid fanboy. "Boone Daniels."

"Nice to meet you, Boone."

They paddled out, and Boone introduced Terry to the rest of the Dawn Patrol, the regulars who surfed that break about every morning before going to work—Johnny Banzai, High Tide, Dave the Love God, Hang Twelve, and Sunny Day. When Terry caught a wave, Dave paddled over to Boone. "You know *Terry Maddux*?!"

Boone didn't mention hauling Maddux out of a bar. "I just met him. Just now."

"Isn't that one of your boards?"

"He misplaced his."

The first of many excuses Boone would end up making for Terry, but all that came later. Right then Boone just surfed with his hero.

It was amazing.

Even with his diminishing skills, Terry surfed with a grace that was ethereal. He made the most difficult moves look easy, the most mundane moves look like art.

"I don't know how to describe it," Boone said later to Duke, trying to put it in terms that the older man would appreciate. "It was like, I don't know, a young sax player doing a session with Miles Davis."

"I think you mean Charlie Parker," Duke said. "But I get the idea."

They say never meet your heroes. They should have added and for God's sake, never make them your friends.

Not a friend like Terry anyway.

A friend who could be so charming in one moment, then try to pick up your girlfriend in the next (albeit with such boyish charm that both you and the girlfriend instantly forgave him) and then stick you with the check.

Who started crashing on your couch and eating your food.

All of which was tolerable, if increasingly annoying.

Then other things started to happen.

The crumpled dollar bills you left on your dresser started finding their way into Terry's pocket. You'd find Terry curled up not on your couch but outside your front door in a pool of his own vomit. He called you for bail money not from a barroom brawl but for a burglary charge.

Duke took the bond.

Boone put up the money.

That charge didn't stick.

The next one did, Terry went away for a year and a half, and Boone had to reluctantly admit to himself that it was a relief not having his hero randomly show up and do embarrassing, tiresome shit.

But it was Boone that Terry called to pick him up when he gated out.

Boone's couch he crashed on until he could get "set up again."

Boone to whom he swore he was kicking the junk for good this time.

It was Boone who found him OD'd on his floor.

Boone who rushed him to the E-Room.

It was Boone who, the next time Terry called him for bail, swallowed real hard and told him no.

Tough love and all that shit.

And now it's Boone who Duke calls to track Terry down.

"You put up the guarantee?" Boone asks.

"A woman named Samantha Harris put up the ten," Duke says, "but yeah, I guaranteed the rest. I can't afford to lose the money. Especially not now."

"No, I get it," Boone says. Duke is about to lose his business, his employees are going to lose their livelihoods, and Boone is going to lose a big chunk of his own income. And he knows Duke, he knows the man is not going to let his employees go out the door without fat envelopes in their hands to help tide them over.

Terry doesn't have the right to take food off their tables.

"I've given the guy every break," Duke says.

"True."

"I know he's your friend," Duke says, "but you're the best guy to find him."

Also true, Boone thinks. He knows the surf community, he knows most of the people that Terry knows—the people who worship Terry and the people Terry has fucked over, often the same set of people. He knows how Terry thinks, the places he goes, the places where he's no longer welcome, which is the larger set.

And Duke knows Boone's standing among surfers. They'll tell him things they wouldn't tell an average bounty hunter, because Boone is not a bounty hunter who surfs, he's a surfer who sometimes hunts bail jumpers, a private investigator who does jobs for Duke (not an unknown personage among the San Diego surf community) and a well-respected "sheriff" on his stretch of beach, one of those guys who keeps things copacetic, ruling with a light but firm hand.

Boone Daniels is a legend in his own right.

So is his crew, the Dawn Patrol, several of whom also help bring in jumpers for Duke, because they are very physical people who tend to stay cool in any circumstance. They won't run hot and get unnecessarily violent, but they won't run at all when confronted by an angry jumper.

Dave the Love God (a play on "Life Guard") moonlights for Duke, usually partnering up with Boone. So does High Tide, the three-hundred-pound Samoan city worker whose very appearance will often persuade the most recalcitrant jumper to step peacefully into the back of the car. Even Sunny Day, five-eleven with a negative body-fat percentage, will sometimes help bring in a female jumper.

The rules of his job prevent Johnny Banzai, the Japanese-American police detective, from moonlighting for a bail bondsman, but he's been known to pass along a tip from time to time.

So when Duke hires Boone, he gets the whole Dawn Patrol as a bonus.

And they're thick, tight together, in the way that people who trust each with their lives in deep water are.

"He could be in Mexico," Boone says.

One of the big problems of being a bail bondsman in San Diego is that the international border is a few miles away and easy to cross. But if you dive into Mexico, you'd better dive deep, because Duke has excellent relations with the Tijuana cops and the Baja state police, both of which have been known to grab one of his jumpers, stuff him in the trunk of a car, and drop him back across the border into the arms of one of Duke's bounty hunters.

Dump the jumper, pick up some cash, and be home for dinner.

Terry Maddux knows this.

He's not going to hang around TJ or Ensenada or even Todos Santos, all places he knows well, because they know him well there, too, and Duke's short, stubby fingers can reach out and grab him in any of his old hangs. No, if he's jumped south of the border, he'll be running hard down to Guanajuato, maybe even to Costa Rica.

But that takes money, and Boone doesn't think Terry has any.

"Why don't you drop in on Ms. Harris?" Duke says.

Normally Duke would telephone the other person on the bond, but in this case it might be better to have Boone show up at her place and see if Terry's there.

Because a lot of times, the same person who can be conned into putting down for the bond can also be talked into harboring a fugitive.

The con uses pretty much the same tactic.

Guilt.

"If you love me, you'll do this for me."

In Duke's experience, mothers are the worst. They almost always go for this one, or if they start to object, there's the similar argument, "If you love me, don't do this to me."

That is, throw him out or turn him in.

Girlfriends are the next worst.

Generally, they fall into one of two categories: an otherwise straight woman who falls in love with a criminal she thinks she can save from himself, or the woman is herself a criminal—usually a drug addict like the boyfriend—so she'll hide him out of habit.

But usually the second category of girl doesn't have $10K to put up for bail.

Then there are the wives. Unless they're the aforementioned co-criminals, they're pretty likely to give up the spouse because they have responsibilities—kids, rent, mortgages—and they can't afford to lose the bond money. To a lot of wives, it's almost a relief when the husband gets picked up—it stops the chaos for a while.

Duke checks her address.

For a short assemblage of letters and numbers, addresses can tell stories. This one—135 Coast Lane, La Jolla—tells an interesting one.

First of all, it's La Jolla, the coastal town that's one of the most expensive zip codes in the country. Second, Coast Boulevard is, as the name would indicate, oceanfront property—the difference between "oceanfront" and "ocean view" moving the needle from six zeroes to seven.

Boone knows right where the place is, just off Nicholson Point, south of the Tide Pools, north of La Jolla Medical Clinic.

Absolutely prime real estate.

Samantha Harris has money.

It's a good news/bad news joke. The good is that Samantha Harris has the money to put down for bail, the bad is that she can afford to lose it. There's probably no financial pressure on her to turn Terry in, which is how you catch most fliers. If she owns property at 135 Coast, she could even be bankrolling him.

It takes money to go off the radar.

Boone rolls up to Samantha Harris's house in his van.

Which is known in the greater San Diego surfing community as the "Boonemobile," but whatever it's called, it's pretty much a disgrace.

Twenty years old, rusted along the edges, stuffed to the gills with boards, wet suits, fins, masks, towels, sandals and the remnants of meals taken from taco stands, In-N-Outs and Rubio's, the Boonemobile looks, to say the least, out of place in La Jolla. If you see the Boonemobile parked on the street in front of 135 Coast, you're going to assume he's there to cut the lawn, fix a leak, or make an ill-advised, meth-inspired effort to rob the place.

The house is a Spanish Neocolonial with pink stucco and a blue-tiled roof. The door is a huge carved wooden Spanish antique.

Boone gets out, walks up, notes the security camera noting him, and rings the bell.

A maid, in an honest-to-God, no-kidding maid's uniform, opens the door. "Yes?"

"I'm here to see Ms. Harris?"

"Is she expecting you?" Her accent is Latina, maybe Mexican, maybe Guatemalan or Honduran. She looks to be in her early thirties.

"No," Boone says. That's the idea.

"Ms. Harris does not see salesmen."

"Tell her it's about Terry Maddux," Boone says.

The maid shuts the door and is gone for about a minute. Then the door opens and she ushers him into a living room five times the size of Boone's whole cottage. She points to a white sofa and says, "Wait there, please."

An enormous window looks out at a garden, a pool and, beyond, the beach. Boone has never understood what people who live a few steps from the ocean want with a swimming pool, which doesn't *do* anything. But he can picture Terry lying out there on a chaise lounge, shades on, sipping on a drink.

Samantha Harris comes in a few minutes later.

She's beautiful in that specific way that wealthy San Diego women are beautiful. Blond hair pulled back tightly into a golden helmet, a black sweater—because it's a California winter—over black slacks. Layers of gold bracelets wrap around her wrists, a large pair of sunglasses hides her eyes.

A PI and a former cop, Boone knows what that too often means.

Samantha gets right to it. "What *about* Terry?"

"He's missing."

"Isn't he always?" She gestures for Boone to sit back down and then sits in an overstuffed wing chair.

"But this time he's jumped bail," Boone says.

"And you're what?" she asks. "Some kind of bounty hunter?"

"*Some* kind," Boone says.

"Well, he's not here."

"Do you know where he is?" Boone asks.

She smiles and shakes her head.

"When did you last see him?"

"Are you a police officer, Mr. . . . ?"

"Daniels."

"Mr. Daniels?"

"No," Boone says.

"So I don't have to answer your questions," she says.

"You don't," Boone says. "But it's in your interest to help us find him. If we don't, you forfeit your ten thousand dollars."

She shrugs.

Boone's aware that she's wearing more than that on her wrists. And that, if he knows Terry like he does, ten grand was probably the least of her contributions to the ELT Fund.

"It's in Terry's interest, too," Boone says.

"And how is that?"

"It's better for him if we find him before the police do."

"I hardly believe that," she says.

Boone's getting tired of her La Jolla Ice Maiden routine. It's one of the pat San Diego personas—Laid-Back Surfer Girl, Hot Soccer Mom, La Jolla Ice Maiden. They're set pieces. She does it exceptionally well, but it's still a tired stereotype.

He stands up and sets one of Kasmajian's cards on the side table by her chair. "Hardly believe what you want. If you have information to give us, call this number. Thank you for your time."

He starts to leave.

"Wait," she says. Then adds, "Please."

He turns and looks at her. Shrugs.

"Do you think they'd really hurt him?" she asks.

"They might not want to," Boone says, "but any arrest has risks, especially with someone who is as erratic as Terry can be."

"Don't I know it."

"Was it Terry who hit you?" Boone asks.

She takes off the shades to show a deep purple bruise that swells under her left eye. "I provoke him."

"There's never a reason for a man to lay his hands on a woman in anger," Boone says. A guy does that, he rips up his man card.

Samantha says, "I think he does it when he feels bad about himself."

"He has a lot to feel bad about," Boone says. "You should help us find him before he hurts someone else."

"Another woman, you mean?"

Now Boone shrugs.

"I know he has other women," Samantha says. "But I really don't know where he is. The last time I saw him was two days ago. He spent the night. Well, most of it—when I woke up, he'd already gone."

"What did he take?"

She looks at him as if reappraising. "How did you know?"

"I know Terry."

"Some loose cash," she says. "A diamond necklace. A watch."

"Worth . . . ? "

"Forty thousand?"

"How much cash?"

"Just a few hundred," she says.

"You should file charges," Boone says.

"I can't prove it was him."

"You can when he tries to move it."

"I don't want to get him into trouble," she says. "I love him, Mr. Daniels. If he came back, I would take him back. Sad, isn't it?"

Yes, it is, Boone thinks.

Because sometimes I feel the same way.

"Can you give me a description of the necklace and the watch?" he asks.

"I have photos," she says. "For insurance purposes."

"If you report this loss," Boone says, "your insurance company will make you file charges."

"Did I say I was reporting it?" She leaves for a few minutes and returns with photos, which she hands to Boone.

"I'll get these back to you," Boone says. "Do you mind if I make copies?"

"These are copies."

"Thank you." He goes to leave again.

"Mr. Daniels . . ."

"Yes?"

"If you do find him," Samantha asks. "Will you tell him . . . that I'm not angry with him?"

It's funny, Boone thinks as the maid shows him out. Terry Maddux can do the most outrageous shit, and the worry always is that you don't want him to think you're mad at him.

Like somehow you need him to forgive *you*.

At the door he says to the maid, "I'm Boone. What's your name?"

"Flor."

"Did you know Terry?"

She nods.

"What do you think?"

"He's a bum," she says.

But he's a bum with money now, Duke thinks as he hangs up from Boone and the photos of the stolen jewelry come across his screen.

Terry Maddux has a little cash (who knows what "a little cash" means to a woman like Samantha?), and some valuable merchandise he'll try to lay off somewhere. The proceeds could be enough to buy him a ticket far away from here, maybe to another country.

As a precaution Duke already had people at the bus depot, the train station and both terminals of San Diego airport. They're good people, and if Terry shows up at any of those places, they'll nab him.

Duke comes out of his office and hands the photos to Adriana.

In her fifties, she's been his right-hand woman for twenty years. He couldn't have run the business without her. Black hair, thin, dressed like she makes more money than she does, she manages the office with style, humor and no nonsense.

"Circulate these to the usual people," Duke says.

He doesn't need to be any more specific. She'll forward the photos to every jewelry store and dealer and every pawnshop in greater San Diego. That way they're forewarned that if anyone shows up looking to sell, the merchandise is hot. And he knows she'll red-tag it, send it out with a request that if a seller does show up, they notify the Kasmajian office immediately.

Most will honor the request. It's good business, and a lot of people owe the Duke a lot of favors.

Adriana looks a little teary this afternoon.

Duke knows why.

This place has been not only her living but her life.

He also knows that if she fell apart, she went into the ladies' room to do it and looked put-together when she came out.

"Don't worry about it, Ad," he says. "It's going to be okay."

"Of course it is."

"Who has the helm tonight?" Duke asks.

"Valeria."

"If anything comes through on this, I want her to call me," Duke says. "I'll be at Carey's."

"It's Thursday, where else would you be?" Adriana says. Every Thursday for the past umpteen years has been poker night at Dr. Carey's house. Jumpers have jumped and been found, marriages have come and gone, the game goes on.

Adriana has called it "The Odd Trio"—Duke, Neal Carey and Lou

Lubesnick. A bail bondsman, an English professor and a cop who play poker, go to baseball games and have endless philosophical debates about meaningless subjects.

For instance, the ethics of refills in fast-food restaurants.

"It says free refills," Lou said, in one of their endless discussions.

"That doesn't mean forever," Neal answered.

"There's no time limit on it."

"Maybe not legally," Neal said, "but ethically."

Duke challenged him on this, because Carey has an annoying habit of claiming the moral high ground. "Okay, what is the ethical span of time in which it's acceptable to refill?"

Neal considered this for a moment and handed down a ruling. "Once you leave the premises, you yield refill rights for that session."

"So say I forgot something in my car," Lou said, "and I go back out and get it. When I come back in, I can't refill?"

"That's different," Neal said, "because it constitutes the same visit."

"But I left the premises."

"Temporarily."

"But that's *always* the case," Lou said, "if I go back."

"Yes, but not a week later," Neal said. "That constitutes a separate visit."

"So it's a temporal issue," Duke said, to keep it going.

"Exactly," Neal said.

Lou was undeterred. Not that he would ever actually go back and refill his drink after a week, but he was stubborn about the principle of the thing. "Nowhere on the cup does it state a time limit."

"So it's forever?" Duke asked.

"For the life of the cup," Lou said. "I purchased the cup."

"But does that constitute rights in perpetuity to the liquid that goes into the cup?" Neal asked. "I don't think so."

"But they don't count by the liquid," Duke said, "they count by the cup."

"But they're still out the liquid," Neal said.

"As they would be if I sat there all day drinking," Lou said. "Would that be more ethical, if I sat there all day refilling my drink *and* taking up space? When you think of it that way, I'm doing them a favor."

The debate has gone on for months. As has the discussion regarding ketchups, mustards and napkins that the kid at the counter puts on the tray. To wit, if there are ketchups, mustards and napkins that you don't use, is it acceptable to take them home?

"I paid for them," Lou said.

Neal is an ethical stickler. "You paid for sufficient ketchup and mustard to season your burger and enough napkin to wipe your mouth."

"But if they give you extra, they intend for you to have them," Lou said. "Besides, I don't think the Health Department lets them use packages once they've gone out to the customer."

"So you're performing a public service," Duke said.

"Someone has to," said Lou.

Now Duke pulls in to the Careys' driveway. Their house is a bungalow on El Paseo Grande they bought twenty years before real-estate prices went insane. Lubesnick's old Honda Civic is already there.

Duke's efforts to get Lou to get a new—that is, *decent*—car have met with abject failure.

"You're a lieutenant in the SDPD," he told Lou. "You can afford a new car."

"Affordability is irrelevant," Lou said. "I can afford a jeweled tiara, too. Does that mean I should buy one?"

"He wasn't speaking to affordability," Neal said. "He was speaking to a necessity that you can afford to meet."

"Define 'necessity,' " Lou said. "My car gets me from Point A to Point B. This is what I need in a car."

"But it looks like shit," Duke said.

"Which is as irrelevant, if not more so, as affordability," Lou said.

"Not necessarily," Neal said. "If, in your role as a police lieutenant, the appearance of your vehicle causes you to lose prestige, it becomes a liability that you can't afford."

"Or," Lou says, "it becomes sort of a trademark. A charming symbol of my refusal to conform to a societal demand for prestige items. Like Duke's Cadillac."

"I drive a Cadillac because I'm big."

"You drive a Cadillac," Neal said, "because you're nostalgic, because you think it brings you back to an era that you consider preferable to the current one."

"I do consider an older era preferable to the current one," Duke said.

As would any sensate being who ever heard Hank Mobley play "No Room for Squares."

"I think it's more a matter of image," Lou said. "Chronic criminals see the Duke rolling around free in a big old Cadillac, they believe he can free them, too."

"I can," Duke said.

"My point," said Lou.

Who had successfully evaded another effort to pressure him into buying a new car.

Karen answers the door.

Amazingly attractive at sixty-eight—tall, leggy— her long white hair is tucked under an eye shade. "Good evening, sucker, come on in."

Both Neal Carey and Lou Lubesnick are *terrible* poker players, perhaps because they're more focused on the Talmudic debates than on their cards.

Not so Karen.

She's a cutthroat, steely-eyed, brutally efficient card player who couldn't care less about ethics and just wants to win, and the end of the evening usually sees her with a stack of chips in front of her. Sometimes Duke has to remind himself that Neal's wife is from Nevada, although not from Vegas, but from some little town way up north in ranch country.

"The other loser's already here," Karen says.

"Lou or your husband?" Duke asks.

"Either," she says, ushering him in. "Both."

The kitchen smells great. Karen's famous "Dreaded Bean Dip" bubbles in a slow cooker, a stack of quesadillas sits on a platter, and her even more famous "Even More Dreaded Chili" simmers in a pot.

The first time Duke had Karen's Even More Dreaded Chili—a recipe she got, improbably, from a Chinese restaurant in Austin, Nevada—she'd warned him about its heat. He'd scoffed and put a big spoonful into his mouth. Then his eyes watered, his cheeks flushed, and he felt as if his actual hair were on fire.

Duke lifts the lid and waves a waft into his nose.

Something's different.

"I made it with turkey," Karen says.

"Why?" Duke asks, distraught.

"Because I don't want you falling face-first on our dining-room table," she says.

"My heart's fine."

"Let's keep it that way."

Karen Carey is one of the best people Duke knows. And one of the kindest. When Marie was first diagnosed, it was Karen who brought casseroles to the house, Karen who drove her to chemo when Duke couldn't, Karen who held her head while she vomited.

When Marie passed, it was Karen, Neal, Lou and Angie who got Duke through the grief, had him over to their houses, came by and drank wine on his deck to shorten those endless nights. It was after Marie passed that Thursday-night poker started and the season tickets to the Padres got purchased, despite Neal's being a lifelong and ardent Yankees fan.

That's been—is it possible?—five years ago now.

He couldn't have gotten through even a year of that—especially that awful first year—without these people.

They're precious to him.

So is this house. He's spent so many hours here, first at couples' dinners when Marie was still with them and before Lou and Angie got divorced, later at Thursday poker, or just those nights when he'd come over to sit and watch TV or listen to music as Neal feigned an interest in West Coast jazz.

It's an academic's house—every bit of wall space is taken up by floor-to-ceiling bookshelves, most of them holding Neal's books of English literature—"Brit lit," as he calls it—some containing Karen's collection of children's books—she'd been an elementary-school teacher—and a small shelf of books that Neal has written.

Highly academic books with titles like *Tobias Smollett and the Origin of the Modern Literary Hero, Samuel Johnson and the Beginning of "Literature," Amazing Grace: The Poetry of Slavery*—books that Duke has stubbornly pretended to have read and Lou has as stubbornly pretended not to have.

Neal is apparently a big deal in his field.

Duke goes into the dining room, where Neal and Lou are standing by the table, which has a green felt cloth thrown over it.

The cards and chips are already out.

"What are you drinking?" Neal asks.

"Grapefruit juice with a sprig of kale," Duke says.

Neal pours him a scotch and clinks his glass with his beer bottle.

Neal Carey, at sixty-five, has hair that is equally gray and brown, unstylishly long down to his collar as befits the raffish street-guy persona that he cultivates to offset the egghead stereotype. But the street thing isn't an affectation—Neal doesn't say much about his early days, but over the years Duke has gleaned that he grew up rough on New York's Upper West Side when *it* was rough, that he never knew his father, and that his mother was a heroin addict who sold herself to pay for her habit.

Students who first take Neal's class are surprised by the New York accent, the black leather jacket, the use of "freakin' " as a descriptor ("You never heard of Smollett, but he's freakin' important, and here's why")—a word he never uses outside the lecture hall. The accent likewise disappears, or at least fades.

"Your students have to be able to imitate you," he explained to Duke.

Lou Lubesnick has a similar philosophy—in addition to the beater car, he sports a black goatee that matches his full, slicked-back black hair, this in the famously buttoned-down, straitlaced, white-bread SDPD, where even the Mexican and black cops listen to country music. In a department full of Republicans who think that Democrats are basically Communists, Lubesnick is a dues-paying member of the ACLU.

Duke knows that neither of his friends could get away with their iconoclastic behavior if they weren't so goddamn good at what they do. Lou's Robbery Unit has a clearance rate that's among the top in the country, and UCSD is afraid of losing Neal to Columbia, just a short subway ride from Yankee Stadium.

They go into the kitchen and "dish up," in Karen's rustic phrase, then go back into the dining room to eat and play cards.

Duke is surprised that the turkey chili isn't as awful as he'd feared.

Ms. Carey plays five-card draw or seven-card stud and doesn't go in for fancy-ass shit with wild cards and kickers and any of that nonsense, so she doesn't hide her disdain when it's Lou's turn and he announces, "Nine-card draw, best five cards, deuces wild, red queen can be an ace, last card in the hole."

"Which hole would that be, Lou?" Karen asks. "Your vagina?"

She kicks their asses.

Even more so than she normally does, and about ten hands in she says, "You're playing even worse than usual, Duke. I expect it from these two, but you generally put up a fight."

"I might be distracted."

Neal asks, "By . . . ?"

"A big-ticket jumper," Duke says.

"Does he have a name?" Lou asks.

"Terry Maddux."

Lou sets his cards down. "You should have known better."

Duke nods. "It was against my better judgment."

Karen asks Lou, "Do you know him?"

"The whole department knows Terry," Lou says. "We arrest him on a semi-regular basis. Why softy here wrote him is a mystery to me."

"You hit the nail on the head," Duke says. "I guess I'm going soft."

"How much are you on the hook for?" Neal asks.

"Three hundred. Thousand."

"Ouch."

"I put Daniels on it," Duke says. "We'll find him."

He reaches into his shirt pocket and jams his cigar into his mouth.

Boone spends the night cruising the PCH.

Because runners are funny. Either they bolt far away or they burrow in, and when they go to ground, it's almost always close to home, in places they know.

Terry is a surfer.

He knows the PCH.

And now that he has some money, he could be at one of the hundreds of motels that dot a tourist town like San Diego. He could be downtown, in the Gaslamp, or he could be up in the northern burbs, but Boone doubts it.

Terry will stay close to the ocean.

Surfers get nervous when they can't smell the sea.

So Boone drives the van up and down the PCH, because it's possible that Terry would wait until the sun sets and then poke his head out looking for something to eat. He'd go to one of the dozens of taco stands or fast-food joints.

Terry Maddux has two conflicting needs.

As a runner he needs a place to hide.

As an addict he needs to score.

The way users hook up with dealers has changed. It used to be there were certain blocks, or parts of parks and even beaches, where sellers would hang out and wait for buyers. So back in the day, Boone would cruise those locales to find his target, but those drug markets don't exist anymore. With the advent of cell phones and social media, addicts phone or text their dealers and arrange to meet someplace indoors, out of sight.

So Boone has had to take a different angle.

He went to High Tide. The charter member of the Pacific Beach Dawn Patrol grew up as a Samoan gangbanger in Oceanside. Now literally a saint, albeit of the Latter-day variety, Tide still has his gang connections, so Boone has asked him to contact them and put out the word that if Terry shows up looking to score, they had better drop a dime if they ever want Duke to bail them out again.

While Boone waits on that, or for Terry to go to a jewelry store or pawnshop, he cruises the coast to see if Terry sticks his head up somewhere.

Dave the Love God rides with him.

If they do find Terry, it's going to be a two-man job taking him in. Plus, they have a lot of people to interview, and at least half of them are going to be women, and women like Dave, perhaps because they sense that he returns the feeling.

"I don't like this," Dave says.

"I don't either," Boone says. "But Terry has crossed the line. And Duke has put a lot of food on our plates."

They start down in Ocean Beach—just "OB" to locals—and work their way north, stopping at motels and fast-food joints. They take turns, one waiting in the car while the other goes and shows Terry's photo and asks the clerks and servers if they've seen him.

No one in OB has seen Terry, or if they have, they're not saying.

Ditto in Mission Beach.

They get up to their home turf in Pacific Beach (PB) and finally get lucky at a little motel just off Mission Boulevard.

Boone goes in and talks to the desk clerk, a middle-aged Indian woman who also happens to be the owner. He shows her the picture and asks, "Have you seen this man?"

"Are you the police?"

"No ma'am, but I'm sort of deputized."

"We respect our guests' privacy," she says.

"So he was a guest here?"

"What did he do?" she asks.

"Among other things," Boone says, "he hit a woman."

She thinks about this for a minute and then says, "He checked in last night."

"What room?" Boone asks, feeling his adrenaline rise. Dave is out in the parking lot keeping an eye out in case Terry is there, sees Boone and makes a run for it.

"Room 208," she says.

"Do you know if he's in there now?" Boone asks.

"He checked out this morning," she says. "Well, this afternoon. Checkout time is noon, and I had to call him at twelve-thirty."

Terry left Samantha's with the stuff he stole and holed up here, Boone thinks. Knew enough to spend only one night, because he knows the process. Now he's finding another place to hide until he can lay off the watch and the necklace for the money that will really allow him to run.

We're in a race.

"Do you know if he was alone?" Boone asks.

He knows she does. The hotel office is neat and immaculate. An owner like this sees who comes in and out of her business.

"There was a young lady," she says. "She came and went to his room."

"Was she there when he checked out?"

The woman is embarrassed. "Yes."

So Terry hooked up with another woman. He has transportation and maybe another place to stay.

"Can you tell me what kind of car she drove?"

"I don't know much about cars," she says.

He thanks the woman and goes back out to the van.

"He was here as of noon today," Boone says. "He's on the move."

"What next?" Dave asks.

"Keep the pressure up," Boone says. "Someone we talk to is going to run to Terry and tell him we're close. If we can keep him moving, we have a chance."

They're up in Solana Beach when the phone rings.

It's Tide.

Terry is going to score.

Tide is waiting for them in the parking lot of the Carlsbad Shore Apartments, off Washington Avenue and Chestnut Street up in North County, just three blocks inland from Tamarack Beach. His truck is parked on the east side of the two-story building, beside a narrow strip of brush with a dirt walking path along the railroad tracks.

Boone pulls in next to him.

Tide rolls his window down. "Do you know Tommy Lafo?"

Boone doesn't.

"You're better off," Tide says. "He's a waste of space, a heroin dealer."

"Is this his place?"

"His grandparents'."

"Are they here?" Boone asks. Because that could be a problem. He doesn't want to get older people involved with this and somehow getting hurt.

Tide shakes his head. "They're back in Palauli, seeing family. They'd die of shame if they knew."

"Why did he flip on Terry?"

"He's in trouble with USO," Tide says. "He knocked up a shot-caller's niece, and they're looking to punish him. He needs help."

He came to the right place, Boone thinks. High Tide quit the United Samoan Organization years ago, but they still look at him as a respected "uncle" who serves as a peacemaker with the Sons of Samoa, the Tonga Crips and other islander gangs. He can get Tommy some slack, maybe a trip down the aisle instead of a one-way ride to a vacant lot.

"We'd better get in there," Tide says. "Maddux is on his way."

"How's he getting here?" Dave asks.

"Tommy didn't say," Tide tells him. "I don't think he knows."

"It's probably the girl from last night," Boone says.

Boone and Tide go into the building. Dave waits outside to spot for Terry and be out there in case he runs. The apartment building is nondescript, basic cinder-block construction. They take the elevator to the second floor.

Tide knocks on Tommy's door.

Tommy Lafo is in his early twenties, small and skinny. His long black hair is tied up into a topknot. Tattoos run from his neck down into his black shirt, and he has inked sleeves. He looks nervous.

He should, Boone thinks.

High Tide is not a man you mess with.

Tommy looks up at Tide and says, "What's up, *uce*?"

"I'm not your 'brother,' *pukio*," Tide says. "I'd introduce you, but you're not worth knowing my friends. Is Maddux on his way?"

"Five minutes out," Tommy says. "He just texted me."

Tide looks around the small apartment—the living room and kitchen they're standing in, an open door to a bedroom, another door to a bathroom. "We'll wait in the bedroom. You let Maddux in, shut the door behind him. Where's your shit?"

Tommy points at a backpack set in a chair. "In there."

"You get his money, give him the dope," Tide says. "He'll be all busy with that, we'll come in and grab him. You just stay out of the way, understand?"

"Sure."

"If you screw me on this," Tide says, his eyes boring into the kid, "*ou e fasioti oe.*"

Tommy goes pale.

Boone doesn't speak Samoan, but he has no doubt that Tide just told Tommy he'd kill him.

They go into the bedroom, leaving the door open a crack.

Boone's phone vibrates. He clicks on and hears Dave say, "Terry just got out of the car. A girl is driving. She didn't get out."

Boone clicks off and nods to Tide.

Tide slips a pair of handcuffs from under his shirt.

Boone hears Tommy's phone bing from a text. It's probably Terry downstairs, letting him know he's coming up.

A minute goes by. . . .

Ninety seconds . . .

Boone whispers, "He fucked us."

They go out the door just as Dave calls. "He's in the parking lot, running toward the car. I have him cut off."

Boone runs out of the apartment, doesn't wait for the elevator but goes down the stairs, hearing Dave on the phone, "The girl took off. I'm chasing Terry south." Reaching the parking lot, Boone turns right and sees Dave running in a vacant lot, then into a narrow alley between an old shed and another apartment building. Boone goes in behind. The alley narrows as it squeezes between two more buildings, and then Boone hears Dave yell "There!" and sees Terry burst out of the alley into someone's backyard.

Then he loses him.

Dave yells, "Right! Right!"

Boone runs after him through the yard onto a wide driveway that opens to a cul-de-sac. He sees Terry run out of the cul-de-sac, through some low bushes and then head south on the dirt path alongside the tracks.

Dave is about twenty yards behind him.

It's no contest. The head start isn't going to help a middle-aged heroin addict against a legendary thirty-something lifeguard in superb shape. In constant training to save people in heavy surf, strong currents and mad riptides, Dave the Love God's cardio is on a par with that of world-class athletes.

Boone's isn't, but it's still pretty damn good from the at-least-once-a-day surf sessions. The paddling looks easy, like the surfer is effortlessly gliding across the surface, but anyone who's never done it can't even guess what a grueling workout it is.

And Tide, carrying three-fifty, is no athlete when he's off his board, but he's now chugging away behind, pissed off and determined, with the DNA of people who paddled freaking canoes across thousands of miles of open ocean.

Terry isn't going to outrun these three, and he's about out of places to duck into as the brush decreases and the trail gets wider and more barren.

Boone knows it's just a matter of time and not much of it.

Then he hears the horn.

And looks over to see the light of a train coming from the south.

Sees that Terry spots it, too, because Maddux stops, looks back at his pursuers and is clearly thinking about doing something rash.

To say the least.

Boone yells, "Terry, don't!"

Yeah, like *Terry, don't!* has ever stopped him. *Terry, don't paddle out into that wave. Terry, don't do another shot. Terry, don't shoot smack.* Terry Maddux has defined his entire life by defying Terry-don'ts and turning them into Terry-dids, and now he's calculating the odds of running across the tracks in front of a speeding train and putting it between him and his pursuers.

Terry's done similar things on Jet Skis, racing beneath a gigantic breaking wave to pull a buddy out of the impact zone. Hell, he's done it on a board, flying down the face of a killer wave and through the tube before it can break and crush him.

He's always come out the other side.

But Boone yells again, "Terry, don't! It's not worth it!"

Apparently it is to Terry.

To Boone's horror he gathers himself and dashes onto the tracks in front of the speeding train.

To Boone's greater horror, Dave starts to go after him.

Boone lunges, grabs him and holds him back.

They stand and watch Terry sprint across the track as the train engineer blasts his horn and the brakes screech in a futile effort to stop in time.

Terry clears the track five feet in front of the train.

"Jesus Christ," Boone says.

And hears, over rattling cars, maniacal laughter and Terry yelling, *"Fuck you, Boone!"*

Dave's pissed. "I could have made it."

Maybe, Boone thinks. Dave's fervent belief that he can perform the impossible has saved a number of lives in the waters off San Diego. But he says, "Not worth it."

Tide hunches over, grabs his knees and sucks air.

Boone says, "He's getting desperate. He didn't score, he hasn't fenced the merch, and he knows we're getting close. He'll make a mistake, and we'll get him."

He says it, but he's not so sure.

They walk back to the apartment building's parking lot.

Tide goes inside to slap the shit out of Tommy Lafo.

"Where do you think Terry went?" Dave asks Boone.

"Back to the girl who drove him here?"

"I got the license plate."

"I figured you did."

They call Duke, who calls a contact (one of many) in the police and gets back to them in twenty minutes with a name and address.

Sandra Sartini.

1865 Missouri Street in Pacific Beach.

Duke answers the doorbell.

Stacy is in her late twenties, redheaded, long-legged and buxom. She has a bit of a throwback look, not surprising for a man of Duke's retro tastes. Indeed, Chet Baker is on in the background, singing "But Not for Me."

Duke ushers her in.

She's been here before, sets her bag on his sofa and smiles broadly. Stacy likes Duke—he's a gentleman, he's not weird, and he's a good tipper. She notices the music and asks, "Is that Harry Connick Jr.?"

"Chet Baker."

"Oh," she says. "Last time it was . . . Gil Evans?"

"Good memory." Duke walks to the bar and pours them each a glass of scotch, hands her one, and gestures for her to sit down. He's in no hurry to get to the main event, and she's comfortable that he'll pay her for her time.

Stacy knows that Duke isn't one of those guys who just likes to talk—he definitely will want sex, but he likes some of the niceties first. She's come to find that she appreciates civility, and she's learned a bit about music, too.

Duke, he's careful about his pleasures. To rush them is to waste them, so he savors the whiskey, the music, the scent of her perfume, the curve of her leg under the skirt, the shine in her green eyes. In a few minutes, he'll set down his glass, hold out his hand, and lead her upstairs into the bedroom.

A man in Duke's business knows a lot of call girls, and he knows the best. Stacy is one of his favorites, but he harbors no foolish-old-man delusions that this is a girlfriend experience. He's both aware and satisfied that this is a strictly commercial transaction, and he feels no guilt about this, with Stacy or any of the others.

He never cheated on Marie, never thought about it, wasn't tempted, even though literally hundreds of women had offered him sex in exchange for a bond. But now Marie is gone, and has been for some time, and Duke is a realist.

A man has needs.

This is the simplest, easiest way of getting them met. He doesn't want a "relationship," knows that he will never fall in love again. This is just sex. Sex is fun, sex is good, sex is necessary, but that's all it is. Stacy is accomplished in the sack. She'll do her job well and with some charm and warmth, and then she'll shower, dress and leave.

He'll wake up alone. Going to bed with someone doesn't feel like a betrayal of Marie's memory, but waking up with someone somehow does, for reasons that he can't articulate and the ethics of which he doesn't want to debate, even with Neal and Lou.

The song ends, and Chet launches into "That Old Feeling."

Duke sets his drink on the side table and reaches out his hand.

"I'm worried about Duke," Karen says as she gets into bed.

"Duke's fine," Neal says, looking up from his Val McDermid novel. The expert on picaresque literature has developed a passion for crime fiction, and a stack of paperbacks—Ian Rankin, Lee Child, T. Jefferson Parker—sits on the side table.

"I'm not so sure," Karen says. "How's his heart?"

Neal shrugs.

Karen frowns at that response.

"We have a rule," Neal says, "that we don't talk about health problems."

Karen shakes her head. These are men who will endlessly discuss whether "launch angle" is ruining baseball, the efficacy or lack thereof of loyalty cards ("How is it loyal to a business to take back ten percent of what you spend there?" Neal has asked), but won't discuss something as literally vital as their health. She says, "He looked tired to me."

"He's worried," Neal says. "About his business and this—what's-his-name—Terry Maddux thing."

Karen is eighty-five pages into Michelle Obama's book. She finds her place, starts to read, and then asks, "Can you help him find this guy?"

"I'm a long way from my people-chasing days."

What Neal used to do before he got his degrees and became an academic, he tracked down missing people for an exclusive detective agency that helped rich people with their problems.

"Maybe it's like riding a bicycle," Karen says.

"I've never ridden a bicycle," Neal says. "I don't intend to start. Anyway, Duke is a pro at this, he has good people who know the streets here. If Maddux went missing in the faculty lounge, I could maybe find him, but beyond that . . ."

Karen goes back to pretending to read. "I just thought you might want to help your friend."

"You couldn't wait for me to get out of that work, remember?" Neal asks.

She remembers. They'd broken up for years because of it, because he was always away somewhere, chasing someone, doing secret things he couldn't share with her. It was only when he promised to give it up, and stuck to it, that she'd agreed to come back to him. And she's much happier as a faculty wife, so she's aware of the hypocrisy of what she's suggesting.

"It's a young man's game," Neal says. "And I hate to break it to you, but I'm not a young man."

"You're young enough," she says, setting her book down and turning toward him.

She's a *good* poker player.

A little while later, he says, "Okay, I'll call him."

He sits there all night.

Boone in the Boonemobile, outside 1865 Missouri.

Another apartment building and another cul-de-sac, Boone thinks.

A large, two-story, U-shaped complex with a central courtyard and a pool.

Sandra is home, or at least her car is parked in the subterranean parking structure. The Boonemobile sits up in the street, across from the driveway that leads down into the structure. Dave is parked over on Chalcedony and Tide on Academy, in case Terry comes in toward a back entrance.

It's the right thing to do, Boone thinks, but probably futile, because an experienced fugitive like Terry will figure that they got the license plate and will stay away from this address. Still, he might be off his game, or desperate for a place to stay, or not thinking because he's strung out, so he might slip up or take a chance on coming back to Sandra.

Boone has already had Duke's people run her. Sandra is an RN at Sharp Grossmont Hospital, in the E-Room. So she's smart, she makes good money, and she isn't likely to panic.

More from boredom than for any real reason, Boone calls Dave. "Anything?"

"I don't know," Dave says. "Has Terry become a shape-shifter?"

"Not that I'm aware of."

"Then I can rule out the cat I just saw," Dave says.

It's coming toward sunrise. Soon Hang Twelve, Johnny Banzai and Sunny Day will be paddling out on the Dawn Patrol and wondering where they are.

The phone rings.

Dave says, "You think Maddux might be in there? Beat us over here and is just holing up?"

"It's possible, I guess."

"Should we go in?"

It's too early, Boone thinks. He doesn't want to scare the shit out of Sandra, guys banging on her door in the middle of the night, causing a scene that might arouse both the neighbors and the police. Better to wait until it's light out and a time when Terry, if he is inside, is more likely to be asleep.

Always best to be a target's waking nightmare.

Then, through the rearview mirror, he sees a car pull up about twenty feet behind him. A guy wearing a baseball cap gets out, jams his hands into his black leather jacket, walks toward the van and knocks on the window.

Boone rolls it down.

"Boone Daniels?" the guy asks.

"Yeah?"

"I'm Neal Carey," the guy says. "Duke Kasmajian asked me to come over, see if I could be of any help."

They go in at 7:00 A.M.

Either Terry is in there or he isn't coming. Leaving Tide and Dave to watch the back in case Terry goes out a window, Neal and Boone go into the courtyard, walk around the pool and ring the bell on Sandra's ground-floor unit.

It takes her two minutes to come to the door, and Neal wonders if she's used the time to rouse Terry. Which would be fine, because in that case he's on his way out the bathroom window and into the waiting arms of Boone's guys, who looked as if they're entirely capable of handling a fugitive.

Sandra's dressed, though, in a sweatshirt and jeans, and doesn't look sleepy. She's pretty, a spray of freckles across an aquiline nose and strong, dark eyebrows. She has a cup of coffee in her left hand and tries to look and sound surprised at someone being at her door at this hour. "Yes?"

"Ms. Sartini," Neal says, "is Terry Maddux inside?"

"Who?"

"Let's not play this," Neal says. "Last night you drove Terry Maddux to a heroin dealer's apartment so he could score."

"I don't know what you're talking about," she says.

"Can we come in?" Neal asks.

"No," she says. "Now, get out of here or I'll call the police."

"Yeah, do that," Neal says. "We can all talk about you harboring a fugitive. And if Terry's in there and he's holding, you'll lose your nurse's license. Or you can just let us come in, we'll take a quick look, and if he's not here, we'll be out of your hair. And we won't see anything that's not Terry."

She steps aide and lets them in.

It's a small one-bedroom. A bar divides the narrow kitchen from the living room. The bedroom door is open.

"Can we go in?" Boone asks.

Sandra shrugs. "You're here."

Neal edges to the side of the door, and Boone stands a few feet behind because Terry's other play would be to wait until Neal steps through the door, smash into him and try to run over him and out the front door.

But Neal doesn't think that Boone is going to let anyone run over him, and they've already agreed that Neal would do most of the talking and Boone would handle the physical stuff, if it came to that.

Neal hopes it doesn't.

He's never liked the physical stuff.

"Terry, if you're in there, just come out," Neal says. "I mean, let's not do this, it's freakin' demeaning."

No answer.

Neal steps into the bedroom.

Terry's not there.

Not in the bed or under it, not in the small closet.

He's not in the bathroom either, not in the shower.

Coming back into the bedroom, Neal sees that the window is closed and locked, but Sandra could have done that after Terry went out. If that were the case, though, Tide would have called already.

Neal goes back into the living room.

"Happy now?" Sandra asks. She's sitting on the couch.

"There's nothing happy about any of this," Neal says. "When did you last see him? When you got scared and drove out of the parking lot up in Carlsbad? Or did he call you to pick him up and take him someplace?"

"I don't have to answer any of your questions," she says.

Neal sits down next to her and says, "Please tell me you haven't taken drugs from the hospital for him."

"I wouldn't do something like that."

"But he asked you to," Neal says.

Sandra shrugs. Of course he did, he's a junkie.

"Did Terry do that to you?" Neal asks.

"Do what?" she asks, reflectively touching her neck.

"Those bruises under your hair," Neal says. "When you told him no, he lost his shit and choked you. Then he got all sorry, begged forgiveness and said if you loved him, the least you could do was give him a ride to his dealer's. He promised it would be his last fix before he turned himself in and got clean."

"How did you know?" she asked.

"My mother was a junkie," Neal says. "I've known junkies my whole life. The more interesting question, Sandra, is what you do now."

"What do you mean?"

"Well, you have choices," Neal says. "You can keep your mouth shut and let him stay out there until he overdoses, or you can tell me where you dropped him so maybe we can find him alive instead of cold and dead with a needle in his arm."

Neal doesn't say another word while she thinks it over. He just looks at her.

It takes a minute, but then she says, "I dropped him off at the Longboard."

Neal looks at Boone, who says, "It's a surf bar in Pacific Beach."

"Why did he want to go there?"

"He said a friend owned it."

"Brad Schaeffer," Boone says. " 'Shafe.' He and Terry go back."

Neal hands Sandra one of Duke's personal cards. "If Terry gets hold of you, will you call this number?"

She says, "I love him."

"It's a bitch, isn't it?" Neal asks, standing up. "If you ever have a problem, Duke Kasmajian owes you a solid."

Then he hands her another card. "This is a police lieutenant named

Lubesnick. He's in a different unit, but he'll get you to the right person so you can file charges for assault."

"I won't do that."

"He beat up another woman," Neal says. "He choked you. Does someone have to die before one of you does the right thing? Think about that, huh?"

In the courtyard Boone says, "You were really good in there."

"I read a lot of books," Neal says.

They drive over to the Longboard, just a block and a half inland from the beach on Thomas Avenue.

Your basic surfer hangout—beer by the pitcher, shots, nachos, tacos, wings, a decent burger. Lately Shafe has reluctantly given in and taken on the craft-beer craze. Boone has been to the Longboard maybe a thousand times.

It's closed now, at seven-thirty in the morning, no signs of life at all.

"Tell me about Shafe and Terry," Neal says.

"Early on, they rode a lot of big waves together," Boone says. "Todos Santos, Cortes Bank, Mavericks. Terry made a career of it, traveled the world with industry sponsorships, made all the magazine covers, the videos. Shafe didn't."

"Why was that?"

"No one is as talented as Terry was," Boone says. "And Shafe is a California guy. Wanted to stay close to his bar business and his local breaks. And he was a devoted father. He had four sons and didn't want to miss their surf tournaments and Little League games. So Terry went on to be a star, Shafe stayed here as a local legend."

"Is he bitter?"

"Not about that."

"About what?" Neal asks.

"His oldest son, Travis," Boone says, "died of a heroin overdose three years ago. Shafe never got over it."

"Who would?" Neal asks.

Boone went to the funeral.

It was brutal.

"With that background," Neal says, "why would Maddux think that Schaeffer would put him up?"

Boone tells him the story—back at Mavericks, years ago, Shafe took a head-first wipeout off a thirty-foot face. Shafe was out of it, dazed, disoriented, tumbling in the cold black water, unable to figure out which end was up or climb his leash to the surface. And the wave was speeding him toward a sunken reef where the impact would kill him if he didn't drown first.

Terry drove his Jet Ski right into the impact zone. With the wave looming above him like a heavy blade poised to crush him, he rode in and scooped Shafe up as the wave crashed over them. Then Terry reappeared, riding out of the tube with Shafe on the sled behind him.

An absolutely classic, epic Terry Maddux move.

"So Schaeffer thinks he owes Maddux his life," Neal says.

"He doesn't *think* it," Boone says. "He does."

"Where does Schaeffer live?" Neal asks.

"Over on Cass," Boone says. "But I don't think Terry is there. Ellen—Shafe's wife—banned him from the house. She didn't want a drug user around her kids."

"Ouch."

"Yup."

"So either Terry's in the bar," Neal says. "Or . . . would Schaeffer drive him to Mexico?"

"In a heartbeat."

Neal sighs. "If Maddux got money from the jewelry theft, he's gone. We lost him."

They sit outside the bar anyway, just in case Terry is still in there and pops his head out.

But if Boone knows Terry, he's already on a beach in Rosarita, sipping on a margarita and grinning about what assholes we are.

Terry always comes out the other side of the tube.

Duke gets a phone call.

Sam Kassem owns one of the largest jewelry stores in San Diego, and now he says, "Those pieces you red-flagged. A guy came in this morning trying to sell them. My clerk told him to hold on, went into the back room and called the police. When he came back, the guy was gone."

"What did the police say?"

"Nothing they can do, because the items haven't been reported stolen."

"Was it Terry Maddux?" Duke asks.

"I don't know who that is," Kassem says. "We got him on the surveillance camera, though."

"Hey, Sam, thanks, huh?" Duke says. "I owe you."

"You don't owe me anything."

Duke looks at the video that Kassem sends. It shows a white male around six-one, in his late forties or early fifties, closely cropped black hair, wearing a black denim shirt and jeans.

It's not Terry.

But it's still good news, because it means that Maddux hasn't turned the merch into the cash he needs to get far away.

Duke sends the vid-clip to Boone's phone.

Because it's a winter morning, Boone can find a parking spot in the small lot on Neptune Place at the bluffs above Windansea Beach.

It's an iconic place, one of those rare locales with a pedigree both in literature and in surf lore. Tom Wolfe made it famous in his book, *The Pump House Gang*, but long before he did, the old-school guys made it known as a center of surfing in San Diego.

The old pump house is long gone, many of the old-schoolers have passed, but the reputation remains.

Terry Maddux surfed here.

Some of his old friends still do.

Only the hard-core are out today.

It's cold, the wind out of the northwest, with a large swell building. The ocean is a dark, slate gray, just a shade darker than the cloudy sky. The surfers who are out are in heavy winter wet suits with booties, some wearing hoods.

Others don't go at all. Some of the old-timers are content to watch the youngbloods and just stand around and talk story. It's axiomatic that the older you are, the colder the water gets. Old men remember summers, not winters.

Boone doesn't get a board out of the van.

He pulls his hood up over his head and walks down the dirt path to the beach, where, as he expected, a gaggle of old-timers are standing around. Some are geared up and have boards, as if they're about to go in. Others haven't bothered with the pretense.

Boone gets a gruff but friendly greeting.

He's from the next generation down, but he has a good rep, so they show him some respect. Everyone on this coast knows that Boone Daniels can flat-out surf, he's made his bones, so they don't give him the hard time they can give to a stranger.

One of them who has a rep for giving newbies a hard time is Brad Schaeffer.

Shafe is old-school. His black hair, shorn close to his head, has a lot of silver in it now, but the man is muscled, like taut rope, and tattooed. If you're looking for a sheriff at Windansea, Schaeffer is your guy. He keeps the interlopers away and the locals in line.

He's not going out today, but Boone is damn sure he'll be going out tomorrow.

When it's bigger.

"You shouldn't be doing what you're doing," Shafe says. "Selling out a brother for money."

"He's jamming Duke for three hundred thou," Boone says.

Duke has bailed Schafe out more than once. When Shafe drinks, he can get aggro. Hell, when Shafe *doesn't* drink, he can get aggro. He's gotten into fights in his own bar, he's gotten into fights just a few feet from where they're standing, when he thought a newcomer was overstepping his bounds. You don't want to fight with Brad Schaeffer, Boone knows. It usually doesn't end well.

Shafe says, "Duke can take the hit."

"Do you know where Terry is?" Boone asks.

"No," Shafe says. "And if I did, I sure as shit wouldn't tell you."

They stand quietly for a few seconds, and Boone can feel Shafe seething. Then Boone says, "Shafe, there's video of you trying to lay off shit that Terry stole."

"Maybe he didn't steal it, maybe it was a gift."

"If you thought that was true," Boone says, "you wouldn't have bugged out of the store. Your good friend Terry is putting you in the way of a felony beef. He'll leave you in the soup to save his own ass."

"He pulled me *out* of the soup." Shafe's eyes go dark. "So get the fuck out of here before you get your*self* in a jam."

Boone doesn't answer, but he doesn't move, either. If you back away from Shafe, you only provoke a charge. But now Shafe's buddies, loyal members of his crew, start to slide over, standing at the edge of the conversation, ready to jump in if Shafe needs them.

So they all can hear, Shafe says loudly, "Terry is a good guy."

Boone asks, "Do you know that he beats women?"

Maybe you do know, Boone thinks. Maybe you know and don't care.

Maybe they all know.

It pisses him off.

"You're hiding him in your bar," Boone says. "Did you score for him, too?"

"You're pushing it, Daniels."

"You of all people know what heroin is," Boone says. "Give him up, maybe he can get the help he needs."

"In prison?" Shafe asks.

"He'll be alive anyway."

He regrets it the second he says it, because he didn't mean it the way it came out, like a reference to Shafe's son.

Shafe swings, a big looping right at Boone's jaw. Boone easily blocks it, but the left lands hard into his stomach. The next right hits him in the left shoulder and numbs his arm so he's late blocking the same right fist crashing into the side of his face. Boone reels back and tries to stay upright, but Shafe sweeps his right ankle and Boone goes down.

They're on him like a pack.

Kicking, stomping, cursing.

Boone brings his forearms up to cover his head and kicks up with both legs to keep them at bay, but he can't cover 360 degrees, so he's taking some damage. He tries to get to his feet, but kicks drive him back down, and then Shafe, standing over him, lurches down with a right punch with the intent to cave his face in. Boone turns his head, and the fist lands in the sand beside his face. Boone grabs the arm and pulls Shafe close to him so he can't get leverage for a heavy punch and so he can be used as a shield, but kicks still come into his ribs under Shafe.

Then it stops, and Boone feels the weight coming off him and looks up to see Tide lifting Shafe like a derrick and Dave standing there with his hands out in front of him as though he's asking if any of them want to go.

None of them do.

They back away.

Dave helps Boone to his feet. "You okay?"

"Better now."

Shafe looks at Boone with sheer hatred. "I didn't buy him dope."

"Tell him to turn himself in," Boone says.

Dave helps him back up to the parking lot.

Adriana presses a washcloth filled with ice cubes up to Boone's swollen cheek.

Boone feels like . . . well, like he had the shit beaten out of him. It could have been worse, a lot worse, if Dave and Tide hadn't come along. Neal Carey, who was watching the Longboard until they came to relieve him, told them where Boone had gone, and they thought they'd better get up there in case he'd gotten himself into trouble.

Carey had stayed by the bar.

"Yeah?" Dave had asked. "You'll be okay?"

"I have a book," Carey said.

They left him in Dave's car parked across the street from the bar.

Now Duke looks at Boone's face and says, "They did a real number on you."

"I sort of had it coming," Boone says. "I said something I shouldn't have."

"I'll call the police," Adriana says. "You should press charges."

Boone tells her not to.

"It might put some pressure on Schaeffer," Adriana says, "to give Terry up."

"If he's not going to do it for fencing stolen property, he won't do it for this," Duke says. "Anyway, Boone's not going to violate some weird surfer code of honor."

"No, Boone isn't," Boone says.

"So now what?" Dave asks.

"Call the police," Adriana says again. "Have them get a warrant, go into the Longboard and get him."

"*I* want to get him," Duke says. He takes a cold cigar from his shirt pocket and chomps on it. "I don't like having one of my people beaten up."

"I'm okay," Boone says.

"That's your opinion," Duke says. "You're going to the E-Room, get yourself checked out."

"No, I'm not."

"You are if you want to get paid," Duke says. He looks at Dave. "Can you drive him over there?"

"Sure thing."

They all stand there.

"Like maybe *now*?" Duke asks.

San Diego, he thinks.

A city where virtually no one honks a horn.

On his way out, Boone asks, "What are you going to do about Maddux?"

"Find him," Duke says.

Terry Maddux is in that bar, he thinks. Forty years in this business, I can *feel* it. He's in there, he's jonesing and getting more and more desperate. The train station, the bus depot and the airport are blocked. The San Diego surf community is tight, and the word of Boone's stomping will get out. A few people will approve of it, but most won't, because Boone Daniels is loved here. So a lot of doors that might have been open to Terry will be closed in his face.

Terry is trapped, and he knows it.

And now he also knows that we know where he is. The thing now is to keep putting pressure on him so he feels forced to run.

And when he does, I'll be there to put the cuffs on him.

A good way to go out.

Because now it's personal.

He clamps down on the cigar.

Neal Carey realizes that he's happy.

Perched on a rooftop from which he can see every exit from the Long-board, he realizes that he's perfectly content just watching, doing the basically nothing that is part and parcel of a stakeout, the tedium of which used to drive him batshit crazy.

But that was a long time ago.

Neal hasn't done this kind of work, in what, thirty years?

It isn't like he wants to go back to doing it again. He likes the classroom, likes teaching, especially likes doing the research for his scholarly books that nobody reads. Even Karen just pretends to read them, but he knows that she really skims so that she can come up with a few complimentary comments. No, he's happy with his career choices.

But now he has to admit to himself that this is kind of fun, that he's missed the excitement of the chase (What "chase"? he thinks. You're standing around a rooftop), the suspense, the adolescent thrill of the illicit.

The rooftop is just more fun than the faculty lounge.

The phone rings, and it's Duke. "You okay?"

"I'm great."

"You don't have to piss?" Duke asks.

"Amazingly, no."

"That girl you talked to," Duke says, "Sandra Sartini. She went in and pressed charges. So I guess you haven't lost your touch. Anyway, I'll get someone up there to relieve you."

"Take your time, I'm good."

"You're having fun, aren't you, Professor?" Duke asks.

"I am," Neal says.

"Like old times."

"A little."

"Yeah, well, enjoy," Duke says. "It isn't going to last forever."

Neal clicks off.

A pickup truck with a surfboard in the back pulls in to the narrow parking space behind the Longboard. A guy—in his fifties, Neal thinks—gets out of the driver's door, looks around, jams his hands into his pockets and walks into the bar.

Neal has seen the nervous look, the stiff walk a thousand times. He'd bet the advance on his next book, all two hundred bucks, that the guy is holding.

And that Terry Maddux is about to get well.

Duke throws a net around the Longboard.

He doesn't bother to disguise it—he wants Shafe and Maddux to know that they're out there, like Indians around the wagon train in those old movies. Duke, he's conspicuous in his Cadillac parked out in front on Bayard. Dave is in Boone's disreputable van out on Thomas, High Tide in his truck in the parking lot out back. Carey has steadfastly refused to leave his rooftop, only taking a quick break to use the bathroom and get more coffee.

Duke made Daniels stay home.

Two cracked ribs, severe contusions, and the doctor is a little worried about internal bleeding. Boone said he'd be fine with a couple of Tylenol and an ice pack, but Duke ordered him to stand down.

Now it's the waiting game.

They've been there all damn day and will be there all damn night if that's what it takes. Which it might, now that—if Carey is right—Shafe brought Terry his get-well fix. Duke's always simultaneously touched and saddened by what people will do for love or loyalty. Love and loyalty trump the law, personal morals, belief systems, sometimes personal well-being. I don't know, Duke thinks, maybe it's a good thing.

It's the best and worst of human nature, but he's seen a lot of both over the years.

He wonders if he'll miss it.

Anyway, it's a shame Shafe got Terry his fix, because it will only prolong the inevitable.

Duke knows that what his people have going for them is patience and discipline, qualities that are in short supply among chronic criminals, or they wouldn't be chronic criminals. Mooks like Maddux are restless by nature. They don't have the patience or discipline to wait something out. And Terry is as addicted to adrenaline as he is to heroin, so he'll force the action. They won't have to close the net around him, he'll swim into it.

On the other hand, Duke thinks as he turns on his car radio and tunes it to 88.3 FM, the jazz station, he has his own adrenaline junkies to handle. Boone's surfer buddies—Dave and Tide—like action themselves, and they're running hot right now, pissed off about their buddy getting beaten up and stomped.

Every hour or so, Duke has gotten a call from one or the other of them, saying basically, "Fuck it, let's go in and get him."

Even though they know this means a fight with Shafe and his crew, who've been drifting in all day long, too, against just such a confrontation. Duke worries that his guys don't want to go in despite this but because of it. They want payback for their boy. He gets it, but he can't allow it.

Patience and discipline.

He's pleased when the deejay puts on Nat King Cole's "Jam-bo," which he recorded with the Stan Kenton Orchestra. Maynard Ferguson and Shorty Rogers on trumpet, Bud Shank and Art Pepper on alto sax.

Capitol Records, 1950.

The sun is starting to set.

Duke wishes he were on his deck.

Boone lies on his couch and watches the sun sink behind the horizon.

Normally this time of day, he'd be out on his porch grilling fish for tacos, but he's too sore to do that.

So he just looks out the window.

And listens to music.

Dick Dale and the Dale Tones.

Boone would lie on the couch and watch television, except he doesn't own one.

He doesn't see any reason he should.

"What about the weather?" Hang Twelve, the neo-hippie, acid victim, soul-surfer member of the Dawn Patrol has asked him. "Don't you want to know what it is?"

"If I want to know what the weather is, I step outside," Boone said. "That's what the weather is."

"But don't you want to know what it's going to be?" Hang asked. "The . . . what do you call it, the forecast?"

"It's San Diego," Boone said.

The forecast is always the same, depending on the time of year. It rains a little in the winter, it's overcast in the spring, what the locals call "May Gray," followed by "June Gloom," and then it's sunny and warm the rest of the year. Sometimes the cloudy marine layer hangs in until about eleven in the morning, freaking out the tourists who've laid out big bucks for Sunny California, but it burns off and then everyone settles down and has a good time.

The television weather folks *do* do a surf report, but Boone gets a better one off the internet, and anyway, he lives on Crystal Pier, so if he wants to know what the waves are like, he does what he's doing now—he looks out the window.

Also, he can feel the surf, literally beneath him.

The big northern winter swell is coming in, full and heavy, pregnant with power. By morning it will be rolling under the pier like a freight train, and the surfers will be out in force. The Dawn Patrol will be there, of course.

But without you, he tells himself.

You're a weak unit who gets himself beaten up, and there's no way you can paddle into those waves with your stupid cracked ribs. Hell, right now you couldn't even lift your board without whimpering.

But Hang will be out there, and Johnny.

And Dave and Tide if this Maddux thing is taken care of tonight.

It will be, he thinks.

Terry is waiting for the sun to go down, waiting for darkness, maybe some rain to obscure vision, if he's really lucky a little fog.

Then he'll try to bust out.

But to where? Even if he makes it through Duke's net, which is doubtful, where is he going to go?

Wherever it is, he can't escape himself.

Boone's been surfing his whole life—literally before he was born, in his mother's belly—and the one thing he's learned is that there's no wave that takes you anywhere but back to who you are.

Terry Maddux sits in the storeroom of the Longboard with his back against cases of Jack Daniel's and his legs straight out in front of him.

The pleasant haze of his last fix is starting to wear off.

He doesn't know if it's night or day out there—there are no windows in the storeroom, just the bay of fluorescent lights on the ceiling—or really how long he's been in there.

Terry does know he can't be in there much longer.

For one thing, they'll be coming in to drag him out—either Duke Kasmaji-an's storm troopers or the cops. For another, he knows he's wearing out his welcome, even with Shafe, because Terry is an expert at wearing out his welcome.

For a third, he's going nuts.

Especially as the high declines.

He has to move.

He has to smell the ocean.

He has to get high again.

The door opens.

It's Shafe.

"How you doing?" Shafe asks.

Terry shrugs. "I could use another fix."

"I can't get you another one," Shafe says. "Duke's guys are all over me."

Terry waits for the other shoe to drop, Shafe telling him he has to get out of here. But Shafe doesn't say that. What he says is, "They're all around the block, they've been there all day."

Terry smiles. "I guess Duke wants his fucking money."

"You have friends," Shafe says. "They're not going to get past us."

Yes, they are, Terry thinks. If the cops come in, they are definitely going to get past a bunch of middle-aged surf dudes. And if Boone Daniels is working for Duke, that means his crew is, too—that guy Dave and the huge Samoan.

They wouldn't be easy to stop.

Terry wishes Shafe and his guys hadn't stomped Daniels.

Boone's a good guy, Terry thinks. He's done a lot for me. But he shouldn't have stuck his nose in this. A veteran like Daniels should have known that you have to stay off other people's waves.

"I have to get out of here," Terry says.

"You can stay as long as you want," Shafe says.

But Terry can hear the relief in his voice, knows that Shafe wants him out of here, too. Oh, Shafe would go to the wall, but he doesn't want to, and who can blame him, not wanting to get thrown in jail himself for "harboring a fugitive." Shit, if the cops found someone in the storeroom with a shooting kit, they could yank Shafe's liquor license.

No, there's no question it's time to go.

The question is how?

I'm trapped, he thinks.

Yeah, but you've been trapped before.

You were trapped yesterday along the tracks, and then that train came and you weren't trapped anymore.

You were trapped at Mavericks when you went in to get Shafe, but you found the seam in the wave and sped through it and you weren't trapped anymore.

Now you're trapped in this building with enemies all around you.

You have to find the chance and take it.

And if you can't find the chance, you have to make one.

There's almost always a way out of a wave if you can hold your breath long enough to find it.

And if there isn't . . .

Well, you die.

Neal pulls the collar of his leather jacket up around his neck and jams his Yankees cap onto his head. It gets cold in San Diego on a winter's night, and it's damp, too, threatening to rain. A brisk wind is coming off the ocean.

He looks at his watch.

9:17.

He's been up here for over twelve hours.

It's not fun anymore. He remembers exactly why he doesn't do this kind of work, but he's not going to punk out on Duke now. Plus, he's getting stubborn, pissed off at this Maddux guy, and wants to see it through.

He sure as hell doesn't want to admit that he's too old for this.

Duke doesn't mind. He calls Neal and says exactly that. "We're getting too old for this shit."

"Speak for yourself," Neal says.

"This is when you separate the boys from the men," Duke says. "The boys stay, the men go home."

"You want to call it a night?" Neal asks, somewhat hopefully.

"Hell no," Duke says. Then, "You?"

"Hell no."

They both laugh.

"What would Lou say if he saw us out here?" Duke asks.

"He'd say we're assholes," Neal says. "And he'd be right."

"Maddux is coming out soon," Duke says. "I can feel it."

Neal thinks he's right.

Because he can feel it, too.

They call it "climbing the leash."

If you're buried under a wave, sometimes you literally don't know which way is up, so you grab the leash and pull yourself toward the buoyant surfboard, which has usually bounced up to the surface.

Most often it works, unless the leash has snapped, in which case you're fucked.

Now Terry climbs.

Not the leash, because unfortunately he's not in the water, but an air shaft. He presses the palms of his hands and the soles of his feet against the metal sides as he pushes his way up. It's grueling, and it would have been a lot easier if he were younger and not strung out, but Terry is pretty sure he can make it up the shaft to the roof.

It's his only choice anyway.

The assholes are expecting him to come out the front or the back door and make a run for it. They'll be looking for him to come out, not up, and if he can make it to the roof of the Longboard, he can jump to the next building and then the next and be outside Duke's fucking net before he comes down.

Disappear into the tube and come out the other side.

He's running out of breath, though.

His arm and leg muscles burning.

Getting old is a bitch, he thinks.

But it beats the alternative.

He stops, takes two deep breaths, and starts to climb again.

Neal sees him come out of the air shaft.

Calls Duke. "He's on the roof."

"What?! You sure it's him?"

"If it's not, it's a hell of a coincidence," Neal says. He watches Maddux hunch over, catching his breath.

"Well, he still has to come down," Duke says.

True enough, Neal thinks. But what is Maddux thinking? He knows they have the building covered. Is he hoping to come down the fire escape and slip off?

Uhhh, apparently not.

Because Maddux straightens up, pulls himself to his full height and then sprints toward Neal, right off the roof of the Longboard.

Terry has gone face-first off longboards before, and from a lot higher than two stories, but at least now there's not a wall of water about to come down on him either. All he has to do is clear a few feet of air and land on the next roof.

Then catch his breath, get his legs under him again, and do it one more time.

He feels free in the air.

Live, die, what-the-fuck-ever.

It feels good, like old times.

Peahi, Teahupoo, Tombstones—he rode them all.

He lands and rolls.

Comes up to see a guy about ten feet away, in a black leather jacket and a Yankees cap, looking at him.

Neal was always a shitty fighter.

Even back in the day, when he was doing this for a living, Neal Carey was renowned for his lack of boxing skills as well as his unabashed lack of interest in acquiring any. He had mostly ascribed to the theory that if you couldn't talk your way out of a problem, you had probably already screwed up and, as a backup, to the fighting philosophy taught to him by his mentor, the one-armed leprechaun Joe Graham: "As soon as you can, pick up something hard and heavy and hit the guy with it."

Unfortunately, there's nothing hard and heavy at hand, the potential for an obscene joke notwithstanding.

He says into the phone, "He's on the roof with me."

"What?"

"What do you want, subtitles?"

"Back off him, Neal," Duke says. "Let him do what he's going to do."

"He's going to get away, Duke," Neal says.

"Then let him get away," Duke says.

His chest feels tight.

His teeth bite through the cigar, and it falls to the car floor.

Duke doesn't want another friend getting hurt, and now his friend is up on a roof with this junkie mutt, and who knows what could happen? Getting out of the car, he speed-dials Dave and tells him, "He's on the roof next door. Go up the fire escape."

"You got it."

Duke eases his bulk out of the car.

He'd go up the fire escape himself, except he knows his knees won't.

All he can do is wait and hope that Neal doesn't get stupid.

"Nobody has to get hurt here," Neal says, putting his hands out in front of him.

"*You* do," Terry says, "if you don't get the fuck out of my way."

"See, I can't do that."

"Why not?"

It's a good question, Neal thinks. For which he has no rational answer. Actually, the rational answer is that he can absolutely do that, he absolutely should wave his arm like a maître d' who's just been tipped a century and let Terry Maddux do whatever he wants to do.

You're sixty-five years old, he tells himself.

On the other hand . . .

Rationality has its limits. You also have to consider, as Boswell might have put it—

"I don't have a lot of time here," Terry says. "Are you going to get out of my way or am I going to have to beat the shit out of you?"

"I guess you're going to have to beat the shit out of me." He drops his head and charges. Smacks into Maddux's midsection, and Maddux, surprised, falls onto his back.

He's no more surprised than Neal, who tries to put all his weight, or lack thereof, centered on Maddux's chest with the aim of keeping him down. He's not trying to win the battle, just fight a holding action until the cavalry arrives.

He's seen a few rodeos with Karen. The idea is you stay on the bull for eight seconds and then other cowboys ride in and haul you off.

Maddux has a different idea.

He gets his arms free, pounds Neal in the back of the head, loops one foot around Neal's ankle, bucks and rolls over, pinning Neal under him. Holding Neal down with his left forearm, he slams two rights to his face, then pushes from his feet like he's getting up on a board.

Neal sees Maddux run for the edge of the roof. For reasons that he can't articulate, he gets to his feet and runs after him.

Duke looks up and sees Terry Maddux flying in the air above him.

Then he sees Neal Carey flying in the air above him.

And what he thinks is, What'll I tell Karen?

Neal lands hard.

He's just grateful he landed at all, on the roof and not in the alley two floors below. Because, you know, what would he tell Karen?

Maddux is standing there, hunched over. He sees Neal and says, "Fuck. *Really?*"

Apparently, Neal thinks. He heads toward him to catch another beating, but this time Maddux turns and runs for the fire escape. Neal takes two big steps and then dives, grabs Maddux by the pant leg with his right hand and holds on.

Maddux drags him and kicks back like a mule, trying to shake him off.

Neal's phone rings.

Seriously, Duke. *Seriously.*

Maddux's next kick shakes off Neal's hand and lands square in his face. Neal reaches out with his left hand and grabs Terry's other leg as Maddux reaches the top of the fire escape and turns to climb down.

Maddux's ankle twists. "God*damn* it!"

He grabs the railing, kicks the hand off and heads down.

Duke is going crazy. "Where is he?"

Dave stands on the roof and looks around. "I don't see either of them."

Duke feels like he did when they first got Marie's diagnosis.

Scared.

Terry hobbles down Reed Avenue toward the beach.

His ankle hurts like crazy, a high sprain. He can barely put any weight on it.

Crossing Mission, he turns his head and sees that the crazy motherfucker is behind him, talking on the phone.

Neal wipes the blood off his face with his wrist as he talks into the phone. "He's headed west on Reed, crossing Mission. . . . I'm maybe twenty feet behind. . . ."

"Let him go," Duke says.

"Fuck that," Neal says. He follows Maddux across Mission. He hadn't realized that it's started raining.

The pavement glistens silver under the streetlights.

Across Mission, Maddux turns and stops.

"I didn't want to do this," he says, reaching into his jacket. "I didn't want to do this, but you made me."

He points the pistol at Neal.

And pulls the trigger.

Neal sees the muzzle flash a violent, angry red.

He feels as if someone smacked him in the chest with a baseball bat.

Then he's lying on his back on the sidewalk, looking up at the light as the rain hits him in the face.

It's cold.

Terry limps on the sand.

But it's good to be on the beach, at the ocean.

It's where he needs to be.

He knows where he's going now, what he needs to do.

The doorbell rings.

"One second!" Boone yells from the couch. He gets up slowly—his ribs angry at the effort—and walks toward the door.

It's probably Dave, or Tide, or even Duke here to tell him that they got Maddux.

He opens the door.

It's Terry.

Dave gets there first, which is a very good thing because as a lifeguard he's also a certified EMT.

Kneeling beside Carey, he sees the entrance wound in the front of his jacket, gently rolls him and doesn't see an exit wound. He checks Neal's pulse at the carotid artery. It's weak, going out, and the man is unconscious.

Then Tide is standing over him, calling 911.

Dave starts to give CPR.

Terry sits down in the chair and holds the gun on Boone. "I need one last favor."

"I'm not driving you to Mexico," Boone says.

"Didn't ask you to," Terry says.

"Then what do you want?"

Terry looks like shit. He's soaked, he was limping, and his hand is shaking, whether from cold or from withdrawal, Boone can't tell.

"I just killed someone," Terry says.

Boone feels a jolt of alarm. Was it Dave? Tide? Duke? "Who? Who did you kill?"

"I don't know," Terry says. "Some guy. Salt-and-pepper hair. A goatee. Yankees fan. What difference does it make?"

Sounds like Carey, Boone thinks, ashamed he feels relief.

"I mean, how did it get to that?" Terry asks. "All I ever wanted was to ride the biggest waves, you know? How did I get from that to killing someone?"

Boone hears a siren scream down Mission.

"I was your hero once, wasn't I?" Terry asks.

"Yeah."

"But not anymore."

"No," Boone says.

"No," Terry says. "Now *I* wish I was *you*. I mean, look at me. I'm a junkie, I can barely walk, I don't have a nickel to my name, and I'm trapped. They're right behind me, Boone. I'm not getting out of this wave, and I'm going to spend the rest of my pathetic life in prison."

"You want me to feel sorry for you, Terry?" Boone asks. "Because I don't. How many people have to get hurt for you?"

"Here's what I want," Terry says. "I want to borrow one of your boards one last time."

"You going to *paddle* to Mexico, Terry?"

"No," Terry says. "I'm just going to paddle out."

"Jesus, Terry."

"It won't jam you up," Terry says. "I had a gun, I forced you to give me a board. Do this for me, Daniels."

"You took a person's life," Boone says. "An innocent, good person. You should stand trial, you should be punished."

"Noble Boone Daniels on his white horse," Terry says. "I had a trial on the beach, I found myself guilty. Now I want to execute the sentence. Give me the board or I'll shoot you in the fucking face. You got a longboard in your quiver? It's heavy out there."

"A nine-three Balty."

"That'll do."

"It's my favorite board."

"It'll drift back."

Neal hobbles over to the far wall, unzips the cover and wrestles the board out. "Here you go."

Terry gets up. "Thanks, huh?"

"Hey, Terry?" Boone says. "If I hear about someone who looks like you hanging out around Todos—or anywhere—I'll come kill you myself."

"That's fair, I guess," Terry says. "You don't have a drink around here, do you? Some scotch or bourbon or something, warm me up a little?"

"I don't know," Boone says. "Look in the cabinet over the sink. There might be something."

Terry finds a pint of Crown Royal someone must have left from a party. He pours three fingers into a glass and jacks it down. "God, that feels good."

He sets the glass down, walks over, picks up the board, tucks it under his arm and nods for Boone to open the door. Terry walks out past him onto the pier, balances the board on the railing, looks out and says, "I was good, though, wasn't I? I mean, in my day. I was the best, right?"

Boone doesn't answer.

"Yeah, all right," Terry says. "I get it. You're mad at me. It's okay."

He tips the board over, and Boone sees it crash into the water and bob up. It's a beautiful board, and he loves it.

Terry climbs up on the railing, turns, gives Boone the shaka sign, grins and says, "Surf on, dude."

Then he jumps, swims to the board and climbs on.

Boone watches him paddle out over the swell, beyond the pier lights, into the dark.

A jogger running with his dog finds Terry's body on Windansea Beach four days later.

Boone's board never makes it back.

Karen Carey is neither a willing nor a gracious nursemaid.

That their bedroom is on the second floor doesn't help her mood as she goes up and down with the meals, drinks, books, articles—whatever her foolish, childish (she rejects the alternative description of "charmingly boyish"), idiotic husband needs during his recuperation from getting shot in the chest.

Or "getting himself shot in the chest," as she prefers to phrase it.

Neal has admitted that his wife's reaction is "totally justified," which touched off an extended debate at Thursday-Night Poker, which had been moved from the dining room to what Karen refers to as his "deathbed."

"I don't think," Lou said, "that you can use a modifier with 'justified.' Either something is justified or it isn't."

"There are no degrees of justification?" Duke asked.

"It's an absolute," Lou said. "You can weigh the pros and cons on justification, but once the decision is made, it's simply justified or it isn't."

"I wasn't using 'totally' as a modifier," Neal said, "but as an enhancer to emphasize the correctness of her justification."

"An enhancer is a modifier," Lou said, sticking to his rhetorical guns to keep the fun going.

"Deal the damn cards," Karen said.

Now she sits down on the bed next to Neal, although not as gently as she has, because he's healing. Although it might someday serve as a good cocktail story, she's still not amused by the irony that it was a book that probably saved her professor-of-literature husband's life, that the dog-eared paperback of *Roderick Random* tucked into his jacket pocket had slowed the bullet that would otherwise have killed him.

"So," she says, "was that it as far as a midlife crisis, or can I expect hang-gliding, or mixed martial arts, or a Harley appearing in the driveway?"

"I could have had an affair," he jokes.

"Yeah, right," she laughs. Neal is as loyal as a golden retriever.

He says, a little sheepishly, "It was kind of fun."

"You're not thinking about going back to it."

"*Nooooo*, I'm good." He sets down his book, turns over and reaches for her.

"Yeah?" she asks.

"Unless you'd rather I get a Harley catalogue."

Outside, the sun is going down.

But it's not down yet, he thinks.

Boone flips the fish over on the grill and admires the light show going on over the ocean.

Reds, yellow, oranges, the narrowing sky a shade of blue that he can't name but can only wonder at.

The rain is over for another day or so, but the swell still surges under the pier.

He'll paddle out in the morning with the Dawn Patrol but without his favorite board. Terry Maddux took that from him, along with his last sense of hero worship, along with a piece of his soul. None of those things are coming back, not with the surge, not with the tide, not with the sunrise.

He slips a piece of the yellowtail into a tortilla and hands it to Dave.

It's a ritual, done more evenings than not, Boone cooking for his friends on the deck outside his cottage as they watch the sun go down.

Dave is there, and Tide, Johnny Banzai and Hang Twelve.

Sunny Day isn't.

She's off somewhere on the pro tour.

He misses her, they all do.

But she'll come back.

Boone feeds his friends and himself, then takes the last piece of fish, puts it in a tortilla, and tosses it over the railing into the sea.

"You think he's hungry?" Dave asks.

"Aren't we all?" Boone says.

They sit and eat and watch the sun set.

Chewing on his unlit cigar, Duke Kasmajian sits on his deck and looks out at the ocean.

He's done now, it's over.

Absent an unlikely rescue from the legislature, his business is dead. He took the money he saved from the Maddux bond and cut it up among his employees. Then he handed out cash bonuses. It won't last them forever, but it will hold them over until they find something else.

Adriana has a pension and says she's going to retire.

Duke wonders how long that will last.

The sunset tonight is nothing short of magnificent, the scotch tonight is particularly smoky and warm, the music—Harold Land's rich tenor sax playing "Time After Time" with the Curtis Counce Group—especially beautiful.

He wishes Marie were here, that's all.

No one who hasn't missed a beloved spouse will ever know the literal meaning of the word "heartache."

Getting cold, he stands up—his knees protest the effort—takes Marie's glass of red, and slowly pours it onto the bushes below.

It's sunset.

PARADISE

Being the Intermediate Adventures of Ben, Chon and O

. . .

Hawaii, 2008
  Fuck everyone.

. . .

Pretty much what O is thinking as she lies on the beach in Hanalei Bay.
  Fuck everyone, I'm on vacation.
  Vacation from *what* is a different question, because when she isn't on vacation, O does basically

Nothing.

  Twenty-three years old, unemployed, uneducated, she lives on an allowance from her South Orange County (read affluent) mother's money—
  —that would be "Paqu"
  (The Passive-Aggressive Queen of the Universe)—
  plus her share of the proceeds from the multimillion-dollar premium hydro cannabis business she helped start with her two lifelong friends and lovers Ben and Chon.
  ("Chon" being the then-five-year-old O's pronunciation of "John," which stuck.)

O (short for "Ophelia"—yes, her mother named her after a girl who drowned herself) is a petite creature.

Five-five in her bare feet—which she is, of course, on the beach—blond hair cut Peter Pan short (in Ben and Chon she has her own mini-set of the Lost Boys but positively refuses to play the boring, mother role of Wendy) and unbuxom (despite Paqu's attempts to "gift" her with breast implants), she is now contemplating getting a tattoo—a large one on her shoulder—maybe of a dolphin.

Not everyone is going to like it, she thinks.

They don't have to, she thinks.

Only I do.

Fuck everyone.

• • •

Ben picked Hanalei for a vacation because he wants to do business here.

He got the idea from Peter, Paul and Mary.

(His parents were hippies.)

Ben explained this to O back in Laguna.

"Peter, Paul and Mary," he repeated to her uncomprehending expression.

"Jesus's parents," O said.

"Yeah, not really," Ben said, unsurprised that O would think that Jesus had multiple fathers. "Peter, Paul and Mary were a sixties folk-singing group."

Chon grunted. He has always taken sort of a John Belushi/Bluto attitude toward folk music. (*Animal House.* If you haven't seen it . . . well, I don't know what to say.)

Ben went on his computer and pulled up a song.

"We used this to interrogate Taliban," Chon said, then sang a few bars from "Puff the Magic Dragon." He served numerous tours in Afghanistan and Iraq, came home wounded and discharged. "They gave it all up after the first verse."

"Be quiet," O said, totally into the song. She cried when Puff died. "He no longer went to play along the cherry lane?"

"I'm afraid not," Ben said.

"Because Jackie came no more?"

"There you go."

"But Little Jackie Paper *loved* that rascal Puff," O said. "He bought him strings and sealing wax and other fancy stuff."

"The living will envy the dead," said Chon. "So why are we listening to this shit?"

"It's in code," Ben said. "The song is about weed."

"How so?" Chon asked.

" 'Puff the Magic Dragon'?" asked Ben. He paused for effect, then said, "Puff the magic drag in."

He replayed the song.

"So a sixties song is about drugs," Chon said. "You find that unique somehow?"

"I find it interesting," Ben said. "Right now we create all our product in grow houses. It's expensive, and I worry about the ecological impact of all the electricity and water we use."

"So . . ."

" 'A land called Honahlee,' " Ben said. "I did some research. Hanalei, Hawaii, gets forty-three inches of rain a year. Average temperature is from seventy-seven to eighty-four Fahrenheit. Between six and eight hours of sunlight a day, UV index between seven and twelve. Rich ferrous soil."

"Sativa," Chon says.

"Bingo," says Ben. "Plus, we don't currently market much in Hawaii. We could kill two birds with one stone. Find a marketing partner and acquire land for a grow operation. When the shit becomes legal—as it will—we'll be in place."

"*Three* birds," O said.

"What's the third bird?" Ben asked.

"Vacation," said O.

• • •

Standing on a cliff at the northern edge of Hanalei Bay, surfboard in hand, Chon watches the best surfer he's ever seen.

Chon has always thought of himself as pretty good on a wave, but now he realizes that he's not.

Compared to this kid.

The waves at the break known as Lone Pine are big and autumnal heavy, and this guy is carving them like Michelangelo on crack. He cuts back into an off-the-lip top turn and tail-slides back down, then does a Superman, flipping into the air and grabbing the board with both hands, then back down into a closeout reentry.

"Jesus Christ," Chon says.

"Close," says a guy who comes up behind him. He's Hawaiian, brown-skinned and big, his long black hair tied up into a man-bun. "That's Kit."

"Who?"

"Kit *Karsen*," the guy says, as if it's obvious. "K2."

Like the mountain, Chon thinks.

Which fits.

It's hard to judge from a distance, but Karsen looks like he goes about six-four, with wide shoulders, a narrow waist, lean and muscled from endless hours in the ocean, long hair bleached by the sun. He'd be Tarzan, Chon thinks, if Tarzan were younger, better-looking and a stronger swimmer.

And he looks like a teenager.

Which means, Cho thinks, he isn't even the surfer he's going to be.

Jesus Christ.

"I take it he's a local," Chon says.

"Everyone here is a local, brah," the guy says. "Except you. You shouldn't be here."

"I'm just watching."

As far as Chon can see, most of the surfers in the lineup look Hawaiian. Karsen might be the only *haole*. He watches Karsen paddle into another wave, cut a line down the face and then bottom-turn and slide back up.

"Don't watch too long, brah," the guy says, hefting his board and stepping to the edge of the rock. "It's not a healthy place for a *malihini*."

"What's a *malihini*?" Chon asks.

"A stranger," the guy says. He tosses his board off the cliff and then jumps in behind it.

For a second, Chon thinks the guy just committed suicide, but then he sees him pop up, grab his board and paddle out.

Chon decides to come back another time.

Chon being Chon, he *has* to jump off that cliff.

• • •

Kauai is a small island, Hanalei a smaller town.

Within a couple of hours of meeting the *haole* on the cliff, Gabe Akuna finds out that his name is Chon, that he's renting a house in Hanalei with two friends from California—a guy named Ben and a woman named O, whatever the fuck that is. He makes a call to some associates in LA and learns that Chon, Ben and O are major marijuana dealers.

And that they sell weed to Tim Karsen.

Tim has dealt small amounts of weed in Kauai for years and the Company has tolerated it because Tim is a local, Kauai is a backwater, his business is small scale, and he's KK's dad.

But things are changing.

The Company is getting more aggressive on taking back control of all drug sales in the islands—all the islands and all the drugs—weed, ice, coke and smack.

There's too much money to allow leakage.

KK's dad or not, Tim has to come into the fold or go out of business.

Then there are these new *haoles*.

It's a problem.

Are they looking to increase their marijuana business with Tim? Start a wider distribution with more product?

That would be bad.

Worse would be if they're thinking of starting their own grow operation here.

That just can't happen.

The Company is buying up real estate, too, and Kauai isn't known as the Garden Isle for nothing. Sugar, pineapples, rice and taro used to be the main cash crops, but marijuana is next. And whether it becomes legal or not, the Company is going to be in place to harvest that green.

Not some *malihinis* from the mainland.

Californication? Gabe thinks.

Fuck that.

The Company is not into Californication.

• • •

Organized crime in Hawaii used to be strictly an Asian affair.

First the Chinese triads, later the Japanese *yakuza*.

But in the late sixties, Wilford Pulawa, a native Hawaiian, decided to take things local and recruited a bunch of local boys to do it.

Gambling, prostitution, unions, the usual mob stuff—the Company had it locked down.

Pulawa went to prison back in '73, his successors fell to fighting among themselves, and the Company had lost a lot of its power by the early nineties. Some people say it's gone altogether, others say it's making a comeback fueled by the ice epidemic.

Then there's this:

A few years past, the mainland mafia sent a couple of hit men from Las Vegas to muscle in on the Company's turf. The story goes that the Company chopped the two wiseguys into pieces and FedExed them back to Vegas with a note that read "Delicious, send more."

· · ·

When he gets back to the house, Chon wants to tell Ben that he's just seen the future of surfing, but Ben has other things on his mind.

"We have business to do," Ben says.

"I guess I'll go to the beach," O says. Paternalism, sexism or just looking out for her safety (choose one or all of the above), the "boys" rarely include her in the details of the business. She spoons a little poke onto a slice of Spam and sticks it in her mouth.

Not half bad.

She decides to call it "Spamoke."

The boys get into their rented Jeep and drive north out of Hanalei on the Kuhio Highway, a two-lane blacktop that hugs the coast. Chon at the wheel, they drive past the spot where he watched KK do his magic, then up past Lumahai Beach to Wainiha, where they take a dirt road inland a couple of hundred yards through thick rain forest.

The road dead-ends in a clearing.

A house that could be best described as ramshackle sits to the left. Single-story, it stretches out along the edge of the forest like a series of train cars, as if each section had been an afterthought. On the right side of the clearing is another building that looks like a workshop. Racks of surfboards are set out in front, the open garage door revealing more boards inside. A small boat and a Jet Ski sit to the left of the workshop, beside a rack of solar panels.

At the end of the cul-de-sac is an enormous banyan tree, and in the tree is . . . well . . .

A tree house.

Under construction.

Not a tree house like a kid would build but a tree *home*, with floors on several levels, carefully and beautifully built, the planks honed and sanded.

Chickens run around the driveway.

The place is isolated, so all you can see is the thick vegetation and a single palm tree that sits in the small, well-tended lawn.

A man steps out of the house.

He looks to be in his mid-fifties, thick, long black hair with a few streaks of silver, slicked back from his head. A small Z-shaped scar over his right eyebrow. Hawaiian floral shirt and baggy board trunks over sandals. A pair of wraparound shades completes the look.

He's smiling broadly. Tips up the shades and says, "Aloha!"

They get out of the Jeep.

The guy stretches out his hand. "I'm Tim."

"I'm Ben. This is Chon."

"Nice to finally meet in person," Tim says.

They've only previously talked on satphones or exchanged encrypted emails.

Tim Karsen is their distributor in Kauai.

They connected in the usual way—friends of friends of friends, but this is the first time they've met face-to-face.

"I'm digging the tree house," Ben says.

Tim smiles. "My son. He's building his own home."

"Very cool," says Ben.

"Come on in," Tim says.

They follow him through the front door, which leads directly into the kitchen. Given the improvised look on the outside, the interior of the house is a surprise—spacious, well ordered, tidy. The floors are polished wood planks, the walls wood paneling with Hawaiian art.

A woman stands at a butcher block, mixing a salad.

"This is Elizabeth," Tim says.

She's beautiful.

Long auburn hair, deep brown eyes, slim in a denim shirt over jeans.

And that voice, Chon thinks. Low, soft, pure sex, even when she says something totally mundane like, "I made a salad for lunch. I hope that's okay."

Chon's thinking that she could have made dog shit on a shingle and that would have been okay, too.

They sit down at a long table in the dining room, which has been set with pitchers of iced tea and guava juice, although Tim comes out of the kitchen with three bottles of ice-cold beer.

"Captain Cook IPA," Tim says. "It's local."

"Local means a lot here, doesn't it?" Chon says.

Tim nods. "We've been here for twelve years, and we're still sort of *malihini*."

"People here are actually very friendly," Elizabeth says. "As long as you respect the local culture."

"Which is basically don't be an asshole," Tim says.

"Words to live by," Chon says.

They clink bottles.

But the funny thing is . . .

Chon thinks he knows this guy.

He knows they've never met, but . . .

He knows Tim from somewhere.

And his name wasn't Tim.

• • •

Tim walks them up a narrow dirt road, more of a trail, through the thick forest.

It's started to gently rain, and the red dirt turns to red mud on their shoes as they climb up into the hills.

A creek runs on their right.

They've been walking for ten minutes when they come to a grass-covered clearing, about two acres, surrounded by thick vegetation.

"Here's where I was thinking," Tim says.

"It's for sale?" Ben asks.

"I already bought it," Tim says. "But yeah, we could work something out."

"Is that on record?" Ben asks.

"I only *look* dumb," Tim says. "I ran the purchase through five shell corps. It can never be traced."

"Perfect location," Ben says, looking around. "Private . . . We'd need to do a soils test."

"Sure," Tim says. "But everything grows here. You could stick a Chrysler in the ground here and it would grow little Chryslers. The real issue will be keeping the jungle cut back."

"It has potential," Ben says. "Could we clear more land if we needed it?"

"I bought fifteen acres," Tim says.

"Can you supply labor?" Ben asks.

Tim nods.

"That we can trust?" asks Chon.

"These people are *ohana*," Tim says.

Chon asks, "What does that mean?"

"Family," Tim says.

Like, subject closed.

They walk back to the house in the rain.

When they get there, Chon sees Kit Karsen lift his board onto a rack in the workshop.

Kit looks back, sees Tim and grins.

"Hey, Dad!"

• • •

Chon's father is a genuine son of a bitch.

One of the founding members of the Association, the largest dope ring in California history, he wasn't very present in Chon's life, and when he was, it wasn't exactly positive.

For example, some of his business associates once took young Chon hostage until John paid them the money he owed.

One of the few times Chon felt actually valued.

Chon always knew that his old man was in the business, but Ben and O had only recently found out that they, too, were *second*-generation dope slingers and not the pioneers they thought they were.

Ah, the beautiful, ignorant arrogance (and arrogant ignorance) of youth— to think they were the first.

But Paqu and Ben's psychotherapist parents were major investors—on the board of directors, as it were—of the Association, and O's real bio-dad was not the man that she thought but instead was the (recently) late Doc Halliday, who had once made Orange County the epicenter of the American marijuana, hashish and cocaine business.

Proving, yet again, that:

A. We don't know our origins.
B. Nothing is new under the sun.
C. Dope has been around forever.
D. All of the above.

Now Chon and his old man have a relationship based on an agreement that the less they see of each other, the better.

But Kit clearly loves Tim.

Just as clearly as Tim loves Kit.

Chon can see it as they embrace each other, as if it's been years, not hours, since they've seen each other.

It makes Chon a little sad.

"Meet Ben and Chon," Tim says. "This is our son, Kit."

"Aloha," Kit says, nodding to them both.

"Ben and Chon are from California," Tim says. "Laguna Beach."

Kit says, "I'd like to go there sometime."

"Anytime," Ben says. "You always have a place to stay."

"Be careful, I might take you up on it," Kit says.

Elizabeth comes out and smiles at her son. "Malia called from town. Your water pump came in."

"Excellent," Kit says.

It's a family, Chon thinks.

He's never really seen one before.

But who are these people?

Really.

· · ·

Gabe is very aggra that the *haoles* are sitting down with Tim Karsen and that he showed them the land he bought.

It doesn't bode well, so he makes a phone call.

· · ·

Red Eddie's hair is more orange than red, and his real name is actually Julius, but no one is going to call the Company boss Orange Julius.

Educated at Harvard and Wharton Business School, Eddie is a Hawaiian-Japanese-Chinese-Portuguese-Anglo entrepreneur with offices in Honolulu, the North Shore and San Diego. Now he's in Honolulu, and he's not happy about what he's hearing over the phone.

A trio of California *haoles* starting a plantation in Kauai?

Hells no.

"Tell them to leave," he says.

"What if they don't want to go?" Gabe asks.

"Did you seriously just ask me that?"

He clicks off and takes a Tylenol.

Running the Company can be a headache sometimes.

· · ·

Ben is totally into the tree house.

This is Ben's kind of thing, right up his alley, so to speak—anything, green alternative, off the grid, crunchy granola—that's for Ben.

(There's no arguing with DNA.)

"Kit and I are building it," Tim says. "For him to live in."

Ben asks to see it.

"Let me show you the plans," Kit says, enormously pleased. They go into the workshop, and Kit unfolds the plans on a table. "I want to live as close as I can to nature."

"I guess you can't get any closer than living in a tree," Ben says.

Soul mates, Chon thinks.

The plans call for a three-level structure, connected by ladders and catwalks. The lower level will be the kitchen, its walls curtains that can be pulled up or lowered, a wood-burning oven and stove, an antique sink with water pumped up from the creek.

A catwalk, railed with coconut wood, will switchback up to the next level, a sitting room with broad plank floors of koa wood and real walls made of monkeywood, with big windows that will look out onto the forest. Another series of catwalks and a ladder lead up to the next level, a bedroom with more plank flooring, walls of mango wood and a thatched roof with a skylight. An attached bathroom ("En suite," Kit jokes) with a gravity toilet and a shower serviced by a Lister bag hung from a higher limb that collects rainwater.

Kit is proud that all the wood is local, from trees that have naturally fallen or had to be taken down for safety reasons. This means that they've had to wait literally years for certain pieces of wood, but they want it right. They've bought the raw wood and lovingly sawed, planed and hand-sanded it themselves. They're also building the cabinetry from *kamani* wood, the shelves and a big table for the kitchen area made from ironwood.

"It's all solar-powered," Kit says.

"Do you get enough sunlight?" Ben asks.

"Enough to battery store," Kit says. "And when there isn't enough power, we have kerosene lamps. And it's not like we have a lot to power."

No television, for instance.

"I like books," Kit says.

No excess lighting.

"I go to bed early," he says. "Get up with the sun."

Kit takes Ben for a tour.

The first level is almost finished. The floors are down, the stove and oven in, the heavy natural bamboo curtains attached and rolled up now.

They go up the catwalk to the next level, a twelve-by-fourteen room with polished floors and beautiful red wooden walls with large windows. Two of the walls are done, the other two only framed out. On the north wall is a stained-glass window bearing the image of a Hawaiian woman walking into the ocean with her surfboard.

"Did you do this?" Ben asks.

"Malia," Kit says. "My girlfriend."

"This is amazing, Kit," Ben says. He feels like he's in an apartment, not a tree house, and yet the leaves brush against the windows and the place is suffused in birdsong.

It's all been done with so much care, so much love.

They climb up to what will be the bedroom and stand on the framing, because the floors aren't down yet.

"I know my dad does business with you," Kit says. "And I know what it is."

"Are you okay with that?" Ben asks.

"I'm protective of my parents, you know?"

"I respect that."

"And I have ethical issues," Kit says.

"I respect that, too."

"As long as it's just herb, I'm good with it," Kit says. "But if it evolves into coke, ice, heroin—"

"It won't," Ben says. "We're on the same page."

They shake hands.

Kit's not even trying to exert force, but Ben's hand feels like it's been crushed.

It would be a good idea not to mess with Kit.

• • •

On the drive home, Chon says, "I know that guy."

"Tim?" Ben asks. "Not possible. He hasn't left the island in twelve years, and you've never been here before."

"I know, but I know him."

"Chononoia."

Chon will cheerfully admit to being paranoid—multiple tours with special ops in Afghanistan and Iraq, it's a predicate to survival—but he doesn't think he's being paranoid now.

Because now he remembers where he knows Tim from, why he looks so familiar.

It's the Z-shaped scar.

An old business partner of his dad's. Chon hasn't seen him in . . . well, at least twelve years—but Tim is a dead ringer for Bobby Zacharias.

The legendary Bobby Z.

Bobby Z was a legendary surfer, one of the best on the West Coast. Chon remembers being a kid and looking up to him. And Z was one of the biggest marijuana dealers in California.

Then he disappeared.

About twelve years ago.

Just fell off the face of the earth.

Landed, Chon thinks, in paradise.

And back in the dope business.

It all makes sense.

Chon remembers something else about Bobby Z.

He was an asshole.

"People change," Ben says when Chon fills him in.

"No they don't," says Chon.

● ● ●

O rejects the idea (the observation, the imputation, the accusation) that she's a hedonist.

"I'm not a hedonist," she told Ben and Chon one day. "I'm a *she*donist."

There's a difference.

● ● ●

O loves it here.

Hanalei Bay is the prettiest place she's ever seen. To her left rise emerald-green mountains, to her right the golden beach stretches to an old pier by a river that runs down from the hills. The ocean (the Pacific, for the geographically challenged) in front of her is a cerulean (O likes that word, "cer*oo*lian") blue, and the whole scene is fringed with palm trees and populated with beautiful men and women.

Hawaiian men are impossibly gorgeous, and so are the women, thinks O, who is bi nature and inclination bi.

No stranger to beauty, she grew up (or failed to) in Laguna Beach, the prettiest town in California (no small claim) among the beautiful people, but Hanalei is on a different order of things altogether.

The scenery, the people, the food . . .

Add to those the happy fact that Paqu is several thousand miles and an ocean away back in Laguna, and this could be paradise.

It rains here at some point almost every day. O doesn't mind—in fact, she likes to walk in the ephemeral showers and then enjoys the warmth of the subsequent sunshine.

She loves the house they've rented, just across a small park from the beach, a beautiful two-bedroom bungalow that has a large living room with ceiling fans and a wraparound porch she's learned to call a "lanai."

O loves that she can have fresh fruit—papaya, guava, mango—for breakfast with strong Kona coffee, and she likes to walk the few blocks into town to have a plate lunch of white rice and macaroni salad with pulled chicken or Spam (more about which below).

They usually go out for dinner to one of the great local restaurants for some kind of fish, although for the last couple of nights Ben and Chon have cooked at home.

Both men are good in the kitchen.

O is not.

O can make:

A bowl of Cheerios
A bowl of Froot Loops
A cheese sandwich
Lasagna (Stouffer's, microwave)
A Hungry Man Fried Chicken Dinner (Swanson's, ditto)

But she does like to eat. When Paqu once observed that "Ophelia eats like a bird," Chon countered that the bird was a turkey vulture. The girl can pack it away like a pregnant horse but no one knows where it goes. The calories just seem to disappear like money in a Hollywood film budget. Nevertheless, her mother often complains that O is carrying somewhere between five to ten pounds of excess baggage on her hips or her thighs, imaginary fat that Paqu has had frozen off her own body.

"Giving yet more credence to the Ice Maiden image," O observed.

Paqu has a Goldilocks attitude toward O's dietary habits—her daughter eats either too little or too much, she's either too skinny or too fat, but never "just right," another reason O is happy she's put half the Pacific Ocean between them.

Because of the plate lunches, O has developed a taste for Spam.

"What is Spam?" she asked Ben one day.

"No one knows," Ben said.

"Even the people who make it?" O asked.

"Especially the people who make it."

O doesn't really care what gets into Spam, as long as Spam gets into her. She just loves the stuff. And poke—chopped-up little bits of raw fish in soy sauce, sesame oil and chili peppers.

Anyway, O loves Kauai.

She loves the culture created by a mélange of Hawaiian, Japanese, Chinese, Portuguese and Anglo traditions.

She finds the food, the weather, the people . . .

Warm and soft.

Something she's been looking for her whole life.

• • •

Once wooden, the pier is now made of concrete and stretches 340 feet out to a canopy at the end.

An old man stands there fishing.

He's handsome, O thinks. White hair and beard, a deep tan, an old ball cap pulled down above the kindest, gentlest eyes she's ever seen. She's too shy to approach him, but the man spots her and says, "Beautiful here, isn't it?"

"Yes, it is."

"They call me Pete," he says, extending his hand.

"I'm O."

"Short for . . . ? "

"Ophelia."

Pete smiles. "O is better."

"Yes, it is," O says. "Do you fish here every day?"

"No," Pete says. "Sometimes I fish at night. Depends on when they're running. Would you like to try?"

"I don't know how."

"I can teach you," Pete says.

She's used to a lot of old guys—some of them stepfathers—wanting to teach her something, except it wasn't fishing.

But this feels different, and she nods.

He hands her the rod and reel and stands behind her, showing her how to cast. And it isn't creepy, O thinks, not at all dirty-old-man sketchy, just a nice guy really teaching her something.

It's nice.

• • •

O tells Pete about her childhood.

The mother who was either absent or obsessively, suffocatingly present, the multiple stepfathers, growing up thinking that her father was someone else. . . .

"Sounds rough," Pete says, rebaiting his hook.

"It was."

"On the other hand," Pete says, straightening up and looking at her, "you weren't poor, were you? You had a roof over your head and food on the table. You had a lot of advantages. What did you do with them?"

Good question, O thinks.

Good fucking annoying question.

Nothing, she thinks as she walks back to the house. I've done absolutely nothing with my advantages.

But O rejects the idea that she's a nihilist.

"Actually," she said when Chon first brought up this notion, "I'm Cleopatra."

"That's a non sequitur," Chon said.

"Not at all," O said. "I'm the Queen of the Nihilists."

• • •

When Ben and Chon get back to the house, O's waiting with an announcement. "I'm joining Mother Teresa."

"Mother Teresa is dead," Chon says.

"Oh." She thinks about this for a second. "Okay, who *isn't* dead?"

"The people we're having dinner with tonight," Ben says. "We want your take on them."

"You want my take?" O asks.

"You're a good judge of people," Chon says.

Which would make me, she thinks, like, useful.

• • •

They meet at a restaurant called Postcards.

Tim Karsen or Bobby Zacharias or whoever the hell he is cleans up well in a white Henley shirt untucked over a clean pair of jeans.

Elizabeth, O decides, is simply stunning. A simple black blouse over (tight) black jeans.

And Malia . . .

Malia *is* Hawaii, O decides.

Tall and lithe, long black hair, shiny like a starlit night, caramel skin, large almond-shaped brown eyes, a voice as soft and low as a sunset.

Smart, funny.

And she stands up to Kit as if he isn't the most beautiful male specimen that O has ever seen.

I'm never leaving, O thinks.

Ever.

• • •

They came to Hanalei when he was about six years old, Kit tells them over dinner.

At first it was hard and he hated it, being the only *haole* kid in his school. The native boys beat him up practically every day, wouldn't play with him, made fun of him.

"What changed?" O asks, leaning over the table, drinking him in.

"Surfing," Kit says.

He went down to the beach one day, and the kids from his school were out surfing. Some had their own boards, most were sharing, taking turns. At first they ignored him, then told him to go away, but he stayed and stood on the beach until finally . . .

An older kid named Gabe walked over with his board and asked Kit if he'd like to try. He showed Kit how to lie down on the board, how to paddle, how to stand up. Then he walked him out into the water and helped him catch the small waves that were coming in.

On his third try, Kit stood up.

He was hooked.

He went down to the beach every day.

He got good.

The Hawaiian kids saw it, started to leave him alone, stopped teasing him, partly because they saw he could surf but also because Gabe threatened to beat the shit out of them.

Gabe started to come to the house. Sometimes he'd bring the other kids, mostly he'd come by himself.

Kit bugged his parents for a board.

He worked for his dad—Tim was cobbling together a living doing handyman and light construction work—doing odd jobs, cleaning up, anything to earn money for that board. It took a year, but one Christmas morning he got up and there it was, used but beautiful, a seven-foot-six-inch Hobie single-fin.

"I still have it," Kit says, smiling over at Tim and Elizabeth.

He became a sensation, one of those wunderkinds who got written up in *Surfer*, got sponsorships from Billabong, appeared in videos. But he never entered any of the competitions or tournaments.

"Surfing's never been about that for me," Kit says. "I've never seen it as a competition or a business. It's just something I love doing, and I never wanted to ruin it."

He got a reputation anyway.

Magazine editors, photographers and just plain surf fans would come from all over the world to watch Kit surf. But Kit wouldn't go to them. He went to Maui to ride the big waves at Jaws and to Tahiti to do the same, but he came right back to Kauai and stayed.

"It's my home," Kit says. "It's all I've ever wanted. I'm happy here."

He loved the island, and it loved him back.

Kit was no longer a mainlander, a *haole*, but a local, part of the *ohana*, a brother.

He's dating a Hawaiian girl, in fact, Malia is the only girl he's ever dated.

So he stays in Hanalei, doing carpentry or working with his dad, occasionally doing a surf video, getting honorariums from the surf companies for wearing their clothes or riding their boards, or posing for an ad, endorsing a wet suit, a board, a pair of shades.

He was fifteen when he made the cover of *Surfer*.

But he isn't just a surfer—he's a waterman— a swimmer, a diver, a lifeguard, as skilled on a Jet Ski, a canoe, a boat as he is on a board.

Kit Karsen is about as happy as a person can be.

"You came here when you were six," Chon says. "Where were you before that?"

California, Elizabeth answers.

We came here from California.

• • •

Ben and Tim walk outside the restaurant.

"So are we going to do this?" Tim asks.

"I don't know."

"What's your hesitation?"

"I can't do business with someone who isn't honest with me," Ben says.

"What am I being dishonest about?"

"Well," Ben says, "let's start with who you are, Bobby."

"You think I'm Bobby Z," Tim says.

"Aren't you?" Ben asks.

"No," Tim says. "I mean, I was for a while."

"What the hell are you talking about?" Ben asks. "Can we stop playing games here?"

"My real name is Tim Kearney," Tim says.

He tells Ben a story.

• • •

O has always lived by the saying that "ignorance is bliss."

This makes her, in her own judgment, one of the most willfully blissful people on the planet.

Of course, she doesn't know the origin of the quote.

That would be counterproductive.

(Thomas Gray, "Ode on a Distant Prospect of Eton College," if you must know.)

"Do you know my friend Pete?" O asks, sitting at the table savoring a dessert of mango sorbet.

"Pete the Bait Guy?" Kit asks. "Sure."

"Everyone knows Pete," Malia says.

"What's his story?" O asks.

Elizabeth shrugs. "He came here about a year ago. Then stayed. Mostly fishes, sells bait to tourists. It happens a lot. People come to visit, fall in love with it, and never leave."

I get it, O thinks.

• • •

Tim Kearney (Tim uses the third person, like he's talking about someone else) was a three-time loser, a B&E artist whose greatest skill was getting caught. Even a stint in the marines didn't change his ways, and he went from Kuwait into the joint.

His only salvation was that he bore a remarkable physical resemblance to a major marijuana trafficker named Bobby Zacharias.

A Mexican cartel was holding a DEA agent hostage and was willing to swap him for Bobby Z. Problem was that Z had died of a heart attack in the shower—at least that's what the DEA told Tim.

They gave him Z's trademark scar and took him to the border to make the switch.

Which is where things went sick and wrong.

Seemed that the cartel didn't want to rescue Bobby Z, they wanted to kill him. So the hostage transfer was actually an ambush. But Tim got out and ended up in a desert hideout, where he met Elizabeth, who was looking after Z's little boy.

"Kit," Ben says.

Tim nods and smiles. "Best thing that ever happened to me. Turns out that the Mexicans wanted to kill Z for knocking up Kit's mom. I went on the run, took Kit and Elizabeth with me and ended up here. Been happy for twelve years."

"And the Mexicans gave up looking for Bobby?"

"All the players are dead now."

"Does Kit know you're not his real father?"

"Kit knows that I *am* his real father," Tim says. "He knows Bobby Z was the sperm donor."

"He really loves you," Ben says.

"I really love him," says Tim. "So now what?"

"I need to talk it over with Chon and O."

• • •

Which he does, on the way back to the house.

"What do you think of them?" Ben asks.

"I can't decide," O says, "which one I want to sleep with more. Tim is like a handsome teddy bear, Elizabeth is the sexiest woman I've ever seen, Malia is exquisite, and Kit . . . Kit is a young Greek god."

Ben tells them Tim's story.

"Do you believe him?" Chon asks.

"Who could make up something like that?" Ben asks.

"So the real Bobby Z is dead," Chon says.

Ben shrugs. "Legends die. So what do you think?"

"I think we should do business with them," O says. "I think we should do business with them and live here forever."

"You can't fuck any of them," Ben says.

"And Mother Teresa is dead." O sighs.

"So are we going to do this thing?" Ben asks.

"We're going to do this thing," Chon says.

It's all good.

• • •

Chon stands at the edge of the cliff—

(No, it's not symbolism. He's standing at the edge of the goddamn cliff, all right? How else is he going to jump in? Jesus Christ.)

—and tosses his board in.

Then he jumps in after it.

Look, Chon isn't the world's best surfer, he's not Kit Karsen Zacharias Kearney, but he's a former Navy SEAL (I'm aware that this has become a hoary cliché, and also aware that "hoary cliché" is an example of itself, but that's what he is), so he knows his way around cliffs and water.

He got out there early, just at dawn, so as not to interfere with the locals, and now he's out there alone as he sinks into a swirling current, fights his way up through it, grabs the board and attaches the leash to his ankle. Then he paddles out into the break. It's not as big as it was yesterday, but it's still big, Hawaii big, and he has to work hard to catch a wave.

But when he does, it's

Awesome

An overused word, Chon knows, worn to the point of meaninglessness, but if anything can inspire genuine awe, it's a big wave on the North Shore of Kauai. If you can't be awed by that, you have no heart and no soul.

He doesn't try any tricks—no top turns, tail-slides or Supermans, just tries to stay on his board on the ride in, which is fast and bumpy, and then he bails out before the wave takes him into the rocks.

He gets four good rides, about all he can take, and then paddles over to the beach on the other side of the rocky point, and that's where the trouble starts.

Actually, the trouble is waiting for him.

• • •

Pete bends down, reaches into his tackle box and comes out with something wrapped in tinfoil.

"You ever had one of these?" he asks O, opening the tinfoil.

"What is it?" O asks.

"A fried egg in an onion bagel," Pete says. "Have a taste. If you haven't had one of these, you haven't lived."

O has a taste.

Decides that she hasn't lived.

• • •

There are six of them, and they're waiting for him to wade in.

It's *Saving Private Ryan* on a beach in Kauai.

The leader, the one who walks up to Chon as he comes out of the water, is the Hawaiian who talked to him the other day. He wears black board trunks, a white T-shirt with the legend DEFEND HAWAII in black, and a black ball cap with the numbers 808—Hawaii's area code—reversed in white.

The other five, all big mokes, come up behind him.

"Hello," Chon says.

"You live here?" the leader asks. "If you don't live here, don't surf here. You *haoles* come over from the mainland, think you own everything. This is *our* break."

"Got it," Chon says. "I'm leaving."

He goes to step around the leader, but the guy moves into his way. "You know who we are?"

"No."

"We're the Palala," the leader says. "You know what that means?"

"No."

"The Brotherhood," he says. "We're brothers. I'm Gabe Akuna."

Chon guesses that's supposed to mean something, but he can't keep the smirk off his face. "Okay."

"You think that's funny?" Gabe asks. "You won't be laughing in a minute, kook."

"I'm not looking for any trouble." Chon goes to move around him again.

"But you found some," Gabe says, blocking him again.

They say that what you don't know can't hurt you.

(Ignorance being bliss.)

They're wrong.

(O notwithstanding.)

By way of example, Gabe doesn't know that Chon has an innate violent streak.

Doesn't know that Chon is a highly trained fighter.
Doesn't know that Chon has used that training to hurt and kill numerous people.
Doesn't know that Chon actually likes to fight.
Doesn't know that Chon isn't used to letting himself be pushed around.
Doesn't know that Chon has a temper.
Doesn't know that Chon is about to lose that temper.

What you don't know can hurt you.

Badly.

"You're in my way," Chon says.

"Move me," Gabe says.

"Is this me and you?" Chon asks. "Or me and you and all your boys?"

Now Gabe smirks. "You call the wolf, you get the pack."

Chon nods.

Before Gabe can move (or blink), Chon grabs him by the front of the shirt, lifts him and throws him into two guys behind him. Then he pivots and hits the fourth guy three overhand rights to the face.

Another moke comes up from behind, wraps his arms around Chon and lifts. Chon hooks his left leg around the guy's left leg, then brings his right foot up hard into his scrotum.

The guy lets go.

Another guy charges, shooting for Chon's legs to take him down. Chon plants his legs in the sand, digs his thumbs into the guy's eyes, forces his neck back and hammer-fists him to the ground.

He turns around just fast enough to see another guy coming at him. Chon steps to the side and plants a front kick into his groin, turns again to forearm a charging guy in the bridge of the nose.

Two of the Palala are on their knees in the sand, grabbing their packages. Two more are flat out, unconscious. Another is on his back, holding his shattered nose.

You call the pack, you get the (lone) wolf.

Which is why Gabe walks to his truck and comes back with a gun.

• • •

O never really had a father.

She had one, of course—even Paqu couldn't pull off a second Virgin Birth, despite her doubtless best efforts—but O never knew him, never even knew who he really was until recently.

O had seven stepfathers that she did know, but she never really bothered to learn their names after the first one or two, so she just gave them numbers.

Sometime after Three, O presented her mother with a Hitachi Wand.

"What's this?" Paqu asked. "Some kind of vibrator?"

Yes, O thought, and Ferrari is some kind of car.

"Just make this Four," O said. "I'm begging you. It won't move a bunch of its personal shit into the house, it won't set a bunch of new rules, and it won't try to be my father. Best of all, when you're done with it, you can just turn it off. No lawyers, no court appearances, no conflicts over assets."

Paqu took neither the gift nor the advice.

She married Four, who was a real dildo, a born-again doofus in Indiana with whom she was going to open a Christian jewelry business. O thought they should have opened a *used* jewelry business so it could be "Born Again Jewelry." But apparently neither the business nor Four worked out, and Paqu moved back to Orange County, closer to her cosmetic surgeons.

Anyway, O never had that paternal figure until Pete.

Pete teaches her to fish.

Pete listens to her.

Pete gives her egg-and-onion-bagel sandwiches.

She falls deeply, daughterly in love with Pete.

• • •

Chon has his Chon up.

He sees the pistol in Gabe's hand and only thinks, Bring it, motherfucker. Get close enough to me with that gun and I'll take it from your hand, stick it down your throat and make you swallow whatever comes out.

But Gabe's too smart for that.

He keeps his distance.

Points the gun at Chon's chest.

Chon goes through a mental process.

People think it's easy to shoot someone with a pistol at close range. It's not—it's hard. Most shooters, even trained cops, usually miss with the first shot. That's part of Chon's calculation as he edges forward.

The next part of the equation is time versus distance—Chon's trying to calculate if he can be on top of Gabe before he can get the next shot off.

Because the second shot usually hits.

One thing he knows for sure:

Standing there waiting for Gabe to shoot isn't an option.

He's about to launch, when—

• • •

"Pau ana!"

Kit yelling "Stop!" in Hawaiian.

Gabe stops.

Lowers the gun and turns to look at Kit, standing at the edge of the beach.

"He aha ana la?" Kit asks him.

What's going on?

"This *haole* disrespected us," Gabe says. "He was trespassing on our break. We needed to teach him a lesson."

Kit scans the scene, sees some of the Palala trying to get up, others just stretched out asleep. "I'm not sure who did the teaching. It took six of you? To not get it done? And a fucking gun, Gabe. Is this who we are now? This is *pono*?"

Chon notes the "we."

"We'll get it done now," Gabe says.

"No you won't," Kit says. "He's with me."

"Say *what*, bruddah?!"

Chon sees the dynamic—Gabe is way pissed, but he's not going to go up against Kit.

Kit Karsen is the A-male here.

"It's *pau*," Kit says.

Over.

Chon picks up his board and walks past Gabe.

They get into Kit's truck and sit quietly for a minute as Kit drives back toward Hanalei. Then Kit says, "Yeah, maybe it's better if you don't surf there anymore."

· · ·

"Who are these guys?" Ben asks.

He and Tim are sitting on the lanai of his house. Chon leans against the railing.

"The Palala," Tim says. "A local gang. Started as surfers protecting their turf, now it's evolved into something else."

"What something else?" Ben asks.

"Word is they're dealing dope," Tim says.

Ben shrugs. Like, *we're* dealing dope.

"It's not just weed," Tim says. "It's ice, coke and heroin."

"Ice is killing the islands," Malia says, walking out from the house with Kit.

"And these are friends of yours?" Ben asks Kit.

"I grew up with them," Kit says. "Went to school with them, surfed with them. And yeah, I helped them patrol the beaches. Keep the *haoles* from trashing everything."

"Aren't *you* a *haole*?" Ben asks.

"By blood, yes," Kit says. "By *blood*, though, I'm Hawaiian. These guys are my brothers, my *ohana*. I'd trust them with my life—"

He points toward the ocean.

"Out there. If I got caught in the impact zone, who would come in to save me? You, Ben? Some tourists? Some real-estate developers? Gabe would. Gabe *has*."

"So that makes it all right for them to sell ice to your other brothers and sisters?" Malia asks.

"They've taken a wrong turn," Kit says. "I'll set them straight."

Tim's worried.

You set someone straight, you have to go on the crooked road yourself. Sometimes you get lost.

Besides, he's heard that Gabe is hooked up with the Company.

• • •

O savors another bagel egg sandwich.

"What did I tell you?" Pete asks.

"I'm hooked," O says. "I'm obsessed."

Pete bends down, reaches into his tackle box and comes out with a new lure. O says, "I've been thinking."

"Oh?"

"I never had the chance to grow up," O says.

"Or you had the chance," Pete says as he carefully fixes the lure to his line, "and you never took it."

Fuck you, Pete, O thinks. But she thinks about that for a minute, wipes a bagel crumb off her lip and says, "You're right. I guess I never *wanted* to grow up."

"Why is that, do you think?"

"I guess I wanted someone to raise me," O says. "When no one did, I just got mad and refused to raise myself."

Pete says, "You're a smart young lady, O."

"And what did I do with all this intelligence?" she asks. "I've wasted my life."

Pete's quiet for a long time. Just looks out at the ocean. Then he says, "So did I."

"I don't believe that," O says. "You're one of the nicest people I've ever met."

Now, Pete thinks.

• • •

Almost everyone who comes to an island, Pete thinks as he watches O walk back down the pier, comes as a refugee.

We don't so much arrive as we wash ashore.

I'm no different, he thinks.

I fled a life that was no longer livable, left behind a person I could no longer live with.

Myself.

Every refugee, by definition, needs a refuge.

The lucky find one.

I've been very lucky.

He hopes the same for this young lady.

• • •

Gabe's pissed.

Pissed that his back hurts from this *haole* tossing him like a Frisbee. Pissed that this same *haole* made them look like a bunch of clowns. More pissed that his *palala* K2 took the *haole*'s side.

What is *that* about? he wonders.

• • •

Ben sits on the lanai reading a Borges novel.

Chon scoffs. "Magic realism."

"What about it?" Ben asks, setting the open book on his lap.

"Which is it?" Chon asked. "You can't have both. It's either real or it's magic. Magic realism is an oxymoron."

Ben says, "It's a paradox."

"There is no such thing as magic realism," Chon says. "There is no magic in the real world."

"But there's no realism in the magical world," O says.

"This is the real world," Chon says.

"How do you know?" O asks.

She's got him there.

• • •

Kit is up in the tree house fitting floor planks when he hears a car engine, looks down and sees Gabe in his truck.

"Up here!" Kit yells.

A minute later, Gabe climbs the ladder. "I need to talk with you."

Kit pulls over two three-legged wooden stools and gestures for Gabe to sit down.

"What was that about yesterday, brah?" Gabe asks. "Why you take that *haole*'s side?"

"Six guys against one?" Kit asks.

"You call the wolf—"

"Yeah, I know," Kit says. "But that's not who we are. Guns aren't who we are."

"Who *we* are?" Gabe asks. "I'm starting to wonder who *you* are."

"What do you mean?"

"I thought you were a Hawaiian," Gabe says. "A *kanaka*. A *palala*."

"I am."

"Then why you helping these *haoles* move in?" Gabe asks.

"They're in business with my dad, not me."

"But you're protecting them," Gabe says. "That has to stop."

"Says who?"

"Come on, brah. You going to make me say it?"

Kit shakes his head. "I heard it, but I didn't want to believe it."

"What?"

"That you're hooked up with the Company," Kit says.

"The Company is for Hawaii."

"Then why are they selling poison to Hawaiians?" Kit asks.

"If they don't, the *haoles* will," Gabe says. "Better to keep the money home, no?"

"No," Kit says. "Better not to sell that shit. If the Palala wants to strap up and throw the ice slingers off the island, I'm on board. One hundred per. But hooking up with them? I'm not doing it. You shouldn't be either, Gabe."

"So we just let the *haoles* take everything?" Gabe asks. "They already stole our islands, now we let them cockroach our land, our beaches, our waves, our breaks, our businesses? That's what you want?"

"I want my dad left alone."

"No one wants to hurt your father," Gabe says. "We want to work with him. We'll let him distribute our weed on the island. We'll buy his land, provide capital or just market his product, if he wants. He can partner up with brothers, not strangers."

"He won't partner with ice slingers."

"Talk to him," Gabe says.

"I agree with him."

Gabe stands up. Finishes his beer and sets the bottle down. "You got to decide whose side you're on. You gotta decide who you are, a *haole* or a Hawaiian. So what you gonna do, K?"

"I'm going to work on my house and surf," Kit says. "What are *you* going to do, Gabe?"

Gabe doesn't answer.

Kit watches him go down the ladder and get into his truck.

I know who I am, Kit thinks.

. . .

I'm my father's son, Kit thinks.

Not "Bobby Z," the guy who abandoned me and my mother, but the guy who rescued me from all that, risked his life to keep me by his side, and brought me here.

To this place I love.

Tim is my real father.

Like Elizabeth is my mother.

He knows that his biological mother was the daughter of a Mexican drug lord. That she died of a heroin overdose after Z left her. That she had left him in Elizabeth's care when she went off on one of her last drug binges.

Kit barely remembers her.

He never met his bio-dad.

He was six when Tim showed up. A six-year-old kid living in a desert compound with a bunch of drug dealers and Elizabeth when Tim took him out of there. It would have been a lot easier, a lot safer, for Tim to have just left him like everyone else did—but Tim didn't do that.

It was Tim who took care of me.

Tim who first put me on a surfboard.

Tim who brought us here, built a life for us.

Did all the things a father does.

Like Elizabeth did all the things a mother does. Tucked me in at night, made breakfast in the morning, hugged me when I came home from school after the Hawaiian kids had beat me, sent me right back out there to make them my friends.

Who explained to me that "father" and "mother" are verbs before they're nouns.

I know who I am, Kit thinks.

• • •

The next morning in the lineup at Lone Tree.

Kit takes off on a wave, is coming down the face when Israel Kalana breaks in on his line and cuts him off.

Kit has to bail out.

Next wave same thing happens.

This time it's Palestine Kalana, Israel's twin brother.

Next time it's Kai Alexander, who jumps into the wave right in front of Kit, forcing him to pull up.

They're crowding him out.

After his fourth bailout, Kit paddles over to Gabe. "What the hell?"

"You made your choice," Gabe says. "You decided you wasn't one of us. So you ain't one of us. You don't belong here."

Kit looks around.

The others guys in the lineup, Israel, Palestine, Kai and the others—his brothers—can't look at him.

"So that's how it is," Kit says.

Gabe shrugs. That's how it is.

Kit paddles over the shoulder, turns and takes off on the second wave of the next set. Gabe comes in from his right to cut him off again.

Kit doesn't bail this time.

He drives down, cutting a straight line right at Gabe. Game of chicken on a fifteen-foot macker as Kit sets the point of his board right at Gabe's head. They collide at this speed, both of them are going to get hurt.

Gabe bails at the last second.

Kit's board grazes over him, the fin almost slicing his neck.

If there's going to be blood in the water, Kit thinks, it ain't going to be just mine.

Having made his point, Kit paddles in and puts his board in his truck. There are lots of other breaks on the North Shore—Tunnels, Kings and Queens, Dump Trucks, Cannons.

If they don't want him here, he doesn't want to be here.

It hurts him, though.

A lot.

• • •

O is walking up the pier to see Pete when a big Hawaiian man steps in her way.

"*Aloha, wahine,*" he says. "*Howz'it?*"

"I'm fine," O says.

"Oh, you're fine all right."

O moves to step around him. "Excuse me."

"I'm just trying to be friendly," he says, stepping in her way. "What, you don't like me? You don't like me, maybe you should leave. You and your friends. Maybe you should leave the island."

"Who are you?" O asks. "What do you want?"

"It can get dangerous here," the man says. "Big surf, big sharks . . . things can happen to a pretty young girl."

"Everything all right, O?"

It's Pete.

"What you want?" the man asks him.

"Leave the young lady alone."

The man laughs. "What are you going to do about it, old man? What are you going to do if I don't?"

"I said leave her alone."

There's something in Pete's eyes that O hasn't seen before.

It scares her.

The Hawaiian man laughs again. "It's all right, old man. It's cool. S'all good. You remember what I said, though, *wahine. A hui hou.*"

Till we meet again.

A promise and a threat.

• • •

Ben walks out of the Big Save market, a shopping bag in each hand.

A big Hawaiian guy bumps into him.

"Excuse me," Ben says.

"Watch where you're going," the guy says.

"Right," Ben says. "Sorry."

"What you say?"

"I said 'sorry.' "

"I boddah you?" the guy asks. "You like beef, boy?"

Ben doesn't know much Hawaiian slang, yet he's pretty sure this guy isn't talking about his groceries but is asking him if he wants to fight.

"I don't want any problem," Ben says.

"I been watching you," the guy says. "You know what I can't figure out?"

"What's that?"

"Which one you're fucking," the guy says. "The blond spinner or the other *mahu?*"

Fag.

"Nice talking with you," Ben says.

"Get off my island," the guy says. "You and your friends."

The shop owner comes out. "Is there a problem here?"

"No problem, Uncle. Just talking story with this *buggah*." He looks back at Ben. "You don't want to see me again, *haole*."

He turns and walks away.

"You know that guy?" Ben asks the owner.

"Palala," the owner says.

• • •

They come on to Chon with more caution.

They already know what he can do.

He's out running on Kuhio Highway, which despite the name is a narrow two-lane road that curves along the coast, sometimes narrowing further to one lane on the bridges that span the creeks.

It's raining.

Chon doesn't care.

He's enjoying the run and the cool rain. He feels lucky to be able to take a run in this spectacularly beautiful place.

Cars pass him slowly, trying to give him as much room as possible. Then he hears a motor approach and slow down. The Jeep doesn't go around him but stays behind him, gets closer and closer.

Chon keeps running.

The Jeep comes right up on him, nipping at his heels.

He hears laughter.

Then, *"Run, tough guy! Run!"*

Chon looks over his shoulder, sees four huge Palala guys in the Jeep.

He runs faster.

More laughter. *"You faster than a Jeep?"*

There's no place for him to get off the road. To his right, on the ocean side, is a steep cliff. He can't risk trying to cross the road and let the Jeep hit him.

Besides, he's pissed.

Chon is stubborn.

He keeps running.

The Jeep keeps coming.

Pushing up on him, pulling back, pushing up again.

A bridge is coming up.

It's one-way, the Jeep will have to stop if there are cars coming, and that's what Chon is hoping for. Sure enough, he sees a white pickup truck drive onto the bridge from the other direction.

He can sprint across and lose the pack.

But the pickup truck turns sideways on the bridge, blocking it.

Two other Palala get out.

With baseball bats.

The Jeep rushes up behind him and turns sideways, blocking any avenue of retreat. The Palala pile out, with bats, clubs, tire irons. *"Hey, tough guy! How tough are you now?"*

Not *that* tough, Chon thinks as they walk up on him from both sides.

I'm fucked.

He looks down at the river below. If it's too shallow he'll break his legs or, worse, his neck or his back.

But if the jump doesn't, these guys will.

He climbs onto the railing and jumps feetfirst.

Hoping that the water will be—

d

e

e

p.

• • •

Chon sinks, grateful for the fact.

He stretches into a diving position to stay under the water for as long as he can in case the mokes have guns.

The current rushes him toward the sea.

After a minute he lets himself come up for air, looks back up to see the mokes at the railing, pointing down and laughing.

The river pushes him into the crashing surf.

Maybe they figure I'll drown, Chon thinks.

Hell, maybe I will.

He lets the current pull him out past the break.

• • •

Ben's concerned.

"Have you seen Chon?" Ben asks O. If these guys fronted Chon, he wouldn't talk nice or try to defuse the situation. If the guys wanted to beef, Chon would go like prime rib. "I can't find him, he doesn't answer his phone."

"He'll be okay," O says. "I mean, he's *Chon*."

• • •

It's a long swim, all the way across Wainiha Bay and around Kolokolo Point, but Chon enjoys it.

Well, he enjoys it a lot more than having his legs broken with a tire iron.

It's not the distance that bothers him—he did a lot more in SEAL training on the cold water of Silver Strand—it's the thought of sharks that worries him.

(Shouldn't—it's the sharks who should be worried about Chon.)

He catches a wave off Lumahai Beach and body-surfs it to shore.

• • •

Tim and Elizabeth are sitting on their lanai having a sundowner drink when Gabe rolls up in his truck.

Gabe gets out. "Uncle Tim. Auntie Liz."

"Gabe," Tim says. "Kit's not here. He's out surfing."

Gabe already knows this. He wouldn't have come if Kit were here.

Tim knows this, too.

"I came to talk to *you*," Gabe says.

"What can I do for you?"

Gabe walks up to the lanai but not up on the porch. Leaning on the railing, he asks, "How long have you lived here, Uncle?"

"About twelve years," Tim says.

Gabe says, "My family has been here since before the *haoles* came."

"*Haoles* like us?" Elizabeth asks.

"I didn't used to think so," Gabe says. "Now . . ."

He lets it hang.

Elizabeth says, "You used to sit in the yard eating peanut-butter-and-banana sandwiches with our son."

"This is our home," Tim says.

"Then why are you selling out to strangers?" Gabe asks. "You could be in business with your own people."

"You mean the Company?" Tim says. "No thanks."

"I'm not *asking*, Uncle." He juts his chin back toward the trucks full of his guys.

"That's how it is?" Tim asks.

"It don't have to be," Gabe says.

"I'm afraid it does," Tim says.

"You need to leave," Gabe says. "I don't want to see you get hurt."

"Who's going to hurt us, Gabriel?" Elizabeth asks. "Are you?"

Gabe turns and gets back in the truck.

• • •

Kit strides down the main street of Hanalei.

Chon sees him from the lanai of Bubba's Burgers. He jumps down and walks beside him.

"You need some help?" Chon asks.

"No." Kit doesn't even look at him. Kit walks through the front door of the Blue Dolphin bar and sees Gabe sitting at a table drinking beer with the Palala. Edging through the crowd, he grabs Gabe, hefts him over his head like he weighs nothing, walks out and tosses him off the lanai. Then Kit vaults the railing, grabs Gabe by the front of the shirt, drags him to the river and pushes his head under the water.

Leaning down, Kit says, "You threatened my parents, Gabe?! You threatened my *mom and dad*?"

He lifts Gabe's head out of the water.

Gabe gasps for air.

Kit shoves his head back down.

Israel Kalana tries to pull Kit off. Kit straight-arms him, and Kalana staggers backward.

"Stay out of this!" Kit yells.

Kalana and the rest of the Palala back off.

Kit holds Gabe down until his legs start quaking, then pulls him back up, turns him around and lifts him till they're face-to-face. "You go near my parents again, I'll kill you. I'll break you to pieces with my hands."

He drops Gabe and looks at the pack.

"That goes for all of you," Kit says.

• • •

"We should pull out of this deal," Ben says back at the rental house. "People are going to get hurt. I'm not sure this market is worth it."

"That's not the point," Chon says. "If we let ourselves get chased from here, people will take runs at us *everywhere* we sell. We'll be out of business. We fight."

"That's always your solution."

"Like yours is always to run."

Ben asks O, "What do you think?"

"I think it's not up to us," O says. "It's up to Tim, Kit and Elizabeth. It's their home, we're just tourists."

"She's right," Ben says.

"She is right," says Chon.

I'm right? O thinks.

Huh.

• • •

They meet at the Dolphin.

Which is in itself an announcement. Within minutes everyone in town will know that not only are the Karsens not going to separate from their mainland friends, they're going to rub it in Gabe's nose—they're dining together in the same place where Kit turned the Palala leader into a pool toy.

"I should have told you about Gabe's possible connection to the Company," Tim says to start things off. "My bad."

"So what do you want to do?" Ben asks. "We understand if you want out of our deal. No hard feelings, no one will think any the less of you."

Tim Kearney was a lifelong loser.

He knows it.

Three B&Es, three convictions, three stretches in the joint. Killed a biker in his last stint (rather than join the Aryan Brotherhood) and would have been serving life without parole if he didn't happen to look like Bobby Z.

Yeah, Tim was losing at everything until life brought him Kit and Elizabeth, and it was taking care of them that made him something. Washed ashore here in Hanalei, worked as a laborer, a cook, a carpenter, dealt a little *pakalolo* and built a home.

A life.

A family.

Kit—his son—is a freaking legend.

Malia—his daughter-in-law-to-be is a wonder.

Life is good.

So why risk it, he thinks, by taking on the Company?

But here's the thing about Tim.

He doesn't respond well to threats.

Just ask the biker in the joint who told him to join the Aryan Brotherhood or else.

Tim chose else.

And you *can't* ask the biker, because he's dead.

So when Ben offers him an out on their deal, Tim is tempted to say . . .

No.

Hell no.

He's not going to let a punk like Gabe tell him how to live. And he sure as shit ain't going to let the Company tell him how to live. But he looks to the rest of his family. "What do you guys think?"

Kit defers to Malia.

Gabe is her cousin, and she's the only native-born Hawaiian at the table.

"I think," she says, "that you shouldn't be in the drug business at all. Certainly not with the Company and—no offense, Ben, Chon, O—with you either. We don't need to be rich, we need to be a family. And . . . we were going to wait to tell you, but . . . well, we're going to have a baby."

Oh.

• • •

"You're seventeen years old," Elizabeth says.

Babies having babies, she thinks.

"Yeah, we didn't plan this," Kit says. "I was careless. But I think we can handle it. I know we can handle it."

I *don't* know, Elizabeth thinks. Kit is physically a man, seventeen going on twenty-five, but he's still a kid, a *boy*. On the other hand, they tend to start families young in the islands, and . . . well, it's a done deal, isn't it?

So Elizabeth throws her arms around Malia. "Sweetheart."

Tim says to Ben, "There's your answer."

"I'm sorry if we've wasted your time," Kit says.

"No, we've had a great vacation," Ben says.

• • •

"Can you imagine," O asks as they walk home, "what that kid is going to look like?"

No answer.

"I mean, *gorgeous*," O says.

"You okay with this?" Ben asks Chon.

"Sure."

"You're worried about our reputation," Ben says.

Chon shrugs. "I guess we can take a hit."

"What about payback?" Ben asks.

"Not everything needs to be paid back," Chon says.

"I want to see your driver's license," Ben says. "Who are you and what did you do with Chon?"

"Maybe I've evolved."

"It's the Spam," O says.

• • •

Gabe takes a gas can from the back of the truck.

The other Wolfpack take more cans and they walk to the tree house.

Gabe didn't want to do this, but then he heard that Kit was rubbing his nose in the shit, going out to eat with the *haoles* at the Dolphin.

You forced me into this, he thinks as he climbs up the ladder.

You didn't give me a choice.

He unscrews the cap and pours the gas around the house.

• • •

Kit sees the flames.

A fire in the sky.

At first he doesn't know what he's seeing—it doesn't make any sense, as if someone lit a huge torch in a watchtower.

Then he gets it.

"NO!"

He guns the engine and races up the road. Jumps out of the truck while it's still rolling into the cul-de-sac, grabs a hose from the workhouse wall, turns on the spigot and runs toward the burning tree.

The top two levels of the treehouse are consumed in flames.

"Kit, there's nothing you can do!" Tim yells.

Kit doesn't listen. He pulls the hose toward the tree and sprays water.

It does nothing.

He drops the hose and starts to climb the ladder.

Tim pulls him back. "No, son! It's too late!"

Kit shrugs him off and climbs into the burning tree. To the first level. He throws down pieces of furniture, rips appliances from the walls, planks from the flooring, anything he can reach through the flames, anything he can free with his hands.

Tim climbs up after him.

Helps him tear out a sink, throw it to the ground.

A mirror from the wall.

The flames are getting worse, but Kit rushes up to the next level.

"We have to go!" Tim yells.

"NO!" Kit is trying to pry Malia's stained-glass window from the wall.

"Now!" Tim yells.

"I have to get this!"

Tim grabs the other side of the window, and together they rip it from the wall.

"Take this down!" Kit yells. "I'm going up!"

"Okay!" Tim puts the window under one arm and then kicks Kit from behind.

Kit falls off the platform, lands on his hands and feet, looks up to see Tim coming down the ladder and tries to go up again.

Tim grabs him and holds him. "You have a kid to think about now. You can rebuild."

Kit grabs the hose again and starts to spray.

It does nothing against the gas-fueled fire.

He finally gives up, drops the hose and watches his beloved home burn, crumble and topple to the ground.

Malia holds him. "It's all right, it's all right."

She's never seen him cry before.

• • •

The rain falls on ashes.

From which nothing will grow.

The stench alone sickens, the gas fumes linger, the acrid char stings the nose.

Standing in the rain with Ben and Chon, looking at the devastation, O can't help but feel that they brought this on these people.

Destruction to paradise.

• • •

The insurance guy arrives later that morning.

He gets out of his Jeep and walks up to Tim. "Jack Wade, Hawaii Fire and Life."

The Jeep has a longboard strapped on the top.

"I'm sorry about your loss," Wade says. As they walk over to the scene, he asks, "How did the fire start?"

Tim looks at Kit.

Kit shrugs. "We don't know."

Wade steps up to the charred tree trunk and says, "I'll run tests, but I can tell you right now it was deliberately set."

"Not by us," Tim says.

"I can smell the gasoline from here," Wade says.

"We didn't set it," Kit says.

"Do you know who did?" Wade asks.

No answer.

Wade does his inspection, taking several samples of the ash at different levels of the tree.

When he comes down, he goes up to Tim and says, "Look, you seem like nice people, and I don't want to jam you up, but this is the clearest case of arson I've ever seen. I have to do an investigation to determine if you set the fire. If you did, the loss isn't covered."

"So, bottom line, you're not paying," Elizabeth says.

"I'd like to," Wade says. "I want to. But I can't until the investigation is complete and I can determine that you didn't set the fire to collect insurance benefits."

"We're guilty until proven innocent," Tim says.

"Not at all," Wade says. "Unless I can show that you had motive, means and opportunity, we'll pay the claim. I hope that's the way this ends, I really do. If you can tell me whether there was anyone else who had a motive . . ."

Kit quickly says, "Not that I know of."

Wade leaves, telling them that he'll be in touch to schedule an EUO, an Examination Under Oath, and suggests they might want to retain a lawyer.

Tim looks at Kit.

"I'm not ratting Gabe out," Kit says. "He's still my brother."

"Your brother burned down your home," Tim says.

Ben says, "We'll pay the cost to rebuild."

"There's nothing to rebuild," Kit says. "The tree is too damaged to support anything. It'll probably die."

"I'm so sorry," O says.

"It's not your fault," Kit says.

O isn't sure he means it.

Tim says he has something to do.

• • •

Tim presses the blade to Gabe's throat.

Gabe never saw Tim, never heard him. Just got into his truck to go surf, and there's a knife against his windpipe.

He hears Tim Karsen say, "Give me one reason I shouldn't, Gabe."

"This isn't you, Uncle."

"You think I haven't killed anyone before?" Tim asks. "Think again. The only reason I don't cut your fucking throat is that I want my family to have a life. Tim and Malia are going to have a kid. Did you know that?"

"No."

"That was going to be their home," Tim says. "And you burned it down. The stupid thing is that you didn't even have to do it. We were going to come tell you we were getting out of the business. You broke my son's heart for nothing."

Tim eases the pressure on the knife.

"Go tell that to the Company," Tim says. "Tell them it's over. *Pau*. We're not going to look for revenge, we just want to get on with our lives."

He takes the knife from Gabe's throat.

"Too late," Gabe says.

• • •

"The Company wants it all now," Tim says when he comes back to the house. "They're demanding we sell them the land for their own grow operation."

"It's like I've always maintained," Chon says. "You take a step backward from someone, they push you two steps more. Because you let them think they can."

We have to change their thinking, Chon thinks.

• • •

Kit wants to go with him.

Chon declines.

"Why?" Kit asks. "I'm bigger, stronger and faster than you. And I know the territory a lot better than you do."

"All of that's true," Chon says. "You train to surf and swim. But this is what I do for a living. Every day I train to do exactly this thing."

"Kill people?" Kit asks.

"Or wound them or capture them," Chon says.

"So which?" Kit asks.

Chon shrugs. "Depends."

Kit says, "I'm coming with you, or I go out and do it on my own."

He's got him there.

• • •

Israel Kalana would have been all right if he didn't have to piss.

But he did have to piss, and he went outside to do it, because Palestine was hogging the one toilet, trying to end a bout of constipation.

Anyway, Israel is outside draining the weasel against a casuarina hedge when he gets thunked on the base of the skull. He wakes up in the back of Kit's pickup truck with his hands plastic-tied behind his back, his feet bound with rope, and a rag stuffed in his mouth.

Palestine's mistake is in going to look for what had happened to Israel. He walks out the lawn to the edge of the pavement and sees the cigarette glowing up the street to the left. That's the last thing he sees until he wakes up next to Israel, similarly bound and gagged, in the back of Kit's truck.

• • •

Kai wonders where everyone went.

He pulls his Glock 9 and steps outside.

Chon's gun is at his neck.

"I will literally blow your head off," Chon says.

Kai drops his gun.

Chon says, "Take me to your leader."

He's been wanting to say that his whole life.

Well, he did say it several times in Iraq, but . . . you know, nobody got it.

• • •

Gabe sits in his house on the south end of the bay along Weke Road.

He's enjoying a very good spliff and *Miami Vice* on the sixty-five-inch flat-screen when he gets a call from Israel. "I need to talk with you."

"You found that guy Chon yet?"

"Yeah," Israel says.

Which is true.

"Where are you?" Gabe asks.

"Outside your place."

"Yeah, okay."

Gabe clicks off.

Suspicious.

Israel sounded hinky to him, nervous. Stepping to the front window, Gabe stands to the side and eases the curtain open enough to look out.

Sees the Jeep in front and Kai squeezed behind the wheel. Kai needs to push away from the table a little more, Gabe thinks. Still suspicious—the line between suspicion and caution being razor thin—he takes his own Glock off the side table and goes out the back door. Sticking close to the wall, he edges his way around the house to the end of the lanai and sees Chon standing by the front door with a pistol held behind his back.

Gabe is a big man, but light on his feet.

He comes up behind Chon and sticks the pistol in his back. "Surprise, motherfucker. Time to die."

Kit steps in and swings the ax handle like he's going after a hanging curve.

Gabe goes down like he's been . . . well, axed.

• • •

"Did you think you were playing with children?" Chon asks.

Gabe is duct-taped to a chair.

Miami Vice is still on.

"My guys will get you," Gabe says.

"I don't think so," Chon says. "One of them is taped to a steering wheel, two others are in the back of a truck."

"So what do we got to talk about?" Gabe asks.

Chon's impressed.

He's seen Taliban and AQ break down and cry by now.

(Usually it was Peter, Paul and Mary.

Or Kenny G that did it.)

"The point is," Chon says, "do you realize how easy this was? I can do this anytime I want. It's what I do. But if I have to do it again, the next time I'll kill you."

"So . . ."

"You didn't take the peace offer the first time it was made," Chon says. "I get it—you thought we were weak. Now you have better information to inform your decision. Take the offer. Don't make me do this again."

"Here's the problem, bruddah," Gabe says. "You think I can go back to the Company and tell them I got beat?"

Chon gets it.

"Do we need to send a message to your bosses?" he asks. "That's unfortunate, but I think we can work that out."

• • •

Gabe and his three guys lie in the back of Kit's truck, all hog-tied and gagged.

Chon hefts a can of gasoline. "You boys like to play with matches, right?"

He pours gas over all of them.

Palestine finally takes a shit.

• • •

Red Eddie looks at the photo and shakes his head.

Four Palala mokes lying in the back of a truck, their mouths duct-taped shut. A big sign is draped over Gabe's neck:

delicious. don't send more.
ps: next time they come back as poke.

Eddie considers this. A former Special Forces stud captures four of my guys. Pours gasoline over them but doesn't toss the match. Has them at his mercy and executed only mercy.

Instead of sending me a photo of four charred corpses, he sends me a joke.

With a warning: "Don't Send More."

And a peace offering: Leave the Karsens alone and we'll leave you alone. We'll leave the islands.

I wish I could accept, Eddie thinks.

It would be the smart thing to do.

Would have been, Mr. Chon (and what the fuck kind of name is that anyway?), if you hadn't exposed me to humiliation. An *ali'i*—a chief—can afford to lose men, can even afford to lose money, but what he can't afford to lose is face.

First it's my face, Eddie thinks, then it's my neck.

And this admittedly comical stunt of yours has cost me face.

I have to get it back.

He calls the phone number attached to the message.

"Funny shit, man," Eddie says.

"So what's your answer?"

"You should have tossed the match," Eddie says.

• • •

"We can't fight the whole Company," Tim says.

Chon says, "*I* can."

• • •

He drives to the other side of the island—the "dry side"—to the small town of Waimea. Where an old teammate lives.

A former medic, Danny "Doc" McDonald chose the place because it's in the middle of nowhere, he can afford a little bungalow not far from the beach, it's sunny and warm, and no one is bleeding out.

He's happy to see Chon. They haven't seen each other since Helmand Province, and they were brothers.

"I need your help," Chon says.

"Anything."

Chon leaves with Doc's offer to come and fight (politely but gratefully declined), two HK 23 So Com pistols, a 12-gauge Remington shotgun, an M14 EBR assault rifle, two grenades, some flares, trip wires, M18 anti-personnel mines and a fully stocked first-aid kit (politely and gratefully accepted).

He needs it all.

He figures Eddie is sending an army.

• • •

Gabe meets the plane at the airport in Lihue.

The reinforcements that Eddie sent are a dozen serious hitters from Honolulu—skilled with guns, knives and jitz— more than capable of taking out this *haole* Chon.

He greets the Honolulu guests warmly but gets only condescending grunts in return. These Waianae boys look at Gabe like a hick who can't handle his own business.

Gabe needs to set them straight. "Remember, I'm still the boss here."

Yeah, okay.

"I don't want Kit hurt."

Yeah, okay.

• • •

Chon tells them all to get on a flight to California.

Except himself.

He's going to stay and fight.

Tim says he's staying with him.

"You'd get in my way," Chon says.

"I was a marine."

"Good for you, ma'am."

"This is my home, my land," Tim says. "I built a life here. I'm not run-ning away and leaving someone else to defend it."

Kit says, "Same."

"No," Tim says. "You're not going to take a chance on leaving that baby without a father."

"I'm not running away," Kit says.

"Then walk," says Elizabeth.

Kit looks at her.

"Seriously, what is this?" Elizabeth asks. "Some kind of bad western com-plete with philosophizing about the meaning of manhood? Let me tell you what manhood is, my son. It's taking care of your family. If that means walk-ing away or running away or crawling away. I raised you to be a man, and that's what I expect you to do."

"Let me suggest a compromise," Ben says.

Because Ben is Ben.

"Not even the Company is going to risk a shoot-out in the middle of town," he says. "You take Malia, your mom and O and go to the rental house. If you need to fly out tomorrow, you'll be that much closer to the airport."

"What are you going to do?" Kit asks.

"Learn how to use a gun, I guess."

"I need you to go with them," Chon says. "There might be some hard decisions to make, and that's what you do best, Ben. You think. Go do what you do best, and let me do what I do."

"What? Make some glorious last stand?"

"I won't be standing, and it won't be the last," Chon says. He hands Ben one of the pistols. "It's kind of like a computer mouse—point and click."

When the others have left, Tim asks, "How are you planning to defend this place?"

Chon looks at him like he's nuts.

"I'm not," he says.

• • •

Too smart just to drive up into a spray of gunfire from the house, the seven Waianae hitters leave their two rented Ford Explorers a hundred yards from the Karsen cul-de-sac and walk in. Their AR-15s at or near their shoulders, they spread out and make a slow approach.

Twenty yards from the house, the leader signals them to stop and get down.

Two tours in Iraq, he's cautious.

Looking over at the workshop, he listens.

Hears nothing.

Not wanting to walk into a crossfire, he signals a couple of his men to loop around the back of the workshop and check it out.

A minute later they signal from the workshop that it's clear.

The leader advances his men ten more yards toward the house. If the Karsens were going to shoot, they'd have done it by now. Leaving them to cover him, he runs to the side of the door, waits a second and then kicks it in.

Nothing.

They search the house.

Nobody's home.

The leader comes out.

Red Eddie isn't going to be happy, he thinks, if I have to call him and tell him we were too late and the targets got away.

Then one of the men he sent to the workshop comes up and points something out. He shines a flashlight at the muddy ground, at fresh tire tracks heading up into the hills.

The hitters get back into their vehicles and follow the tracks.

• • •

Driving toward the rental house on Weke Road, Kit spots a vehicle full of Hawaiians he doesn't know.

Problem is, Kit knows every Hawaiian in Hanalei.

Who does and doesn't belong.

These guys don't.

All mokes, all with that hard look, that Waianae look, and their rented Toyota Highlander is driving slow, cruising, as if the guys inside are looking for something.

Us maybe, Kit thinks.

But the Highlander slides past the house without even slowing down.

Kit drives past the house, too.

Elizabeth says, "Kit—"

"I know."

He keeps a distance but follows them down the road, then stops and sees their car take a hard right to avoid going into the Black Pot beach parking lot and then continue on Weke until it takes a left down the short dirt road to a boatyard that sits along the river.

"Stay here," he says.

He gets out of the car and watches the Highlander park at the boatyard. Four men get out and walk to a twenty-foot rigid-hull inflatable boat—the kind they use to take tourists out on snorkeling trips—pulled up in shallow water beside the small beach.

What are they going to do with that? Kit asks himself.

He sees Gabe get out of the car.

It's a shame, Kit thinks. He walks back to the car. Says to Ben, "Take them back to the house and wait."

"What are you doing?" Ben asks.

Taking care of my family, Kit thinks. "Just do it, please."

Malia says, "Kit, what—"

"I'm not doing anything stupid or rash," Kit says. "I'm going out in the ocean, where nobody in the world can touch me."

I'm going to take the guys out, Kit thinks, but I'm not going to kill them.

The ocean will do that.

Kit walks upstream from the boatyard to a little cove where he knows that Ty Menehe's Jet Ski will be sitting in the water. He feels a little bad about taking Ty's ski, but Ty had told him "anytime," and this is anytime.

Straddling the ski, a Sea-Doo RXP-X , Kit starts it up and heads downriver toward the boatyard. He doesn't try to be inconspicuous but drives right into the moonlight on the river.

Looks over and sees that Gabe spots him from the shore.

Kit guns the engine like he's surprised and alarmed, and he races toward the mouth of the river.

Praying they'll follow him.

• • •

Lying in the trees at the edge of the clearing, Chon watches the vehicles' headlights come up slowly, the cars navigating the narrow, curving, bumpy trail that's slick with mud.

It's what he hopes will be the first mistake of many. They should have walked, humped it in.

Laziness, he thinks, is always punished.

He hopes Tim, on the other side of the clearing, sees the headlights, too. Hopes he's ready when this goes off. Tim was a marine—all jokes aside that's a big deal—but his skills are two wars old, and that's no joke either. He has to trust that Tim will have the patience to wait and not fire before the targets are in the kill sack.

Kit looks back, sees the inflatable speeding toward him.

With all four mokes and Gabe on board.

Good, Kit thinks as he hits the incoming surf on the bay and busts through the inside break. He doesn't turn to cross the bay toward home but keeps the ski pointed straight out of the bay.

Toward the break known as Kings and Queens.

• • •

Tim watches the headlights.

It's been a long time since he's set up a night ambush.

Kind of like riding a bicycle.

• • •

Kit hears the whiz of bullets past his head before he hears the crackling of the automatic rifle.

It's scary, but not that scary.

Unused to guns as he is, Kit thinks it's probably pretty hard to hit someone from a moving boat bobbing in the increasing swell.

He revs the engine, though.

He has to reach Kings and Queens before the mokes reach him.

And they're gaining fast.

• • •

Ten feet from the clearing, the lead car's bumper hits the trip line.

The mine goes off.

Chon sees the flash of light before he hears the sharp crack of the explosion and the shouts.

The Explorer jumps sideways.

The driver opens the door and dives out.

The front-seat passenger isn't going anywhere. His left hand holds his right arm, trying to keep it attached to the shoulder. Two men in the back, both hit with shrapnel and blinded by the flash, spill out of the car.

Chon finds one of them.

Green in his night scope.

The old expression is "shoot to kill," but Chon shoots to wound. Not out of some humanitarian concern—fuck that—but when you're outnumbered, wounding the enemy can be more effective than killing him, because at least one of his buddies has to tend to him, taking two men out of action instead of one.

Chon hits him in the hip. The force of the bullet spins the guy before he goes down. Sure enough, his buddy bends over, grabs him and drags him back out of the open.

Or tries to.

Chon's next shot hits him in the back of the leg.

Now there are three wounded.

Chon stops firing.

Hopes that Tim won't shoot yet.

• • •

Gabe knows what Kit is doing.

Taking them into the face of the enormous waves at Kings and Queens. Luring them out into the death zone, where only the best watermen can survive.

I'm one of the best, Gabe thinks.

These Waianae mokes aren't.

And even I would have a tough time making it out here without a board, just me in the water without a life jacket or a bruddah on a ski coming to pull me out.

He yells, "We need to go back!"

The Waianae boss turns and points a gun at him. "Keep going!"

"We'll get killed!" Gabe yells.

• • •

The leader is a cold, cool mother-jumper.

Cold because he's going to let the wounded take care of the wounded. He still has four men left, and they're going to fight.

So fuck this buggah Chon.

Cool because he's been here before—a night ambush off an IED in Ramallah—so he lies down and marks exactly where the shooting came from.

So fuck this buggah Chon.

He spreads his men out, ten yards apart, and they belly-crawl into the clearing. Then he takes careful aim, sights in on the shooter's position, and squeezes the trigger.

Hears this buggah Chon yell in pain.

• • •

Even in the moonlight, Kit hears Kings and Queens before he sees it.

The huge waves—thunder crushers—blast onto the reef like cannon fire. KA-BOOM.

• • •

Chon has rolled five feet away from his last shot.

Experience has taught him that it's preferable to let them shoot you where you were, not where you are.

The bullet zips close enough, though, and he yells like he's been hit. He crawls away, moving along the side of the clearing, abreast of the Waianae hitters.

Now it's up to Tim.

• • •

Kit's sorry that Gabe is driving the boat.

He's a great waterman, and it gives them a better chance.

He looks ahead and in the moonlight sees the first wave of a set—a giant, but still a little brother to the ones that will follow—coming directly at him.

He points the ski straight at it.

To climb the thirty-foot wall and go out the other side.

If he doesn't, if the ski can't get over the top before the break, the wave will throw him upside down and then crush him.

• • •

The leader waits.

No return fire.

He gets up slowly, signals his men to do the same, and they start across the clearing to go collect the shooter's body or put him out of his misery.

The leader feels pretty safe.

It's dark.

Then the world lights up.

Kit slides down the back of the wave, looks quickly behind him and sees the boat tottering on the top.

Then it slides down the backside.

Gabe is good.

But Kit can't look back anymore.

The second wave is rising in front of him.

A bigger mountain than the last.

Chon fires the flare.

The clearing looks like a baseball park during a night game.

Tim can't miss.

It's the bicycle thing.

The guy closest to him goes down, opening a shot at the second guy. Ducks-in-a-row kind of thing.

The third guy hits the dirt before Tim can get a shot off.

The night goes black again.

Kit climbs and climbs.

Seems like it takes forever.

He looks up and sees the lip of the wave, the spindrift whipping on top, hissing like the fuse of a bomb before it goes off.

He hopes it does.

If he can just make it over the top, the wave will crash on the boat and swamp it.

Then he's in the air, above the wave.

Two shooters, the leader thinks.

Who knew?

("What you don't know can hurt you.")

Fuck Red Eddie, he thinks. If he wants this guy so bad, he can come do it himself.

Time to bug out.

He hisses, "Can you guys move?"

Hearing affirmative answers, he gets into a low crouch, gathers his wounded and moves back toward where the shooters aren't.

Right into Chon's line of fire.

He's moved again, back along their probable lane of retreat.

The maneuver has a name—a "swinging-door ambush."
Chon opens fire.
Shutting the door.

Kit pitches forward as he comes down the backside.
Almost falls off the front of the ski.
Rights himself, holds on and looks back to see:
Gabe makes it.
The boat slides crazily down the back, almost goes over, but somehow
Gabe keeps it upright.
There's only one wave left in the set, Tim thinks.
If I don't take them down on that, I'm finished.
They'll catch me in the flat water outside the break.
He heads toward the next wave.
It's the big brother.

The leader knows he's fucked.
If you can't go forward, you can't go sideways and you can't go back, what
you are is . . . fucked.
He has only one thing going for him.
Firepower.
"Lay it down!" he yells.
Wounded, scared or fucked, doesn't matter—they're going to blow the
back door open.

The night blazes with muzzle flashes.
Chon flattens himself in the mud.
Bullets zing just over his head, kick up the ground around him.
He's pinned, he can't move.
You fucked up, he thinks. You thought they'd freeze in the kill sack or try
to get out a side or a front door. Instead they're coming right back at you,
using superior firepower as a shield.
You can't run and you can't stay.
You're fucked.
They're going to overrun and kill you.
The only question now is how many of them you can kill first.

From the top of the wave, Kit can see the lights of the entire bay.
And the boat in the well below him.
Gabe keeps charging.

He has no choice. He's in the impact zone, and if the wave falls on him, he's done.

And if it doesn't, Kit thinks as he plummets down the back side, I'm done.

As any child knows, everything is worse in the dark.

Sound is magnified, distance warped, the imagination of the unseen makes monsters.

Night ambushes are the worst.

The shouts of anger, the screams of the wounded, the hissing of bullets, the crack and boom of explosions. The enemy is nearer than he is, then farther away, then nearer than ever.

The monsters are real.

Real enemies, real bullets, real shrapnel, real blood, real pain, real death.

Anyone who's ever been on either side of a night ambush knows the true meaning of chaos.

The concepts were always related.

In Greek mythology there first existed chaos, darkness and hell.

The Greeks had it right when it comes to night ambushes.

But—

If you've been through them before—

If you were skilled and lucky enough to survive—

You might have learned something.

You might have learned to keep your head enough to read bits of structure in the confusion.

You might have learned to read muzzle flashes—streaks of light in the darkness—to discern patterns of movement.

You might have learned to hear sound—the salvation of the blind—to find out what's going on around you.

Tim Karsen (né Kearney) is one of those survivors.

He hears the gun battle to his left.

Sees the multiple flashes of the Company gunmen going one way, sees the single, intermittent flash of Chon's rifle coming back.

Knows what's happening.

Knows what's going to happen.

What he can't let happen.

If he can help it.

He can't shoot for fear of hitting Chon.

So he stands up, steps out of the trees, and charges.

Screaming like a banshee.

To draw fire.

To let Chon escape.

Kit turns to look behind him.

Gabe and the inflatable slide down the back of the wave.

They made it, Tim thinks. They made it, and they'll kill me, and they might go back and kill the rest.

He starts to turn the ski.

One last desperate shot—

Ram the ski into the inflatable at full speed and tip it over.

Drown all of us.

• • •

What the triple fuck? the leader thinks, hearing the screaming.

He turns around but can't see in the darkness, can only hear someone charging toward him, screaming like a night demon.

He shoots toward the sound.

Tim keeps going.

One thing in mind.

Close the distance.

To grenade range.

• • •

Then Kit sees it.

A fourth wave.

Impossible, but there it is.

A rogue wave.

A giant's giant.

If the last was the big brother, this is the father, the grandfather, the ancestor, God.

Forty feet on the face.

Looming over them like judgment.

Rushing toward them with murderous intent.

The kind of wave you don't survive.

• • •

Adrenaline shrieking, Tim launches the grenades.

The blasts shatter the night.

He hurls himself flat to the ground, so jacked-up he doesn't realize that he's been shot and is bleeding.

• • •

It's a nightmare

surfers have
children have
some adults who've never been in the ocean inexplicably have

this nightmare of sitting in a deep valley beneath a wave, a gigantic wall of water—unstoppable, unforgiving, relentless, omnipotent—looming above, rising until it blots out the sky until there's nothing but water and imminent doom.

The lucky wake up, shaken, trembling but alive.

The unlucky are in the water when the wave comes down on them.

They never wake up.

• • •

The leader can't hear and can barely see.

The bright grenade flash has all but blinded him, his ears ring and whine, the concussion has him reeling, he's bleeding from shrapnel wounds.

But he's tough.

He gathers his people, also wounded, and half drags, half carries, half beats them back to the surviving vehicle. Loads them in and on the car, gets behind the wheel and starts back down the trail.

Chon hears the grenade blast.

He moves along the side of the trail toward the sound, knowing it could only have been Tim.

Knows it means that he's likely to be spotted by the enemy, but he's not going to leave a man behind.

Or a man's body.

He heads for Tim.

But stops to perform a small task first.

• • •

Gabe looks up.
  Sees the NBW.

  Nothing But Wave.
  Nothing But Water.

  He tells God he's sorry and begs forgiveness.
  Hears the other guys screaming.
  Not yelling—*screaming.*
  The wave comes down on top of them, then
  NBN
  Nothing But Nothing.

• • •

Plunging in the dark.
  Falling in the cold black.
  Tumbling down
  head over heels over head.
  Kit fights to keep his arms tight so the wave doesn't rip his shoulders out
of their sockets.
  Fights to hold his breath.
  He's trained for this.
  Since he was a kid.
  But nothing can train you for this.
  The wave pushes him down and holds him down.

• • •

The vehicle hits the second trip wire.
  (Synchronicity is a beautiful thing.)
  The leader hears a pause, then a click—
  Then—
  Nothing.

• • •

Chon finds Tim.
  Stretched out
  in the grass.

Bleeding out from the legs.
Chon grabs the compress on his belt.
Presses it, applies pressure, says,
"Don't you fucking die on me."

• • •

They say what you don't know can't hurt you.
Ben—who prides himself on his knowledge—doesn't know that—

there wasn't one hit squad—
there weren't two—
there are three.

(Eddie's not fucking around.)
What you don't know . . .
But we've covered that already.

• • •

There are three of them, and they're already on edge.
They haven't talked with the two other teams, but Eddie's strict instruc-
tions were "radio silence."
"Do you know what phone records are?" he asked. "Evidence."
He just wants one quick call. "It's done."
So although Hani's name means "happy" in Hawaiian, the hitter ain't
happy at the moment. He's stressed, because he has to just trust that the
other two teams have done their jobs.
Stick with the plan, Eddie had ordered.
Just stick with the plan.
What freakin' plan? Hani wonders as he walks toward the house. We don't
even know who's going to be in there. The place could be empty, there could
be one person or seven, one of them could be this guy "Chon" who is serious
business. And one of them could be KK, who is not going to go down easy.
Eddie had instructions about this, too.
(Eddie has instructions about pretty much everything.)
Don't hurt KK if you can help it. Don't hurt any Hawaiians—especially
Eddie's cousin—if you can help it.
The *haoles*, the mainlanders? Take them out in the ocean and give their
bodies to the sharks.

A block from the house, Hani and his two boys pull hoods over their faces.

· · ·

O is in the kitchen when the glass of the back door shatters, a gloved hand comes through and opens the door.

A second later she's face-to-face (so to speak) with a hooded man holding a gun on her.

Two more men follow him in.

Then Ben comes in behind her.

Holding a gun.

"Three to one, buggah," Hani says. "How you want to play this?"

Ben doesn't know.

Hani sees that, sees that this isn't that Chon guy. He just steps up and swats the gun out of the guy's hand. "Now you don't have to t'ink about it."

He cracks him in the side of the head.

· · ·

Ben's never been hit like that.

Actually, Ben's never been hit.

His head whirls.

He staggers back against the counter.

· · ·

This is going to be easy, Hani thinks.

"Just the *haoles*," O hears the man say.

Elizabeth glares at him. "*I'm* a *haole*."

"You're KK's mom," the man says.

"If you take them," Malia says, "you take us."

"You're not in charge here," the man says. He turns to his guys. "Tie the two *wahini* up."

O watches as they tie Elizabeth and Malia up, wrap duct tape around their mouths and set them on the sofa.

"Sorry, Auntie," one of them says. Then he turns to Ben and says, "Let's go, buggah."

"Where are we going?" Ben asks.

"Nice ride in a boat," the man says.

They walk them outside.

The one guy leads, the other two stay tight behind Ben and O. She can feel the gun barrel poking into her back.

She thinks about trying to run, but she's too scared.

The men pull off their hoods.

O knows that can't be good.

• • •

Tim hefted over his shoulder, Chon trudges back down the trail. With his free hand, he pulls his cell phone out of his pocket and calls Ben.

No answer.

He tries O.

Same.

This is not good, Chon thinks.

"What's wrong?" Tim asks.

"Nothing," Chon says.

He picks up the pace.

• • •

Hani walks down the pier.

Doesn't see a boat.

Where are dose buggahs?

There's a man at the end of the pier, fishing,

An old man.

Hani steps up to him. "Hey, old man, maybe bettuh you be someplace else, eh?"

The old man looks right past him.

At the *haole* girl.

Pretty damn rude.

• • •

"Everything all right?" Pete asks O.

She's too scared to answer.

Even in the moonlight, he can see her eyes fill with tears. He sees the guy standing too close behind her, the man standing too close behind her friend what's-his-name, Ben.

"Hey, old man," one of the guys says. "Maybe you not hear so good. I said mo' bettuh you leave."

"I heard you," Pete says.

• • •

Air.

Kit sucks it in.

Fills his lungs.

So beautiful.

The wave had held him down but pushed him forward. Slammed him, rolled him, bounced him off the reef, scraped him across and then, having punished him for his insolence, let him go. Kit pushed to the surface.

Bleeding, battered, exhausted, his left shoulder dislocated, he takes a few deep breaths and starts swimming, with one arm, toward shore.

• • •

O sees that look in his eyes again.

She says, "Maybe you'd better leave, Pete."

He nods, sets down his fishing pole and reaches into his tackle box. Comes out with a pistol and shoots the three men between the eyes before they can as much as move.

Sometimes what you don't know can save you.

His real name isn't Pete, it's Frank.

Frank Machianno.

"Frankie Machine."

Once the most feared mob hit man on the West Coast.

The life he left behind to come to paradise.

He looks at O and says, "You'd better go. Don't worry, I'll take care of things here."

"Pete—"

"It's all right," he says. "Go."

Frank loads the bodies into the boat, goes out into the deep water and dumps them in.

The sharks will dispose of them.

They're sort of . . . bait.

• • •

Eddie gets a call, but not the one he expected.

He hears the *haole* say, "Your people met with a series of unfortunate mishaps. They aren't coming back."

Ben has skills.

They're not gun skills, not fighting skills, not Chon skills.

Ben has negotiating skills.

What he says next is, "You don't want to spend the rest of your life looking over your shoulder. Neither do I. So we leave this island alone, and you do the same."

"I'd lose respect," Eddie says.

"For what?" Ben asks. "Something that never happened?"

A long silence, then Eddie says, "Aloha."

• • •

O goes to say good-bye to Pete.

"I'll miss you," Pete says. He reaches into his tackle box, comes out with an onion-bagel egg sandwich, and hands it to her. "For the trip."

"I'll miss you, too."

"You can always come back."

"No, I can't," O says.

She looks around at the blue ocean and the green mountains, sunshine glimmering off a distant waterfall, and feels sad that she can never come back.

Banished from paradise.

Me and Adam, she thinks. And the other Adam.

O puts her arms out and hugs Pete. "Good-bye, Pete."

He kisses her hair and says, "Good-bye, daughter."

Paradise.

THE LAST RIDE

_____

The first time he saw the child, she was in a cage.

Ain't no other word _for_ it, Cal thought at the time. You can call it what you want—a "detention center," a "holding facility," a "temporary shelter"—but when you got a bunch of people penned up behind a chain-link fence, it's a cage.

He thought about what his daddy said when Cal called his old man's cancer his "health problem."

"Call it what it is," Dale Strickland told his son. "Ain't no point in calling it what it ain't."

So that was bone cancer, and this was a damn cage.

Cal still don't know what it was about the girl that struck him special. Why her, why that kid out of so many? Hell, they had hundreds of kids behind them fences, why this one so damn particular?

It could have been her eyes, but _all_ the kids had those big eyes staring out from behind the fence—eyes like you see in them paintings of kids they sell out at the gas station up on the highway. Maybe it was her fingers twined through the links like she was trying to hold on to _something_. Maybe it was the runny nose, the dried snot caked over her lip.

She couldn't have been more than six years old, Cal figured.

Their eyes met for just a second, and then Cal moved on.

Walked past that cage so jammed it looked like a feed lot, except these were people, not cattle, and they wasn't "mooing," they was talking or shouting or asking for help. Or they was crying, like that little girl.

Cal Strickland saw her and then walked past her, and how a man can walk right past a crying child would be a good damn question, except the answer was that there was so damn many there was nothing else a man _could_ do.

Call it what it is, don't call it what it ain't.

So that was the first time he saw her, at what they called Ursula, the big holding center in McAllen. Cal wasn't stationed there anyway. He was just trying to grab some supplies to take back to Clint, where they didn't have enough of anything—blankets, soap, toothpaste—to handle the people they had there.

He didn't expect to see her again.

Then he did.

Just yesterday.

At Clint.

Now he rides his ATV along the barbed-wire fence and finds what he expected to find.

The wire has been cut and the grass tamped down where illegals camped the night before. A charred patch where they'd built a small fire and garbage they left behind—old cans, a couple of plastic water bottles, a dirty diaper.

"Fuckin' Mexicans," he mutters as he gets off the ATV and grabs his repair kit. Except he knows that it probably wasn't Mexicans but Salvadorans, Hondurans or Guatemalans. Mexicans still come, but not so much anymore, not like they were in the nineties, when he and his daddy used to ride the fence and find it cut about every damn day. They rode horses then, not ATVs, and much as his daddy used to cuss out the "wetbacks" and threaten to shoot the coyotes who brought them up there, Cal remembers his reaction when the guy from the vigilante group came and asked him to join.

"Get off my ranch," Dale Strickland said. "And if I see any of you here again with your dumbass cammies and your ARs, I'll shoot you myself. All I got is a Remington thirty-aught, but it'll do the job, I guess."

A few days later, when they were riding fence, his old man said out of nowhere, "That ain't about them trying to defend the land, it's about them being scared their dicks ain't big enough. I ever hear about you joining them assholes, I'll figure you ain't inherited what's rightly yours."

Cal didn't join them assholes.

He signed with the Border Patrol.

Mostly because it was a job, and jobs was hard to find around Fort Hancock, Texas, in them days, after he got out of the army.

He couldn't stay on the ranch, especially not after his daddy died, because the ranch was barely enough to support Bobbi, if his sister even managed to hold on to it.

It was mostly just six hundred acres of dirt and dry grass getting drier every year, and there was no money in cattle anymore anyway. They tried a little bit of everything—growing cotton and even fruit trees, but there wasn't enough water for the fruit, and cotton . . . well, most of the cotton was grown across the border in Mexico, and they couldn't compete with the cheap labor. Bobbi was selling off pieces of the place in order to keep the rest of it.

Cal tried cowboying for a while, working on ranches all over the area— the Woodley ranch, the Steen place, Carlisle's big spread—but there was less and less of that work, too. He gave a thought to trying rodeo, but while he was a pretty good roper and rider, pretty good wasn't good enough to make any money at it.

You had to be great, and he knew he wasn't.

So he went with the Border Patrol.

It paid well, had good benefits and was steady. The Border Patrol snapped Cal right up. He had the military background, was used to hierarchies so knew how to follow orders, spoke border Spanglish and knew the territory better than the back of his hand, having been born and raised here. Hell, Stricklands have lived on the border before it *was* a border.

"I've been patrolling the border my whole damn life," he said when he took the job.

So Cal don't live on the ranch anymore, he got a little apartment in El Paso, but he comes out a few times a week to check the fence. The immigration had slowed to a trickle the past few years, but now it's started again, and a cut fence is a *problem*, because they don't need what few cattle they got wandering into Mexico. In the old days, at least so he was told, the ranchers and the *vaqueros* used to ride back and forth across the border all the time, stealing each other's cattle, which would probably be frowned upon these days.

These days what comes across the border is people and dope.

He twines a new piece of barbed wire into the cut fence, twists it with pliers and reminds himself to come out later in the week with the stretcher to tighten it up.

Fuckin' Mexicans.

He drives the ATV to the old corral and gets off. Leans against the pipe-rail fence. Riley ambles over and snorts his reproach at being replaced by the machine.

"Sorry, boy." Cal scratches the horse's sorrel muzzle. "I've picked up a few pounds you don't need to carry."

Truth is, the gelding is getting old. Was a damn fine cutting horse, a good worker back in the day when they had more cattle to cut.

Cal scoops up some grain from a bucket and the old horse eats out of his hand.

"See you in a few days," Cal says.

He takes the ATV back into the barn.

His old man's pickup truck, a red, 2010 Toyota Tacoma—is still sitting there because neither Cal nor Bobbi has the heart to get rid of it. Shit, the keys are still lying on the front seat, his old 30.06 rifle still in the window rack.

Dale Strickland loved that truck, although Cal was always busting his balls about buying a foreign vehicle.

"Them Jap trucks," Dale said, "you keep 'em in oil, they run forever."

Cal, he has himself a white Ford F-150.

He buys American.

Bobbi has breakfast waiting for him when he gets back to the house. Four eggs over hard, sausage links *and* bacon, black beans, scorched tortillas and coffee that could have made it to the table on its own.

"Angioplasty on the side," Bobbi says as she sets the plate on the table. She has yogurt and fruit and NPR on the radio.

"How can you listen to that shit?" Cal asks.

"Same way you can watch Fox News," Bobbi says.

Bobbi is a West Texas liberal, which don't make her a unicorn but something much rarer. Compared to a West Texas liberal, Cal thinks, unicorns are a dime a dozen.

Actually, Cal don't watch much Fox News, but he won't tell Bobbi that. He don't watch much news at all—sure as hell not the "Communist News Network"—because it's too damn depressing and the Border Patrol is always in it these days, journalists swarming around the detention centers like flies around fresh shit. They say they're just doing their job, but Cal wants to tell them that he's just trying to do his.

Would tell them also, except he ain't allowed to talk to them.

"They'll come on like they're your friends," his boss told him, "but they're really only trying to fuck you."

The other day, a reporter from the *New York Times* (or the *Jew York Times*, as Peterson would have it, but Peterson's an asshole) came up on him in the parking lot asking if he'd answer some questions.

"I'm interested in what it's like to work here," the reporter asked.

Cal kept walking.

"You won't talk to me?" the guy pressed.

Apparently not, because Cal kept on walking.

"Were you told not to?" The guy pressed a card in his hand. "Daniel Schurmann, *New York Times*. If you ever want to talk."

Cal put the card in his shirt pocket. Talking to a *New York Times* reporter wasn't the last thing he would ever think of doing, but it would be the *next-to-last*, after maybe wiping his ass with a wire brush.

Bobbi looks tired.

Her long red hair is thin and dirty, and she has on the same old T-shirt she had on three days ago.

Why shouldn't she be tired? Cal thinks. The strain of trying to keep the ranch going, waiting tables at Sophie's in town and an eighteen-year-old son with an "opioid problem."

Jared's supposedly living with his useless father in El Paso and has a job in a body shop, but Cal doubts either of those things is exactly the case. He suspects that Bobbi thinks the same, that her son is living on the street and shooting heroin, so why shouldn't she look worn down?

She is.

Now she asks, "How's work?"

"It's work." He shrugs.

"I watch the news."

"I thought you just listened," he says.

"We rip children from their parents and put them in cages?" she asks. "Is that who we are now?"

"I'm just trying to do my job," Cal says. "I don't always like it."

"Hey, you voted for the guy."

"Didn't see you in the booth," Cal says.

"I just assumed."

You assumed right, he thinks. Like you usually do. I did vote for the guy, because there was no way I was going to vote for a woman who thought the country owed her the White House because her husband got a blow job.

And a Democrat to boot.

"We need to do something about Riley," Bobbi says.

"I know. Just . . ."

"Just what?"

"Just not yet," Cal says.

"We're going to have to do it sooner or later," Bobbi says. "The vet bills alone . . ."

"I pay the vet bills."

"I know you do."

Cal gets up. "Gotta go put some kids in cages."

"Come on, don't be like that."

He gets up and kisses her on the forehead. "Thanks for breakfast. I'll be back later in the week, check on the fence."

Cal walks out to his truck. It's seven in the morning, and he's already sweating. They say it's a "dry heat," but so's an oven.

He saw the little girl again yesterday.

She'd been transferred to Clint.

Which means we haven't found her parents, Cal thinks.

Well, since we took her from them.

The Clint facility sits four miles from the border amid neat rectangular fields along Alameda Avenue southeast of town.

El Paso is just six miles west on Route 20.

The facility is a group of nondescript buildings powered by big solar panels, which makes sense to Cal, because the one thing they got plenty of out here is sun.

Clint was never designed to hold people.

It was built as sort of a forward logistical base from which to launch patrols. Which was what Cal mostly does. He and two other agents take horse trailers from Clint and go ride the border, scouting drug trails and immigrant tracks.

Kind of like one of them old black-and-white John Wayne movies his old man used to watch on TV.

"You're the modern-day cavalry," Bobbi said to him one time.

Cal don't quite see it that way, but he knows what she meant, and he loves his job, spending long days in the saddle doing a good thing, protecting the country. And helping people, truly, even though the "media" rarely give them credit for it, because from time to time he tracks down a group of illegals who, judging from their footprints, are clearly lost and would otherwise die of dehydration or sunstroke out there in the hundred-degree heat, and those are real satisfying moments for Cal, saving people's lives like that.

Other days, though, they wouldn't find them in time, they'd only find the bodies, and those are the not-so-good moments, especially if it's a woman or a kid, and Cal curses the coyotes that dumped them out there with no food or water or no other directions but a finger pointing north.

If Cal had his way, he'd shoot the damn coyotes and leave their bodies on the fence or the wire. It ain't like he don't know who they are—hell, he went to high school with one of them.

Jaime Rivera used to come back and forth across the border like it didn't exist. Sometimes he'd be in school at Fort Hancock, then he'd just be gone, and then he'd be back again.

Cal played football with him, lined up right beside him at left tackle while Jaime played tight end. They was friends, used to drive across the border to a remote flat out in the desert, sit in their trucks and drink beer together, that sort of thing.

Jaime eventually settled on the other side of the border, decided he could do better in Mexico smuggling a little weed, which Cal didn't find particularly offensive. But then he started trafficking people, and even that Cal wouldn't have taken personally, just considered it the usual sheepdog-versus-coyote border business, except that Jaime just took the immigrants' money and then didn't give a shit what happened to them once he had it.

So yeah, they was teammates back in the day, but now if Cal was absolutely, positively sure he'd get away with it, he'd put a round in Jaime's head and leave him as a buffet for the vultures and the *real* coyotes.

Told him so, too.

One night after Cal found the bodies of a mother and child out in the desert, he had one too many adult beverages, looked up Jaime's number over in El Porvenir—shit, he could probably shout over there—and told him he'd like to leave his corpse out in the sun.

"Why don't you come over here and try, hoss?" Jaime asked. "We'll see who ends up meat."

"You know, you had pretty good hands," Cal said, "but you couldn't block for shit."

"Never wanted to," Jaime said. "But hey, Cal, no offense. If you ever want to make some real money, I guess you have my number. You might even be able to hold on to that dogshit ranch of yours."

Much as Cal hates Jaime, Jaime hates him right back, because Cal Strickland has been hell on his operation. By far the best tracker the Patrol's got, Strickland knows every trail and piece of brush in this country, he's hellacious at setting ambushes, and he's put more than a few of Jaime's people behind bars.

If Jaime could put a price on his old friend, he would.

And it would be a big price.

Now Cal rolls up to Clint and finds a parking spot, which ain't easy, because half the lot is taken up with huge tents set up to house the overflow of inmates. The storerooms and warehouses have all been converted to makeshift holding cells.

Cal gets out of the truck.

The protesters are out early, holding signs in English and Spanish: FREE THE CHILDREN. There's only a couple of reporters. Most of them have gotten bored and moved on to the next story, Cal figures.

Fine with him.

He walks past the protesters into the office.

Twyla is behind the desk.

She's what Cal's grandma would have called "big-boned." Tall, broad-hipped, wide-shouldered, with short black hair and blue eyes. And awkward as a newborn filly—watching Twyla walk is like waiting for an accident to happen. She has what the same grandma would have called a "hitch in her get-along," and the word around Clint is that she got blown up by an IED in Iraq and there's still a piece of metal in her hip.

Cal don't know if that's true.

He does know that he likes her.

A lot, maybe too much.

They're pals.

Or as Peterson told him, "You're in the friend zone, brother. And once you're in the friend zone, you don't get in the end zone."

But Peterson's an asshole.

Twyla smiles when she sees Cal walk in. "Another day in paradise, huh?"

"Gonna be a hot one."

"Already is."

When he'd first introduced himself as "Cal," she'd asked, "Is that short for California or Calvin?"

"Calvin."

"Like in *Calvin and Hobbes*," she said.

"Huh?"

"The comic strip?" she asked. "A boy and a tiger?"

"Which one was Calvin?"

She thought about it for a second. "I don't remember. The boy, I think."

"That's good," Cal said. "I'm not a cat guy."

"Dogs?"

"Horses."

"I've never even been on a horse."

"Where are you *from*?" he asked, because this was well-nigh inconceivable.

"El Paso," she said.

"A city girl."

"I guess."

Now he asks, "Anything new?"

"Same shit, different day."

"Well, I'm headed out on patrol," Cal says. He can't wait to get the hell out of there.

"No such luck, mister," Twyla says. She holds up a clipboard. "You're on guard duty until further notice."

"The hell—"

"All hands on deck until the crisis is over," Twyla says. "Welcome to my life. Time to do the count."

"The what?"

"You're a jailer now, cowboy," Twyla said, "and we got to count the prisoners, see that we got 'em all."

That's when he sees the girl again.

The "detainees" at Clint are held in several buildings—or tents—around the facility, and Cal and Twyla are assigned to the largest one.

She's not in an actual cage now but alone in a corner in a cinder-block room that serves as a large cell. Alone, because almost all the kids still left are boys, and she has to be segregated. From adults, too. They're held on the other side of the room, a chain-link fence between them.

She sits on the floor and looks up at Cal.

Those damn eyes.

"What's her story?" Cal asks.

"Luz?" Twyla asks. "Same old story. Salvadorans seeking asylum. She and her parents were processed at McAllen, then separated. Forty-one, forty-two, forty-three . . ."

The number of kids changes about every day, as some are released to families in the U.S., others to group homes, a few reunited with their parents and deported, while most are transferred to facilities all over the country.

"How long has she been here?" Cal asks.

"Three weeks? Forty-four, forty-five . . ."

"That's a little longer than seventy-two hours," Cal says.

By law children were supposed to be processed out, reunited with parents or sent to approved family or friends within three days.

"We can't locate her parents," Twyla says. "Best we can tell, they were deported. They could be in Mexico, El Salvador, anywhere."

"They have to be looking for her."

"I suppose," Twyla says. "But how do they know where to look? Forty-six, forty-seven . . ."

Yeah, Cal thinks. The system, such as it is, is chaotic. Kids have been taken to multiple holding centers, spread out all over the country. In Texas alone they're being held in Casa Padre, Casa Guadalupe or the tent city in Tornillo. Shit, there are kids in *Chicago*.

"So now what?" Cal asks. "What's the plan?"

"When has there been a plan?" Twyla asks. "Forty-eight, forty-nine . . ."

Cal looks at Luz and says in Spanish, "It's okay. It's going to be all right."

She doesn't answer.

"She's stopped talking," Twyla says. "About four days ago. She used to cry. Now nothing."

"Has she been seen by anyone?"

"An ORR counselor comes in a couple of times a week," Twyla says. "But there are two hundred eighty-one kids here. As of this morning. We have sixty-five in our unit if you want to help me count."

"You seem to be doing fine." He forces his eyes away from the girl and follows Twyla across the room.

"Cal, don't get pound-puppy syndrome."

"The hell does that mean?"

"You know what it means," Twyla says. "When you go to the animal shelter and fall in love with every puppy but you can only take one of them home? We can't take *any* of them home."

"She belongs with her people."

"I agree," Twyla says. "But what are you gonna do?"

The best we can, Cal thinks. What the protesters and the media don't understand is that we're not monsters, we're people doing the best we can with what we have. Which ain't enough. Not enough soap, toothpaste, feminine stuff, towels, clean clothes, medication, doctors, staff, hours in the day or night.

The guy I voted for started a war with no preparation or plan on how to wage it, and here we are.

Kids have lice in their hair, kids are getting sick with chicken pox, kids have scabies, kids cry all the time. It's a constant backdrop, like NPR droning at Bobbi's all the time, except it's heartbreaking and you can't shut it out.

Unless you're Roger Peterson.

"I don't hear it anymore," he tells Cal. "It's a mental discipline."

It's mental all right, Cal thinks, but he ain't so sure about the "discipline" part.

"The parents should never have brought their kids in the first place," Peterson says. "It's not our fault."

"It's not the kids' fault either," Twyla says.

"What are we supposed to do," Peterson asks, "throw open the doors and let every suffering kid in the world in?"

"Maybe," Twyla says.

Peterson says, "I think Iraq scrambled your eggs."

"That's enough," Cal says.

Peterson smirks and walks away.

"I can defend myself," Twyla says.

"I know. I was just trying—"

"I know what you were just trying to do," Twyla says. "Don't. When I need a knight in shining armor, I'll read a fairy tale."

"Got it," Cal says. "We got all the kids we should have?"

"All present and accounted for," Twyla says.

Why was I such a bitch to him? Twyla asks herself when she gets back to her apartment that night.

She strips off her clothes and puts them right in the washer. One of the things about working in Clint is that your clothes smell from being around all the dirty inmates and *their* dirty clothes. It sticks to you, and people in town sometimes hold their noses when agents walk into a room.

Twyla gets into the shower and lets it beat on her for a long time as she tries to scrub the smell out of her skin.

She knows it's not the only reason she feels dirty.

There's also that little girl traumatized into near catatonia.

Maybe that's why I was such a bitch to Cal. Or maybe because Peterson stumbled onto being right, which for him would *be a lucky accident. Or is it because I have feelings for Cal that I probably shouldn't oughta have?*

Twyla has seen the way he looks at her sometimes, and she's not used to men looking at her that way. Even in woman-starved Iraq, the guys in her unit thought that she played for the other team, and not one of them ever made a play on *her*.

She knows that she's awkward and appreciates the irony of her mother, an art-loving wannabe bohemian misplaced in El Paso, naming her for the famous dancer Twyla Tharp.

Shit, even my last name is awkward.

Kumpitsch.

In high school the mean girls used to call her "Lumpitsch."

Twyla Lumpitsch.

After those horrible four years and a pointless semester at community college, she decided her best bet was in the army, and she enlisted. She'd done almost her whole deployment in Iraq when she got blown up. When she was let out of the hospital with an honorable discharge, an artificial hip socket and a slight limp, she signed on with the Border Patrol, which was always looking for female agents, even if they were a little dinged.

Twyla looks at the big scar on her left hip, something else bound to make her unattractive, if a man ever got so far as to see her naked hip. She had a couple of casual boyfriends before Iraq, none after, not only because she doesn't want one seeing her scar but because she also doesn't want one to see what else comes with sleeping with her.

Getting out of the shower, she dries off, puts on a robe and walks into her little kitchen to make what passes for dinner. Every Saturday, Twyla goes to the supermarket and buys seven microwave dinners. She has one plate, one fork, one spoon, one knife, a drinking glass and a coffee cup.

Twyla likes it that way, clean, spare, uncomplicated. Easy to make, easy to clean up. The little apartment is immaculate—the bed made army style, the towel folded neatly on its rack.

Twyla controls everything she can.

She nukes her Salisbury steak, mashed potatoes and corn and sits down in front of the television to eat. A Rangers game is on. Twyla likes baseball because it has neat lines and numbers. Three strikes are always an out, three outs always half an inning.

Cal isn't what you'd call exactly handsome, she thinks. His hair is thinning, and there are probably more holes on the left side of his belt than the right. But he has nice eyes, and he's funny and soft-spoken, and most of all he's kind and he looks at her that way, like she's pretty.

And you were so mean to him, she thinks.

The game is in the top of the seventh when it starts to come on.

It doesn't happen every night, but it happens too many, and she knows the symptoms. It starts with a sick feeling, then a headache, and then she starts blinking and can't stop.

She gets up and goes for the bottle of Jim Beam in the cupboard above the sink. Twyla always pours it into the glass, because drinking from the bottle would mean she has a drinking *problem*, which she doesn't have.

Twyla belts it down like a dose of medicine, which it sort of is. She doesn't really like the taste. What she likes is the calming effect and the hope that it might forestall the inevitable, for a little while anyway.

When she puts the bottle away, her hand is shaking.

She goes into the bathroom, shuts the door and pushes the towel against it to muffle the sound. Then she lies down on the cool tile floor, and before she knows it she's curled up into a fetal position back inside the armored vehicle, her head pounding from the concussion, her side a mass of shredded flesh and shattered bone, she's trapped inside the burning vehicle and there's bleeding and yelling and her buddies hurting and dying, and she hears herself screaming.

Twyla puts her hands over her ears and waits for it to pass.

It always does, just as it always comes back.

Cal can't get her out of his head.

The little girl, Luz.

Them eyes.

Looking up at him . . . accusing?

Or asking.

Asking what?

Can you help me? Can you find my *mami* and *papi*? Asking, maybe, What kind of man are you?

Good goddamn question, Cal thinks as he unwraps the silver paper from his fast-food burrito. It takes some skill—one hand on the wheel, the other extracting half the burrito and getting it into his mouth. But he's had lots of practice. The attendants at the drive-thrus know him by name.

He's thirty-seven, no wife, no kids, lives on the east side of El Paso in a nondescript one-bedroom apartment with rented furniture. Had a fairly serious girlfriend a couple of years ago, a nice woman named Gloria, a kindergarten teacher, but she broke it off because she couldn't "reach him."

"You're so inside yourself I can't reach you," she said. "And I'm tired of trying. I can't do it anymore."

Cal pretended not to know what she meant, but he did. His mom used to say something pretty similar about his dad, which is probably why she up and left. He knows he's the same way, but he also thinks it's true of most people, that the best part of ourselves is trapped inside the worst part of ourselves and just can't manage to get out.

Biting the little packet of hot sauce open and squeezing some out on the burrito, he thinks that maybe the same thing is true of countries, that somehow we lock up the best part of ourselves and don't even realize it, maybe not even when we put children in cages.

So what kind of a man are you? he wonders.

Good goddamn question.

In the morning he goes into the office and asks Twyla, "You got the file on that girl Luz?"

She don't look good, pale and tired like she didn't sleep.

"ORR has all the files," she says.

"Can you get hold of hers?"

She looks at him hard. "Why?"

Cal shrugs.

"Yeah, that ain't gonna do it," Twyla says.

"Thought I might take a shot at finding her folks," Cal says.

"So the Office of Refugee Resettlement, Health and Human Resources,

Homeland Security and the ACLU can't find them," she says, "but Cal Strickland can?"

"I just wonder how hard they're trying," Cal says. "I mean, they got a few thousand kids to deal with, I just got this one."

"*You* do?" she asks. "I warned you about this, Cal."

"I can take care of myself, Twyla."

"Well, I guess I had that coming," she says. "Okay, I'll have a beer with the ORR lady. She ain't a bad type. But no promises."

"Thank you."

There's this moment.

Except neither of them can reach out and take it.

Next morning Twyla hands him a thin file folder.

"It cost me three beers," she says. "That lady can drink. We're not supposed to have this, so read it and shit-can it."

"I'm appreciative."

It's the perfect opportunity to offer to take her to dinner or even just a beer to pay her back, but Cal can't make the words come out of his mouth, so he just takes the file and goes to his truck.

The girl's last name is Gonzalez, and she is Salvadoran.

Her mother is Gabriela, twenty-three. She and Luz were caught wandering on this side of the border on May 25, processed at the big station at McAllen and held for two days before Luz was taken from her mother and moved to Clint.

Every detainee has an Alien Number.

Luz's is 0278989571.

Gabriela was deported out of McAllen on June 1.

Put on a plane back to El Salvador.

Without her daughter.

She has to be out of her mind with worry, Cal thinks, but nothing in the file indicates that she's made any contact. There's no note that she's called the ORR hotline, but it was only just set up, and she might not even know about it. There's no record of calls to any of the processing centers, ORR, Homeland, or Immigration, but she might not know who to call.

Hell, even Legal Aid lawyers are having a hard time wading through the alphabet soup of agencies, never mind an unsophisticated young woman who doesn't speak the language and is scared out of her wits.

If she's even alive, Cal thinks.

There was a reason she fled El Salvador, and that reason might have been waiting for her when she got back.

And where's the father?

The file shows no family in the U.S., so no potential sponsors to release Luz to.

Then what are we going to do with the kid? Cal wonders. Farm her out to a group home, foster care? Keep her in custody until she's eighteen? And then what? She'll be no more legal than she is now.

What she'll be is messed up.

Luz might get real lucky and end up with a warm, loving family who takes good care of her, but there'll always be a part of her that wonders why her mom abandoned her. Or she might get unlucky and end up in a horror-show group home or a fucked-up foster family and get abused, emotionally, physically or sexually or the whole trifecta.

So we have to find her mother.

He starts in the cells.

Of the several hundred inmates at Clint, probably a third are Salvadoran, so maybe one or more of them knows Gabriela Gonzalez.

Except ORR won't let him go through their records.

"I already gave you a break on one file," the ORR lady says. "I can't let you go fishing through all of them."

"Are you trying to tell me," Cal says, "that we're in charge of these people's welfare but we're not allowed to see their files? Why not?"

"HHS is embarrassed enough already by this clusterfuck," she says. "The media is all over every sad story. You think we need you spreading more?"

"I'm not going to the damn media," Cal says. "I'm just trying to find a little girl's mother."

"That's not your job, it's mine."

"Then maybe you should do it."

"I'm doing the best I can," she says. "But let me ask you this, Agent Strickland: Is the mother trying? You've seen the file. There hasn't been a single outreach, a single phone call. Have you ever considered the possibility that the mother doesn't want to be found? That she simply abandoned the girl? I've been in human services a long time. I've seen babies left in garbage cans."

Cal feels his face get red. "No, I hadn't thought of that."

She looks at him for a few seconds and then says, "Maybe if you came in tonight, you'd find the office door unlocked. But if you make a Mongolian opera of this, Strickland, my hand to God I'll get you transferred to the Canadian border, where your balls will freeze off and drop in little crystals down your leg."

"Thank you."

"No," she says. "Don't thank me. Don't *ever* thank me."

When he comes back that night, Twyla is there.

"What are you doing here?" he asks.

"Pulling a double," she says. "I can use the overtime. More to the point, what are *you* doing here?"

He doesn't say anything.

"It's a pretty simple question, Cal."

"I don't want to pull you into this."

"Pull me into what exactly?"

"The less you know—"

"Fuck you." She turns her back on him and walks away.

He goes down to the ORR office and finds the door unlocked.

It takes him hours to go through the files, which are a damn mess. No consistency of format or requirements. Some note national origin, others don't. Some have the date of arrest, others only the date of intake into a facility.

He does the best he can.

First he takes out every file that identifies a Salvadoran.

There are 280 of them.

He copies the names in a notebook he bought at 7-Eleven on his way in. Then he goes through those to see if any of them were arrested near McAllen on or around May 25, because when the illegals come across the river, they often come in groups.

He gets lucky.

There are seven.

Cal photocopies their intake photos, underlines these names in his book, and then he replaces all the files the way he found them.

When he walks back out into the hallway, Peterson is standing there.

"What brings you here at night?" Peterson asks.

"I left my damn wallet in my locker."

Peterson smirks. "Twyla's on duty."

"Oh, yeah?"

"You didn't know that?" Peterson asks. "I thought maybe you came back to get you a little somethin'."

"You're an asshole, you know that?"

"Take it easy, I'm just joking," Peterson says. "You need to lighten up a bit there, Cal. It's grim enough around here already, all these kids crying."

"I thought you didn't hear them."

"You know what these little bastards are to me?" Peterson asks. "Fat over-time checks. They're gonna buy me a new truck."

"I'm happy for you."

"I'm happy for me, too," Peterson says. "But hey, listen—if you and old Twyla there need some alone time, I'll cover. What can it take, a couple of minutes? Lighten up, just joking."

"I'm gonna go now."

"Give Twyla my best," Peterson says. "Or *your* best."

On the way out, Twyla asks him, "Did you get done what you needed?"

"I'm getting there."

"Cal—"

"What?"

"I'm worried about you," she says.

"Yeah, I'm kind of worried about me, too."

He walks out the door.

First thing in the morning, Cal goes behind the chain-link fence into the adult holding area and calls out the names of the seven Salvadorans.

He calls them by name and by A-numbers.

No one answers.

They avoid his eyes or look back at him with fear and suspicion. Why shouldn't they? he thinks. It's a man in my uniform who put them here in the first place.

"Sólo estoy tratando de ayudar," he says. "I'm just trying to help."

They don't believe that.

He points across the room toward Luz. *"Esa niñita por allí."* That little girl over there.

They don't believe he wants to help her either.

Tired, dirty, hungry, scared, angry—they don't believe in much of any-thing anymore.

They don't believe in America.

"Okay, we'll do this the hard way," Cal says. He goes through the holding area with the photos and one by one finds his people. And one by one they tell him exactly shit.

None of them know Gabriela Gonzalez.

None of them know her daughter except for seeing her here.

None of them came up through Mexico with her.

Or crossed the river with her.

No sé, no sé, no sé, no sé.

"What are you doing?" Twyla asks him.

"Trying to find that girl's mama."

"How, by bulling your way through the pens?" Twyla asks.

"You got an idea that I don't?"

She says, "No, but I have an X chromosome you don't."

"The hell does that mean?"

"I'm a female," Twyla says. "Look, the men in here aren't going to say anything. The women might, but not to a man. Half of them have probably been raped or at least assaulted on the trip up here. The other half are running away from violence perpetrated by men. And then you go in there threatening—"

"I didn't threaten—"

"You're big, Cal," she says. "And you're in uniform. That's an implicit threat."

" 'Implicit'?"

"I had a semester of community college," she says. "Look, let me see what I can do."

"I already told you—"

"I know what you told me," Twyla says. "But you don't tell me shit, Cal. I do what I want."

"Okay."

"Okay."

Okay.

The last three nights have been bad.

Usually the attacks come only once a week or so, but Twyla's had them three nights running now, and she doesn't know why. Maybe it's the long hours, she thinks, or maybe the stress.

Twyla goes into the adult section of the pens to see a woman from El Salvador named Dolores. She has a fourteen-year-old son they located in the Tornillo camp, and ORR is trying to reunite them, but the paperwork is taking forever.

It's hard to find space in the cramped cell, but they move to a corner, and Dolores gives the others a stern, leave-us-alone-a-minute look.

"Is it a problem?" Twyla asks. "You being seen talking to me?"

"If it is, it's their problem, not mine."

True that, Twyla thinks. She's observed that no one messes with Dolores in here. She's a leader among the women, and probably among the men, too.

"What do you want, *m'ija?*" Dolores asks.

Twyla thinks it's funny Dolores calls her "daughter." "My friend Cal—"

"The big one."

"The big one."

"What's he thinking?"

"You know men."

"Oh, I know men," Dolores says. "So this one of yours—"

"He's not mine."

"Lie to yourself, *m'ija*," Dolores says, "not to me. Your man, he's trying to find that Luz's mother."

"Can you help?"

Silence.

"Woman to woman," Twyla says.

More silence.

"You're a *mother*, Dolores."

Twyla waits for it.

"Maybe I can find someone here who knows something," Dolores says.

"I'd be grateful."

"Enough to get me a phone call with my son?"

"I think I can work that out."

Woman to woman.

Dolores gets her phone call.

Cal gets his guy.

His name is Rafael Flores, and he came up from El Salvador with Gabriela. Crossed the river the day before she did, was arrested the same day, ended up in Clint because McAllen was overcrowded.

"When I asked you before," Cal says, "you didn't know nothin'."

"That was before."

"Before Dolores talked to you?"

Rafael nods. Thirty-four with a wife and two kids already in the States, up in New York, he went back to El Salvador for his grandfather's funeral and got caught coming back in.

"What did Dolores promise you?" Cal asks.

"Granola bars."

"Granola bars?"

"She said you'd give me more granola bars," Rafael says. "Did you bring them?"

"First the talk," Cal says, "then I'll get you your granola bars."

There are no humanitarians in cages, Cal thinks.

Turns out Rafael's from the same *barrio* in San Salvador as Gabriela Gonzalez.

"So you know her," Cal says.

"A little."

"What's her story?"

The details differ, the story is always the same.

Gabriela's husband, Esteban—Luz's father—belonged to Marasalvatru-cha. Didn't want to join the gang, but on that street in that barrio you were in the gang or you had to pay *renta*, a bribe to stay in business. Esteban had a little taco stand, so he joined, got his tattoo, became a *marero*.

Until a government *Mano Dura* death squad, cracking down on the gangs, forced him to his knees in the middle of the street and shot him in the head in front of his wife and child. Then the chief of the squad told Gabriela that he was coming back that night.

She could take his pistol or his cock in her mouth, her choice.

Gabriela grabbed up her daughter, joined one of the caravans that was headed for El Norte and hoped to apply for asylum.

"Does she have people up here?" Cal asks.

Not that Rafael knows about. "But I barely know the Gonsalvez family."

"*What* did you say?"

"I barely know the Gonsalvez family."

Five minutes later Cal is in the ORR office.

"It's possible," the lady says. "Yes, it's possible that if a call came in asking about a Luz *Gonsalvez*, the computer search would not come up with a Luz *Gonzalez*."

"We're talking one letter here."

"I'm aware of that. If she had referred to the girl's A-number—"

"Would she have had it?"

"Not necessarily," she says with a sigh.

"So we wrote her name down wrong, and now a mother can't find her child."

"Agent Strickland, you know the volume of—"

Cal walks out.

Turns out Rafael has a cousin who has a friend who has a sister who works with Gabriela Gonsalvez's aunt.

Who has a cell phone.

"Give the number to ORR and let them take it from here," Twyla tells him.

"Because they've done such a great job so far?"

"Because you're getting in over your head," she says.

"My daddy used to say, 'When you're halfway across the river, it's a little late to start worrying about how deep the water is.' "

"He have any other great folksy sayings?"

"Lots of 'em," Cal says. "Like, 'When you want a job done right, do it yourself.' I'll give ORR all the info after I've made the call."

He calls the aunt.

And hears, "No, Gabriela is not here."

"She came back, didn't she?" he asks.

"Yes, but she left again."

At least she's alive, Cal thinks. "Do you know where she went?"

"Mexico," the aunt says. "She's trying to find her daughter."

"We have her. Do you have a pen or pencil or something?" He gives her Luz's A-number and the incorrect spelling of her name, then asks, "Does Gabriela have a phone?"

"No, no phone, but she said she would call."

"When she does, please give her this number."

"I will," the aunt says. "How is Luz? Is she okay?"

"She misses her mom," Cal says.

It's the best he can think of.

Jaime gets on the horn. "Hey, what's up? What's happening? What do I need to know?"

"Your old *cuate* Strickland," Peterson says.

"What about him?"

"He's asking a lot of questions about some *cerote* named Gabriela Gonsalvez. We got her brat here."

"What's his interest?"

"Hell if I know," Peterson says. "But he's rattling cages."

"Okay, okay. Keep an eye on it."

"Keep my envelopes coming on time."

"I'm on the pill, my little white brother," Jaime says. "I'm never late."

Jaime clicks off.

The fuck is that shitkicker Cal up to? he wonders. What does he care about some Salvadoran and her kid?

More important, how can it benefit me?

Cal hitches a rope to Riley's bridle and walks him out of the corral. The horse expects to be saddled but is bound for disappointment—Cal don't want to put his weight on him.

So they're just going to go for a walk down the old dirt road toward what used to be the cotton field. A lot of people are planting peppers now, jalapeños for a growing market, but that takes irrigation, and Cal knows Bobbi don't have the capital to lay out for all the new equipment it would take.

The old man would have gotten a kick out of it, though, Cal thinks. The man put sliced jalapeños on *everything* and then doused it all with tabasco, jabbing the bottle at his food like he was stabbing it with a knife.

"You sure you ain't part Mexican?" Cal asked him one time, watching him mix jalapeño in with his eggs.

"If I am, you are," Dale said.

"There are worse things, I suppose," Cal said.

"True enough. You could be part banker."

Fat chance of that, Cal thinks now.

There are a lot of Stricklands in this part of Texas, generally categorized into two distinct groups. You got your "Money Stricklands" and your "No Money Stricklands," and he definitely hails from the latter category.

Riley gives him a push from behind: Can we please walk a little faster?

"You got somewhere you gotta be?" Cal asks. But he steps up the pace. It's getting hot, and the horse probably wants to get back in the shade under the ramada Cal built.

So Luz's mother, Cal thinks, the woman who "abandoned" her, who didn't care enough to make a phone call, apparently cared enough to get back to El Salvador, turn clear around and make the long, dangerous trip back to the border to try to find her child.

Well, she's got a better shot at it now.

He looks at the failed cotton field for a few seconds, then turns himself around and leads Riley back to the corral.

When he gets to Clint, the ORR lady wants to see him.

Toot sweet.

"I hear you located Luz Gonsalvez's family," she said. "Would you like to share that information with me?"

Cal tells her what he knows and gives her the aunt's phone number.

"I'll contact the aunt and tell her that if Gabriela calls her, she should tell her to call me," the lady says. "We'll take it from here. Are we clear about this?"

His boss tells him pretty much the same thing. Cal runs into him in the hallway, and the post commander tells him he won't put up with any "cowboy shit" in his unit.

Then you probably shouldn't have hired a cowboy, Cal thinks.

Luz looks at him.

What those eyes have seen, Cal thinks.

"I got her to eat a little something," her caseworker says.

"We keep trying," Twyla says.

"There's a possibility of getting her back with her mother soon, I hear?" the caseworker says.

"Yeah," Cal says.

"That's good," she says. "Because otherwise . . ."

Yeah, except it is otherwise.

Two days go by, then three.

No call from Gabriela.

They don't hear from her, neither does her aunt.

Then Cal hears that it don't matter anyway.

"The hell do you mean?!" he hollers.

The ORR lady says, "I'm only telling you this as a courtesy. It really is literally none of your business. I thought you might want to know."

That Esteban Gonsalvez had resided illegally in the United States for several months in 2015, was convicted on a DUI and deported. So ORR will not return an unaccompanied minor to a custodian with a criminal record.

"In addition to that, he has a gang affiliation," the lady says.

"He's dead!"

"But by extension the wife also has a gang affiliation," she says. "Furthermore, she hasn't made contact—"

"Because we got her goddamn name wrong!"

"—this is going to be deemed a case of abandonment."

"You're telling me that even if we locate the mother," Cal says, "you won't give Luz to her?"

"That's what it amounts to."

"What's going to happen now?" Twyla asks.

"Seeing as there is no family in the United States to take sponsorship," the lady says, "the girl will be put up for adoption."

Cal leans over the desk. "The. Girl. Has. A. Mother."

"Where?" the lady asks. "Where, Agent Strickland? Where is she?"

Cal's never been much of a drinker.

He is tonight.

Him and Twyla hit Mamacita's up on the 10, order a pitcher and then another.

"This is going to sound stupid, but I went to Iraq because I loved America," Twyla says. "Now I feel like I don't even know this country anymore. We're not who I thought we were. Something's broken in us."

"We can't let this happen."

"What are we going to do about it, Cal?"

"I dunno."

There's happy drunk, there's angry drunk, and there's sullen drunk, and they sit there in sullen-drunk silence until Cal says, "You ever get tired of losing?"

"What do you mean?"

"It's just that it seems the past few years we've been *losing*, you know?" Cal says. "Losing our jobs . . . our land . . . losing what we used to be. I'm just sick of losin', ain't you?"

Twyla shakes her head. "You can't lose what you never had."

"What did *you* never have?"

She looks over the pitcher at him for a few long moments, then says, "It doesn't matter."

"Matters to me."

"Yeah?"

"Yeah."

Then she says, "Cal, I'm . . . self-conscious, you know . . . about my hip . . . the limp."

"It don't bother me."

"It bothers me," she says. "I mean, I'm not, you know, exactly, you know, *beautiful.*"

"I, on the other hand," he says, "constantly get mistaken for Brad Pitt."

She looks at him with new appreciation. "That was the perfect thing to say."

They're that close. That close to getting up, going to his place or hers, falling into bed together, maybe falling in love.

Except Cal's phone rings.

He looks at the number, sees it's from Mexico.

"Is that you, Cal?" Jaime says. "Hey, I hear you're looking for a woman named . . . let me check my notes . . . Gabriela Gonsalvez?"

"What about her?"

"Well, she's right here," Jaime says. "You want her so bad, why don't you come down here and get her, hoss?"

They sit out in his truck.

"Let the higher-ups handle it," Twyla says.

"Already seen how they handle it," Cal says.

"Jesus, what are you thinking of doing?"

"Taking the girl to her mother."

"I knew it," Twyla says. "You take that girl, it's kidnapping, it's a federal crime. They'll put you away for the rest of your life."

"Maybe."

"Or Jaime Rivera will kill you."

"Maybe."

"Good," she says, "go all cowboy stoic on me. This is crazy, Cal. You're going to do something crazy."

"What we're doing now ain't crazy?" he asks. "Ripping kids from their mothers ain't crazy? Putting kids in cages ain't crazy?"

"Totally," she says. "But you're not going to fix it by throwing your life away."

"Ain't gonna fix it by throwing that girl's life away either."

"She's one child out of thousands," Twyla says. "You can't save all of them."

"But I can save one."

"Maybe."

"Maybe's gotta be good enough," he says. "I don't want you being part of this. They can't hold what you don't know against you."

"I'm not going to let you do this."

"You're going to rat me out?"

She looks out the window away from him. "No."

"Didn't think so," he says. "That ain't you."

"I'm begging you, don't do this," Twyla says. "You do this, I'll never see you again. That's not what I want."

"We're not people who get what we want," he says.

"I guess not," Twyla says.

She opens the door and gets out. Slams it behind her.

He watches her walk to her car and drive away.

Twyla gets back to her apartment and figures she doesn't need the bottle above the sink, she's already drunk enough to head it off.

  She isn't.

Cal sits for a while, then drives toward his place thinking about Luz Gonsalvez and Gabriela Gonsalvez and Twyla.

He turns the truck around and drives to her apartment.

Sits in the parking lot and thinks about changing his mind. Sometimes opening your truck door can be the hardest thing you ever do, but he does.

Walks up the exterior stairs to the second floor and then stands there trying to make himself ring the bell. Stands there for probably five minutes, and five times in those five minutes he starts to walk away.

Trying to figure out if she wanted him to come or she didn't.

He rings the bell.

Hears "Go away!"

"Twyla, it's Cal!"

Thirty seconds of eternity, and the door opens a little and he sees her face. White as oncoming headlights. Tears streak down her cheeks. She's quivering, her eyes wide with what looks like fear.

No, not fear.

Terror.

"Go away, Cal," she says. "Please."

"Are you okay?"

"Please."

"Can I come in?"

Her face twists into something he's never seen. She screams, "Go away, Cal! Please! I said *go away! Leave me alone!*"

What he should do is push his way in.

Push his way in and wrap her in his arms and protect her from whatever is hurting her so bad. Stand between her and her terror.

That's what he should do.

But he don't.

She told him to go, and he does.

The door slams in his face, and the last door he remembers slamming like that was when he was eight years old and his mother walked out of the house and the door never opened again, at least not with her coming through it.

So now he walks away.

Twyla staggers back into the bathroom and collapses to the floor.

Everything in her wanted him to hold her. Thought that maybe the feel of his skin on hers might hold her in the moment, pull her out of the burning coffin she lives in. He could lie with her through the long night until the sun came up on another broken day. Maybe together they could limp through in this strange and foreign country.

But she sent him away.

Forced him away.

Threw him away.

Because we're each in our separate cages.

No one can break in.

We can only break out.

Most often we don't.

Cal walks the fence line.

It ain't been cut anywhere.

His daddy used to say that most people will do what's right when it don't cost much, but very few will do what's right when it costs a lot.

"And no one," Dale said, "will do what's right when it costs everything."

"You would," Cal said.

"Don't you believe it."

But Cal did believe it. He was young then. Ain't young anymore, but truth is, he still believes it.

He visits Riley. Gives him some feed, strokes his muzzle and says, "You've always been a good goddamn horse, you know that?"

Riley bobs his head, like, Yeah I know that already.

Cal has the pistol behind his back. He steps back and raises it.

The horse looks at him—what are you doing?

Cal holsters the pistol.

When he goes back in the house, dinner is on the table and he sits down to eat. Beefsteak, roast potatoes, green beans.

"You couldn't do it, could you?" Bobbi says.

"No."

"I'll call the vet."

"Give it a day or so, okay?"

"Why?"

"Just because," Cal says. "You heard from Jared lately?"

"He's back in rehab."

"What's that costing?" Cal asks.

"More than I got."

"Sell off a few more acres."

"Going to have to," she says. "They'll throw up some shitty town houses and call it 'Something or Other Meadows.' "

"The owners can play cowboy," Cal says. He stabs a potato and puts it in his mouth. Then he asks, "You remember that record Daddy used to play nonstop?"

" 'Blood on the Saddle,' " Bobbi said. "I hated that damn song. Jesus, what made you think of that?"

"I dunno." He gets up. "Gotta go. Thanks for dinner."

"What's the hurry?"

"Pulling a night shift." He kisses her on the head. "Love you."

"Love you, too."

Cal goes out and drives his truck over to the barn. Inside, he tries to start his daddy's old Toyota, but the battery is dead. He goes back to his own truck, gets the jumper cables, and the Toyota fires up.

"Them Jap cars," Cal thinks.

He pulls the Toyota out of the barn, then pulls his Ford F-150 in.

On the drive out, Cal thinks, the right thing is the right thing is the right thing.

Call it what it is.

Not what it ain't.

He's in his truck when Twyla calls.

"I'm sorry about last night," she says.

"You don't need to apologize," Cal says. "I know you were pretty mad at me and all."

"It wasn't that," she says. "It was . . . Hey, Cal, last night, what you said you're going to do, that was just drunk talk, right?"

"Yeah," he says. "That was the beer talkin'. Me shooting my mouth off, being a big man. In the sober light of day . . . you know . . . I thought it over. I wouldn't do anything like that."

"I'm glad," she says. "I guess I'll see you later? You on night duty?"

"Yup."

"Well then, I'll see you," she says.

"Twyla. You okay?"

"Yeah, Cal. I'm good," she says. "I mean, better *now*."

Twyla wonders why Cal doesn't show up for his shift.

She calls him.

Straight to voice mail.

She doesn't leave a message.

Luz is asleep on the concrete floor. She barely wakes when he picks her up and cradles her in his arms.

"Está bien, no voy a lastimarte," he says.

It's all right, I'm not going to hurt you.

Across the room, behind the chain-link fence, most of the people are asleep. But Dolores peers out, watching him.

He looks back at her.

She nods.

Cal carries Luz down the hallway and out a side door. He puts her in the passenger seat of his truck, fastens the seat belt, gets in and drives away.

Twyla starts her count.

One, two, three . . .

Still hasn't heard from Cal.

Where the hell is he? What happened?

Twenty-two, twenty-three . . .

Did he just quit, say to hell with it, he's not doing it anymore?

Forty-four, forty-five . . .

Sixty-six, sixty-seven . . .

Sixty-seven.

Not sixty-eight.

Oh, no, Cal. Oh, no.

She goes running back through the room.

No Luz.

Oh, shit. Oh, no.

She sees Dolores staring at her. "Where is she?"

Dolores shrugs. *"Ida."*

Gone.

Twyla feels dizzy, she leans her back against the wall.

Then she slumps down to the floor.

A few seconds later, she gets up and sounds the alarm.

Cal pulls in to a truck stop out on the 10.

Calls Jaime Rivera. "Where and when?"

"You gotta know *now?*"

"Right now or you won't hear from me again."

"Okay." Jaime thinks for a minute and then says, "You remember that spot outside of town we used to go and drink beer?"

Cal remembers it—a deep gully southeast of El Porvenir— rough, isolated brush and chaparral running down into the desert. "When?"

"Tomorrow morning, first thing."

"I'll be there."

"Looking forward to it, hoss."

Cal clicks off. Tells Luz, *"Ya vuelvo."*

I'll be right back.

He walks over to where the westbound eighteen-wheelers are parked, finds one with California plates, looks around to see no one is watching, then jams his cell phone behind the rear bumper.

Back in his own truck, he pulls out on the highway and drives east.

He has to find a place to hole up for the day.

Twyla is getting grilled.

They have her sat down in the boss's office, and him, the ORR lady and an ICE agent go at her.

"Where is he?" the ICE agent asks.

"I don't know."

Her boss says, "You and Strickland are friends, aren't you?"

"Not really."

"Agent Peterson says you are."

"I mean, Cal and I work together," Twyla says. "We always got along fine. . . ."

"Did he ever say anything about taking this girl?" the ICE agent asks.

Twyla makes a point of meeting his eyes. Thinking, What have you got for me I didn't see in Iraq? "No."

"You sure?"

"I would have remembered something like that."

Her boss says, "This happened on your watch."

"I'm aware of that, sir."

"You're responsible."

"Yes, sir."

"Further disciplinary action might be considered," he says. "In the meantime you're suspended. Go home until you hear from me. Not a word to anyone about this."

"Yes, sir."

The ICE agent says, "And for God's sake, don't say anything to the media."

She walks away from the office to the locker room. Sees Peterson getting something from his locker, grabs him by the shirt and slams him against the wall. "If my name ever comes out of your mouth again, Roger, I will *fuck . . . you . . . up.*"

"Ok*ay.*"

She lets go of him and walks away.

Goddamn it, Cal, what have you done?

"This is a disaster," the ICE agent says. "If this gets out . . ."

The media is already all over them for the child-separation policy, he thinks, then for the substandard condition the kids are being held in. First we can't find the parents, and now we have a kid missing? And a *guard* took her?

Jesus Christ.

"How is it not going to get out?" the boss asks. "Finding him is going to take ICE, Border Patrol, local law enforcement, state law enforcement, Homeland Security. He could be in New Mexico by now. If he's crossed state lines, this is an FBI matter. . . ."

"It's kidnapping," the ICE agent says. "It's already an FBI matter."

"And who takes charge of the investigation?" the boss asks.

"We do," the ICE agent says.

"Tell the FBI that," the BP boss says. "In any case we're going to have to alert Washington."

"They're going to blow a gasket," the ICE agent says.

"You want them hearing it in the media first?" the BP boss says. "Because this *is* going to get out."

"Rock, paper, scissors who makes the call?" the ICE agent asks.

"I hate to interrupt here," the ORR lady says, "but are we giving any thought to the actual child?"

Cal pulls off the highway in Fabens, Texas, and goes into a McDonald's drive-thru.

Orders a sausage-and-egg biscuit, coffee, a Happy Meal and a milk. Then he drives up North Fabens to a motel.

"Espera aquí," he says to Luz.

The girl just looks at him, like she always does. He knows she'll stay in the truck—she always seems to do what she's told.

He goes in and up to the desk. "You have a vacancy for one night?"

"How many people?" the clerk, a middle-aged lady asks.

"Just me."

"I only got a room with twin beds ready," she says.

"That'll do fine."

"Eighty-nine dollars," she says.

Cal pays cash.

She slides a paper at him. "Name here, initial here for the rate, here that says you won't smoke. License plate, make of vehicle, and sign down here."

He makes up a license plate and signs. He ain't used to lying, but he guesses that he's in the dishonesty business now.

"Thank you, Mr. Woodley."

He sees the MAKE AMERICA GREAT AGAIN sticker behind the desk.

I'm trying, he thinks.

He carries Luz to the room and sets her on one of the beds.

Hands her the Happy Meal and the milk and says, *"¿Tienes que comer."*

You have to eat.

The room looks like a thousand other motel rooms. Green walls, a print bedspread, striped curtains, one of them noisy air-conditioning units by the window already struggling against the heat and losing.

Cal turns on the TV.

Finds some cartoons.

"Te gustan . . ." He can't think of the Spanish word for cartoons. *"Te gustan* cartoons, *¿verdad?"*

"SpongeBob."

First words he's ever heard her say.

"Yeah, okay, SpongeBob," Cal says. Whatever the hell that is. *"Ahora comes, bien."*

You eat now, okay.

Her eyes on the TV, Luz picks up the little burger and takes a bite.

Cal opens the cardboard carton of milk. He don't know nothin' about kids except that he was one once, a long time ago, and remembers he drank milk. *"Esta también, ¿sí?"*

This, too, okay?

She takes a sip.

"Buena niña," Cal says, smiling at her.

Good girl.

She doesn't smile back but alternates sipping the milk and eating the burger while her eyes are glued on the TV.

Cal goes into the bathroom and runs warm water into the tub. When he comes out, the burger is gone.

"Banera," he says.

Bath.

"Ven, ahora. Los cartoons *seguirán aquí."*

Come on, now, the cartoons will still be here.

Luz gets up and follows him. He hands her a bar of soap and says, *"Sabes que hacer, ¿verdad?"*

You know what to do, right?

She hesitates.

"No te preocupes," Cal says. *"No te voy a mirar."*

Don't worry, I'm not going to look.

He turns his back. *"¿Ves?"*

See?

A few seconds later, he hears her clothes fall on the floor. Then he hears a swish of water and asks, *"¿Hace suficiente calor?"*

Is it hot enough?

"Sí."

"¿Demasiado caliente?"

Too hot?

"No."

"Hay una de esas pequeñas botellas de . . . uhhh . . . shampoo," he says.

"Champú."

"Sí. Champú."

Luz washes her hair.

Cal reaches behind him to turn on the tap so she can rinse it, and she sticks her head under the tap.

A few seconds later, he reaches behind and hands her a towel. She gets out of the tub, dries herself off and wraps up in the towel. When they go back into the room, he points to the TV and says, "I'll be back in a few minutes."

She doesn't seem to care.

She has the television.

He takes her clothes, goes down to the office and asks if they have a laundry room. They do, and he gets quarters to buy detergent and run the machines.

Her clothes—an old red sweatshirt, a yellow T-shirt, some jeans, a pair of white socks—are filthy and stink. He shoves them into the washer, pours in the powder, sticks the quarters into the slot and pushes.

The machine starts with a rumble, and he figures he has twenty minutes so he goes back to the room.

Luz is asleep.

He takes the spread off his bed and covers her with it.

Then he takes the remote and changes the channel to Fox News.

Sees a picture of himself staring back at him.

The suit from Homeland Security took over from McAllen.

Put out a BOLO to all agencies—Border Patrol, ICE, local and state police, DEA—and calls the FBI office in El Paso. Then she calls all the media and asks for cooperation—put out the story and PSAs, please—a rogue Border Patrol agent of questionable mental state has kidnapped a six-year-old girl named Luz Gonzalez.

The public is asked for its assistance.

If you've seen this man or the girl, please contact this number immediately.

An 800 hotline number.

The Border Patrol boss, Peterson, and an ICE agent drive out to Fort Hancock and find the Strickland ranch.

What's left of it anyway.

Bobbi sees the cars pull in and walks out of the kitchen.

Terrified that something's happened to Cal. That he's been shot or something. She's only had NPR on, and they haven't picked up the story.

The ICE agent takes charge.

"Roberta Strickland?" he asks.

"Is Cal all right?"

"Have you seen him?"

"Tell me if he's all right."

"As far as we know," the ICE agent says. "You mind if we take a look around?"

"Why?"

He explains what Cal did.

"Have you seen him, Bobbi?" Peterson asks.

"You two know each other?" the ICE agent asks.

"We went to high school together," Bobbi says. "About a hundred years ago. I saw Cal last night."

"What time?"

"I dunno," Bobbi says. "Dinnertime."

"And you haven't seen him since," the ICE agent says.

"Nope."

"So do you mind if we look around?"

"Knock yourselves out," Bobbi says.

They start in the house.

Don't see Cal or any sign of him.

"Your brother really fucked up," Peterson says to her.

"You still trying to get a hand job, Roger?" Bobbi asks. "Or you still helping yourself?"

They go into the barn.

Bobbi follows them so they all see Cal's truck together.

"That's his," Peterson says.

"No shit," the ICE agent says, looking at the plates. "Any other vehicles here?"

"Just mine," she says, pointing out to her old Chevy.

The ICE agent steps outside and looks down. "There are other tire tracks coming out of the barn. And they're not from that 150."

Bobbi shrugs.

"Ms. Strickland—"

"Benson," she says. "I was married for about fifteen minutes. It didn't take."

"Mrs. Benson," the ICE agent says. "Your brother kidnapped a child. If you withhold relevant information from us, you are aiding and abetting a federal fugitive and obstructing justice—you could do twenty years. I'm only going to ask you once more: What vehicle did he take out of here?"

"I'm searching for the words," Bobbi says. "Oh, yeah—go fuck yourself."

He's weighing whether or not to put cuffs on her when his phone goes off—they've picked up cell-phone pings. Strickland is between Las Cruces and Lordsburg, New Mexico, headed west on the 10 at eighty per.

"We'll be back," the ICE agent says.

"I'll put the coffee on," Bobbi says.

The ICE agent and the BP boss go, but they leave Peterson at the end of the road to watch the place.

Ila Bennett, the woman who runs the motel, watches Fox News.

Pretty much 24/7.

The guy they said took the girl checked in this morning.

And he was washing a little girl's clothes.

She knows she should call the number, but on the other hand she don't want to get involved.

Ila writes down the number, though, and thinks about it.

They set up a roadblock on the 10 west of Lordsburg and stop every vehicle.

Then a check of vehicle registrations in El Paso County show that a Dale Strickland registered a red 2001 Toyota pickup, plate number 032KLL.

Except that no red Toyota with those plates appears on the 10, even though the phone keeps pinging that way.

Helicopters fly the freeway and the off roads.

Nothing.

"The son of a bitch put his phone in a different vehicle," the ICE suit says.

So if Strickland picked a westbound vehicle, she thinks, he headed east.

She redirects the chopper searches east of Clint.

Twyla sits in her apartment glued to CNN.

Every fifteen minutes there's "breaking news" on Cal, which is generally that there's no news at all.

In fact, it's mostly old.

They show Cal's high-school yearbook picture.

A photo of him in his football uniform.

They've dug up his military records and say that he served in Afghanistan and was honorably discharged. A panel of "experts" on a split-screen give background on the family-separation policy, the crisis at the border, the conditions at the holding centers. One of the experts speculates whether Calvin Strickland suffers from PTSD, although he doesn't say if he meant from Afghanistan or Clint.

None of them talk about Luz Gonsalvez.

They don't name her.

She's just "the missing girl."

No calls come in with a sighting of Strickland.

"We have to turn the heat up," the ICE suit says.

He has Fox News on speed dial and uses it.

The announcer looks into the camera and says, "There is a troubling development in the Clint abduction case. Authoritative sources tell Fox News that there is legitimate concern that Calvin Strickland, the rogue Border Patrol guard who kidnapped the six-year-old girl, might be a pedophile and that the girl is in extreme danger. Authorities ask the public to please call if they have any information. . . ."

Twyla clicks from news channel to news channel and gets on her laptop.

A story is emerging from mainstream and social media that Calvin John Strickland is a potential child molester possibly mentally unbalanced from his time in Afghanistan.

On Twitter, Facebook and Snapchat, calls are going out for vigilantes to comb the area. Some say that Strickland should be shot on sight, while others say that shooting is too good for him.

Cal sees the news, too.

Luz is still sound asleep on the bed as he sees his face plastered on the screen and hears the word "pedophile."

He digs through his pockets and finds a card.

Goes to the motel phone and dials the number.

Dan Schurmann answers. "Hello?"

"Mr. Schurmann, this is Cal Strickland. I ain't got much time."

Strickland tells him the whole damn story.

How ORR lost contact with the girl's mother ("It's Gonsalvez, by the way, with a *v*"), how he found her, how they was going to put the girl up for adoption anyway, how he took her, that he's going to take her back to her mom.

"Where?" Schurmann asks. "When?"

"I guess I said too much already," Cal says.

"You can trust me."

"Can't trust anyone," Cal says, and clicks off.

Schurmann writes the story and calls his editor.

The question is whether to put it out right away or save it for print in the morning.

"We should put it out now," Schurmann says, "for Strickland's sake. People down here want to kill this guy."

It goes out online.

An Amber Alert goes out to every smartphone in the general El Paso area. Gives the make and color of the Toyota and license-plate number.

Ila sees the news report.

It tips the scales.

The sick son of a bitch has that little girl in one of her rooms right this very moment, and God only knows what he's doing to the poor dear thing.

She calls the 800 number.

The yahoos are out in force.

From El Paso to Socorro, Lubens to Clint to Fort Hancock, all the way down to Laredo and McAllen, the pickups are rolling. U.S. flags stream from their beds as the boys look for Calvin John Strickland, the kidnapper, the pedophile, the child molester.

Down on the border, along the Rio Grande, the vigilante groups are out in their four-wheelers, their Jeeps and ATVs, with their radios and night scopes, their assault rifles and all their toys, ready to keep a fugitive from doing what so many try to do, cross the river to the other side.

They're all on the lookout for a Jap pickup truck with a dirtbag behind the wheel.

Cal pushes the curtain aside and looks out.

They know about the truck, he thinks, I'm over twenty miles from where I need to cross the border, and they'll be covering the roads in all directions.

He hears the helicopter rotors.

Up there with spotlights searching for the truck.

I'm trapped.

He sees the motel manager come out the office door and look in his direction. She quickly turns and goes back when she sees him.

She knows, Cal thinks.

Luz is sitting up, looking at him.

"We have to go," he says.

Where, he thinks, is another question.

He gets Luz into the truck and fastens her seat belt.

"*¿Adónde vamos?*" she asks him.

Where are we going?

"*Para ver a tu mami,*" Cal says.

To see your mama.

Cal knows an old dirt farm road that leads off Fabens Road before it hits the 10.

If he can reach that before they come down the road, he has a chance. He races the truck up Fabens, expecting to see flashers coming down the other way. The choppers have moved off, scanning to the south. But Cal drives north, spots the old road and turns.

Cal sees the police cars coming up on the 10, flips his headlights off and stops underneath the overpass. Then he relies on the full moon as he crosses under the freeway and then into the high, sparse brush country. He's going in the opposite direction of where he needs to get but knows from working these ranches back in the day that this road will connect with a cattle road running southeast down toward Fort Hancock.

A collection of cop cars—sheriffs, Border Patrol, ICE—roar into the motel lot.

Ila is out front of her office.

"He left!" she yells. "You're too late!"

The *Times* article blows up the narrative like a hand grenade.

As any good reporter would, Schurmann had his tape recorder going for the phone call, so not only are Cal's quotes in print, they're sound bites in twangy good ol' boy on the audio.

"I ain't no pedophile."

"The girl is a helluva lot safer with me than she was in Clint."

"Hell, they was just going to give her away like some glove in the lost and found at Walmart."

"Post-traumatic stress disorder? I was a supply-room guard at Wagram. I ain't got post-traumatic stress disorder, pretraumatic stress disorder or current traumatic stress disorder.

"You know who's got stress disorder? Them kids we got locked up, taken from their folks."

"Hell yes, they're cages. Call 'em what they are, not what they ain't."

"I ain't no bleeding-heart lefty liberal either. Hell, I voted for the man. But I sure as shit didn't vote for *this*."

And the kicker—

"These colors don't run," Cal says. "But . . . maybe they weep."

The whole story of Esteban, Gabriela and Luz Gonsalvez comes out, the fact that a widowed mother is waiting in Mexico for her child, and even when Cal finishes with, "I guess I said too much already," most people don't agree, and most of them have no doubt about what he intends to do.

Now a big part of the public is on his side.

It's, as they say in the media, "polarizing."

Depends which side of the great divide you're on.

Ten miles down the cattle road, he gets caught.

Cal was driving slow on the bumpy road with only the moon for illumination. Last thing in the world he needed was to run into a ditch and damage a tire or the suspension or something.

He was out there with the mesquite, the sage and the *real* coyotes, one of whom ran across the road in front of him and then stopped to look in surprise, like, What the hell are *you* doing out here?

It was quiet.

Except for Luz talking.

"Donde esta mi mami?"

Cal points ahead. "Down there a ways."

A little silence, then, *"Mi papi esta muerto."*

"I know. I'm sorry."

"Los hombres malos lo mataron," she says.

The bad men killed him.

"Hay hombres malos aqui??" she asks.

Cal thinks a bit before answering. Then he says, "Si, there are *hombres malos* here. Pero . . . no dejare que te . . . lastimen."

I won't let them hurt you.

"Okay."

A few minutes later, the spotlight hits him, almost blinding him, but he can make out a pickup truck pulled sideways along the road, blocking his way. A man is standing behind the open door of the truck, pointing a rifle at him.

"Cal Strickland!" the man yells. "Don't be thinking about reaching for that rifle! Come out of the car, and keep your hands where I can see them!"

Cal doesn't reach for the rifle, or for his service weapon, an HK P2000 pistol in a holster at his hip.

He don't want to kill anybody.

"Be careful where you're aimin'!" Cal yells. "I have a kid in here!"

"I know that! Get out of the truck!"

Cal looks at Luz. "It's going to be all right."

Although he don't know how.

He slides out and keeps his hands high in front of him. The man steps out from behind the door, rifle raised and pointed. He's an older man, squat and thick, wearing a gray Resistol. "You're trespassing on my land."

"I didn't have much choice, Mr. Carlisle."

"You're Cal Strickland?"

"Yes, sir."

"Didn't you used to work for me?"

"For a little bit," Cal says. "A long time ago now."

"You were a good worker, as I recall," Carlisle says. "But not much of a cowboy."

"Why I gave it up."

"You're famous, son," the man says. "Seems like the whole country's looking for you. They got a twenty-thousand-dollar reward on your head."

"Most I've been worth in my life," Cal says.

"First I heard you was molesting that little girl," Carlisle says. "Then I heard you was taking her back to her mama. Which is it?"

"Taking her back."

"To Mexico?"

"If I can get her there."

Carlisle thinks it over. Then he says, "Well, you ain't gonna get her there in *that* truck. Every good ol' boy this side of the Red River's looking for that vehicle. I guess you best get in mine."

"Sir?"

"I don't need their darn money," Carlisle says. "I'll take you down to the end of the road. Will that do you?"

Cal goes back to the truck to collect Luz and his rifle.

The girl is pushed flat against the seat, afraid. *"Es un mal hombre?"*

"No, he's a very *good* man," Cal says. "Come on."

He carries her to Carlisle's truck.

"Hello, young lady," Carlisle says.

"Hello."

They drive down from the high country.

Bullets strike metal.

Flames crackle, then roar.

Balled up on the bathroom tiles, Twyla clamps her hands over her ears, but the sound is coming from *inside* her head and won't fade.

It only gets louder.

So loud she can't hear herself cry.

"Is the girl hungry?" Carlisle asks. "I got some sandwiches in back of the seat. Beef, I think."

"¿Tienes hambre?" Cal asks.

Luz nods.

He reaches back and finds a brown paper bag, takes out a sandwich wrapped in waxed paper and hands it to her.

"I'm a little hungry myself," Cal says.

"Help yourself."

"You sure?"

"Don't ask me again."

The sandwich, beef with mustard and jalapeños, tastes damn good. A few minutes later, Cal asks, "Mr. Carlisle, if you don't mind me asking, why are you doing this?"

He knows that Carlisle is a die-hard Republican who probably thinks that "Democrat" is just a code word for "Bolshevik."

There's a silence, and then Carlisle says, "Well, I got a lot more days behind me than ahead of me. What am I gonna tell my Lord and Savior? You read the Bible, son?"

"Not much."

" 'Truly I tell you, whatever you did for the *least* of my brothers and sisters, you did it for Me,' " Carlisle says. "Matthew 25:40."

Then they see headlights in a valley down the road, maybe half a mile off.

"Shit," Carlisle says.

"What are they?" Cal asks.

"I dunno," Carlisle says, "but I think it's one of them vigilante groups. I think you and the girl had better get in the back."

They get out and lie in the bed of the truck.

Carlisle pulls the cover over it.

It's tight in there.

Close.

Cal feels like he can't breathe.

Luz puts her index finger to Cal's lips and whispers *"Callate."*

Silence.

Cal has a feeling she's been in this situation before. He holds the rifle tight against his chest and feels for the trigger. He don't know if he's going to have to use it or even if he would, but at least it's ready.

Ten minutes later he feels the truck come to a stop and hears Carlisle ask, "What are you boys doing out here this time of night?"

"Looking for that bastard Strickland."

"Well, I just come down this road, and I ain't seen anybody."

"I'm afraid we're going to have to search the truck, Mr. Carlisle."

"Well, don't be afraid, son," Carlisle says. "But you ain't searchin' my truck. Last I checked, this was still the United States of America, and it sure as heck is still Texas, so you ain't gonna stop and search me on my own ranch. Which, by the way, you are trespassing on."

"Gonna have to insist, Mr. Carlisle."

"Son," Carlisle says, "I take orders from one man, and you ain't Him. Now, I got places to be, so move your little toy Jeep out of my way before I forget I been born again and go all Old Testament on you."

Five long seconds.

Then, "Well, Mr. Carlisle, you probably are the last person who'd be hiding a child molester. Sorry to have bothered you."

Cal hears an engine start, cars move, and he feels the truck go forward.

It stops a few minutes later.

The cover comes off and Carlisle says, "I guess it's safe now."

"That was close," Cal says.

"Not really," Carlisle says. "Them vigilantes are generally more hat than cattle."

A few miles down the road, he says, "You know they're going to have people watching your place."

"I know."

"You got a plan for that?"

"Mr. Carlisle, I been pretty much making this whole thing up as I go along," Cal says.

"It does have that feeling about it." He stops the truck.

Cal sees the 10 a couple of hundred yards away.

"This is as far as I should go," Carlisle says. "The police will be watching for any vehicle that gets any closer."

Cal and Luz get out of the truck.

"I don't know how to thank you," Cal says, offering his hand.

Carlisle takes it. "Get that girl to her mama."

Cal watches him turn around and head back up the road. He looks down at Luz and says, "I don't know Spanish for 'piggyback,' so just hop on."

She jumps onto his back, and they set off hiking.

Cal lies on the top of a low hill and looks at the ranch house.

The lights are on, Bobbi is up.

Probably worrying herself sick, he thinks.

He sees the Border Patrol vehicle sitting outside with the dome light on. Looks like Peterson sitting inside, but he can't be sure.

The truck is still in the barn, but he can't drive it down to Mexico. They'll have roadblocks everywhere and will be surveilling the crossings. But there's no way he can walk with the girl all the way to his rendezvous with Jaime. There ain't time for that, and she wouldn't make it through that rough country anyway.

He crawls back down the hill to where he left Luz waiting.

Takes her by the hand and walks along the base of the hill for a few hundred feet, until he's out of sight of the house, then through a cut in the hill and down to the road that leads to the old corral.

Riley walks over to him.

"Hey, boy," Cal says, "we got work to do."

He saddles the horse, puts Luz up, then sits behind and takes the reins.

"Uhhh . . . ¿Un caballo antes?"

Best he can do for, You ever been on a horse before?

She shakes her head no but turns back to him and smiles. First sign of childish joy he's seen from her.

"¿Cuál es su nombre?" she asks.

"His name is Riley."

"Voy a llamarlo 'Rojo.' "

"I guess he won't mind," Cal says. "Okay, Riley Rojo, let's get at it."

He takes the horse on a gentle walk out of the corral.

Comes to the barbed-wire fence a few minutes later, untwists the stitching he did a few days ago and rides through.

Twyla gets up off the floor.

Looks at her watch.

Three-fifteen in the morning.

She goes back into the living room and checks her computer for news of Cal and is relieved to see that they haven't caught him.

Yet.

They almost had him in Lubens, but he "evaded capture."

She wonders where he is, *how* he is, how Luz is.

Twyla walks into the kitchen and takes the bottle down from the cupboard. Drinks directly from it, because what the hell anyway. Figures she's going to need a few stiff hits to do what she knows now she has to do.

She takes the bottle, sits down on the sofa and picks up her service weapon from the coffee table.

Takes it out of her holster and lays it on her lap.

The sun won't come up for another three hours.

It's too long.

Cal knows this country.

So does the horse.

It's easy riding, a dirt road along flat farm terrain, plowed fields almost to the river, where there's a strip of brush near where the border fence ends.

Then it's the river.

Then Mexico.

The river ain't far, only a mile or so.

Except now he sees he ain't gonna make it.

Three Border Patrol SUVs are clear in the moonlight, moving back and forth only a quarter of a mile away to his right.

Spotlights sweep the fields.

Then hit him.

The vehicles stop, Cal hears men's voices, and then they come toward him.

At speed.

Cal leans down over Riley's neck. "Boy, you think you got one more in you?"

The horse lifts its head up, like, The hell you talking about? You think you got one more in *you?*

Cal says to Luz, *"Espere!"*

Hold on!

She grabs Riley's mane.

Cal jerks the reins, and they gallop.

He runs for a wash that he knows leads to the river.

The cars are faster than the horse and gain ground, rumbling right behind him. Cal knows that no one is going to shoot and risk hitting the girl, but he keeps his head low. One arm around her, one hand on the reins, he gives Riley a nudge with his boot to get a little more speed out of him.

The horse responds, surging forward.

It ain't enough.

A BP Jeep draws beside him, then races ahead and turns in front of him.

Riley don't need the reins to know to cut. The horse plants, then veers right, great goddamn cutting horse doing it from memory. Gets around the Jeep and keeps running like he knows it's his last gallop, his last free run through open country, plunges down into the wash.

The Jeep comes down after him. Cal turns his head back to see the SUVs coming, too. The sandy soil will slow them a bit but not stop them, and his only chance is to gain sufficient ground to get into the brush ahead and lose them long enough to get to the river. He knows a narrow smugglers' trail that will take him there.

Then a light comes from above, and Cal hears the helicopter rotors whirring low over him.

"Come on, Riley!" he yells. "I need more!"

Knowing he's killing the horse.

But also knowing that most horses got more heart than most people and that this one sure as hell does, because Riley kicks it up a notch he doesn't have, they gain ground, and Cal can see the heavy brush just a hundred yards ahead of them, and he has to get to that to lose the chopper.

They're almost there when an ATV comes down from the left out of nowhere and turns in front of them.

The driver raises his rifle, aims at Cal's head.

Cal grabs Luz tighter.

Riley jumps.

Clears the vehicle and its rider by an inch, but clears it.

Then they're in the brush.

Riley barely slows as they dodge back and forth along the trail between the bushes, headed toward the water.

The terrain opens up again, flat, treeless for a few feet, and they're at the fence.

Fifteen feet of metal, concrete at the base.

They ride alongside it.

Cal turns and sees the vehicles coming from behind.

"Come on, you damn horse!" He can almost hear Riley's heart pounding, sees flecks of foam streaming from his mouth. "Come on!"

The fence ends.

Cal whips the reins, turns Riley to the right, and they're past it.

Into an arroyo and to the river.

Silver in the moonlight.

Riley descends the bank into the water.

It ain't so deep in summer, the currents aren't so bad, and the water only comes up to Cal's ankles as the horse swims across.

And then they're in a different country.

Semi-drunk, Twyla contemplates whether to stick the barrel in her mouth or under her chin.

Or against my temple? she wonders.

Twyla doesn't want to mess it up, end up a vegetable full of needles and tubes, and she doesn't want it to hurt either.

She just wants it to be over.

The ICE suit is foaming-at-the-mouth furious.

"He's in Mexico?!" she says. "Are you goddamn sure?!"

"My people saw him cross the river," the BP boss says.

"On a goddamn *horse*?!"

"Yes."

"And the girl is with him," she says. "Do you have any idea what the media is going to do with this?! 'A lone, heroic cowboy on horseback defies the resources of the federal government and returns a child to her mother'? Do you know how this makes us look?!"

"Like shit."

"We'd have to look a whole lot better to look like shit!" she says.

She picks up the phone to call Washington.

Decisions get made.

Change the narrative.

Contact the Mexican authorities and have them bend every effort to find the mother, take Strickland into custody, and reunite that family. As was always our intent, as we were making progress doing when Strickland stepped in and endangered the child.

The suit is in front of the cameras half an hour later.

"We have made every effort to reunite families," she says. "As I'm sure you understand, this is a complicated process. But it has always been our policy to reunite children with their parents, as we are in the process of doing with the Gonsalvezes."

"Do the Mexican authorities have either Luz or Gabriela Gonsalvez in their custody?" Schurmann asks.

"We're not taking questions at this point."

"Is Cal Strickland in Mexican custody?" he asks.

"We're not taking questions at this point."

"If he is arrested, will he be extradited to the United States?" Schurmann asks. "And if so, what charges will he face?"

"We're not taking questions at this point."

"Will you indict Cal Strickland for carrying out the policy you now say has always been in place?"

"We're not taking questions at this point."

She's not taking questions, but she knows the answer—she'll charge Strickland with everything she can think of and a few things she hasn't thought of yet. Once the media moves on to its next story, she'll put that son of a bitch bastard in prison for life.

Longer, if she can figure out a way to do it.

Cal rides through the thin strip of fields on the Mexican side of the border.

It's morning now, the sun just rising pale yellow.

A few *campesinos* stare at the cowboy with the little girl in front of him, but none stop him or ask questions.

They know not to ask questions in this country.

Cal feels Riley's legs weak underneath him. He'd like to get off and just walk him—the horse is exhausted, played out—but he has to get out of this exposed terrain and down the slope into the arroyo before the Mexican police spot him.

"*¿Estás bien?*" he asks Luz.

"*Sí.*"

"*Veremos a tu madre pronto.*"

We'll see your mother soon.

Luz just nods.

Yeah, I'm not sure I believe it either, Cal thinks.

They make it through the fields and come to the edge of the slope. Below them, for as far as they can see, is just desert.

Rock and sand.

He finds the mouth of the arroyo, and Riley gently picks his way down the tricky slope with its ankle-breaking stones.

Two miles to go is all, to the rendezvous spot.

They're about a mile in when Cal feels Riley shudder.

Sweeping Luz in his arm, he jumps off.

Riley's forelegs buckle.

He goes down to his knees, then rolls over onto his side. His eyes are wide, his breathing labored, belly heaving.

"Rojo!" Luz screams.

Cal walks her a few feet away and turns her so her back is to the horse. *"No mires."*

Don't look.

He steps back and squats next to Riley's head. Strokes his neck and muzzle. "You were always one good goddamn horse. You never let me down."

Cal gets back up, takes his pistol from its holster and shoots twice.

The horse's legs kick out.

Then are still.

Cal lets his holster belt drop to the ground and tucks the pistol in the back of his pants behind his shirt. Then he turns and takes the crying child's hand.

They walk down the arroyo.

Four Ford Explorers sit in a shallow pan at the base of the canyon.

Cal sees Jaime and seven of his boys standing around smoking cigarettes, drinking from plastic bottles of water. They're armed with AKs and machine pistols.

It's hot now, the sun fully awake and on the job.

Cal unslings his daddy's rifle and holds it in front of him as he walks toward Jaime.

All the guns are pointed at him, but Jaime gestures not to shoot.

"You made it, hoss!" Jaime says. "I was about to give up on you!"

"Where's the woman?" Cal asks, aiming the rifle at Jaime's chest.

Jaime jerks his thumb at one of the SUVs. "She's here. The question is, why should I give her to you? I mean, Cal, the deal I was going to make was that I give you the bitch and you go back and work for me. But you've totally fucked that up by taking the *niña* here. You can't go back, and even if you could, you'd be no use to me. I can get a good price for a mother-daughter team in Juárez."

"Don't."

"Why the fuck not?"

"Because I'll kill you."

"You pull that trigger," Jaime says, "my boys will blast you into pozole."

"But you won't see it."

"And then they'll kill the woman and the girl," Jaime says. "After they've had some fun with them."

Cal lowers the rifle.

Jaime is right—killing him would do no damn good at all.

"Do the right thing for once in your life," Cal says. "How much money can you spend? How many more burritos can you eat? How many cars can you drive? And think of the story, Jaime: 'Mexican coyote does what the American government won't.' It'll go viral. They'll sing songs about you."

"I have to admit, it has some appeal," Jaime says. "But so does killing you."

"Do both, then," Cal says.

In this life, he knows, you take the deal you can get. It ain't always what you want—hell, it almost never is—but as his daddy used to say, "If good enough wasn't good enough, it wouldn't *be* good enough."

This is good enough, Cal thinks.

Jaime nods his head toward one of the cars. His guy opens the back door and takes Gabriela out.

She runs to Luz, lifts the child in her arms.

"Touching," Jaime says. "I'm deeply moved. Okay, hoss, you got it. I'll dump them off at a shelter, get a blessing from the nuns. The other part of our deal, though, that's on, ¿*comprende?*"

"*Comprendo.*"

Jaime snaps some orders. One of his guys takes the rifle from Cal. He don't think to look for a pistol.

Gabriela Gonsalvez walks over to him. Her daughter is the spitting image of her. "Thank you."

"It should never have happened in the first place," Cal says. "I'm sorry."

Luz wraps her arms around his waist, puts her face into his stomach and holds him tight.

"*Está bien,*" Cal says. He reaches down and holds her. "It's all right."

They stand like that for a few seconds, and then one of Jaime's guys takes them and leads them back to the car.

"Get them out of here," Jaime says. "No need for the kid to see this."

Cal watches the car go.

He did what he came to do.

Jamie goes to the back of the Explorer and pulls two bottles of Modelo out of a cooler. "You want one, hoss? For old times' sake?"

"Sure."

Cal takes the cold beer, and it feels great going down.

"High school feels like a long time ago," Jaime says.

"It *was* a long time ago."

"Where did it go, huh?" Jaime asks.

"I dunno." Cal takes another long draw, almost finishing the bottle.

"What happened to us?" Jaime asks.

"I don't know that either," Cal says.

"You scared, hoss?"

"Yeah." He is, he feels like he could piss himself.

"Good," Jaime says. He pulls a pistol from his belt. "That makes it better. Finish that off and start walking."

Cal drains the bottle and drops it to the ground.

He walks away.

Can't stop his legs from shaking.

They feel like old wood fence posts rattling in a north wind. First the posts blow down, and then the wire.

Jesus, Jaime, why don't you shoot?

Then he hears, "I can't do it, hoss! Just don't have it in me! You just keep walking! Enjoy prison, okay!?"

Cal hears doors open and shut.

Then motors start.

He keeps walking.

The pistol under her chin, Twyla sees the news on her computer screen. Tape of a suit saying that Cal made it across the border with the girl.

Good for you, Cal, she thinks.

Good for goddamn you.

You got out.

She lowers the gun.

Picks up her phone to start looking for some kind of help.

Can't live inside this anymore.

Cal walks back up the arroyo.

Staggers is more like it. The sun beats on his head like a hammer, and the climb makes his legs ache. He's thirsty, the beer was good, but now he needs water he don't have.

He comes to where Riley lies and sits down beside the horse. Waves the bottle flies away from Riley's eyes.

Exhausted, Cal looks out at the empty terrain. Below him he sees the caravan of cars taking Luz and her mother away. Behind him, up the slope, are green fields fed by irrigation, then the river, then the fence, then his country. The only thing waiting for me on the other side, he thinks, is more wire.

They'll put me in a cage and I won't ever ride this country again.

His daddy used to say that most people will do what's right when it don't cost much and no one will do what's right when it costs everything.

But sometimes it does cost everything.

Cal takes his pistol, sticks it under his chin, and pulls the trigger.

His head falls back on his horse's neck.

The first time he saw the child, she was in a cage.

The last time he saw her, she was free.

ACKNOWLEDGMENTS

I harbor no illusion that I'm a self-made man, or that this volume, like any of my work, comes from the sole efforts of one person. My parents saw that I always had books, public school teachers taught me how to read them. Friends and family give encouragement and support, fellow writers, past and present, inspire me. Publishers work so hard to get the books out there to libraries, booksellers, and readers. My agent sees that I have the financial means to sit down and write. My spouse cheerfully shares the uncertainties of a writer's life.

We writers like to think that we work in splendid solitude. But every morning when I go to work, other people make the lights go on. When I drive to do research, taxpayers and workers built those roads. When I work safely at home, military and police provide that security. I'm grateful to them all and to so many others.

There are people I want to thank specifically:

Shane Salerno, my friend, fellow scrivener, agent, and partner in crime fiction had the idea to do a volume of novellas in the first place. I'm glad he did, and, as always, I owe him more than I can repay.

Liate Stehlik at William Morrow agreed to publish it, an act of confidence for which I am humbly grateful.

Jennifer Brehl was a wonderful and discerning editor, and Maureen Sugden saved me from many embarrassing errors. Thank you both for your hard, creative work and care.

I owe Brian Murray, Andy LeCount, Sharyn Rosenblum, Kaitlin Harri, Jennifer Hart, Julianna Wojcik, Brian Grogan, Chantal Restivo-Alessi, Ben Steinberg, Frank Albanese, Juliette Shapland, and Nate Lanman debts of gratitude.

And to all the publicity, sales, and marketing folks at HarperCollins/ William Morrow, know that *I* know that without you I would be unemployed.

To Deborah Randall and all the people at The Story Factory, my sincere appreciation.

To my lawyer, Richard Heller, thanks for all the care and hard work.

To Matt Snyder and Joe Cohen at CAA—as always, thanks.

To the people at Kids In Need of Defense, thank you for your help and for everything that you do.

A shout-out to the following people for reasons they will understand: Teressa Palozzi, Drew Goodwin, Right-Click, Colton's Burgers, Drift Surf, Jim's Dock, Java Madness, TLC Coffee Roasters, David Nedwidek and Katy Allen, Miss Josephine Gernsheimer, Cameron Pierce Hughes, Tom Russell, Quecho, El Fuego, and Andrew Walsh.

To my mother, Ottis Winslow, for the use of her porch.

Finally, to my wife, Jean, for all her tolerance, enthusiasm, sense of adventure, and love.

ILYM.